GROSS OUT

DUNCAN RALSTON

SHADOW WORK PUBLISHING

Cover art by Anton Rosovsky
Nightchilde and Danse Macabre fonts
by Iconian, used by permission.

ISBN 978-1988819310

Also by Duncan Ralston

Gristle & Bone (Collection)
Salvage (Novel)
Wildfire (Novella)
Woom (Novella)
The Method (Novel)
Video Nasties (Collection)
Ebenezer (Novella)
Ghostland (Novel)
The Midwives (Novel
In Every Dark Corner (Collection)
Afterlife: Ghostland 2.0 (Novel)
Ghostland: Infinite (Novel)

For more, visit
www.duncanralston.com.

AUTHOR'S NOTE

If you haven't read my previous "extreme horror"/transgressive novella, *Woom*, and if you think you have the stomach for it, I'd advise you to read it before you dive in to this novel. *Gross Out* resides in the same universe—let's call it the *Woomiverse*, for lack of a better term—and contains characters and spoilers for that book. Yes, dear Woomies, this book will fill you in on what happened to Angel and Shyla after the events of that fateful night in Room 6. It also expands the mythology of the Lonely Motel itself, which will be further explored in later works.

The usual legal preamble, modified slightly: This story is a work of fiction. Though the "Gross Out" contest is a tradition at a handful of conventions, the characters and incidents within this book are fictitious. No identification with actual persons, living or deceased, is intended or should be inferred.

Also, it should go without saying, but the behavior and thoughts expressed within are not indicative of the author's own beliefs. Reader discretion is very strongly advised.

Writers aren't people exactly. Or, if they're any good, they're a whole lot of people trying so hard to be one person.

— F. Scott Fitzgerald

I recognize terror as the finest emotion and so I will try to terrorize the reader. But if I find that I cannot terrify, I will try to horrify, and if I find that I cannot horrify, I'll go for the Gross Out. I'm not proud.

— Stephen King, *Danse Macabre*

Artist, cancel thyself.

— Anonymous

From The Buffalo News,
Monday, November 29th edition

Events that transpired at an annual horror convention over the weekend have left local police baffled. The convention, held over a three-day period at the Plaza Hotel and Conference Center in Downtown Buffalo, ended in tragedy when violence broke out during the final day's "Gross Out" contest, allegedly instigated by a reading of one author's short story entry.

The affectionately named "Splatterfest" has become a fan favorite in the ten years since its inception, but organizers Frank K. Wallis and Jane Cockcroft have stated their concern that this year's event may be its last. By the end of the weekend, dozens of attendees, mostly horror writers and critics, had been hospitalized from their injuries, several were arrested, and at least two, dead.

An investigation is ongoing.

SPLATTERFEST, DAY ONE
FRIDAY, NOVEMBER 26TH

ARRIVALS

1

THERE SHE IS, thought Clay Kayden. It was two years since he'd seen Moira Mead in person and she was just as radiant as ever, even huddled up in a winter coat and knit hat with a pom-pom, her breath pluming ahead of her as she shivered on the sidewalk in front of the Arrivals terminal at the Buffalo-Niagara International Airport.

Clay pulled up alongside her and zipped down the window of his rental car. Moira bent to peer in, a tangle of dark curls spilling from her hood. In the falling snow she had to squint to see inside.

"Looking for a good time?" he called out, grinning.

"Oh, Clay, thank *gawd*!" She uttered what he suspected was a curse word in her native Welsh. "Open the bloody boot."

Clay opened the trunk and got out, hurrying around to grab her suitcase. In his rush, with the snow and Moira freezing her ass off in the late-November chill, he took her suitcase from her and then, following some strange urge, decided to shake her now empty hand.

She blinked at him, flabbergasted.

Clay stood there awkwardly a moment, holding her bag in one hand and her hand enclosed inside its mitten with the other. Then he said, "It's so good to see you," making the situation even worse.

"Yeah," she agreed, obviously still trying to work out what was going on here, to figure out the dynamic, but she masked her confusion with a polite smile. "Thanks for picking me up."

Clay nodded, smiling stupidly himself. *A handshake?* he thought, bringing her suitcase to the trunk. *What the fucking fuck, Clay?*

The passenger door shut.

Clay slammed the trunk, cursing himself.

When he got back in the car, brushing snow off his shoulders as he slipped in behind the wheel, Moira was already buckled in to the passenger seat. Too late to course correct with a hug now that his hands were free.

"Well, should we get moving?"

'Should we get moving?' When did I turn into my dad?

Moira smiled and nodded. "I suppose we should."

This was only the second time the two of them had met in person. The first time they'd met was at the previous convention in San Diego almost two years ago. Clay still tried to think about the event as little as possible after what had happened following the Gross Out contest, but his time with Moira had been one of the few high points of an otherwise disastrous weekend.

Moira was a fellow horror author, often called the "Queen of Extreme," due to the lack of boundaries in her short stories and one published novel. She and Clay had met online after their mutual publisher went bankrupt a few years before the last in-person con, throwing each of their first novels into limbo. They'd bonded over the shared frustration.

In the time between the San Diego con and this one, they'd chatted over Messenger and eventually added Zoom calls to their daily routine. They knew practically everything about each other, and had taken their online and phone seduction just about as far as it could go.

Yet instead of hugging her, instead of the kiss he'd been planning to attempt if she'd seemed into it after their hug, he'd shaken her fucking hand.

"It is good to see you, Clay." She took off her mittens and tucked them into her lap to warm her hands at the heat vents. "Are you staying at the hotel?"

"Couldn't get a room anywhere," he half-lied, not wanting to burden her with his hopefully temporary financial woes. "I'm at this shitpit little motor inn near here. The Lonely Motel. Heard of it?"

She chuckled. "No, but it sounds ominous."

"It *looks* ominous, believe me. I'll probably sleep in my clothes on top of the comforter."

"There's an image. I hope you brought some coffin dirt to sprinkle under the bed."

Clay laughed. He signaled to get onto the expressway.

They fell into easy conversation from there, Clay asking about her daughter, Genevieve, and her mother who was taking care of the eight-year-old and her brother, who had health issues. Moira had been divorced six years. Clay had dodged both the offspring and marriage bullets. He'd been living single in San Francisco, trying to make it as a writer while working a mind-numbing nine-to-five data entry job. But as the rent that had skyrocketed over the past few years became a struggle to pay, he'd begun to think about moving to L.A. with some people he knew, a struggling actor and an up-and-coming comedian. It was either that or ask his parents if he could stay with them until he got back on his feet, which should be any day now.

Just waiting on that windfall. How in the hell is this thing between us gonna work? he wondered for the hundredth time. *We've both got so much baggage.*

Maybe it wouldn't. Maybe all they had was this one weekend together. If so, was that so terrible? A weekend together was better than a lifetime apart.

Clay promised himself, despite everything else he hoped to accomplish this weekend, he'd make it count with Moira.

2

Three days of convention entry cost three hundred and sixty-five dollars. One day cost one-fifty.

Tyler Grody justified paying for the entire weekend rather than the one day he needed in order to give himself an extra two days to prepare. But the added cost meant he had to stay at a dump all the way across town, near the airport. It had snowed overnight, and his car—technically it was his grandma's Datsun, but he was allowed to borrow it whenever he wanted—hadn't been able to start. He'd had to take the Metro to get here, which was an experience he didn't wish to repeat.

Tyler had *hoped* to be able to cover the cost of the flight, convention and hotel with his royalties from this year, but he'd only managed to sell two of the twenty-six short stories he'd submitted, pulling in less than twenty bucks for each one, not even enough to qualify for Active Member status in the Horror Writer's Association. Judging by their ranks and reviews, the anthologies themselves probably hadn't even sold enough to cover the cost of contributor copies.

The late-great Harlan Ellison said "pay the writer," and Tyler had always believed art had *intrinsic* value—even objectively bad art. But Ellison had never mentioned a *specific* dollar figure. He'd never said, "pay the writer *this much* per story," or "per word." So Tyler had parted with his darlings for less than what they were worth, and he'd waited patiently for someone, *anyone*, to mention them *by name* in the handful of reviews those anthologies had garnered.

Alas, in eight months his first professionally published story hadn't garnered a *single opinion* worth writing about. He supposed the fact that no one had mentioned *hating* them was something. But even *dislike* was an emotional response. The fact that no one mentioned them at all made him wonder if anyone had even read them. Most readers had likely skipped the stories from newbie authors and gone straight for the famous ringers the publisher had likely paid *far more* than Tyler. Like fucking Anderson Ackerman, the big-name dark fantasy writer Tyler had seen lording over his minions at the bar.

The convention hall was way too hot, compensating for the poor weather, and Tyler had already broken out in a sweat under his hood. Not a lot of people wore costumes, but Tyler was determined to keep a low profile. Some people knew him by reputation, if not sight. It was easy enough to remain anonymous on the internet, but not when you were trying to build a following under your real name. Agents these days seemed to require writers to have their own ready-made "platform." God forbid they had to do some of the actual heavy lifting for their fifteen percent. All this meant comments he made about certain writers, especially big-name hacks and self-publishers who'd somehow managed to crack the algorithm, gaining a decent readership of mainly cretins, were tied to his real name and face.

Other writers called Tyler a "troll." Tyler thought of himself as the world's last realist. Every artistic endeavor needed its harsh critics, unfettered by the opinions of the common man. Without them, you ended up with a convention full of hacks, like this one. Not a single one of these so-called "authors" deserved their stardom—*More like star*dumb, he thought, and made a mental note to write that one down when he got back to the motel. They were all just ass-kissers and glorified fan fiction writers, standing upon the shoulders of giants.

It made Tyler physically sick seeing the pretentious drivel or outright crap some of these editors chose to publish over his own work. Skimming through the magazines and anthologies he'd been rejected from, he had to laugh or he'd puke. Rejection was a necessary part of any artistic endeavor, he knew, but when his own work was constantly being passed over for people who were so clearly *beneath* him, he'd begun to wonder if there wasn't something—or some*one*—actively preventing him from reaching the level of appreciation he knew he deserved.

He'd soon discovered *exactly* who that someone was—it had come to him as a sudden revelation during the last convention. The answer was *so obvious* he'd berated himself for days for not having seen it sooner.

Two days to prepare should prove sufficient.

In two days, the author of Tyler's misery would pay *this* writer. He would pay dearly.

3

"There he is," Moira said. "Are you going to speak to him?"

Clay peered across the throng of moving bodies in the Plaza Hotel's convention hall to where Moira had indicated with a nod.

David Ennis sat at his vendor table, chatting with a couple of young female attendees, critics or authors, Clay wasn't sure which. Stacks of brand-new paperbacks adorned the folding table, along with boxes of pins and stickers, and colorful boxes containing things Clay couldn't determine from the distance.

Two large standees featured a black-and-white Ennis in a pose more suited to a professional wrestler than a best-selling author. Each standee declared him the *UNDISPUTED MASTER OF SPLATTER HORROR!* Beside him, a young, besuited writer with a manbun—*This year's model*, Clay thought bitterly—sat pecking at the screen of his cell phone. Ennis wore all black, from his jeans to his T-shirt, the black leather jacket from his photos slung over the back of his folding chair. He often prided himself as a "blue-collar writer," and this was his uniform.

The event was much bigger this year than the previous in-person event, the November before the pandemic hit. They'd managed to score quite a few "names" in the horror world this time around, from C-list actors who'd died screaming in a couple of films only available on low-tier streaming sites, signing glossy 8x10s for a fee, to wizards of special effects makeup and prosthetics, selling masks of their creations, to midlevel heavy-hitters in the genre like Ennis, Ackerman and a handful of others. The convention had gained a fair bit of infamy in the horror world after the more intimate affair two years ago—thanks in part to the controversy Clay Kayden had inadvertently caused, no doubt—and now it looked the part.

I should get royalties, Clay thought, nursing his Coke Zero, the only thing he'd allow himself to drink in public anymore.

"Nah," he said, answering Moira. "He'll expect me to kiss the ring, and I'm not gonna debase myself like that again."

Moira sipped her cocktail, nodding in sympathy, eyeing Ennis across the conference room. The two starstruck young women pressed themselves against the author, smiling for a photo, the white bread in an asshole sandwich.

"God, he's such a cockwomble," Moira said. "Why don't

people see it?"

"Starry eyes. Speaking of which, did you see your favorite director's here?"

Moira's own eyes went starry as she looked around. "*What?* She wasn't on the guest list."

"Must've been a late addition." Clay grinned. He loved to torture Moira about her mild obsession. "I saw her checking in on my way through the lobby."

She turned to face the doors. The convention lighting was garish, too bright, but Moira Mead had a bright, cheery face that never failed to shine in any environment Clay had yet to see her in. When she failed to find the object of her obsession, her shoulders slumped, her lower lip pooched out, and she polished off her drink, the ice clinking. "I guess she's probably still in her room."

"Probably."

"Did you get her autograph, at least?"

"I'm not really an autograph kind of guy. I said hello to her, though."

She popped her eyes. "That's it? *Hello?* The greatest living horror director and you said—"

"Hello," Clay repeated, his grin widening. "That's it, yeah."

"Did she say anything *back*?"

"She said 'hello,' but I think she was just being polite. I think she didn't want to seem starstruck."

Moira swatted his chest. "Arsehole. You didn't see her."

He chuckled again. "No, I didn't see her. But she is on the guest list. Just added last night, I saw on the message board. I guess they didn't have time to change the posters in the lobby. Honestly, I don't know how these guys scored such a heavy hitter."

Moira regarded him with narrowed eyes. "I swear, if you're lying to me…"

"I wouldn't lie about that. I'm as big a fan as you are."

She was still pretending not to be looking around the hall for Kendra Pleasance, writer/director of *Creep City*, *The Stain* and *Abaddon Mountain*, among many others.

"Well," he admitted, "maybe not quite *that* big. Anyway, they say she's writing the script for her new movie. I bet she'll be working on it in her room this weekend."

"Oh, to be a fly on that wall," Moira said.

They fell into a silence, the two of them watching people go by. The music was loud—some classic hard rock song Clay didn't recognize—too loud for a proper conversation, easy to let time lapse between exchanges.

With the crowd momentarily parted, Clay saw David Ennis had left his table. The young up-and-comer with the manbun was keeping Ennis's seat warm behind stacks of paperbacks, stickers, bookmarks and other merch. At the last in-person con, Clay had been in that place. Now he was *persona non grata*.

A cheaply printed paperback appeared between himself and Moira, causing the malicious smile Clay didn't know he'd been wearing to slip from his face. The book had an equally cheap-looking matte cover—its title, *BLOODLESS*, spelled out in a pixelated blood splatter font—the corner of it smothered and smudged by a thick thumb.

Clay turned to see who'd presented it to them, a middle-aged man with black-rimmed glasses and a long, shaggy hairdo. "I hate to be That Guy," he said, "but perhaps I could interest you in a signed copy of my new apocalypse nov—"

"No," Moira snapped.

"It's got over a hundred reviews on A—"

"*No*," Moira said again, slapping his hand away. The book fell on the floor, creasing the spine.

Moira held back snickers as the guy bent down to pick it up. "No need to be rude," he grumbled on the way back up.

Clay considered intervening, but it seemed like Moira had a good handle on it. He stood back and watched with a grin.

"It's *rude* to inject yourself into a private conversation for a sales pitch," she said, scolding him like a child. "It's *rude* to persist when a lady says no."

"Calm your tits. I'm just trying to make a living."

"Jog on, you prat," she said, waving him away.

The jilted salesman slipped his damaged book back onto the

stack cradled in his other arm and proceeded to harass the next group of people he saw.

"Honestly, you'd have to be awfully pathetic to think that's okay," Moira said. "It's sad, really. Is it odd I feel bad for him?"

Clay shrugged. "I wouldn't. It's the unsolicited dick pic of the literary community."

She raised an eyebrow. "You might want to keep that little analogy to yourself."

He chuckled. Considering what had nearly got him banned from the convention the last time, she made a good point.

"Well, what d'you say?" she asked, eager to change the mood after an awkward silence. "Shall we go mingle?"

"If I have to."

She eyed him sharply. "You should *want* to. Why the hell else would you drive all the way to *Buffalo*?"

He shrugged again.

"Tell you what. I'm gonna get another one of these—" She jiggled the slice of lime in her otherwise empty cocktail glass. "—and scope out the scene for friendly faces. Wait here and I'll come get you?"

"Sounds good."

She pointed at his Coke. "Shall I grab something stronger for you?"

Clay forced a smile. "Not after last time, thanks."

She nodded. "Wise choice. I'll be right back."

"We're horror writers, Moira. You should know better than to say that."

"How about, 'if I die, don't shag my corpse'?" she said, already moving sideways into the crowd.

He watched her sashay away, greeting people on her way to the convention bar. Until the airport pickup, it had pretty much been a given the two of them would hook up before the end of the weekend. They'd flirted heavily at the last Splatterfest but hadn't acted, too nervous to put their feelings ahead of professionalism. Before she'd gotten on the plane that morning she'd told him she was going to "jump his bones" when she saw him in person again—but the handshake had probably put a damper on all of that. He'd salvaged it somewhat with a hug in the lobby, but the awkwardness remained.

Moira disappeared into the crowd, and Clay returned his focus, and his anger, toward Ennis and his new protégé.

Revenge was much simpler than love.

And often, in Clay's limited experience, it could be much more rewarding.

4

"But it's a *dangerously* slippery slope, isn't it?" Anderson Ackerman pronounced, already slurring his Ss. He'd been holding court at the hotel bar since it opened, and now, at just after two p.m., his wheelchair—and possibly his overinflated ego—was the only thing holding him upright.

"Take the laughably titled 'Gross Out' contest from our last cattle call, *par exemple*. How many of you attended?" His bleary-eyed gaze surveyed the crowd of writers, young, middle-aged and older. Several hands shot up. "Right. Now hands up if you know what I mean when I mention The Controversy?"

Every hand shot up, some reluctant, some fervently.

"All right, how many of you believe the punishment for that apparent transgression fit the crime? Do *any* of you sincerely believe the perpetrator of said 'violent act' deserved to be punished in the manner he was?" Without providing time for a response, the award-winning author pushed on, stroking his long, silver beard like a pontificating wizard. "Allow me to put it to you this way: if you had made a similar mistake, under the apparently naïve belief that *anything goes*, as was the common wisdom at the time, would you think the reaction was just?"

"It was a Gross Out contest," a young man in a black zoot suit and fedora ventured, raising a hand to shoulder height as if to ask for permission to speak. "The intent was to make the audience react in disgust, right?" He looked around at the others for confirmation. "The story—and I'm not saying whether it crossed a line or didn't, that's not what I'm saying—but that story *disgusted* people. It disturbed *me*, and I write that shit—*stuff*—myself. Hashtag Slobby-Poo-Poo-4-Eva." This bit of apparent gibberish got a few light chuckles from some of the others. "The story got the reaction he wanted, so I think, whatever else you wanna say about it, it shouldn't've been disqualified from the contest—it probably should've *won* the contest, considering the reaction—and people who felt violated or whatever by it, maybe they need to think about why it made them feel that way, instead of lashing out at the author."

"I disagree," said a man about Ackerman's age, with a shiny bald head and no neck to speak of. "It's our job as writers to present an approximation of the truth to our audience. Fiction is truth repackaged. There was no *truth* to that story, in my opinion. People like that aren't deserving of sympathy. It's like, *A Serbian Film*. Is that art? Or is it just pornography?"

"Pornography *is* art," a tall, sensuous-looking woman with multicolored braids said. Several onlookers nodded at this.

"*Some* of it is," No Neck replied. "Some of it's just for getting off."

"Getting off's an art, too," the woman shot back. "Maybe it's not one *you're* familiar with…"

The crowd *ooh*ed and laughed. No Neck's cheeks reddened, appropriately chastised.

"Ah," Ackerman said with a raised finger, "but our sexually challenged friend *does* have a point. Is art not meant to contain an element of truth? Don't we, as weavers of dreams, have a responsibility to, if not present the truth as the *world* sees it—to use the common parlance—share *our own* truths?"

"Are you implying the story was autobiographical?" the sex expert asked.

"All stories are autobiographical, in a sense. There is an element of each of us in all of our work, whether we're conscious of it or not."

"Right," Zoot Suit said, rolling his eyes. "Bret Easton Ellis is a brand-obsessed serial killer and Stephen King is a rabid Saint Bernard. Hashtag Not All Writers, dude."

"Not *literally*, of course not," Ackerman pronounced. "But

25

it could be said that Cujo the dog was an *aspect* of King's persona, crying out to be heard. It's a novel he barely remembers writing, from his own account. So thoroughly blitzed was he on cocaine and beer he couldn't remember writing an *entire novel*. A novel, I might add, which may or may not be about his fear that his own personal demons might in fact have been terrorizing his young family as Cujo terrorized young Tad Trenton and his mother."

"If all stories are autobiographical," said the young woman with the braids, "what does that say about *your* back catalogue? You've made a career out of what some people call 'torture porn.' Are you the victims, or the perpetrators?"

"I'm both victim *and* perpetrator." Ackerman gave the woman a smug smile, as if he'd discovered a way out of a fiendishly constructed trap. "When I write from the perspective of the psychopath, I squeeze my size tens into their shoes as comfortably as I'm able. And when I write for the victim, I attempt to do the same. *Empathy* is the key to writing any sort of fiction. *Story* is merely the transcription of a struggle between the author and the multiple aspects of his or her Self. To strive for anything less is intellectual cowardice."

"Are you excusing him then?" No Neck asked. "You think he had the right to tell that story?"

"'Authors, full of evil thoughts, lock up your typewriters.' That quote is from *Fahrenheit 451*, in case it wasn't featured on your high school curriculum. It seems my dear late friend Ray Bradbury may have predicted the future."

"Bullshit," said the sex expert.

"I beg your pardon?"

"Look," she said, "I respect your body of work and your... *unique perspective* on the genre, but I think maybe you're just a little out of touch—"

"'Okay, boomer,' in other words," No Neck said with a dismissive shake of his head, which didn't seem capable of the action.

The woman continued, unabated but more forcefully, "— and *now* you're making excuses for people like you to act like

26

colossal dickheads with zero consequence."

Ackerman goggled at the woman, and the crowd watched awkwardly, awaiting his reaction. Finally, he burst out in hearty laughter, his chins jostling. A smattering of relieved laughter from the others joined him.

"Someone buy this woman a drink! And *relax*, everyone, for God's sake. Art is *intended* to push us out of our comfort zones. *Especially* our beloved, transgressive 'splatterpunk.' Go forth and *offend*, my dears!"

The crowd dispersed, leaving Ackerman alone at the bar with the woman who'd challenged him. While she leaned over the bar to order a drink, he looked her up and down lasciviously.

Oh yes, he thought, stroking his beard. *This one will do just fine.*

5

"Oh, *shit*! It's the Poo-Poo Man!"

Archie Schneider merely wanted to reach the bar and get a drink without being spotted by anyone, but *of course* that was too much to ask. When you were notorious among a group of misfits, you became a sort of anti-pariah, a hero among rejects.

That King of the Losers was him: the Poo-Poo Man.

"Here he is!" An arm slipped around his neck and pulled him in for a hug. Archie recognized Conor O'Malley from Facebook, a writer/small press publisher who was also the vocalist and lead guitar for some virtually unknown band. He sometimes called himself a "double hyphenate." In fact, Archie recognized the entire group huddled around a vendor table, stacked with books and adorned with logos and advertising copy from O'Malley's small press, Gorehounds Publishing.

A chant began: "*Poo-Poo! Poo-Poo! Poo-Poo!*"

Archie pictured the scene from Tod Browning's *Freaks*, with the sideshow troupe seated around the dinner table chanting, *Gooble gobble! One of us! We accept her!*

"Yo, dude, we were literally just talking about you," Conor

said, then as if he'd only just noticed he squeezed Archie's right bicep. "Bro, you are *jacked*. Was he this pumped last time?"

"I think I'd remember," said the one woman in their crew.

"You been working out, bro?"

Archie made to respond, but another voice interceded.

"My guy," said Steve Pilkington, a Canadian author who wrote gritty and visceral revenge fiction, "*tell* me you're doing the Gross Out contest this year. Puh-lease!"

Archie nodded meekly.

Miller pumped a fist. "Yes! Your story was so good I totally almost puked in my mouth! I mean who even *thinks* of that shit?"

"The Poo-Poo Man, that's the fuck who," Conor said.

The others laughed at this: Steve, Shawn Anders, Mike Miller and the woman Archie had prior to now only known by her pen name, Jessica Tuffet. Her day job was teaching grades one and two, and the types of things she wrote would likely put her on an FBI watch list. Her real name was Aubrey something.

"Aw, man…" Aubrey shook her head in reverential disgust. "I can't even *think* about using a public toilet anymore without picturing that *story*. Just thinking about that *eye*, peering up through the mirrors in the pipe like a submarine periscope…" She shuddered dramatically, hugging herself.

The others laughed.

"'Launch torpedo!'" Conor and Steve said in unison.

The group laughed harder.

"'Their eyes locked: her brown eye with his blue eye,'" Mike Miller said, misquoting the story. The line was "his blue eye with her brown *one*," because the punchline needed to be at the end of the sentence for maximum effect, and because Archie had felt the second repetition of "eye" didn't flow quite as well. It wasn't worth the trouble to correct him. He'd learned from years of childhood bullying, the less he reacted, the more likely they were to drop it.

"Actually, that reminds me of a story of mine," said Shawn Anders, known as "Shawnders" to his friends.

The others groaned.

"Here we go," Aubrey said with a dramatic roll of her eyes,

causing the rest of them to laugh. "Something *always* reminds you of one of your stories."

Shawnders laughed amiably along with them, though it was clear he felt teased. "This one really does."

There was a dynamic here Archie didn't quite comprehend. Some kind of inside joke, he supposed. But then, he'd never been very good at making friends with people his own age. The elderly loved him. He supposed it was a perk of the job.

"Did you just get here?" Steve asked, seeming to notice the awkwardness oozing from Archie's every sweating pore. "You want a drink, buddy? I'm buying."

Gorehounds had been courting Archie ever since the last Gross Out contest. Conor O'Malley had stepped into his path as he'd left the stage with his eyes downcast, his entire body still shaking with adrenaline—from fear and excitement—while the crowd roared with laughter and applause. He'd only wanted to get back to his room, but Conor had convinced him to stick around for a drink. He'd calmed down after a few sips as the thick brown ale slid down his throat, and the two of them had talked about his future. A future Conor O'Malley hoped would involve Gorehounds.

Archie hadn't promised anything, but he did say he'd consider the offer. In truth, he didn't want to get pigeonholed into splatter horror. He liked to gross people out, sure. But it wasn't where his passion lay.

That night had been the first time he'd heard his most hated of nicknames. From across the hotel bar, someone had shouted, "Hey! Poo-Poo Man! Sick story, dude!"

And a shit-eating grin had spread across Conor O'Malley's face over his neat whiskey. Archie had seen a small, distorted version of that grin reflected in the brown liquid, goblin-like, as the publisher said, "We could *market* this shit."

From that day forward, the Poo-Poo Man nickname stuck. In Facebook groups and reddit threads, the legend of the Poo-Poo Man grew, and with it, Archie's resentment.

He dreamed of making them all eat shit the next time he saw them. While he toned and strengthened his body, honing it into a well-oiled machine, classical music playing in his earbuds—not always but usually Mozart—he imagined the things he would do to them all, but especially to Conor.

When he wasn't writing or working out, Archie was a nurse in an elder care home. Stained with the vile moniker they'd given him, he couldn't help but think about it each time he wiped shit from between the wilted buttocks of an elderly patient, when he emptied their stinking colostomy bags, when he reached his fingers into their hemorrhoidal anuses to dig out hardened clumps of impacted excrement, like a California panhandler searching for gold nuggets in a damp, fetid crevasse.

He loved his job. Even during the most difficult moments, the reward he felt helping his patients live their everyday lives was uplifting. But the nickname haunted him. It was just a story. He wasn't some kind of sick fecophiliac. He didn't *like* the smell of shit. He didn't savor the gritty feel of diarrhea between his gloved fingers, or the slippery, wormlike texture of a supplement enhanced bowel movement plucked up from the bathroom tiles. It wasn't like he'd strip off his gloves and *smear* it on himself, reveling in its grotesque stench.

It was just a story. A silly little story meant to disgust and amuse some people in a Gross Out contest.

He'd always had the ability to gross people out, since he was a little kid forming fake poop out of dirt and saliva, pretending to discover them like little cat turds to the dismay of the other children in the sandbox.

The performance he'd prepared for this year's Gross Out Contest would teach them all a lesson. He'd been saving it up for months, letting it fester, imagining the shock on their faces. In two days, he planned to spring it on them.

After that, *nobody* would be calling him the Poo-Poo Man anymore.

They wouldn't *dare*.

HAS-BEENS & NEVER WAS

DAVID ENNIS, MULTI-AWARD-WINNING author, blogger, and mentor to several other award-winning writers, couldn't write a single word to save his life.

After a career spanning twenty-six years, sticking to it while so many of his peers had fallen by the wayside—to depression or drugs, from lack of sales or enthusiasm or emotional support, to illness or death—he'd achieved every one of his goals along the way, from contracts with dream publishers to graphic novels to produced movies. And now here he was, addressing a room full of fellow horror authors, most of them younger than him, *hungrier* than him, and he felt like a complete and total imposter.

"My friend David J. Schow," he said, looking over the audience, "helluva writer, by the way—he's often credited for coining the term 'splatterpunk.' David once said, 'I like to keep one hand over your heart, with the other poised to rip out your guts and strangle you with them, as a fallback.' And that, I feel, is the heart and soul of this genre. We're not a bunch of sociopaths and nihilistic reprobates."

Some guy in the crowd shouted, "Speak for yourself!"

David chuckled along with the smattering of laughter from the crowd. "All right, *most* of us aren't," he admitted. "Many of us have spouses and children. A large majority of us aren't lucky enough to be able to write full time, and hold relatively normal day jobs. We're responsible members of society. We eat and shop and fuck like the rest of the world—we just happen to enjoy scaring the shit out of people." This was met with light chuckles. "And we're not too proud, as Stephen King famously wrote, to 'go for the Gross Out.'"

David paused for laughter and applause, which he received. It was a good crowd this year. After the last in-person event, two years back, he'd wondered if Frank and Jane would put on another, what with the so-called "violence" at the Gross Out contest, and several sexual harassment allegations. David had to admit, he was glad they'd stuck with it. They'd implemented the changes requested for reporting incidents and promised to beef up security, which David had noticed on his way in.

Other conventions were great, but he was happy to be back here, among his people. If not for these cons, and the admiration and appreciation he felt showing up here, he couldn't be sure if there was any value in keeping up the pretense.

He shuffled his notes, this little speech the only thing he'd managed to write for weeks. Before it, his well had been dry for going on three years.

"This convention was created, as you know, because our beloved splatterpunk has been largely overlooked by the gatekeepers of mainstream horror. The author of *Psycho*, Robert Bloch, once said, 'There is a distinction to be made between what inspires terror and what inspires nausea.' Charles L. Grant, notable writer of what's sometimes called 'quiet horror,' went so far as to say, 'Explicitness is lazy writing. They don't know how to suggest it so they spell it out.'"

A handful of boos erupted throughout the crowd.

David held up a mollifying hand. "Look, I think Grant was a fine writer, and Bloch was one of my earliest influences. But they were dead wrong. And I think we've proven that, with outstanding writers like Clive Barker, Ed Lee, Wrath James White, Skipp and Spector, Poppy Z. Brite, Brian Keene and Matt Shaw—there he is, the lovely gentleman giving me the finger," he said, pointing into the audience—"just to name a handful. Yes, we could easily be accused of too-often plucking the low-hanging fruit. But it's just hanging there, waiting to be picked, isn't it? Is it somehow more noble to ignore it?"

Heads shook in the sea of faces, rapt on his every word.

"It's easy to pick on our characters as human beings, or our abilities as writers, because of the subjects we concern ourselves with. We peer deep into the darkness and interpret what we see without holding back. We refuse to pull punches, and we enjoy it, and it's something none of us should be ashamed of, whether it's what we enjoy writing or reading or both."

General applause, punctuated by whistles and cheers.

"We may be horror writers, but we're horror *fans* first. We're horror *writers* second."

I'm not even sure if I'm that anymore, he thought.

"Anyway, that's my five minutes. Get out there, mingle, meet your favorite writers, get some autographs. But most of all, have fun!" He glanced over, saw the convention manager signal him, and added, "Oh, and I hope to see some of you at the panels and readings, and of course, my personal favorite, the topper on the cake, Sunday's Gross Out contest."

David left the stage to a roar of the crowd. He took the bottle of water the convention manager offered, twisted off the cap, and took a healthy gulp. The stubby bottle was adorned with the convention logo on its label, and the product tasted as expected. But David was beyond thirsty. He would've downed a bottle of his own piss if it was chilled enough.

"Exceptional speech, David," the convention manager said, following Ennis into the crowd. "Truly exceptional."

David nodded at his friend, Frank K. Wallis: a subpar writer but a decent publisher for a mid-sized press and all-around good human. He had a little Van Dyke beard like Lenin, wore a Che Guevara T-shirt with a bright green trucker cap like some young L.A. hipster, and frequently espoused, on his social media, the benefits of ingesting "microdoses" of lysergic acid diethylamide and other psychedelics to cure depression and anxiety.

"Could I get your autograph, Mr. Ennis?"

A kid had stepped into their path, wearing some kind of cloak. *Is that a druid costume or is he playing one of the dudes from* Eyes Wide Shut*?* David wondered. Either way, the kid's sweaty, pimple-spotted face was partly obscured by its hood. In a bandaged hand the kid held out a weathered copy of *Medusa's Curse*, one of David's early novels, currently out of print.

"Sure, kid. Call me David."

The kid grinned, showing teeth dotted with what looked like poppy seeds. Even the sharp smell of bleach wafting up from him couldn't disguise his Comic-Con-worthy B.O.

David took the book and pen—normally he'd only use one of his own signing pens, but he'd left them at his table—scrawled a vaguely humorous message on the title page along with his signature, and handed them back. The kid nodded thanks, and headed off seemingly pleased into the moving crowd.

Frank dutifully squirted hand sanitizer from a small bottle into David's waiting hand as they continued to his table. David rubbed his hands together vigorously. It was one of the things he disliked about cons: shaking hands with strangers, using their pens, holding their books and cell phones, visibly smeared with streaks of their sebum, spit, crotch sweat, snot and ear wax. He wouldn't put it past some of them to inadvertently imprint their belongings with shit and piss, semen and vaginal discharge.

To be honest he loved *most* of his fans, but he was a bit of a germaphobe, especially since the pandemic, which made him even more skeptical of the general public's hygiene than he'd been in years prior.

The problem was, some of his readers got a little too close for his comfort, acting overly familiar with him, like they were close friends he hadn't seen in ages rather than people he'd only ever interacted with on the internet. He'd been an early adopter of social media for writers, and had spoken with readers online well before big names like Stephen King and Joyce Carol Oates were easily accessible to fans. Before agents and publishers began suggesting it to all of their writers.

Even on the best days, sifting through tags and replies on Twitter was like navigating a fire swamp. Young writers tried to topple his career on a regular basis, as if he was a statue of some awful historical figure. What they didn't seem to grasp was that standing on the shoulders of giants offered little benefit if you've clipped them off at the knees.

But I digress, he thought with an inward chuckle, and took another slug from the plastic bottle. There was an off taste to the water. He handed it back to Frank. "This water tastes bad."

"We got a discount for bulk orders with the logo. If you want, I could get you an Evian?"

"I'm good." He raised a fist to his sternum and let out an acrid belch. "I'm gonna head on up to my room for a few. Let Dean know, would you?"

David nodded toward Dean Foster Towne at their vendor table. He was handing back change for some buttons, while surreptitiously trying to sell the customer on one of his own books. The customer looked like she was dreaming up an excuse to get the hell out of there.

David didn't begrudge Dean his hustle. It was the least he could allow the kid, considering.

Only Dean knew David's Dark Secret—*And Clay, don't forget him*, he reminded himself, as if he could ever forget. Even Vanessa didn't know, and they'd been married since he sold his first novel in the late-'90s. She didn't know his creative well had run dry. And as long as the bills got paid, she would never *have* to know.

But his Dark Secret was much worse.

If anyone found out, it would *ruin* him. Fortunately, non-disclosure agreements prevented either Towne or Kayden from making it public, and he aimed to keep it that way.

David handed the empty water bottle back to Frank, who took it dutifully. "Thanks, Frank. I'll be back down in a few."

He had to pass the bar on the way to the exit. Normally passing a bar came with its own aggravations—he'd been off the sauce for three years, for reasons he didn't like to remember—but it was worse with that arrogant prick Ackerman slouching in his bar stool, slurring every second word. Drunk at a hair past happy hour. Probably hitting on every young piece of tail who ventured into his orbit. If there was anyone in the horror community David wanted to take a slug at, it was that lazy, sleazeball piece of shit.

Serenity now, Dave, he thought, picking up his pace. *Just a few more steps and you're in the—*

"David, my dear!" the old has-been called out. "Not planning to walk by without saying hello, I hope?"

Ennis sighed. He turned reluctantly, wearing a phony smile. "Later, Andy. Duty calls."

Ackerman appeared sufficiently chastised, but returned his attention to the young woman with colorful braids leaning against the bar beside him, drinking something fruity from a martini glass. She raised the glass to him with a slight smirk. Ennis vaguely remembered speaking to her briefly this morning, as he was setting up behind his table. Something about the new assault policies, from what he recalled. Whether they were strict enough.

Yeah, that's it. I remember she seemed to place a lot of emphasis on the word "strict." Weird crowd this year.

"Oh, David!" a woman called in sing-song, as he turned back to face the lobby.

A woman in her forties approached him, wearing a heavy gray shawl with a bunchy, pleated denim dress underneath. If not for the arms full of thick notepads and hardcover books, David might have mistaken her for a sister wife recently escaped from some Mormon pluralist compound.

She stopped right in his path. The lobby was so close. He shot a glance behind himself, caught a glimpse of the kid in the—*It's a druid, definitely*—cloak vanish into the crowd. For a second there he was sure the kid had been watching him.

David returned his gaze to the woman, who was looking at him expectantly. Though she looked nothing like Kathy Bates, she had a sort of Annie Wilkes quality to her. His first instinct was to ask, *Do I know you?* But of course, he didn't know her. And asking would do him more harm than good. Better to pretend he remembered her from wherever it was they'd met before, then quickly excuse himself.

"Hi," he said.

"Rosalee," she prompted. "Rosalee Adams. We met on Facebook. We've spoken several times on Messenger."

Reason number 111 why I don't use Farcebook anymore, he thought. "Of course, Rosalee. Listen, I'm kind of in a rush—"

"I promise I won't take up much of your time. I know you're a very busy, *extremely* busy man, that's why you missed my last message over a month ago, but what I wanted to ask, and maybe this is a bit presumptuous of me, but what is your advice to a writer who receives poor criticism from a reviewer? I know the common wisdom is to ignore it, but I've been having such a terrible time with this pernicious review, it's costing me sales, I believe, and if I could only just *talk* to the man he'd understand and take it down, but he's ignored several emails and I'm just about at my wit's end—"

"Have you considered physically assaulting him?"

The woman goggled at him, her mouth open but finally, mercifully, no longer producing words.

"I'm kidding," he said, and barked a laugh. She didn't laugh along with him. She didn't even close her mouth. "Common wisdom is right, in this case. Ignore it. Even bad reviews are sales pitches to someone, especially in our market. Now, if you don't mind…"

The woman—he'd already forgotten her name—shut her mouth audibly with a soft jiggle of her jowls and David sidestepped her, moving briskly into the lobby.

2

6:30 P.M. Reading from Shawn Anders,
Conference Room 3:

This story is called, "I Wish I Could Do That."

I was thirteen when I figured out how to give myself a blowjob.

My dad and me used to repeat this joke when our dog, a Golden Lab named Stan, licked his own privates. Dad would turn to me and say, "I wish I could do that." And I was supposed to say, "Why don't you ask him?"

You know that expression, "If I could do that, I'd never leave the house"? Well, it's true: once I learned how to suck myself off, I *never* left the house, aside from going to school.

Look, I'm not implying I've got a huge dong. I was short and skinny back then. I started learning karate when I was twelve to deal with neighborhood bullies, and that led to being incredibly limber, as well.

There's this story that Marilyn Manson got his two lower ribs removed so he could blow himself. I think before him the story was attributed to Prince. And Prince was pretty short. I bet he could've blown himself if he really put his mind to it. But while I spent my teens gobbling my own man meat, Prince spent his learning how to shred guitar. I'll leave you to decide which youth was better spent. I mean, *look* at me.

We all know Manson and Prince probably didn't remove their ribs to blow themselves, just like Richard Gere never put a hamster up his ass. It's rumors. It's a funny way to break the ice at parties.

But there is a guy who *did* blow himself, and that's confirmed. It was filmed, back in the '70s. *Multiple* times. People called him the Hedgehog, for obvious reasons.

Okay, if you need me to spell it out for you, he curled himself into kind of a ball to suck himself off, like how a hedgehog curls into a ball to protect itself from predators. Now you know why Sonic's always shooting up those loop-de-loops so fast. He doesn't give a shit about those coins, he's up there slurping on his schlong!

What? Can you blame the poor guy? He's got constant blue balls.

Anyway, obviously I'm talking about Ron Jeremy. If you don't believe me, look it up. I'll wait.

Sorry. I've got the image saved.

Actually, it's my screensaver.

Anyways, if somebody says it's impossible without removing your ribs, they're wrong. I should know, I used to do it every day.

The trick, the way I figured it out, was to sit on the couch or my bed and bring my knees up so they're level with my shoulders. Again, short and skinny. You're not exactly sitting on your butt, you're on your tail bone. You gotta get hard first, otherwise you likely won't be able to reach.

Look at this guy, taking notes.

At first, I was only able to lick the tip. It was weird, tasting my own precum the first time. You know, I'm a relatively straight guy, I never expected to taste cum. I got used to it pretty quick, and after a few tries the whole thing got easier. I also started doing a lot of crunches to make sure and keep off that belly fat. Less meat between me and my meat.

Oh, I wish I had an Oscar Meyer wiener…

Eventually, I was able to get the whole head—the glans as they call it, in doctor school—I got the whole tip in my mouth. Now, straight guys—and gay women—if you've never had a dick in your mouth, this next part might sound weird. You know that feeling, when you put your tongue on the head of a battery? That's the way it felt when I was about to cum.

To be honest, as much as it was a really good orgasm, it was also kind of *empowering*. Who needs a girlfriend when you can do this yourself? I was the ouroboros. The Alpha and the Omega. The sucker and the sucked.

Most times, I'd get ready with the tissue or whatever was close at hand, and shoot in that. But once, I got a little curious. So, I let a bit shoot into my mouth before reaching for the rag. It did not taste good. As a kid who used to eat his own boogers, I honestly expected it to taste like butter cream in comparison.

Anyway, the last time I did it, the last time I was *able* to do it, I came home from school already anticipating a night of self-romance, since Dad had to go to parent-teacher night after dinner. I waited until the headlights left the driveway, put on some nice music, lit some candles.

Oh, yeah, I was *really* into it. Oh, and my home life wasn't exactly typical if, uh, you couldn't already tell. It was just my dad and me and Stan, the dog. My mom left when I was a kid, I suspect because she was psychic and saw things like what I'm about to tell you in my future.

So my dad, he was gone for a few hours. And I stripped down to my socks—yeah, I'm a socks-on guy, for traction, mostly, and also because I get cold feet, just ask my girlfriend—then I climbed up onto my dad's bed.

Now, to be clear, that's not a weird father complex thing. He just had the better mattress. Mine was too hard, and his let you sink into it just enough that it was more conducive to sucking myself off in this position, what I called "hedgehogging." Anyway, I put down a towel. It's not like I was doing it on his *sheets*. I'm not a *Philistine*.

So, I'm deep into it—well, not *physically*, I was still only able to get the tip in my mouth—but I'm really going to town, I'm churning butter, and lo and behold, I hear scratching on the door. It's Stan. Did I lock it? I can't remember. But I'm getting close, if I stop now, I won't be able to finish and I've wasted a rare evening entirely to myself. So, fuck it, I keep going. I'm *pounding* my balls at this point, you know, desperately trying to make the butter to come out.

Then it happens. The door swings open. Stan comes trotting in, sees me with my knees up to my head and my dick in my mouth, I don't know *what* he's thinking, but he runs right over to me and starts sniffing my butt, his cold wet nose *literally* between my ass cheeks.

And as much as I want to push him away, I realize this is actually *working* for me. Like, it's gross on a *mental* level, but so is sucking yourself off. I've already crossed the Rubicon here—this is just a particularly filthy tributary that has yet to be explored.

Anyway, I hadn't showered, so I was pretty salty down there. And Stan's going to town. He's eating my butt like a can of wet food and I'm gobbling my knob and George Michael's singing "Careless Whisper" on the radio and I'm about to pop.

And then, Dad walks in….

You wouldn't believe how long it took to wash all the cum out of Stan's fur.

Needless to say, my Dad and I stopped telling the "Why don't you ask him" joke after that. It turned out, I didn't even *need* to ask.

3

Tyler followed Ennis out of the hall and back to the lobby. He stayed a good distance away while Ennis spoke to some plumper in a jean dress. Ennis must've said something pretty awful because he left the cow blinking like one of those baby dolls with the eyes that flutter when you turn them upside down and shake them around.

Ennis crossed the lobby to the elevators. Tyler hung back as two elevator doors opened in succession, while Ennis was accosted for a photo by a female Ash Williams from *Ash vs Evil*

Dead, followed by a group of gender nonspecific cenobites. Tyler hurried across the lobby as Ennis stepped into the elevator.

"Tyler?" someone said. "Tyler Grody?"

His hood had fallen back in his rush to follow Ennis. He drew it back over his head, but it was already too late. The interloper grabbed him by the arm.

Tyler turned with his lips pulled back in a sneer.

"Whoa, take it easy," the lanky guy in a black fedora and pinstripe suit said, throwing up his hands. "Hashtag Peace and Love, brother."

Tyler returned his gaze to the elevators. Ennis was gone. It was like a shell game. The two elevators that had spilled their costumed freaks into the lobby ascended simultaneously. He couldn't tell which one the son of a bitch got on.

"Do I know you?" he snapped at the guy in the zoot Suit.

"It's *me*, dude. Jackson Rawlins. The Hashtag King?"

"Right. Great."

"Yeah, I knew you remembered me. Hey, what's with the wizard cloak? It's a bit of a Hashtag Red Flag, dude, gotta say."

"What about you? What are *you* supposed to be?"

The guy gave him an offended look, then grinned and looped his thumbs under his red suspenders. "This is my *power* outfit, bro. Never underestimate the appeal of a dude in a suit, even a weedy dude like me."

A couple of spooky chicks entered the lobby through the revolving doors. "Ladies," the Hashtag King said, bowing slightly and removing his fedora. His scalp shined through a thinning head of dark hair.

Of course, they laughed at him and hurried away.

"Well, okay, it doesn't work on *everyone*, but it looks like they're more into the dark side. I'll wingman you. With that outfit you could pretend you're into Anton LaVey. Ladies of Darkness dig that old perv for some reason."

"I have to go now," Tyler said. The idea that he'd not only go to a club but go to a club and let this beta-male wingman him was preposterous. The guy didn't even have facial hair but he was acting like a total neckbeard.

"Go?" the Trashbag King said. "Dude, I *just* found you. We gotta catch up. Hashtag Bro Out! Where ya going?"

Tyler crossed to the concierge desk, trying his best to ignore the idiot in the zoot suit.

"Fine!" Rawlins called after him. "Let's chop it up later. Hashtag Beef House, my dude!"

Tyler slapped his sweating palms down on the desk, forgetting for a moment the injury to his palm from two days prior, which split open excruciatingly under the bandage wrap. The concierge, a genteel looking man with a thin Prince mustache, turned around with a startled look.

"May I help you?"

"Ennis. David Ennis. What room is he in?" He'd left a smear of blood on the desk. The concierge didn't seem to notice—yet.

"I'm terribly sorry, I can't give out that information."

"But I, um… I have a package for him."

The concierge looked him up and down. "You don't *look* like a courier. And even if you weren't dressed like a Franciscan monk, I'd have to take the parcel myself and hold it for Mister…?"

"Ennis," Tyler said angrily. "David Ennis."

"Oh, *Ennis*." He seemed relieved. "I thought you said something else. Yes, I would have to accept the parcel on his behalf."

"But what if it was urgent?"

The concierge made a dubious look Tyler would have loved to wipe off his face. "An urgent parcel?"

"His insulin," Tyler blurted out.

"Does Mister…"

He slapped his palms on the desk again, wincing from the pain. "Ennis!"

"Sir, I'm going to have to ask you to please calm down."

Tyler glanced up at the security camera above the office door, aimed at the desk where he stood. He took a calming breath. This was a bad idea. The concierge would remember him. The footage would be shown on the six o'clock news. Grandma would see it and then it would all come tumbling down.

But then, he'd never expected to *get away with it*. He'd only ever needed to make his point.

"Now, does Mr. Ennis *require* insulin?" the concierge asked with very little patience.

"Yes. He's diabetic."

"Then I would still have to accept the parcel at the desk. It's hotel policy."

The telephone rang. The concierge glanced at it.

"But… but he could *die*."

"Sir, that's a risk the hotel is willing to take to protect our guests. Now if you'll *excuse* me, I need to answer the phone."

Tyler walked away, shaking his head and cursing under his breath.

Jackson Rawlins stood in his path. "Dude, does David Ennis really need insulin? I've got syringes upstairs, I could probably spare one—"

Tyler ignored him and headed for the wide, carpeted staircase. He'd found himself woefully unprepared for this. Despite all of the crime fiction and true crime stories he'd read, and all the meticulous planning he'd done of the deed itself, he hadn't accounted for obstacles he might encounter—unhelpful staff, crowds, annoying social media randos and Ennis's rabid fans—which would make abducting the man far more difficult.

"Wait, you're not playing a *prank* on Ennis, are you? I fuckin love pranks, but diabetic comas are no joke."

If I could kill you right now I would, Tyler thought. *I'd slit your throat and make you a human fountain.* "Would you *please* go away?" he said aloud.

"*Harsh.*" Rawlins pouted. "Hashtag Do Better, dude."

Tyler bounded up the stairs two by two. According to the old-fashioned numbers above the elevators, Ennis had gotten off either on the third floor or the fifth.

He would pick a floor and wait, watching the elevators, for

Ennis to come out of his room.

Tyler glanced at his cell phone, the wallpaper a sketch of H.P. Lovecraft's long, dour face surrounded by tentacles and darkness.

He wouldn't be waiting long. Ennis had a reading in less than an hour.

It was time to get serious.

#CANCELED

1

CLAY APPROACHED ENNIS'S vendor table, playing cool. This year's model, a young writer by the name of Dean Foster Towne, looked up from his cell phone, held up for a selfie video. "Greetings from Splatterfest Day One in Buffalo, New *Yawk*," he said, pronouncing the state with a fake New York accent very different from his native English. He swung the phone in a sweeping arc to face the crowd.

Clay turned away to avoid being caught on camera. Ennis was in the main hall, MCing the opening ceremonies. No chance of an encounter, though it was possible someone might recognize him and later inform Ennis that Clay had been at his table. The boxes Clay had noticed on the table earlier were Ennis's very own custom-made Funko Pops, the heads of which were just about large enough to fit the man's ego.

Towne finished his video and set down his phone. "Sorry, mate. Doing a TikTok."

Clay tried not to smirk. The app was teeming with writers, desperate to grab hold of the gnat-like attention span of the younger generations in the hope of making a buck. Meanwhile, Towne started straightened the stack of his own paperbacks, in an obvious ploy to draw Clay's attention toward them. "See anything you like?" he asked. His accent was posh, very different from Moira's working-class Welsh.

"Yeah, actually. I'm a big fan of your work," he lied. From what he'd read in the Amazon samples, Towne's prose lacked passion and was heavily influenced by Ennis's *Lee Stark* series, which in Clay's opinion were Ennis's laziest commercial efforts, begun during a low point in his career when he'd been deep in an alcoholic binge, cheated on his wife repeatedly and come very close to divorce. These were all things Ennis had admitted to Clay during their time on the road together, crossing the country slinging his books.

Towne brightened at the compliment, an impossibly white smile spreading across his tanned face—*Or is that makeup?* Clay wondered. He had to admit this year's model was better looking than him. Younger and far more polished.

"That's brilliant," Towne said. "Were you looking for a signed copy then, or…?"

Clay reached for one of Towne's books, then passed over it to pick up a special convention edition of Ennis's *Medusa's Curse*. "Actually, I was hoping to get one of these signed, but I guess I picked a bad time."

The man's shoulders sagged but the smile remained on his face, like a poorly made wax statue of a Hollywood star. "David's at the opening ceremonies at the moment."

"Right, yeah."

"He does have some flat-signed—"

"I'd rather get one personally inscribed. Hey, listen, do you wanna grab a drink when you're done? I'm a writer myself and it'd be a real honor if I could pick your brain. I'm buying."

Towne shrugged. "I'm *supposed* to be doing a thing with David…."

Clay thought he knew what "doing a thing with David" meant. It was something Towne would probably be eager to get out of, though not so eager that he could bail for just anything. Clay picked up a cheap-looking hardcase of Towne's debut novel, *Castles Made of Bone*. "How much did you say one of these was?"

Towne smiled again. He nodded at the sign in front of the stack of books. "Twenty dollars, signed. Or fifteen for two paperbacks."

"What's that in pounds?" Clay asked.

Towne shrugged with a look of vague annoyance. "Haven't a clue, mate."

The second book was an anthology Ennis had published, featuring one of Towne's short stories and a reprinted novella from Ennis. Since Clay had no intention of reading either, he chose the *Castles* hardcover. Give the guy a thrill.

"Who should I make it out to?" Towne asked.

"To James," Clay said. "James Lovecraft."

Towne poised with the pen over the title page, then blinked comically. "Wait. *Lovecraft?*" His eyes narrowed. "Is that a pen name, mate?"

"No, actually. Howard was my great grandfather."

"*The* H.P. Lovecraft was your…? I mean you've got to be joking."

"Wish I was. Having a Stoker or a King for a relative might be okay, but I bet you can't guess how many times I've been told how racist my long-dead ancestor was so far today."

"Have you considered a pen name?"

"I have, but I figured someone would find out anyway and expose me, like Joe Hill. So I just decided to embrace it."

Towne nodded thoughtfully. He appeared to be making up his mind as he signed the book. "You know what, I think I can get out of that thing tonight…."

He handed the book to Clay, who took it with a smile.

"Terrific. Why don't you text me when you've wrapped up for the night and we can meet in the lobby?"

Towne nodded. "Brilliant. H.P. Fucking Lovecraft. That is *wild*. You must've heard some crazy stories growing up, mate."

"Oh, you wouldn't believe the stories I've heard." Clay grinned. "Do me a favor, though?"

"Name it."

"Don't tell David what you're doing."

"Absolutely. I'm an impenetrable vault. Your secret is safe with me, mate."

Clay wondered if that was the case, and hoped to find out

tonight. He wandered through the crowd, back to where he'd been standing with Moira.

"You should be fucking ashamed of yourself," a familiar woman said, stepping into his path. She had frizzy brown hair, thick black glasses, a perpetual sneer, and one of those bull nose-rings that were just starting to come into fashion when Clay left college and now seemed ubiquitous among the progressive youth.

"Excuse me?" he said.

"You heard me." She seemed drunk. He smelled vodka on her breath. What a silly thing it was to put a bar in the middle of a room full of writers. "I know who you are."

For a moment, he wondered if she'd overheard him lying about being related to Lovecraft. Then it clicked. It was *her.* Fiona St. Claire. She'd been in the front row during his Gross Out Contest reading, one of the first writers to try and get him blackballed from Splatterfest, and likely from the industry as a whole. She'd claimed his story had caused her "trauma," that his words were an "act of violence," and that she hadn't "consented" to the "verbal assault" of his story.

He took a deep breath, holding it in long enough to prevent himself from saying what he *wanted* to say to her. He knew exactly what she wanted. She wanted a fight. He refused to give it to her.

"You're right," he said. "What I did was inexcusable."

She stared at him blankly. "I… what?"

"I just hope that you can find it in your heart to try and forgive me."

"Your story was racist. It was *sexist.* It was anti-gay!"

It was none of those things, but he nodded. "And I'm trying my best to do better, Fiona." She flinched at the sound of her name. "I'm putting in the work."

Fiona St. Claire suddenly appeared to be on the verge of tears—of rage or shame or relived trauma, Clay didn't know. And honestly, he did feel bad for her. If she truly had been hurt by his words, she was a fragile thing, too delicate for this world.

And if she hadn't, if she'd been virtue signaling or whatever people like her called it, that was sad in a different way. Chasing clout by faking offense was a sickness of the online world.

But social media wasn't real life. If it was, all hell would break loose on a daily basis. People would constantly scream at each other, never listening, never looking the person they spewed their bile at in the eye. Never recognizing them as a fellow human being, only ever as an "other" to be shouted over and shamed, chastised into oblivion.

"I just hope that we can move forward together, as a community," he said, reaching out to touch her shoulder.

"Leave me alone!" she shouted, violently shrugging off his hand. "You don't get to *touch* me! Don't you *ever* touch me, you *fucker*! You piece of fucking sexist *shit*!"

She stormed off then, and a few people in the crowd paused to figure out what happened, who the piece of shit was, then continue on with their day. Only a tall, lanky guy who looked like the trumpet player in a ska band with his fedora and suspenders, remained staring at him.

"Are you nuts?" the guy asked. "You wanna get thrown out? Hashtag Respect Women, dude."

"Namaste," Clay said with a small, clasped-handed bow. He returned to just about where he'd been standing with Moira before she'd left for the bar. He finished his Coke, scanning the crowd for Ennis or Fiona St. Claire or one of her friends. After a moment, Moira returned.

"I'm back," she said, holding up her refreshed drink. "Did I miss anything?"

Clay shrugged. "Nothing much. Ready to mingle?"

Her eyes lit up, and she smiled. "Changed your mind, did you?"

"I guess so. Maybe we'll spot Kendra Pleasance," he said, knowing the name of Moira's favorite director would get her excited.

She flushed, as if he'd embarrassed her somehow. "That'd be tidy," she said, which Clay had discovered via context seemed to mean *great* in Wales. "Shall we?"

She held out her arm. He'd never been comfortable looping his arm with someone else's—it made him think of those embarrassing three-legged races from back in grade school—but he indulged her.

He really couldn't get a read on women today, and as they walked into the crowd arm in arm, Clay started to think he never had.

Am *I a sexist piece of shit?* he wondered.

2

Tyler waited by the third-floor elevators for forty-five minutes, according to his phone, before finally admitting to himself he'd picked the wrong floor.

He probably should have stayed in the lobby, but the idiot concierge would have been a problem after the fiasco with the insulin, possibly even sicced security on him for loitering. He'd made a mistake asking for Ennis's room number. He should have been patient. Impatience was the enemy of the assassin. He'd learned that when he was a kid playing *Hitman* on his dad's old Pentium II.

Now it was clear Ennis's room was on the *fifth* floor, unless he'd skipped his reading. Tyler supposed it was possible, though highly likely. Ennis was a very punctual man. He held deadlines and contracts with a great deal of respect. He was the "working man's horror writer," according to his bio, and according to his autobiography he considered lateness a sign of laziness and poor business acumen that would follow a writer "like a bad smell" (his words). Ennis was a recovering alcoholic—alcoholics were always either "on the wagon" or "recovering," they were apparently never "cured"—and his behavior during his "rock bottom" still haunted him.

At least I've narrowed it down. When he leaves the con tonight, I'll hurry up ahead of him.

Ennis's reading was meant to start in five minutes. He was likely off-stage drinking a bottle of Splatterfest-branded water, moistening his larynx to speak without pause for five minutes straight.

Tyler still worried about his own reading for the Gross Out contest. He'd made certain to get the final slot of the weekend, intending his performance to be the curtain call for Splatterfest, save the best for last, the "topper on the cake," as Ennis had said in his opening ceremony address. Some leprechaun with the comically Irish name Conor O'Malley booked his reading in the online form minutes after Tyler's, and Tyler had quickly canceled and rescheduled, just seconds before the cutoff time.

He wasn't so much worried about the piece he'd written itself—he'd gone over it so many times he could recite it while suffering at the hands of the Spanish Inquisition—but he was mildly concerned he might not be able to perform the action that went along with it. He'd practiced on an anatomical dummy, slashing it with a utility knife to punctuate certain pivotal sentences, hitting each one like musical stings.

But a mannequin wasn't the same as a live human being. Mannequins didn't talk back, for one thing. They didn't cry out. They didn't *bleed*.

When Gramma had discovered his dummy in the closet, she'd been very concerned about it. She hadn't said anything because he'd gotten so mad that she'd gone into his room, but she'd clucked her tongue disapprovingly. He'd wondered what she thought of it but didn't dare ask.

After his parents died in that car accident it was just the two of them in that big old house, Gramma in the attic, himself in the basement. The second floor had always been off limits, but since his parents had passed he'd sneaked around up there more and more often. He liked to look at old photos of his mother. She'd been so beautiful. Gramma had apparently looked very similar in her day but that was fifty years ago. These days she looked like an off-white Raisinet and smelled like baby powder and stale urine.

How did I get to thinking about Gramma? I need to get my head out of the clouds and get to that reading.

He hurried to the elevators. David's reading was scheduled to begin shortly.

3

7:00 P.M. Reading from David Ennis,
Conference Room 3:

This is an excerpt from my latest novel, *Dead Heat*, which is book—six, I think?—in my Lee Stark crime thriller series. Just a little preview for any diehard Starkers in the audience.

Now, before we go on, I should mention that this excerpt has several trigger warnings. Should go without saying at a splatterpunk convention, but if you're at all sensitive to violent sexual assault and graphic depictions of torture, please feel free to leave the room. Don't be shy. I'm not holding you at gunpoint, unlike Stark would.

A little background: this time around, Lee Stark's hunting down the so-called Devarim Killer, who's been using the Book of Deuteronomy as a guide to punish people he considers "wicked" or "sinful." Stark's just witnessed the Devarim's latest atrocity, where the killer replaced the lube in a fetish club with hydrochloric acid, with appropriately nasty results.

Needless to say, Stark's mad as hell, and he's got the man he thinks is Devarim in his hot seat, eager to get answers.

Without further ado, here goes:

Stark raised the confession chair higher. There was something satisfying about having this man's exposed genitals at eye level. With what the psycho had done at the Red Riding Hood Club, the hands and faces and pricks of his victims mutilated, flesh and muscle bubbling, stripped to sinew and bone, he deserved everything he'd get and worse.

Stark moved lithely to his table of instruments. The chair swung in midair behind him as Devarim struggled against his restraints. It was no use. Stark had held many killers, child rapists and human traffickers within the chair's bonds. None had escaped it without giving him what he wanted first.

If not quite *justice*, at the very least *closure*.

The killer had snapped awake the moment Stark waved the bottle of amyl nitrate under his nose. He'd blinked furiously against the bright lights but quickly narrowed his gaze. He wasn't afraid to die, at least not yet. What came next would convince him otherwise.

Stark stepped aside, giving Devarim a clear view of the stainless-steel instruments and various other implements of torture laid out on a roll of black velvet draped over the workbench. His fingertips grazed their smooth surfaces. He would enjoy playing with them. He was no sadist, at least not technically. He derived no sexual gratification from torturing these men. This was a job. But there was no rule against enjoying your work. He would have to ask Devarim what Deuteronomy might've thought of that, once he was finished with him.

If there was anything left of him to ask, when all was said and done.

Stark selected a rake-like tool and casually returned to the chair.

Devarim didn't move a muscle. He sat there, staring at the instrument with a clinical detachment. His eyes, almost pure black, stared dead into Stark's own. But Stark knew the man feared him. The sharp tang of the killer's sweat excited him. He knew the smell of fear from experience.

This man would break.

4

"This man would break," Ennis read, pacing the stage in his black jeans, T-shirt and Converse sneakers.

That's the plan, Clay thought with a grin. The rest of the torture scene was typically grim for Ennis, only Clay knew for a fact Ennis hadn't written a word of it. If he had, he might have noticed the shift from the typically sterile, all-business Lee Stark to the almost overtly closeted homophobe Lee Stark of the excerpt. He might also have noticed the not-so-subtle hints of antisemitism in this latest book of his most popular series.

Clay felt the atmosphere of the room shift as Ennis's brutal descriptions and sparse, telling dialogue continued. The subtle frowns, the raising of eyebrows, the squirming in seats. He heard people talking quietly in the rows behind him, and they weren't amused.

When the reading concluded the applause clearly wasn't as uniform or enthusiastic as Ennis had expected. Clay avoided eye contact as the man left the stage, but his former mentor did the same, hiding behind what Ennis would have called "business" if he'd written in a story, taking a guzzle from a bottle of water.

Once he'd passed where Clay and Moira were seated, Moira leaned over and asked, "What the heck was that?"

"I was thinking the same thing."

"Is it just me or was that... kind of *hot*?"

"If that's what you're into, I'm not gonna knock it."

She looked at the empty stage in thought. "So... is Lee Stark a dom or something now?"

"It would appear that way. And possibly homophobic. Maybe antisemitic, too. I'm not sure about the Devarim name, but I think it's from the Torah."

"Does he know it, do you think? Was all of that intentional?"

"Ennis hired a few competing sensitivity readers once a few years back, none of them aware of the others working on the same book. They all eviscerated it, of course, it's Ennis, and it's their job to find stuff to be offended by. But here's the thing: they barely agreed on a single element. Since then, he's privately called it a scam and just gone with his editor, this senior citizen who chain-smokes a pack a day. She's pretty clueless about any of this progressive stuff."

"Clearly," Moira said, snickering. "Lee Stark, cleaning the streets, one sexual domination session at a time." She stood up. "Got to pee. Meet you out front?"

"Wouldn't miss it. Meeting you," he clarified, "not the peeing."

"Ha ha," she said, and excused herself to slip past the woman seated beside her.

The moment Moira left, Clay slipped his phone out of his pocket. He pulled up the message board for the convention, signed in under one of his fake email addresses, and started to type.

Within seconds, his post got a reply. Then two more in rapid succession. People were angry. He could hear it in the crowd, alerts pinging.

Clay grinned, the replies scrolling up the screen faster than he could follow them, reflected in his dilated pupils.

This was going to be *fun*.

5

David felt fairly decent about the reading from the applause, but the few baffled looks and amount of huddled chatting as he left the stage did concern him. Clearly some audience members were offput by the excerpt. He hoped it would prove a good omen for fans of the series. Starkers liked hardboiled, dark-as-hell crime fiction with gruesome deaths and vicious torture. If the Chatty Cathys were upset by the brutality of his reading, at least they couldn't say he didn't warn them.

As Frank Wallis handed him a bottle of water—Evian, this time, not that bottled tap water—David spotted Clay Kayden in the crowd, chatting with a woman who looked something like David's wife, Vanessa. He took a healthy sip and quickly turned away before Kayden could make eye contact.

Vanessa had tried to make him feel guilty about the way he'd left things with Clay, but he'd been too mad at the time. He'd felt betrayed and he'd lashed out. He could have stood beside his friend—they *had* been friends, at least he felt as much—but David had a career to think about, a brand to protect. Twenty-six years was a lot of work to waste in support of someone who'd likely bounce back on his own after a few years out of the spotlight. The incident would be dead and buried by then.

Most of the writers in the room probably knew very little if anything about what happened at the previous Gross Out contest, back in San Diego, and certainly very few readers did. Most of David's fans had little to no interest in how the sausages were made. It was a very vocal minority of writers and reviewers who'd made it impossible for him to support Clay any longer. He'd been painted into a corner. Clay had *painted* him into that corner.

Out in the main hall, he returned to his table, where Towne was selling a few of the pre-signed Lee Stark hardcovers to two young women. Towne pushed his own book on them, but they declined and left with a roll of their eyes.

Again, David couldn't blame Towne for trying. The kid had to eat, and he could sing and dance with the best of them. Unlike Kayden, who just wasn't cut out for the business side of writing, in David's opinion. Clay was a bright kid and a competent writer, maybe even a better writer than David and certainly better than Towne. He had promise, and David knew he'd make something of a career despite what happened, if he didn't quit or flame out like the majority of young writers seemed to these days. But he didn't have an eye for business. He wasn't savvy like Towne.

"Hey, boss," Towne said, tucking his phone back in his suit

jacket.

"How's business?" David asked, sitting in the folding chair beside him.

"Three-hundred clams in half an hour, I'd say business is pretty good."

"Good work. How many of yours did you sell?"

Towne shrugged. "A couple. How'd the reading go? What'd they think of the new Lee Stark?"

"It went pretty well, I think. Some chatter in the back, but then there's always chatter, isn't there?"

"People do like to talk," Towne nodded. "Listen, about tonight…"

David frowned. "You're not bailing on me, are you? We're at a pivotal moment, Dean."

The kid tapped his head with a grin, showing too much of his chemically-whitened teeth. "It's all up here, Dave. But some business just came up."

"If you mean you met someone, far be it from me to stand between a man and some strange."

Towne patted his shoulder. "Thanks, boss. I promise I'll put in the extra push tomorrow night. I think I really tapped a vein just now. I was writing notes on my phone between sales."

Probably sexting his latest conquest, David thought but didn't say. The reading had gone well and he couldn't fault Towne for wanting to stretch his wings a little. He'd just have to put in more effort tomorrow.

"Why don't you take a break?" David told him, feeling generous. "Go make some contacts." He grinned. He had to admit he enjoyed living vicariously through Towne. Married life had its virtues, and he certainly didn't want to be out on the market these days, with all the apps and whatnot, but there were times when he envied the young and single, especially since he'd climbed back on the wagon. "Or break some hearts," he added.

Towne tapped his nose. "Will do, boss."

6

Ennis was in the midst of his reading when Tyler Grody entered the conference room and made his way to a seat in the back.

After the excerpt, Ennis left the stage to applause, meeting up with the convention director, who handed him a bottle of Evian. As people began chatting, a group of people Tyler wouldn't have associated with outside of social media began talking loudly about the "latent homosexuality" in Ennis's work.

"That was worse than Joe Rogan, *and* Jordan Peterson, *and* KK-Kayden's Gross Out story all put together," said the woman with multicolored braids.

"It's just more cishet White Savior power-tripping," said another. "We lowly queers couldn't *possibly* be given the agency to take revenge for ourselves in a David Ennis novel."

Tyler hadn't considered how homophobic and possibly homoerotic the Stark character was before, but it all made sense. Stark never had a love interest, throughout all five previous books. When asked by a police detective friend about his lack of "meaningful relationships" he'd said women just "complicate things," whatever that meant. He'd often inflicted genital torture on men, particularly the child rapists and human traffickers, and he'd always used amyl nitrate, more commonly known as "poppers," to rouse his victims in the confession chair.

Given the context of this particular scene, the use of poppers—allegedly used in the "gay community" to enhance sexual performance and relax the muscles of the anus—felt like it *must* have been a conscious choice. Did Stark *know* he was gay? Did *Ennis* know Stark was gay? Was all of this leading up to some big epiphany in a later novel in which badass private detective Lee Stark "came out" to his audience, or would he be made retroactively gay, like Dumbledore and Grindelwald, or Bert and Ernie?

The group in front of Tyler kept discussing Ennis's "small dick energy," his "*raging* heteronormativity," and his "toxic masculinity." Tyler thought maybe they were taking it just a bit *too seriously*—it was fiction, after all. Rather than interject he pushed his way through the small crowd already leaving their seats. He had to beat Ennis to the fifth floor.

But Ennis didn't go back to his room. He returned to his table, and after a brief exchange with his latest pet project, a barely literate crime thriller writer with three names, he let the other man go and remained seated at his vendor table.

Now Tyler stood at another crossroads. Did he stay with Ennis and wait for the man to get up and leave? Or did he follow the protégé, who could just as likely be going to take a squirt as heading up to Ennis's room?

It could be hours before Ennis left the table. If he followed the protégé, Dean Foster Towne, it was possible he'd discover Ennis's room number within a few minutes.

With an exasperated sigh, he turned and followed Towne through the crowd.

Towne did head straight for the washrooms, and Tyler waited a moment before following him in. A man with dreadlocks was drying his hands with paper towels as Tyler went and stood in front of a urinal. He glanced under the stalls and saw the back of a pair of well-shined brown loafers.

Loud sniffling came from the stall. The bathroom door opened and a large-shouldered bald guy washed his hands at the sink quickly, dried them off, then stood at the urinal directly beside Tyler's.

Tyler stood awkwardly, staring at the white tiles while the man unzipped and unleashed a torrent of piss into the bowl. He saw the man turn to him in his peripheral vision.

Vehement snorting came from Towne's stall, as if he was trying to snort up an especially pernicious booger.

"What are you supposed to be?" the guy at the urinal beside Tyler asked.

"Pardon?"

"What's with the robe?"

Tyler clenched his jaw. "It's a costume."

The man shook twice and zipped up. "Yeah, no shit. But what's it a costume *of*?" He stood there staring at Tyler, a bald white guy with no visible division between his head and shoulders.

"Do you mind? I'm trying to pee."

The man looked down at Tyler's hands cupped in front of the crotch of his cloak. "There's no opening on the front."

Tyler thought quickly, willing this man to go away, to slip on a wet tile and crack his skull on the urinal, to spontaneously combust, for the door to burst open and an active shooter to fire round from an AR-15 into this troglodyte's big shiny head.

"I have a urostomy bag," he said.

"Then why are you standing at the urinal?"

"It's psychological."

The man huffed a laugh. "*I'll* say. I need to remember that one." He turned and left the bathroom without washing his hands.

"Gun shy, eh?"

Tyler startled, forgetting for a moment that he wasn't alone. Towne had stepped out of the urinal, smoothing his suit jacket. He was sniffing and wiping his nose with the back of his right hand.

"Mate, don't let anyone make you feel bad for having a disability." Towne went to the sink and ran his hands under the tap. He checked his manbun, which was pulled tight, wiped under a nostril with his thumb, and flashed a smile at himself in the mirror. "You've probably got twice the strength as him, just from dealing with your day-to-day."

"Thanks," Tyler muttered, still looking at the tiles.

Towne used the blower to dry his hands, smoothed his eyebrows and left the bathroom. Tyler hurried out after him, pausing only briefly to consider washing his unsullied hands.

Towne was surprisingly easy to follow. He didn't appear to be extremely aware of many externalities, mostly concerned with his hair, his suit and his cell phone. One exception appeared to be attractive women, many of whom seemed equally intrigued by him. Tyler supposed it was the suit, as the Hashtag King had mentioned earlier, though he didn't suspect dressing any less like a gargoyle would garner a similar response for himself.

The protégé's peacocking quickly began to grate on Tyler. Fortunately, Towne sauntered and swaggered through the main hall but didn't stop, heading directly into the lobby. He crossed to the elevators.

A woman stood behind the front desk, sparing Tyler further embarrassment. The concierge from earlier had likely gone home. Tyler didn't expect the woman would be any more candid with the whereabouts of their guests, but hopefully it no longer mattered.

He rushed to the stairs, bounding up them two by two. By the time he reached the second flight he heard the elevator ding.

He was winded by the time he reached the third floor, and absolutely exhausted by the fifth. He burst through the doors just as the elevator doors slid open a little way down the very generic hotel hallway. Towne reached into the pocket of his jeans as he walked, heading down the hall in the opposite direction. Tyler followed, watching Towne take a left at the T-section.

The opening bars of Britney Spears's "Oops!... I Did It Again" blasted down the hall as Tyler crept up to the corner and peered around. He recognized it as a Britney Spears song, and wondered if Towne actually liked it or if the ringtone was another part of his persona meant to help him score with low-value women.

Towne slipped the cell phone out from his inner jacket pocket. "Towne." A pause. "Yes, David. I'm at my room right now. A what? What the hell is a Mr. Pibb? Oh, a fizzy drink. I'll have a look and get back to you. Is the adjoining unlocked on your side? Right, shouldn't be a minute." He hung up the phone, muttering, "Silly twat," as he used his keycard on the door.

Tyler hurried over in a crouch as the door to 503 swung shut. It was the second from the corner, which meant Ennis was probably in 501. He heard the sound of a door opening inside. A moment later, Towne's muffled voice came from behind the door to the adjoining room.

"Yes, there's two left in the minifridge, David. Shall I bring one down? Oh, you don't? All right. No bother. *Ciao*."

Tyler sneered. He hated people who weren't Italian and said *ciao*. It just sounded so pretentious and dumb. *Chow*. Did it count as cultural appropriation? He wasn't sure, but the gender-fluid snowflakes he'd been sitting behind at Ennis's reading would probably think so.

Regardless, his work here was done. He could follow Towne some more but there didn't seem to be much point to it. He wasn't keen to make himself feel more inadequate. Writers on the internet always said not to compare yourself to other writers, but this was a whole different thing. Good-looking people annoyed Tyler on a gut level. Good-looking *and* talented hardly seemed fair.

All he needed now was a good vantage point to spring his trap on Ennis. He spotted a soda machine between their rooms and the elevators, and squeezed himself in between the machine and the wall, hoping Towne didn't choose that exact moment to step into the hall. *Yes, I am the same gargoyle you met in the washroom. I dropped a quarter behind the machine. Oh, there it is. I'll just be on my way.*

The hiding spot gave him just enough room to watch the hall for Ennis. He didn't suspect he'd be easily spotted unless someone actually used the machine itself.

Ennis had a panel tomorrow morning but after that he was free and clear of convention obligations until the Gross Out contest on Sunday. It would give Tyler nearly a full twenty-four hours alone with him. He'd have to make sure Towne was out of the room when he finally worked up the courage to do the deed, but they seemed to be sharing table duties, which meant the probability was high.

Ciao, Dean Foster Towne, he thought, with surprising good cheer. *Arrivederci, David Ennis.*

SPLATTER

1

CONOR O'MALLEY AND his Gorehounds cronies dragged Archie Schneider into the crowd for the opening ceremonies. It was a blast this year, with fire eaters and knife throwers, a surprisingly lucid reading from Anderson Ackerman—the man had appeared drunk off his ass mere seconds before launching into apparently memorized passages from his latest dark fantasy novel—then the Guest of Honor came on for his speech.

"So Archer, how come you never got back to me about that book we discussed?" Conor said, talking over the legend on the stage.

Archie hadn't gotten back to him because he'd wanted nothing to do with it. He wanted to be respected as a serious writer. The Gross Out contest was just something he'd whipped up for, as one writer put it, "shits and giggles."

"Look, I get it. I've read your other stories. They're good. *Really* good. You want to be known for more serious stuff. Weird fiction and shit. Cthulhu mythos. And I respect that. But extreme horror *sells*, Archer—"

"Archie."

"—extreme horror sells, *Archie*. It's probably the fastest growing niche in the horror scene right now. People gobbled up your toilet peeper story, no pun intended. But they are absolutely *slobbering* for that Schneider *scheisse!*"

Archie gritted his teeth. Kids had called him *Schiesse*, the

German word for "shit," ever since they'd heard about it in the *South Park* movie, since it rhymed well enough with Schneider. Like shit to the bottom of his shoe, the name had stuck with him all the way to high school graduation.

"—the heart and soul of this genre," David Ennis was saying from the stage. "We're not a bunch of sociopaths and nihilistic reprobates."

"Speak for yourself!" Conor cried, draping an arm around Archie's shoulder and shaking him vigorously. Laughter erupted around them, mostly from Conor's cohorts. At home, when she wasn't writing, Aubrey was a teacher in New Jersey. Shawn Anders worked the line at a meat processing plant in Iowa. Conor was a dentist in Austin. Steve Pilkington sold used cars in Niagara Falls, on the Canadian side of the border. Mike Miller was a stay-at-home dad. His wife was apparently a lawyer for a "very big" firm in Des Moines.

On the stage, David Ennis continued his speech despite Conor's interruption.

"What do you say?" Conor said. "Are you gonna do a reading this year? Blow everyone's asses out of their seats?"

"So to speak," Steve Pilkington added from Archie's left.

Onstage, Ennis said, "The author of *Psycho*, Robert Bloch, once said, 'There is a distinction to be made between what inspires terror and what inspires nausea.'"

The quote spoke to Archie. He wanted to inspire dread, horror, terror. Gross Outs were no better than jump scares in his opinion, overused and often poorly done.

But they *could* be done effectively, under the right circumstances. The buildup had to be just right, parceling out the clues, the pressure constantly building until it finally burst onto the page, catching the reader off guard—and the shock of it, the *disgust*, might remain with them *forever*. They'd find themselves thinking about That Scene in the shower, or on the toilet, or making love. It would disrupt their lives. Spoil their holidays. The moment would fester within their minds like trauma, to be relived and analyzed. A *mind virus*.

"I'll do it," he said.

Conor's eyes popped. "Oh *shit*, he said yes!"

The others cheered quietly, gathering around and shaking Archie's hand, patting his back, as if he'd just told them he was having a child. Archie stood there meekly accepting their praise, quietly judging them all.

Now all he had to do was make sure they were front and center, cheering him on.

2

Tyler had drawn his winter coat over top of his cloak and stepped outside, eager to head to the bus stop and get back to his hotel, when he heard a familiar voice.

"Dude? You leaving?"

The Skintag King stood smoking a joint under the hotel awning, shivering in the cold.

"What business is it of yours?"

The man chuckled, exhaling smoke. "Hashtag Touché. I was thinking about your prank."

"What prank?"

"On David Ennis? I just wanted to tell you, I'm game."

"Game?"

"I'm in. I'm down to clown. Somebody's gotta take that guy down a peg and who better than Tyler Grody and the Hashtag King, huh? We'll be legendary!"

"Legendary," Tyler repeated. Yes, he had considered what he'd planned to do to Ennis would go down in the annals of history. But he had no desire or need for a partner, for someone to share in the glory. And the Hashtag King didn't have a clue what he was signing himself up for.

"No." Tyler shook his head. "I don't think so."

"Aww, come *on*, dude." The Hashtag King flicked the butt of his joint. It hissed in a patch of snow. "Every prankster needs a sidekick. Or at least a hype man. Trust me, you won't find a better shit-talker than the Hashtag King."

Tyler had to admit, that did sound accurate. "What can you do for me?"

"What are you planning to do?"

"I can't say specifically, but it involves video."

"Video. Dude, I *work* in video. I shoot weddings for my day job. I was *born* to do this with you, my man!" He stuck out a hand, palm up. Tyler looked at it impassively until the Hashtag King lowered it and stuck it back in his pocket. "So what, you gonna humiliate him, *blackmail* him? What? I'm all in, buddy. Hashtag I'm Your Huckleberry."

Tyler didn't understand that last one, but he realized he would need someone to help him, at least on the day of the Gross Out contest. Someone would have to make sure there were no problems with sending video into the conference room. The Hashtag King, whatever his name was, didn't even need to know about what Tyler planned at all, and he'd likely be implicated simply for helping him with the video.

"Okay," Tyler said.

A goofy grin spread across the Hashtag King's face. "Right on, brother! Dude, come up to my room, let's hash this thing out."

"I don't think so."

"Come on. Just for one drink. Nobody wants to party," he said in an incredibly whiny tone that almost made Tyler feel sorry for him. "I'm bored as shit in this place. There's a couch in my room. You can crash on it if you want."

He considered it. The alternative was to stand out in the cold for potentially a half an hour waiting on the bus.

"Okay, fine."

"Yes!" The Hashtag King pumped his fist, then patted Tyler on the back.

"Please don't touch me."

"Hashtag Duly Noted. Hey, did I tell you about the new book I'm writing? It's about this zombie killer, right? And he's on his last mission—"

As they reentered the hotel lobby, Tyler already began to regret his decision.

3

Archie hadn't been to a strip club since college, when his dorm buddies had dragged him there for his birthday before realizing he was a drag to bring just about anywhere fun. Unfortunately, that was where the Gorehounds decided to go after they gathered outside the conference room following Shawnders's raunchy story of self-pleasure.

Despite his objections to objectifying women, Archie knew it was best to tag along. He needed to stay on their good side if he wanted them to be cheering him on from the front row on Sunday. Without the Gorehounds crowd up there, he saw very little point in going through with it. Besides, it wasn't as if he'd never seen a naked lady before, and these women would have far less wrinkles than what he experienced day to day working at Wellspring.

The Canadian Ballet was a half-hour drive from the hotel. Steve Pilkington had heard about it on an internet chatroom, specifically about a show that, according to him, would blow their minds. He'd gone ahead the night before—for "recon," as he'd called it, to which Aubrey had said, "How many lap dances can you get on recon budget?" Steve confirmed the place was relatively sleazy, though typical for a strip joint near an airport. He'd asked a few regulars about the show they were going to see tonight and those that had witnessed it firsthand confirmed it was a one-of-a-kind experience.

The five of them piled into Steve's car, Steve driving, Archie—as Guest of Honor—sitting shotgun. Conor and Aubrey sat in the back, with Shawnders "riding bitch," as Aubrey put it. Mike Miller had "pussied out"—another Aubreyism—because he had an early reading tomorrow and his wife would kill him if she knew he'd gone to a strip club.

"So don't tell her," Shawnders suggested.

"If my daughters ever found out," he'd said, "it'd just break my heart."

"Sex work is real work, square," Aubrey said.

"Well, sure. But I'd prefer they got into STEM."

"I'm a big fan of STEM," Shawnders said, surprising the others. "All I wanna see is *stem titties*."

Conor and Michael shook their heads.

Aubrey scowled. "Gross, dude. That's his *kids*."

"Sorry. Got carried away."

They left Mike behind with a chorus of simulated whip sounds, and drove past the airport under the dark, empty sky. Snow had clumped on the roof of the flat, two-story building, and on several cars in the small lot, as if they'd been parked there for hours. The wet asphalt shone red and white from the neon sign, its red maple leaf between CANADIAN and BALLET, spelled vertically in red to represent the flag's stripes. Beside it was a neon ballet dancer who appeared to be nude.

The five of them piled out of the car, doors thunking as Steve Pilkington took the lead toward the club. Music pounded from inside. Everything about this made Archie anxious. The others looked back to see if he was following. He quickened his step, shoving his hands into his coat pockets.

As they passed a rust-speckled Camaro near the doors, Archie saw the driver in the front seat smoking from a glass pipe. A blonde woman raised her head from the driver's lap and he exhaled a cloud of drug smoke into her glossy, pursed lips.

"This is fine," Archie said to himself. "Everything's fine."

Steve held the door open for him with a sly grin. "Come on in, big guy. Cover's thirty-five bucks but I've got the newbie's."

"*Thirty-five dollars?*" Aubrey whined. "How much are the *drinks*?"

"Yeah, they don't serve alcohol here," Steve said.

"No fucking booze? Are you *kidding* me?"

Conor nodded at the Camaro. "I guess that explains Smoky and the Bandit."

"It's New York State law," Steve said. "Fully nude clubs can't serve alcohol. But these guys wanna compete with the clubs across the border, so they nixed the booze."

Aubrey sulked. "What am I supposed to do with my *hands*?"

"Why is that even a question?"

"It's a nervous habit. I need something to do with my hands. Smoke, drink, *something*."

"Why not put em between your legs?" Shawnders suggested with a snicker.

"I'm about to put my foot between yours."

"You know, we don't have to do this if it's too expensive," Archie said meekly.

"*No*." Steve sliced the air with his hands, as if he was cutting prices at his discount car lot. "No, I drove all this way, we're not pussying out now."

"Guys," Conor said, waggling a large metal flask with a grin. "Don't leave home without it."

"Probably won't make it past the bouncer with that thing," Aubrey grumbled.

Conor shrugged. "Well, we can shotgun it now."

That seemed like a good idea to everyone but Archie, who didn't bother to voice his concerns. They passed the flask around. Steve wiped the mouth and said, "You know, we could all get drunk off this if we boofed it."

"Boof?" Aubrey asked.

"You know. Butt-chugging. Boofing."

"I'm not putting a bottle up my ass, Steve."

"Don't knock it 'til you've tried it," Shawnders said, and took a healthy slug from the flask. He grimaced and wiped his lips.

When it came around to Archie, he took it reluctantly, wiped the mouth of it vigorously, then tilted it back.

"*Chug! Chug! Chug!*" the others chanted.

Shawnders lifted the flask from the bottom and Archie choked on a scalding mouthful of what he guessed was whiskey. He never drank alcohol, only protein shakes and water. It burned all the way down and when he coughed, he wouldn't have been surprised to see flames.

Aubrey finished off the flask and the five of them entered a small vestibule with a glassed-in booth for cover and coat check, stationed by a visibly pregnant woman in a tight black T-shirt and jeans. The small space was dark and loud, everything white glowing green from the blacklights, even their teeth. Archie noticed neon green flakes of dandruff and brushed them off his shoulders. Steve and the others paid. They traded their coats for numbered ticket stubs.

"Aren't we supposed to get ponchos?" Steve asked the pregnant attendant.

"Thanksgiving Special tonight," the attendant said, pointing to a sign. "Poncho Night next week."

"Are you *kidding* me? We drove all the way out from the fucking Plaza for the Poncho Show!"

The attendant shrugged. "Enjoy the show."

"For fuck's—" He gritted his teeth. "You could've said that before we paid for cover, you know. This is *extortion*."

Aubrey put a hand on his shoulder. "Relax, tiger." She nodded toward the bouncer, a burly bald guy dressed in black, watching him closely, like he'd enjoy the opportunity to toss Steve onto a fire hydrant.

"This fucking Thanksgiving Special better be good," Steve said, jabbing a finger toward the pregnant woman behind the counter. She just blinked at him.

"*Seventy bucks*," he grumbled, tucking his wallet back into his jeans. The gang followed him into the club. The bouncer patted them down. He was more thorough with Steve, Archie noticed, far less with Aubrey. They met up just past the bouncer, looking for a free table.

The place was packed with men in dress shirts and ties Archie suspected might be on layovers or here in Buffalo on business. He spotted some gang-looking types near the back, getting a table dance from two topless, sparkly women. On stage, a tall, lithe dancer in clear platform heels shuffled lazily around the brass pole while a repetitive beat blared. The incessant refrain assured listeners there were "whores in this house," and while Archie didn't want to make assumptions, he figured there were at least a few.

They found a table up front and watched several dancers of varying quality take the stage one after another. The first was what Shawnders called a "goth chick," which was apparently his type. She called herself Severin, danced enthusiastically to loud rock music, shook her black hair around, and for some reason licked the toe of her shiny black boot several times. A dancer named Thicc—"That's with two Cs," the DJ informed them—came on next to some smooth R&B. True to her name she was quite large and had to lift her stomach to play with herself, a show a small group of businessmen seemed quite fascinated by. She spent most of her three songs lying down in front of them.

Archie watched the show unenthusiastically. Every so often a dancer would sidle up to their table, uncomfortably close, and offer to take them for a private dance in the back room. They seemed to zero in on Shawnders and Steve, as if they knew who would most likely to succumb to their wiles. Eventually, the goth dancer Shawnders had fallen for came around wearing a black two-piece bikini so small it could have belonged to her daughter. She batted her heavy eyelashes and Steve shot up from his seat immediately. Taking her hand, he followed her up the stairs to the VIP Room, making Archie think of a vampire and her familiar.

"Want a bump?" Conor shouted very near Archie's ear.

"What?"

"A bump!" Conor leaned over with a small heap of white powder on the mound between his thumb and forefinger.

"No, I don't do that stuff," Archie said, unsure what "that stuff" was exactly, if it was cocaine or some other drug.

"Come on, man. It'll loosen you up."

"What is it, a laxative?"

The others laughed uproariously. Embarrassed, only hoping to deflect their attention, Archie quickly leaned over and snorted the powder up his nose. The others cheered him, then focused on their own "bumps." Whatever it was tingled and burned in his sinuses for a moment, then filled him with a warm feeling, like sliding into a hot bath after a long shift at the care center.

He leaned back in his seat, getting comfortable, watching a whirling dervish in a Canadian flag bikini spin around the pole with a big bright smile too cheery for her surroundings. The spotlights started to leave trails in Archie's vision and for a few seconds she looked like a candy cane spinning around the pole. When she finally twirled away, a server briefly wiped down the stage and pole with Windex, and the DJ announced the main event: the Thanksgiving Special.

"Gentlemen, put your hands together for… *Vixen*!"

Applause and wolf whistles filled the club as red spotlights lit the stage. An old doo-wop song began, and a dancer burst through the velvet curtains, flapping brown-and-orange wings. She wore a cartoon-yellow beak with a red wattle that flopped beneath her chin, and large plumage on her rump. Beneath this she wore nothing but burnt-umber G-string and beige leather kinky boots.

"What the fuck?" Steve shouted. "We missed Poncho Night for *this*?"

Conor leaned forward. "Hang on, this could be interesting."

Aubrey slugged him in the arm. "Connie just discovered a new fetish: turkey porn!"

"Yeah, yeah," Conor said, "gobble-gobble me. I meant for research purposes."

The Turkey Lady skipped and flapped across the stage, her perky breasts jostling. Archie had to admit, as odd as it was, he was strangely aroused. Embarrassment burned his cheeks.

"You know, as a Canuck I find this kind of offensive," Steve said.

Conor frowned. "How's that?"

"This place is called the Canadian Ballet, but they have the Thanksgiving Special on *American* Thanksgiving. Canadian Thanksgiving was over a month ago."

Aubrey snorted. "Quick, somebody call the Prime Minister."

The curtains parted again, this time for a rolling chef's table with a steel bowl laid on it. A burly, bearded man with sleeve tattoos, dressed in butcher's whites, pushed the table to the center of the stage. The Turkey Lady peered over her shoulder, while the doo wop girls sang about mashed potatoes.

The butcher gestured her over, removing the bowl from the table. She beat her wings and leaped high onto the pole, grabbed it and twirled around it, sliding down until she landed with her bare ass cheeks on the table, straddling it, to the applause of the crowd.

The butcher placed the bowl between Vixen's legs. He took out a pair of clear plastic gloves from his apron and snapped them on. The Turkey Lady lay back against the table, raising her legs as if they were in stirrups.

"I've been a bad bird," she said.

Aubrey turned to the others, looking distraught. "*What is happening?*" she asked, shouting to be heard over the music.

The butcher dug a hand into the bowl. He came up with a fistful of what looked like Stove Top stuffing.

The crowd went wild. Archie cringed. Aubrey covered her eyes, then peeked out from under her hand.

Turkey Lady's labia parted and the chef pushed his entire gloved fist into her vagina, stuffing and all. Moist bits of bread and mirepoix fell to the sides, splatting on the table, smearing on her inner thighs.

"Yeah, stuff me!" she cried, throwing her head back in real or faked ecstasy. "Stuff this bad bird!"

"I think I'm gonna be sick," Steve said, though he didn't turn away.

The butcher reached in for another handful, which he proceeded to stuff into Turkey Lady's moistened cavity.

Aubrey leaned in to shout over the music. "I don't mean to kink shame, but I don't think that's sanitary!"

Steve frowned. "Why not? He's wearing gloves!"

"For *her*, you meathead!"

"Oh." Steve leaned back in contemplation.

"They should've played Madonna," Conor shouted, then sang off-key, "*Like a turkey... stuffed for the very first time.*"

Steve laughed and gagged.

"*Like a tur-ur-ur-urkey—*"

Aubrey rolled her eyes. "Okay, we get it!"

Conor said, "You know, if I wrote this in a story nobody would fucking believe it."

"And yet, donkey shows exist," Aubrey said. "People rub their genitals together dressed in cartoon animal costumes. Kink is the last truly transgressive act, even though I don't personally think *this* particular kink would pass health regulations."

"In Canada," Steve said, "there's this performance artist who sharpened pencils with her vadge. She got a government grant for it. She dressed up as Kermit the Frog and had some woman playing Jim Henson in up to her wrist while she sang 'It's Not Easy Being Green.'"

"I'd like to see someone do *that* at the Gross Out contest." Aubrey got out her phone. "Should we be taking notes? I feel like we should be taking notes."

Archie ignored their chatter, unable to look away from what was happening on stage. Was all of this talking considered rude? Did the people he'd come with even *experience* things, or did they see everything through a lens of fiction, of how something might be utilized in a story?

Despite their disruptive behavior, Archie found himself uncomfortably erect, and crossed he legs self-consciously.

"*Yes! Stuff me!*" Turkey Lady cried, accepting another fistful of stuffing.

"Is human meat considered vegan?" Steve asked.

"Only if you eat a vegan," Conor said.

Fully stuffed, Turkey Lady climbed off the table. The chef took his bowl and left the stage, rolling the table away with him. Turkey Lady then waddled up to the edge of the stage, where the businessmen sat in rapt attention, still flapping her wings. She squatted in front of them and the cords in her neck and tendons in her inner thighs stood out, as if she was forcing a bowel movement.

Oh no, Archie thought, not wanting to see what would happen next yet unable to look away.

A moist glob of stuffing oozed out of Turkey Lady's vagina like lumpy, autumn-colored Play-Doh and splatted on the stage in a wet clump.

Archie caught the table in a death grip, desperate to keep from moaning or crying out as he ejaculated in his underpants. He flinched as Conor patted his back.

"Hey, Archie, buddy, you all right?"

"Oh, the poor baby's sick," Aubrey said with an audible pout.

Archie stood abruptly, glad he'd kept his coat, and held it over his lap as he scurried off in horror to find the bathroom and clean himself up.

"Hey, guys," Shawnders said, returning to the table with a rosy glow in his cheeks and the tail of his shirt poking out between the zipper of his pants. "What'd I miss?"

Authors Behaving Badly

1

ROSALEE ADAMS HAD missed the opening ceremonies that evening but she'd ended up passing David Ennis on his way to the lobby, and had stopped him in the lobby to ask for his advice.

It was wonderful to see so many faces she recognized from social media and dust jackets, though most of those she'd already spoken to personally online seemed not to remember or recognize her in person, which was troubling.

Even worse: David himself didn't seem to remember the conversation they'd had only a few months prior, which had spanned several weeks. She'd passed off his ignoring her last message over a month ago because he'd written on his blog that he'd left Facebook "indefinitely." Rosalee couldn't say she blamed him. If she didn't need it for her group and promotional posts, she might have dumped it herself.

Ennis's advice had taken her aback. Obviously, while reading the hateful review she'd considered reaching through the internet and throttling the reviewer, but when Ennis had told her to physically assault Ignacio Ortega, she'd fallen into a sort of feedback loop of action and consequence, going over what she might do and how she might go about it.

I'll only talk to him. I'll convince him it was wrong to post that hateful review and ask him kindly, again, to take it down. There's nothing wrong with asking.

And if he says no, okay, what then? I'll... I could slap him.

Yes, I could slap him right across his smug face. What's the worst that could happen? A slap on the wrist. Ejected from the convention. Banned? Big whoop. These people don't even remember my name. What good are they to me, anyway?

Yes, that was what she would do. She'd confront him, just as Ennis had suggested. Physical assault—a good hard slap to knock some sense into him—would only be used as a last resort.

She returned to the convention hall, seeking out Ortega. He was a small man with a small beard and a small mind. People seemed to find value in his reviews, which explained why her sales had floundered almost immediately after his review of *A Life Extinguished*. Rosalee considered the type of people who enjoyed his brand of snark and sarcasm to be generally not very nice. It was the lowest form of comedy, taking pleasure in the ridiculing of their betters. Most of them wouldn't appreciate true art if they were staring right at it. They would sneer at the *Mona Lisa*, asking why da Vinci had painted her without eyebrows. All they understood was how to tear down, they knew nothing about how to create. They were no better than art vandals, slashing and desecrating what they feared or failed to understand.

Rosalee realized she was clutching her purse in a death grip, and released it, flexing her now sore hand. She spotted Ortega standing with several women and another man. She suspected they were a group of critics and reviewers, as that was the circle he tended to gravitate toward on Twitter. They connected via the hashtag CriticCrew, and often used it to dogpile writers who'd violated their specific code of ethics.

That was how they'd damaged *A Light Extinguished*. To his credit, Ortega considered himself a professional, and wouldn't have sullied his reputation by naming and shaming Rosalee on his reviewer account. She had simply asked him in the comments on Goodreads if he could reconsider his review, and at the very least tone down some of the snarkier comments—especially the repeated use of the terms "clichéd language" and "laughable dialogue"—and to please remove a few spoilers. She'd been as polite as possible, considering her anger in the heat of the moment and the two Chablis she'd downed, not to mention the rest of the bottle her Maine Coon cat Church had knocked off the table, spilling on the rug.

Ortega himself had not replied, but two other critics did, chastising her "unprofessional" behavior, arguing that "reviews are for readers," a phrase she'd often seen hurled at writers who dared take exception to something said of their own hard work.

It wasn't long before she saw screenshots of her comment all over Twitter, under the CriticCrew hashtag. It took only minutes for someone to tag her with a retweet and the words: "This you?"

From there it had quickly spiraled out of control. The one-star reviews came fast and furious. Rosalee—who wrote under the pen name D.M. Carpe—had spent the entire night fielding angry replies to her Goodreads comment, furious quote tweets and replies and threats of violence on Twitter, as well as downvoting, flagging and replying to one-star reviews with threats of suing them for libel.

One of them had even found out her address using internet wizardry and posted it for everyone and their uncle to see. Fortunately, the tweet didn't last very long, and the account itself was banned for violating the terms of service.

But the harassment didn't stop there, causing Rosalee to take her concerns right to the source. She emailed Ortega through his website, in what she thought was a very considered and polite letter, given the circumstances.

It was several days before he replied. He apologized for the behavior of his "contemporaries" and promised her he would put a stop the harassment right away. As for her initial comment that started the firestorm, he understood her concerns but it was his policy that he did not retract reviews, and he would not take down or alter his review for *A Life Extinguished*. In his opinion, he wrote, it would open the door to authors bullying him into submission, and though he didn't think that was what Rosalee had intended, if he deferred to her, he'd be setting what he called a "dangerous precedent."

She'd tried to bargain with him, tried to reason. She'd

promised him "no one would have to know but the two of us."

To this and the subsequent emails, which even she had to admit had sounded more and more desperate and whiny as she'd read them aloud to Church, he hadn't responded. Church had merely yowled as if annoyed.

Again, to his credit, Ortega issued a brief statement about the incident, urging his Critic Crew to "stand down," following it with a numbered thread—twenty-three tweets long—against cyberbullying, which seemed to take no side in the current situation. In fact, it left Rosalee wondering if he'd considered her polite and reasoned comment to his review "harassment" itself.

Unfortunately, it was too little too late to stop the one-star reviews, and by then her sales had dried up entirely. Her publisher, also harangued online for daring to work with her, told Rosalee he had no choice but to back out of her contract.

And so, her career was extinguished before it even had a chance to burn.

With her rights back under her control, she could have republished the book under her real name or a different pen name—in retrospect "D.M. Carpe" was a tad childish—and even changed the title. She could give it a second chance at life. But self-publishing was no better than vanity press, a dead end for losers and bad writers with poor spelling and grammar and even worse taste in cover art.

Ortega broke away from the group, who seemed genuinely displeased by his departure, pawing after him and calling for him to return. Rosalee straightened her shawl and followed him, losing and finding him again and again as they moved through the thinning crowd. It was getting late. The night was almost over, and Rosalee suspected Ortega wanted to get a good sleep for the critic panels tomorrow morning, featuring such hot-button topics as "The Old Guard: Dismantling Power Structures in Horror," "Should We Separate the Art from the Artist?" and "'Othering' in Fiction."

Ortega took the stairs, and like Stephen King's Gunslinger, Rosalee followed. He glanced back at the top of the second flight, and she quickly busied herself, pretending to be looking for something in her purse.

The critic got off on the first floor, thankfully. Rosalee's calves were already starting to get sore and the two flights had winded her. Aside from Ortega, the hall was empty. She followed him at a far enough distance, removing her keycard from her purse just in case he decided to turn around again. She was staying in an entirely different hotel, a discount place, but it wasn't like he'd be able to see it was a card for the wrong hotel.

He turned the corner and removed his room key from the pocket of his vest. Before he could slip it into the maglock, Rosalee cleared her throat loud enough for him to hear.

"So you *were* following me," he said with a suspicious look.

Rosalee clutched her purse to her chest to bolster her courage. "Yes," she said. "I wanted to speak to you—"

"You're a fan of my work?"

"Actually, I'm a writer. We've spoken before. I'm D.M. Carpe," she said, more brusquely than she'd meant.

"Ah, yes." He grinned and stroked his small beard. "The infamous Rosalee Adams. You know, my husband told me to ignore you. He said if I replied to you, it would only spur you on. I don't like to be proven wrong, Rosalee. Especially by my husband."

"I just wanted you to see it from my perspect—"

"I've dealt with writers like you many, many times," Ortega said, cutting her off. "'Entitled,' we call it in the business. I don't owe you my time, Rosalee. I replied to you as a courtesy and I asked that my followers leave you be. And yet, you persisted. *You called my agent*, Rosalee. That, in my esteemed opinion, is crossing a line."

"But you don't understa—"

"I understand *perfectly*, Rosalee."

Why does he keep saying my name like that? she thought. He was using it like a punctuation mark. Hurling it like an insult.

"You see, I am a writer myself. I understand the urge to defend one's own work, regardless of its merit. When I first started out, as a young man in Cartagena—"

Rosalee snapped. She spotted a room service tray in front of the room across the hall. Two plates of food mostly eaten and an empty bottle of Chablis. She grabbed the bottle by the neck and, without a second thought, swung it at Ignacio Ortega's small head.

The bottle didn't break. It split Ortega's head open at the temple and blood gushed out from the wound. He screamed in horror. Rosalee screamed in tandem, staggering back with the undamaged bottle still in hand, smeared with the critic's blood.

Ortega's scream became a battle cry. He ran at her, hands extended, blood pouring from the wound. His gore-slicked fingers slipped around her throat and he squeezed. Rosalee toppled backwards, knocking over the room service cart, and fell to the floor with a gasp.

She'd never *seen* so much blood in her life. It pattered down on her face, into her eyes and nose and mouth. She spat it out as his small thumbs dug into her larynx. Little black dots floated in her vision. She rolled over and suddenly she was on top of Ortega, striking him in the head with her purse, his grip on her throat loosening.

Finally, his hands fell to his side with a defeated gasp, a black stain spreading from his head on the carpet. His eyes were closed.

"I'm calling the police," a man said, startling her from her shock. She looked up at a man and woman dressed in white bathrobes, standing in the door across from Ortega's.

"This isn't what it looks like," Rosalee said, still lying on Ortega's prone body.

But of course it was *exactly* what it looked like, and only after she'd said it did she realize it was the same sort of clichéd dialogue Ortega had criticized her for in the first place.

2

Archie spent an inordinate amount of time in the bathroom, trying to clean the inside of his boxer shorts, before returning to the table. Everyone made their jokes, but fortunately most of them were about him pooping his pants. Nobody seemed to know that he'd ejaculated while watching the Turkey Lady give birth to globs of wet stuffing. They all just thought the cocaine was probably cut with laxatives, and it had hit him harder because it was his first time.

While Steve drove them all back to their respective hotels, Shawnders regaled them with a tawdry story about his sexual encounter with the goth stripper, who charged him two-hundred dollars, "and I didn't even blow my load," Shawnders said. "Not that she wasn't hot. I just kept worrying the bouncer was gonna walk in on us and throw me out with my pants around my ankles."

"See, that would work for me," Aubrey said. "But I don't pay for sex."

"Women don't *have* to pay for sex," Conor said. "You could literally drop your pussy on the street and someone would pick it up."

"Not all women."

"Sure they could," Steve said. "They just have to have no standards, like Shawn."

"Hey, I just paid two-hundred dollars for twelve minutes with the hottest woman in the Canadian Ballet—sorry, Aubrey, *hottest heterosexual woman who isn't practically my sister*—and you're critiquing *my* taste? Actually, that reminds me of this story I wrote—"

Aubrey rolled her eyes. "Gawd! We get it! You've written a lot of stories."

Fifteen minutes later, Steve dropped Aubrey and Shawnders off at a Super 8 in North Tonawanda, and Conor at his Airbnb condo near Delaware Park. Then he drove Archie back to the

Plaza Hotel, telling him about all of the things that were different here than they were in Canada. Archie tuned him out. After a few blocks it started to remind him of Bubba's shrimp speech from *Forrest Gump*.

"...so that's why we get milk in bags," Steve said as he parked the car in the hotel lot. "And they sell it in liters, not quarts and gallons. Same with gas."

"Oh yeah?" Archie said, not really paying attention as he removed his seatbelt and got out of the car.

"Yeah. Everything's metric. Except for height and weight— we still use pounds, feet and inches, I dunno why."

"Huh."

"It's not as weird as the British, though. I mean, what's up with measuring things with stones and hands? What if you've got small hands? And who decided what size stone to use? It's weird."

"That is weird," Archie agreed. They were inside the lobby now, already warming from the chilly night.

Steve headed for the elevators. "You coming?"

Archie's room was on the first floor. He said he'd take the stairs.

"Suit yourself. Have a good one, dude. Sorry about the other guys, by the way. They can be a bit much."

Archie shrugged. "Thanks. It's fine."

"Nah, I could see you weren't enjoying yourself. You were just playing along. I appreciate that."

Archie wasn't sure what to say. He nodded.

"And sorry again about the Turkey Lady, eh? Poncho Night would've blown your mind. Bit messier, though."

As they left the Canadian Ballet, Steve had described what he'd heard about Poncho Night, in which a performer sprayed the audience like a garden sprinkler with a several gallons— Steve said "liters," which he probably even spelled differently— of colorful liquid she'd squirted into her vagina and anus during the show. It sounded pretty unappealing to Archie. Then again, if someone had described the Turkey Goddess's performance to him, he never would have imagined he'd end up basting the inside of his jockey shorts from it.

Back in his room, he flicked on the lights and removed his belt and khakis on his way in. He slipped off his underwear—white crust still streaked the inside, despite all the scrubbing he'd done in the strip club toilet stall—and picked up a roll of saran wrap from the vanity, beside his leather briefcase.

He brought the plastic wrap to the toilet, lifted the seat, rolled some out and spread it over the bowl. After a minute he'd formed a pouch. He put the seat down, pinched the head of his penis to prevent himself from urinating into the pouch he'd made, and squeezed out a triple-coiler onto the plastic wrap so smoothly he doubted he'd even need to wipe.

Baby laxative, he thought, feeling a phantom tingle in his nostrils from the cocaine. *Maybe I should look into some of that.*

3

Clay and Moira were at the hotel bar, seated in a pair of big comfy couches near the back in dim mood lighting beside a gas fire made to look like a real hearth. While Clay nursed his third Coke Zero, Moira guzzled her—it had to be fifth—gin gimlet and was looking a little tipsy, stretched out on the sofa with her shoes kicked off on the floor, wiggling her toes. She wore what they used to call "nude" pantyhose under her pleated slacks.

"You *apologized* to her?" She laughed disbelievingly.

"I know. It's the exact opposite of what I've always said I'd do if someone confronted me about it, but honestly, if I didn't apologize, I would've just spewed a whole year's worth of bile all over her, and it's not like she was the lone culprit. Then some asshole would've recorded it, and that'd be the end of my short-lived career."

"Clay…" Moira pushed herself up to sit, leaning forward with her elbows on her knees. "You were harassed so badly you avoided social media for an *entire year*. I'm sure *most* people would understand…"

"These people? It's all crabs in a bucket, Moira. Every one of them clawing over each other in their struggle to get to the top. But most of them are just gonna fall right back to the bottom. Sometimes…" He trailed off, thinking about his plan.

"Sometimes what?"

"Sometimes I think about burning this whole damn scene to the ground."

She blinked several times, her eyes glassy, before responding. "You think that would make you happy?"

"I don't know if it'd make me happy, but at least I'd feel like I *accomplished* something."

"You've got a novel coming out in a year with a major publisher."

"But it's all tainted. My Gross Out story, the controversy over it, it'll follow me around for the rest of my life. You can't erase the whole internet. Much as I'd like to."

She nodded, though her eyes looked heavy, as if she might pass out on the sofa at any moment. "I get it. You feel like the horror community, whatever the hell that means, like they turned their backs on you. Rightly so, I'd say. Only a handful of people had the courage to defend you in public. Even Ennis, who'd championed you as a Young Writer of Promise, even he threw you under the bus the second he realized defending you might tarnish his own image. Do you remember James Frey?"

"The guy from the Eagles?"

"That's Glenn Frey. James Frey wrote *A Million Little Pieces*, what he claimed was a non-fiction book about his life as a drug addict. None other than Oprah made it one of her Books of the Month. Then it came out that it was mostly made up, and Oprah's fans got out the pitchforks. Rather than defend it as an outstanding piece of fiction, Oprah condemned it. She condemned *him*. Ennis did the same to you. He chose to side with a toxic portion of his fanbase over his friendship with you. And you were hurt. After nearly a year on the road together, I'd say understandably so."

Clay sat back, considering her words. He was about to reply when his front pocket vibrated. He pulled out his phone. A text from Dean Foster Towne, asking him to meet in the lobby.

"I think you need to forgive him, Clay. You don't have to agree with what he did, but you've been so angry since it happened. You need to let go of all that rage."

Clay nodded, but he didn't agree. Rage was a good motivator. Anger had fueled his latest novel, sold for a decent first-time advance. Without the rage he'd stored up over the past two years, since the Gross Out contest, he'd still be writing silly, high-concept ghost fiction. True horror was other people, to paraphrase Sartre.

"So, Clay Kayden, I've had one…" She looked at the empty cocktail glass on the low table between them, licking a few granules of sticky sugar off her lips, moistening them. "…*a few* too many gim ginlets," she said, mixing up her words, "and I'm afraid I'm too tipsy to make it to my room without a handsome man to escort me."

"You're drunk," he said.

"Are you just going to repeat what I say, or are you going to take me to bed?"

"Moira, I…"

Another buzz.

"I'll get you to your room but I'm not going to sleep with you."

Her expression flattened. "You don't want me."

"Of course, I want you, Moira. I wouldn't have shown my face at this fucking con if not for you," he said, though it was only half true. "But not like this."

"Clay, I drink to lower my inhibitions. To let loose. It's *deliberate*. I'm not unconscious. You wouldn't be taking advantage. *Two years*, Clay."

"I know."

The phone buzzed insistently.

Moira nodded. "Oh, I see. You've got a more interesting prospect on the line."

"This is business."

She glowered. "Go then. Take care of your 'business,'" she said, emphasizing her distrust with scare quotes.

"I'll take you upstairs—"

"*Go*, Clay."

"Honestly, Moira—"

"*Go*," she said, not looking at him.

He stood. "We'll talk tomorrow?"

She was staring at the fire.

"Are we good, Moira?"

"We're fine," she said, the fire reflecting in her glassy eyes. "I'll see you tomorrow."

Clay nodded, though he was wise enough to know they were anything but fine, and left. He just hoped Moira wouldn't be too angry. With any luck, she'd had enough gin gimlets to forget all about the incident in the morning.

4

David walked with Towne to the lobby, rolling the boxes of their respective books and merch on a dolly. After the last con he'd done, where two stacks of his hardcovers and a box of pins had been stolen, David no longer trusted the hotel staff to keep his wares under lock and key overnight.

Red and blue lights flashed on the snow outside. David only noticed it on a subconscious level. His mind was on the new King novel—it was a massive tome, as usual—that was waiting for him in his room, and one of two ice-cold cans of Mr. Pibb left in the minifridge. They went by Pibb Xtra now, but when you were that delicious, in David's opinion, you deserved to be called Mister.

Towne pressed the button for the elevator, what he'd earlier argued should be called a "lift" everywhere, with what seemed to be his trademark colonialist attitude—in contrast to David's admitted Americentrism—since "lift" was only one syllable and thus easier to say. They stood there together, watching the floor numbers above the doors. The second elevator seemed to be stuck on the first floor.

"I'll be fine, Dean. Do your thing, kiddo."

Towne patted his shoulder, giving him a million-dollar smile. "I'm meeting my friend in the lobby, David."

The elevator stuck on one finally descended, and the doors opened with a polite ding. What emerged was hectic and took a moment for David to fully grasp. Two EMTs rolled out a small Hispanic man on a gurney. He was dressed in a three-piece tweed suit without the jacket, a bandage wrapped around his head, blood already seeping through, his expensive-looking cream dress shirt and vest spattered with it.

"You bitch! You catty, illiterate bitch!"

The EMTs rolled the man on the gurney past David and Towne. Waiting inside the elevator, a female uniformed police officer said to her male counterpart, "I told you we should've taken the stairs."

They escorted a frumpy, vaguely familiar woman in a gray shawl and denim dress, her hands handcuffed behind her back, out after the gurney.

"You ruined my life!" the woman in handcuffs shouted. "I'll sue you for libel! You won't get away with this!"

Towne and David watched the spectacle, along with about a dozen others standing in the lobby, as the EMTS, the cops, the victim and the apparent assailant all headed out into the snow.

"Was that Ignacio Ortega, the famous critic?" Towne said finally.

"I think it was."

"Who the hell was that bird shouting at him?"

David shrugged, ambivalent. "I have no idea," he said. He rolled the dolly into the elevator. "See you at seven?"

"Bright-eyed and bushy-tailed, *mon ami*," Towne said, tapping his temple.

The doors closed and David went up.

5

Clay found Towne waiting for him in the lobby, peering out the glass-front doors. Police lights flashed through the windows, flickering in Towne's eyes.

"What the hell was all that racket?" Clay asked.

"Some woman appears to have beaten the piss out of Ignacio Ortega," Towne said amusedly. "Was that Moira Mead I saw you with at the bar?"

Clay followed Towne's gaze in time to see the cops push a woman into the back seat of the cruiser. "What's it to you?"

"Just curious," Towne said, turning from the scene with a predatory grin. "Speaking of, as it turns out, someone hasn't been exactly forthcoming with me."

"You found out Lovecraft didn't have any children."

"I did. I thought perhaps he'd sired an illegitimate son unbeknownst to Lovecraft scholars, but if the dweebs at the Miskatonic Society weren't aware of it, chances are quite good none exists. So… tell me your goal, Mystery Man."

Clay sighed heavily. "I'm Clay Kayden."

It took Towne a moment to get it. When he did, his tanned face shifted through flashes of disparate emotions—shock, anger, annoyance—before settling on wary. "Last year's me," he said. "I thought I recognized you, you crafty cunt. So you thought you'd get the skinny on my working relationship with David, is that it?"

"Get the skinny?" Clay said. His patter was as corny as his characters' dialogue.

"I thought that was something you Americans say. Like in the movies."

"Not since the '40s. I was just curious if you'd signed any sort of non-disclosure agreement with Ennis as part of your working relationship."

"If I had," Towne said, his eyes narrowed to slits, "I *certainly* wouldn't be at liberty to tell you, would I?"

"And if you hadn't, you would've just said 'no.'"

The two men stared each other down until Towne grinned. "Touché."

"I'm not a lawyer, but I don't think saying you signed an NDA falls under the purview of an NDA."

"Yes, I've signed an NDA with David," Towne admitted, in a blasé tone indicating he'd grown bored with the conversation. "What business is that of yours?"

"It's something we have in common. I wonder what else we have in common? I didn't see you at David's reading tonight."

Towne shrugged. "I've read the book."

"What did you think of it?"

"Not his best effort, but certainly not the worst."

"Did you notice anything different about it?"

Towne grinned. "If you're referring to the homoerotic overtones, I did, in fact. I thought it was an interesting choice for the character. Stark always struck me as a bit... *fastidious*, but I never assumed—"

"That's because he's not. At least, not in David's mind. *I* wrote that book, Towne. Just like I suspect you're writing his next however many novels. Because Ennis hasn't been able to write a word of fiction in years, not since he quit drinking. I figure he's been lying to himself for so long, he must've forgotten how to do it for a living."

Towne said nothing. He didn't need to. The way the younger, more polished man's jaw tightened, Clay knew he was right.

"I wrote it because I *knew* he wouldn't get the subtext. He's not a subtext guy, is he? He'd let it pass on to Joanna, and she'd hand it off to the publisher, and the second people outside of the industry started to read it, he'd get called out all over the internet. He'd get *canceled*, Towne. Just like they canceled me."

Towne looked at him with a mixture of awe and disgust. "How do you manage to stand upright with such a large chip on your shoulder, mate?"

"Just wait," Clay said, beginning to walk away. "You ain't seen nothin' yet."

"You Yanks still say that, do you?" Towne called after him.

"*This* one does," Clay called back, and stepped through as the automatic doors opened, out into the chilly night.

SPLATTERFEST, DAY TWO
SATURDAY, NOVEMBER 27TH

TRIGGER WARNING

1

AT ELEVEN MINUTES past midnight, Tyler Grody finally decided on a plan.

Earlier in the evening, after he and the Hashtag King had watched the hubbub outside with the cop car and ambulance from the balcony in Rawlins's massive suite, Rawlins outlined his gripes about the horror scene. The infighting, the constant callouts, the ass-kissing and cronyism. It was late, and Tyler had listened to Rawlins bitch for nearly an hour before deciding it was safe to illuminate him with his own theory.

"Ennis is behind it all," he said. "You know that, right?"

Rawlins scowled. He'd been drinking a bit of vodka from the minibar, but not too much, because of his diabetes. "What makes you say that?"

"I figured it out at the last con we were all at. The way everyone kept deferring to him, even the convention organizer, Frank Wallis, as if Splatterfest was more for *his* benefit, not for the horror writing community. The way they buzzed around him like flies on rotten fruit. Then they gave him the Lifetime Achievement award and I *knew*—I could see it in their eyes, the way they *idolized* him—that this wasn't just a convention, see?" Tyler's eyes alighted with pure awareness. "It's a *cult*," he said. "And the people who step out of line, writers like that sniveling wimp Clay Kayden, who commit thought crimes, or critics like Ignacio Ortega, who refuse to kiss the ring and recognize Ennis's genius, they get excommunicated. They don't get *banned*, see, because that'd be something *tangible*, something you could *prove outright.* It's more like a shadow ban. They put you on *mute.* So, you can come to the con and hang around in smaller and smaller circles of fellow rejects, but the horror elites and their cronies will never *acknowledge* you. Guys like you and me, we'll never get asked to do readings or panels. We'll never get lifetime achievement awards."

"Kinda have to have some achievements first," Rawlins muttered. Tyler ignored him.

"They *laugh* when people like us call them 'gatekeepers,'" he said, feeling the buzz of finally letting all of this out, of putting his thoughts into words for someone other than himself to hear. "But they *orchestrate* all of this, see, exactly what you were talking about. They're always the first to point out the presumed transgressions, the crimes of thought, of politics, of whatever they decide is in or out this year. You like the wrong movie, or the wrong artist, or the wrong politician, and suddenly you're on the bad side of a firing squad. Only they don't actually *do* anything to you. It's all *covert.* Shadow ban. Stories you *know* are better than half the stuff in those anthologies you subbed to, or were *asked* to submit to, suddenly they don't have enough room, or it didn't fit the theme. *They all do this,* don't you see? It's a… a what do you call it?" He showed his teeth in a snarl. "It's a *conspiracy.* That's the only way to describe it. The whole industry is *insidious.*"

"I want some of the drugs you're on," Rawlins said after a long moment, sitting on the edge of his bed. "Hashtag *Poco Loco,* Bro-Bro."

Afterwards, still buzzing from his rant, undeterred by the Hashtag King's lukewarm reception to his theories, Tyler had gone to the bathroom to call his grandmother. She was fine. She said she was missing him, the house wasn't the same without his "video game noises" and his constant grumbling, but fine.

When she finally let him hang up, he'd returned to the room to find Rawlins sprawled on his back on the bed, arms splayed like a drunken angel. His hat lay on the floor between his feet. The top of his head shined in the lamplight.

"Rawlins?" Tyler said. It had taken him the distance from the bathroom to the California king-sized bed to remember the Assrag King's real name.

The man didn't wake. Tyler tapped him with the toe of his shoe. Nothing. He pushed Rawlins's leg. The man didn't blink.

Then he saw it: the little brown glass bottle lying on the carpet in a dark, wet stain. The medicine bottle from his coat pocket. He'd originally wanted to use amyl nitrate, Lee Stark's drug of choice, but found it inaccessible, and had instead spent days perfecting the chloroform the bottle on the floor had contained. He'd poured it in various rags, huffing it and passing out again and again, getting the formula just right for a man of David Ennis's weight and build. Now there it was, the lid discarded, all of his hard work soaking into the carpet.

"Ohhh, no no *no no NO!*"

He fell to his knees and picked it up. The stench of bleach and rubbing alcohol wafted up from the stain. Closing one eye to peer into the small bottle, he gauged what was left. Little more than a few drops. It wasn't even enough to knock out Gramma's cat, Otis—a stunt he'd pulled twice to determine it was safe for his own consumption. He stood, cradling the bottle, his mind reeling. First the gun, then his car and now this. Was he cursed?

He kicked the Hashtag King in the calf. Hard. "You stupid piece of shit!"

The man didn't even flinch. But he was still breathing, so at least whatever the hell he'd done hadn't killed him—judging by the dribble of liquid spilling from the corner of his lips he must have *drank* some of it while Tyler was in the bathroom, calling home—but he'd be out like a light for several hours. At least Tyler wouldn't be forced to explain what he'd been doing in the hotel room of a corpse.

He crossed to the vestibule and sank into the sofa, staring at the Hashtag King in seething contempt for several minutes, rotating the empty medicine bottle between his fingers.

Finally, his gaze fell on the vanity. On the box of insulin syringes he'd noticed earlier, on his way to call his grandmother.

Rawlins had mentioned earlier that if Ennis didn't require insulin it could put him in a diabetic coma. Tyler found himself wondering how long, exactly, one would last. Would it plunge the man directly into unconsciousness, or would he have time to struggle? Would he wake in a few hours, or days, or not at all?

Tyler crossed the room, pausing briefly to be sure Rawlins wasn't awake, wasn't faking it.

Cautiously, making as little noise as possible, he opened the box. By a quick count there were eleven, make that thirteen, syringes left. Would the idiot miss a single one? Did he count them every day as his supply began to dwindle?

No matter. Rawlins had already ruined his plan to surprise Ennis in his room with a rag soaked in chloroform. Though, frankly, the amount of effort it would take to keep the rag over the man's mouth while he struggled and potentially overpowered Tyler had never felt quite like an acceptable risk. It wasn't like in the movies, one breath and they're out. You really had to hold it there for a decent amount of time for the victim to pass out.

So, another change of plans. Grampa's service pistol, which he'd at first planned to use in order to force Ennis to breath enough chloroform to knock himself unconscious, had been working fine until two days ago, when Tyler decided to give it another test run. Not that he'd ever intended to actually *shoot* Ennis, but if you held a gun on someone you had to be willing to put your money where your mouth was. Or a bullet, in this case.

He'd set up a few cans in the back nine, stood back with his right eye squeezed shut, and pulled the trigger. Only instead of firing, the barrel had split and burnt his hand, leaving a scalding piece of shrapnel in his palm that he'd had to pull out with pliers while running his bleeding hand under cold water. He'd told Gramma he'd hurt himself climbing a tree, and buried the remains of Grampa's service pistol behind the barn.

This was it. The new plan. The gun had backfired, the car had stalled, and his entire bottle of homemade chloroform was drying into the hotel carpet, but Providence had intervened once more, had shown him the way.

Tomorrow morning, Ennis would begin to learn the true meaning of pain.

2

Clay awoke at seven-thirty on Saturday morning with slats of sunlight blasting into his retinas like a prison searchlight. He'd stayed up late using several dummy accounts to stir the pot on the message boards. Many attendees seemed less concerned about David Ennis than with the altercation between Ignacio Ortega and an "unknown author," which had landed him in the hospital with a concussion, or Anderson Ackerman's continued presence at the con (he'd apparently been accused of sexual harassment a few years prior). But Clay's taunting had actually convinced half a dozen or so that a campaign to protest David Ennis for yesterday's reading was the next logical step.

He'd even recognized, with a sardonic chuckle, a handful of usernames, Fiona St. Claire's "hauntedwaif"—her handle on Twitter—among them.

Wouldn't it be ironic, he thought, *to have my very own Grand Inquisitor leading the charge against my worst enemy?*

He was exhausted. The small bed was as uncomfortable as it looked, and he'd slept on top of the covers, in his clothes, as he'd told Moira the day before, only removing his shoes, belt and the items from his pants pockets. But the eagerness to see his plan put into motion this morning got him moving quickly, undressing and stepping into the shower, rinsing off the drive to the airport, the flight, the drives back and forth, the night spent in his clothes on a too hard bed. The water, lukewarm and hard, was at least invigorating. It was starting to get cold when he'd decided to get out anyway, fresh enough to face the day.

He'd typed out a brief apology text to Moira while still wrapped in a towel, then left it unsent. It was still much too early. She'd probably be hungover, sleeping in. When they'd spoken over messenger there'd been a seven-hour time difference: Clay in San Diego, Moira "across the pond" in Wales. They were always poorly timed.

Outside, a car engine gasped and wheezed like a dying horse. Clay changed into fresh clothes from his suitcase and peered out through the blinds to see who was murdering it.

A kid with a mug like a young Wilfred Brimley, only studded with acne, sat behind the wheel of an old Datsun, the driver door open, one booted foot in the exhaust-blackened snow drift. He kept turning the key, over and over, the definition of insanity, and the engine coughed its death rattle. The kid beat a fist against the steering wheel in aggravation.

"Gonna flood the engine, kid," Clay muttered to himself. He put on a jacket, his shoes, and stepped out into the cold morning air. "Need a boost?"

The kid looked up through the windshield with the purest animosity Clay had ever seen. Then his expression softened. The kid didn't smile, his face just went flat. Devoid of emotion.

"Sure, if you don't mind," he said, leaning out the door.

Clay got the jumper cables from the emergency box in the back of his rental and helped the kid get them attached. He seemed to know less about cars than Clay did, which wasn't much at all. Once they got the Datsun running the kid thanked him—still without an emotional response—and Clay sent him on his way.

"Was it just me or did he not seem all that grateful?" a woman said.

Clay turned. He'd seen the woman in the fur coat the other day when he'd checked in, pushing a bald man in a wheelchair into one of the rooms perpendicular to his side of the L-shaped building. She was a large woman, pillowy in all the right places, and despite the heavy application of makeup at the ass-crack of daybreak there was a softness to her features that made Clay feel immediately at ease.

He smiled. "I thought it was just me."

"Nope." She took a drag off her e-cigarette. "I'm Shyla."

"Clay. Nice to meet you."

"Clay. That's a nice, strong name."

She held his gaze too long for his comfort. He looked off at the highway, scratching his head. Was she flirting with him? "I saw you yesterday with your… boyfriend? Husband?"

Shyla chuckled, exhaling a cloud of vapor. "It's a little more complicated than that."

He shrugged. "Complicated is interesting."

"Interesting is an understatement."

"Color me intrigued."

She gave him a direct look under her thick, doe-eyed lashes. "Clay, you wouldn't believe me if I told you."

"I'm a writer. You'd be surprised what I'd believe."

"A writer, huh?"

Clay smiled despite himself. Often when he told normal people he was a writer they'd ask, "Have you written anything I'd know?" (To which he'd invariably say, "Probably not.") Or they'd tell him they were thinking of writing a book but they just needed to "find the time." Or they'd ask if he'd write their life story. Shyla asked, "What kind of writer?"

He laughed. "Not a very good one, it turns out. Or too good. That's still up for debate."

She pouted, pooching out her shiny red lower lip. "I meant what do you write?"

"Horror and transgressive fiction."

"Transgressive—is that like queer stuff?"

"Sometimes. It focuses on characters living on the fringes of society and societal taboos. Often graphically."

She seemed to find something intriguing in this. "Oh, so you like taboo stories?"

"They're… interesting," he said.

"And complicated," Shyla added.

He grinned. "Exactly."

"Well, Clay, if you're around later and the light's on above the door—we're in six—" She nodded behind her. "—feel free to knock. Maybe we could… share some stories."

Again, Clay couldn't tell if she was hitting on him or sincere. But her offer did intrigue him. Meeting new people, hearing their stories—maybe lifting a detail or two here and there—was one of the most beneficial things he learned from his time on the road with Ennis. Listening to different perspectives and voices. Shyla and her... whatever the man in the wheelchair was to her— *Brother? Pimp?*—looked like she might have a story or two worth cribbing.

"I'll keep that in mind," he said. "You have a good day, Shyla."

"You too, Clay," she said, exhaling through her cherry lips. "Nice to meet you."

Clay got in his rental car and drove to the closest diner, a hole in the wall called Lester's Place. The name Lester always made Clay think of those old *Hustler* magazine cartoons about "Chester the Molester," the one by the guy who was later accused of molesting his own daughter, hiding it in plain sight.

This place was old enough—and sleazy enough—that the owner might have gotten the reference. Clay bet the old guy with the coke nail behind the front desk at the Lonely Motel would've been a fan. But Lester, for whatever he lacked in cleanliness and modern style, made a mean stacked pancake breakfast, and the bacon was greasy and charred to perfection. Clay didn't even care that the cutlery had water spots, and the old green glasses that looked like holdovers from when Mobil used to give them away free with gas had chips in them.

He'd need all the energy he could get to make it through the day. With the Hit Squad's attention successfully deflected toward Ennis—or so it seemed on the message board—he could worry less about their targets on his own back. But once Ennis got a whiff of what he'd done, how he'd screwed him with the Stark book, the old hack would be out for blood.

Clay needed to be ready for a showdown.

3

Moira woke with a screaming hangover and rolled over to find herself in bed with a snorer.

The man's face was buried in the pillow, his back turned to her, only his slightly mussed manbun—what she typically referred to as a twat-knot—visible above the pristine white hotel comforter. She recognized him immediately. Streaks of his tan-colored foundation were smeared on the pillow. His saliva was crusted on her nipples, their mingled juices on her inner thighs. There was a condom—she crossed herself briskly—on the carpet beside the bed, between her knickers and his bunched-up underpants, thick and gooey with dead sperm.

"Fucking hell," she muttered, slipping quietly out of bed.

Dean Foster Towne was the absolute last person she would have wanted to wake up beside. It was *supposed* to be Clay. That was the plan. They'd flirted at the last in-person con but neither of them had worked up the courage to ask the other to their room. Between then and now the sexual tension had been palpable. She supposed she had to respect that he'd declined her rather unsubtle offer, considering Clay no longer drank, and she did seem to have gone a bit over her limit with the gimlets. The hangover was testament to that. Even the thick, dark curtains couldn't keep out enough light to quiet her throbbing headache.

Speaking of throbbing, she thought, practically duckwalking to the loo. They must've either gotten up to some Olympian-level sex or David Ennis's protégé had a hog between his legs.

Whichever it was, she couldn't remember much of it. Towne had approached her in the lounge a short time after Clay left, that much she did know. He'd bought her another gimlet, and she'd been so disappointed by Clay's hasty departure she'd accepted it out of spite.

After the first sip the night was a blur until they got into the elevator, where she vaguely remembered kissing him, followed by his awkward attempt to finger her down the front of her pants.

Not that she'd tried or even wanted to stop him. There'd simply been too many layers with her buttons, her tights and knickers.

Moira ran the shower, waited for the mirror to get foggy, then stepped in. She washed away Towne's saliva and whatever else of him was left on her skin. The thought of actually *fucking* him caused another wave of nausea. She leaned over and puked between her legs, the running water making it circle down the drain like a Hitchcock scene. Gingerly, she squished the larger chunks of undigested—were those bits of cocktail shrimp?— through the grate with her toes, thinking how horrible it was to her but for someone else, it was likely a fetish. There had to be some crossover in the emetophile community with those into splosing or crush videos, at the very least foot partialism.

Chucking it up now meant she wouldn't have to vomit quite so much before her reading this afternoon, which tended to be an integral part of her pre-public speaking ritual. She just wished she'd known she had to before she'd gotten into the shower.

Clay hadn't texted her this morning. Thinking back on what she remembered of last night, she felt foolish. She'd practically thrown herself at him and he'd rejected her. Whatever "business" had kept him from her bed, it better have been important.

Maybe it was another woman, she thought. Of course, it was also possible he'd been stringing her along, or simply not wanted to hurt her feelings.

She kicked the mattress. "Rise and shine, sleepyhead."

Towne rose on his elbows with a beleaguered groan, picked up his sunglasses from the bedside table and slipped them on. "What time is it?" He rolled over, scowling at the sun blasting in between the curtains, his slender, tanned chest bereft of body hair.

"Time for you to get your skinny arse out of bed."

Towne grinned. "I knew there was a reason I liked you."

"Couldn't possibly be that I was the only woman drunk enough to spread her legs for such an obvious fuck boy as you." She threw his jeans at him. He caught them deftly before the leather belt could hit his face. "Up, up, out."

"Take it down a peg, Missus Fawlty. Where are my shorts?"

Moira picked the white briefs up off the floor with her toes and flung them at him.

"That's quite a skill," he said, flipping off the covers to slip them on un-self-consciously. His pubic hair was trimmed to a very deliberate V. She had to admit, he had an attractive pelvic region, reminiscent of Brad Pitt in *Fight Club*, and his cock was a bit larger than she was used to. "What else can you do with those feet?" he asked.

"Besides kick your arse?"

He grinned. "I like a feisty woman, I do."

"I like an expedient man."

He slipped his tattooed arms into his dress shirt. "Is Clay Kayden *expedient*?"

She flashed him a look of annoyance. "You weren't such a great shag you can act like the cock of the roost."

He grinned up at her. "But have you read my book?"

This, she didn't dignify with a response.

"All right, I'll go quietly." He slipped sockless into his loafers and stood, his shirt hanging open on his boyish chest. "Let's do this again."

"Not likely."

He kissed her cheek on his way to the door, his permanent five-o'clock shadow prickling her skin. She wiped away his spit with the back of a hand, and locked and latched the door the moment he stepped out into the hall.

The business card Towne left on the entryway table—it turned out he ran a swanky barber-slash-cigar shop in London called The Boys' Club—she tore into bits before throwing it in the bin.

She sprayed the room with her perfume to get rid of any lingering scent of his cologne, then gave up and called the front desk, asking if they'd change the bedlinens. They were spoiled with sex, sweat and Towne's overpowering L'Homme by Yves Saint Laurent. Satisfied she'd done all she could, she dressed, putting on a delicate blouse and a mid-length twill skirt with black tights. The idea was to look presentable and feminine but not overtly sexy. She wanted the focus to be on her words, not how she dressed.

Still no text from Clay. No matter. She had a morning filled with panels and her reading at two. She gathered everything she'd need and left the room, heading down to the lift.

"Hold the elevator," a woman called from the hall as Moira entered one.

She pushed the Close button first, only realizing her error as the doors began to slide shut—the woman in the hall noticed, muttering "*Son of a bitch*"—then repeatedly mashed Open until it reluctantly obeyed.

The woman entered, looking harried, holding a stack of loose papers and spiral notebooks. She muttered "Thanks," but didn't look at Moira. She wore her blonde hair knotted in a French braid beneath a black beret, a T-shirt with the slogan "On Wednesdays We Smash the Patriarchy," parachute pants and Doc Martens. She stared at the doors, waiting for them to close, then waiting again for them to open on the lobby.

Even standing in profile, Moira recognized her. It was really *her*. The critically acclaimed writer/director of *Creep City*, *The Stain* and *Abaddon Mountain*, amongst many others, three of Moira's all-time favorite not just horror movies but treatises on being a woman in male-dominant industries, standing in the lift beside her, pretending not to notice her staring.

Forget Clay, Moira thought. *It's Kendra bloody Pleasance*.

The doors opened, and Kendra Pleasance stepped out into the lobby. Moira stayed in the lift, watching Ms. Pleasance scuttle toward the convention hall, until a man stepped toward the doors asking, "Going up?"

She shook her head, stepping out briskly.

No, she wasn't going up. But she *could* be if Kendra bloody Pleasance came to her reading.

4

1:30 P.M. Reading from Fiona St. Clair,
Conference Room 3:

"It's a sickness," he tells her.

Already she's hiding scratches on her arms and legs. Bite marks on her breasts and neck. She's walking bowlegged from the abrasions between her thighs.

"It's a disease. I can't help myself."

He reminds her of this on the mornings after. Not during. During, he can't speak. Then, it's like he's a different person.

Slobbering. Slavering. Panting.

But no words.

At least, none she can understand.

She considers herself demisexual. She can't start a physical relationship with someone without first having a romantic attraction. But that's the problem, see? That's the trap. Once she's gotten a man in bed it's already too late. She's already hooked. It's not like an online hookup. It's not like how she wears an off-the-shoulder Prada dress for a gala opening, careful not to leave any spills or stains, and returns it the next day folded just so, telling the clerk it didn't fit the way she'd expected when she got it home. With men, she's already cut the tag by the time she wears them to bed. She can't just put it back in the box once the seal's been broken.

It's because of this she's suffered through the worst sex, the most aggravating habits, the lies and cheating and neglect. For months. Sometimes *years*. All because she's already in love, these are things she tolerates.

"I'm a different person when I'm in a committed relationship," she tells him, on their third date. "Once you see the real me, you'll want to run."

"I wouldn't," he says.

Because we're all hiding something, aren't we?

That ex we're still in love with. That girls' trip to Cancun, where we got a little too drunk and high and did some things we regret in front of strangers. The sex tape we were sure would get erased. Shameful experiences. Horrible breakups.

We all have things we're too afraid to share while we're dating, things we keep secret until we hope it's too late for the other to back out. It's then we realize the little black dress has a crusty white stain that won't come out before the "return by" date. It's then we reveal the packaging is too damaged to return without the clerk getting suspicious.

So when he tells her a couple of months into their relationship, "It's a sickness," when he says, "I can't help myself," she tells him she understands.

Whatever he's going through, whatever it is, they can get through it together.

But *this*—this is different. This is unlike anything she's ever experienced. This isn't just a "he farts in his sleep" thing. Or humming while he eats. This isn't a cute character flaw she can have a good laugh about with her girlfriends over margaritas, or work into the novel she's been talking about writing since grad school.

This, she has to actively *hide* from her friends.

Because she already loves him. The stain was there when she took it home, it was just hidden in a place she hadn't thought to look. In a place she never would have *thought* to look.

There's a crazy popular literary genre she reads, it's called "shifter romance," or "paranormal romance," but a lot of it is erotica. It's porn. A woman falls in love with a man who can *shift* into a wolf or a dragon or a bear. Or he's a vampire, a demon, a fairy.

Sometimes the shifter, these "alphas," they're the

last of a dying breed and need to mate with a human woman to have their hybrid baby and continue their lineage. They're *destined* to be together. It's the old trope: the Fated Couple.

People love the idea of that *perfect someone*. The One. Soulmates. They sell it to us with every fairy tale, with every teen drama, with every diamond commercial, this heteronormative fantasy relationship, and we buy into it and we seek it out, and when we can't find it, we *manufacture* it. We say to ourselves, "This is the guy." We ignore the danger signs. The red flags. Or we tell ourselves he can be fixed. He just hasn't found the Right Woman. The Right Woman obviously being us, even though every other Right Woman thinks the same thing until she's lost all of her friends and he's having parties in her apartment while she's at the office.

Inevitably, the Strong Female Character in these shifter romances somehow finds herself dominated by the alpha male, or an entire "reverse harem" of alphas, engaging in intercourse whether she wants to or not— often overpowered, or at least *entranced*, unable to help herself—and it's all packaged in a fun little story about some kingdom that needs to be saved or a war between races of shifters.

She reads it for fun. A little harmless fantasy before bed or in the bath.

She doesn't think, *It would be so hot if I could find a werebear for myself.* Or a vampire, or a monster. She's not going to the zoo and hanging out in front of the exhibits, praying for a cage to burst open, creaming herself over the thought of getting ravaged like Leo DiCaprio in that movie with the horny bear.

When he finally tells her about his sickness, his disease, he makes her promise not to laugh.

Of course, she can't actually *promise* that. Laughter is an involuntary response. Like gagging, or cringe, or falling in love. But she promises she will.

Then he tells her, and she laughs.

"It's not funny," he says.

But it *is* funny. It has to be a joke. Because what he's talking about, there's no such thing. It isn't real.

He tells her he changes. Like she told him she'd changed in a committed relationship. This is months down the road, when they're talking again about taking "us" to the next level.

"I change," he says, "... *during*."

"During the full moon?" she asks, trying not to laugh again.

He was perfectly fine with holding out, with fooling around over the clothes, a little bit of hands down the pants or up the shirt action, which seems rarer and rarer these days unless you're into dating Mormons or doing foodie calls, where you're just there for the free meal.

Now she knows why.

He tells her he's a werewolf, only it's not like in the movies. He doesn't change when the moon is full. He changes when he's sexually stimulated. When he's fully aroused. When he's "making love."

Clinical lycanthropy, it's called. She looks it up after their discussion, after his confession. It's a rare mental disorder, a delusion. It's been shown with neuroimaging that when someone with clinical lycanthropy believes they're changing, they're *shifting* into an animal, that the areas of the brain in charge of body movement and body image actually light up with "unusual activity." Proof that it's *real*, at least for the sufferer.

That first time they have sex, she prepares for the worst. She's had bad sex before. The impotence, the going in dry, the guys who assume she's into the same kink they're into and do it without consent. Fish-hooking from behind. Ass play. Spitting.

None of that has prepared her for this. *At all.*

He's howling and clawing at her. He's pulling out to scurry off and piss on the carpet, then turning around and sniffing the puddle. He's flipping her over and burying his nose in her ass cheeks, which admittedly she kind of finds kinky and fun, but *still*. The way he sniffs and laps at her isn't all that sexy. It reminds her of the family dog.

All of these things she bears, because she loves him. All of these things she never tells her friends because he's "such a nice guy."

And they're right. He is a Nice Guy.

He's just an animal in bed.

When they talk about it the next morning, she says, "If it's an illness it can be cured." He's reluctant but he wants to do his part, he wants to make this work between them.

So they go to counseling. Group couples therapy, for people dealing with rare mental illnesses.

It's clear he doesn't want to go, but he does it for her. Even when she jingles her car keys, like they used to do with the family dog, he's definitely not excited.

At group therapy they meet a lesbian couple where one partner has something called Cotard's syndrome, she believes she's dead, she feels like her flesh is rotting off her bones, that she's turning to dust. She's disgusted by her partner and calls her a necrophiliac in front of everyone sitting on plastic chairs in a semicircle in the children's room at the public library. The same place they read *Yertle the Turtle* and *Charlotte's Web* to kids barely old enough to use the bathroom by themselves, they're talking about sexual dysfunction and bizarre, violent delusions.

They meet a straight older couple, twenty years ago the man was so certain the poor woman was cheating on him he threw acid in her face. She's still got the scars, her new skin gnarled pink. In jail the prison shrink diagnosed him with Othello syndrome. They wrote letters to each other while he was locked in a cage and after he got out, she took him back. He hasn't hurt her since but they've been doing group therapy and she makes sure every day he takes his meds.

They meet a poly throuple, two men and a woman. One of the men has Ekbom's syndrome. They all love each other and want him to be well, to stop hurting himself. He used to be addicted to cocaine, when he was a hedge fund manager. Now, every so often he feels like he's got bugs crawling under his skin, burrowing and biting him. And when the scratching doesn't help, he gets a razor blade, like he used to use to chop up lines of coke. He's got scars up and down his arms, his legs. Infected ones. Angry red. Suppurating. But the worst are on his back where he can't reach, where he had to scratch himself on a rake leaned up against the wall.

After group, she feels much better about him, her pseudo-lycanthrope. Her latent shifter. Her faux furry. Sure, she's got bruises and scratches and tears in her vagina but at least he's not *these* people.

But he says he's not like them. Those people were mentally ill, he says. And nothing they try works. Group therapy. Talking it over rationally. Taking a "neutral" approach, like a therapist would.

That's when it hits her. This whole time, she's been doing things to convince him he's not what he says he is. What if the only way to "cure" him is to play along?

The next time they do it, she's ready.

She abhors animal abuse. She donates to PETA. She has an aunt who regularly posts pictures on her Facebook of animals who've been abused. Just scrolling past them makes her literally sick to her stomach.

When she goes to the pet store and asks what the best kind of choke collar is, and the clerk gives her side eye and asks what kind of dog she has, she blurts out,

"It's for my boyfriend."

Like that makes it any better.

They strip down at her apartment, in her bedroom. Before he can touch her, before they touch each other, she commands him to sit on the floor.

He slumps into a cross-legged position on the floor, more like those kids listening to the librarian read *Where the Wild Things Are* in the children's room at the public library than a wild thing himself.

"I've bought you something," she tells him, and she shows him the collar.

He gives it the kind of wary look you might give a plate of food with something you're deathly allergic to as the main ingredient. "What is this?"

"It's a collar for my wolfman," she says. "I want you to wear it. It'll be sexy."

"I'm not a domesticated animal."

"That's why we need this," she says. "If you want to be *my* wolf, you're going to have to be housetrained. When you're being bad, I'll give it a little tug."

So he gives in. She wraps the chain links around his neck and holds on to the handle while they make out. She feels him change, feels the *shift*, just like he does, and in that moment when he first starts to slobber and growl and lose his human traits, she pulls the handle, tightening the chain.

Instead of getting angry, instead of cursing her out, he whimpers.

She tells him it's treat time and shows him his treat. He starts lapping away at her, like a Shar Pei drinking from a puddle, *lap, lap, lap*, completely unsexy and barely pleasurable.

There's a magazine on the bedside table, the copy of *Modern Dog* where she got the idea for the choke collar. She rolls it up tight and smacks him sharply on the nose.

He looks up from eating her out with puppy dog

eyes.

"Slower," she commands.

Her man, her dog, he does as he's told.

"Good boy," she says, patting his head.

5

"*Racist, sexist, anti-gay!*" the protesters cried. "*David Ennis, go away!*"

The rallying cry of the activists followed David to the elevator, but he was too quick for them. He thumbed the Close Door button repeatedly until they finally closed on his pursuers, their chant silenced by the car's upward movement.

"Oh, thank God," he sighed, collapsing against the elevator wall. The protesters had first accosted him outside of the "Toxic Fandom" panel discussion. They seemed to think his reading the day before had been "homophobic" and "antisemitic," which was news to David. Afterwards, they'd stood beside his vendor table, frightening off potential customers. Frank Wallis had tried to intervene but the trio reminded him, as per Frank's own new convention rules, they retained the right to protest. Unless they resorted to violence, his hands were tied.

Rather than cost himself and Towne potential sales, David decided to spend his time between panels out in the cold, certain they wouldn't follow him. He'd been right. He was colder than a witch's tit each time he returned to the con for another discussion, his cheeks rosy and his knuckles raw, but the trio remained in the lobby awaiting his return, repeating their mindless chant as they followed him to the conference rooms.

Except they multiplied each time he returned to the lobby. Like cockroaches in a filthy kitchen, every time he came back in there were more of them, joining in on that nonsensical mantra.

They shouted it outside the conference rooms as he and several other authors and publishers discussed "Trauma Porn vs Positive Representation," and "Harmful Tropes: Depictions of

Mental Illness in Extreme Horror." They all did their best to ignore the protesters but David felt increasingly humiliated, the sort of embarrassment he'd only ever experienced the morning after a fall off the wagon. Somehow he was able to maintain his composure, but he didn't find he was able to contribute much to the discussions, and told Frank Wallis he'd like to sit out the day's final panel.

Even though he'd already paid David for the full weekend, Frank had agreed it was probably for the best. David would judge tomorrow's Gross Out contest, and spend the rest of the weekend in his room, bingeing reality TV. Let Towne handle the table. The kid was a natural.

The bell dinged and David stepped off the elevator on the fifth floor. After the awful morning, what he wanted more than anything was an ice-cold Mr. Pibb.

Except that's not quite true, is it? What I want more than anything is a visit to Brown Town. But we can't let that happen again now, can we, Davey?

On his way down the hall, toward the corridor where the pop and ice machines stood, he suddenly felt… *watched.* Despite his many years writing horror prose, there was no more an accurate way to describe it. If pressed to beef up his word count, he might add that it felt like a laser-scope target had been painted on the back of his head, the hairs on the nape of his neck standing at attention.

He turned at the corner, expecting to discover the protesters had followed him upstairs, and saw… nothing. No one.

With a relieved chuckle—*Got yourself worked up for nothing, David*—he pulled out his keycard from the front pocket of his jeans and swiped it in the lock. At the *ka-thunk* of the lock disengaging, he pushed the door open and entered his room.

He kicked off his shoes and crossed the carpet in tube socks, heading for the minifridge. His knees popped as he bent. *Why do they have to put these goddamn things on the floor where kids can reach it?*

He opened the fridge. Rows and rows of colorful mini liquor

bottles met his eye, from Grey Goose to his former drink of choice, Wild Turkey, what he used to call the "Brown Demon." When on a bender, which was most of the time during his many-year stint as an alcoholic and occasional coke abuser, he used to say he was "downing the brown." He used to call getting sloshed on the Turkey getting a "Kentucky hug" or visiting "Brown Town."

When he hadn't wanted to get *too* smashed, if he'd had an on-camera interview or a panel or a book signing, he'd mix the Brown Demon with Mr. Pibb. He found the cherry of the soda was a nice addition to the vanilla and caramel of the bourbon, like an ice cream sundae with a kick.

He'd gone cold turkey from the Turkey, but the Pibb was something he refused to give up. It was a reminder of how far he'd come from the brink of losing everything he cared about, and a reminder never to go back. In a way, it felt like a middle finger to those blurred days, to the Turkey, to his life on the knife edge of oblivion. Drinking a Pibb without spiking it showed the alcoholism who was in the driver's seat.

Christ, wouldn't you know it? Not a single Mr. Pibb in the fridge. Must've finished the last two.

The machine in the hall probably had some, or at the very least a Dr. Pepper, which he'd often gone with in a bind.

He got up—the rifle crack of his knees like the first shots in a firing squad—and went back out into the hall, counting change from his pocket. The Coke machine held bottles of several Coke varieties, Sprite, iced tea and—

"When you're this tasty, they call you Mister," he said with a pleased grin. He fed a handful of coins into the machine and punched the button.

6

Tyler had been waiting on Ennis in the nook between the soda machine and the wall for nearly twenty minutes when the man finally stepped off the elevator. He'd attempted to lunge at Ennis the moment the hotel room door opened, but he found he was stuck.

Panic only made it worse. His breaths came quick, filling his diaphragm, wedging him in tighter. By the time Ennis's door opened again and the man himself reemerged in the hall, Tyler started to feel lightheaded.

Ennis's door came open and the man himself reemerged. He padded down the hall in his sock feet, heading straight for Tyler and the machines. If he looked up right now from the palmful of coins he appeared to be counting, he'd make direct eye contact with Tyler.

Tyler held his breath.

When Ennis looked up, he was already out of Tyler's line of sight. He said, "When you're this tasty, they call you Mister," then dropped coins into the slot. This close, Tyler could smell the man's aftershave, the same brand Tyler's father used to slap on his cheeks and neck after shaving his face with a rusty double-blade Bic razor: Aqua Velva. That was before Mom and Dad had their accident. Before it was just him and Gramma in the big old farmhouse alone.

The machine rumbled and the soda thumped into the tray. Ennis picked it up. He wiped off the condensation on the hem of his T-shirt, and turned, heading away from the machine.

Tyler breathed a sigh of relief and realized while he'd been holding his breath, he'd gotten unstuck.

Now, Ty!

Ennis unscrewed the cap on the way back to his room, and took a good slug as he pushed open his door.

Tyler ran at him. The needle had sunken into Ennis's bicep before the man managed to turn halfway. Tyler pushed the plunger, pumping the entire dose of insulin into his enemy's bloodstream.

Ennis's eyes went wide in rage and he dropped the bottle of Pibb Xtra, its contents spilling on the carpet. He grabbed Tyler by the wrist and Tyler threw his minimal weight, all one-hundred and thirty-six pounds, against the larger man.

Despite their size difference, Ennis stumbled backwards into the room. He clutched his chest. "What the... what the *fuck* was in that thing?" he gasped.

What have you done? Tyler thought. *You can't take this back. What if he dies before you can get him back to the motel?*

Ennis staggered backwards, his mouth opening and closing like a fish suffocating in a wet stain on the carpet.

The back of Ennis's calves struck the bed and he plopped down on it, still clutching his chest.

"Oh, thank God," he said. His gaze was unfocused, looking beyond Tyler, rather than at him.

Tyler turned, realizing too late that the door to the hall was still open, and someone had caught him.

Jackson Rawlins, the Cashgrab King, stepped through the doorway.

"This kid attacked me," Ennis gasped. "Call an ambulance. I think I'm... I think I'm having a heart attack!"

Rawlins pulled the door shut swiftly, locked it and threw the security latch.

"He—" Ennis moaned. "Help!"

His cry was feeble. Already his eyes were fluttering shut. He looked like he was on the verge of collapse. The syringe was still sticking out of his arm.

"Pl-please," Ennis gasped, reaching out to Rawlins.

"Hashtag What the *Fucking Fuck*, man?"

"What was I supposed to do? " Tyler snapped. "You *drank* all my chloroform!"

"*Chloroform? That's* what that was?"

"I told you, *it's not a prank.*"

Ennis fell backwards onto the bed with a grunt.

"We gotta get my glucagon kit."

"We're not *getting* anything."

"He's in an insulin coma!"

"I looked it up while you were passed out. Doctors used to do this all the time on addicts and psychos."

"That's a *specific* dose, man! Also, Hashtag *You're Not a*

Doctor!"

"Enough with the hashtags!" Tyler approached the bed. As he'd done with Rawlins the night before, he pushed Ennis's leg with the toe of his shoe. Ennis didn't make a sound. "He's out," Tyler said, and reached out to check the man's pulse.

Ennis sat up abruptly, unclouded fury in his gaze, and shot out a hand toward Tyler. Tyler yelped but was too late to deflect the grasping hand. It clasped around his larynx and Ennis's thick fingers squeezed, cutting off his air. His vision started to fuzz around the edges as he weakly slapped at Ennis's wrist.

Rawlins brought his right hand down in a swift chop against Ennis's neck and Ennis collapsed back on the mattress.

"Now you're..." Tyler gulped a breath. "...an accomplice."

Rawlins stood there shaking his head, looking down at Ennis's comatose body. "Hashtag Fuck My Life, man."

7

Word had traveled quickly about the unknown self-published author's assault on Ignacio Ortega, one of the horror genre's leading critics.

By the morning's panels on trigger warnings and diversity in fiction, along with various other hot topics, people were already spreading rumors that several writers at the con meant critics "legitimate physical harm." Saner minds suggested this was a random incident, but some wouldn't be swayed. To them, this was the first salvo in a war between authors and critics. This was a *warning shot*, fired across the bow. First it was Ortega, then it would be all of the top reviewers. Then any of the rest.

No critic left standing.

"Not to mention," said Kelly Lumpkin, aka "Sugar" from Sugar and Spice Reviews, "the author was *white*, and Mr. Ortega is a dignified Person of Color."

"Isn't Iggy white Hispanic?" a woman in the group asked.

"Why does any of this matter?" asked Beth-Anne Roe, aka

"Spice" from the same reviewer blog, though she was clearly the sweeter of the two. "Do you really think this was a hate crime?"

"Oh, it's a *hate* crime, all right," Sugar said. "They hate *us*, as a community. Laughing at our reviews, harassing us in emails when we've got *clear* 'not open for submissions' messages on our sites, getting readers to *dogpile* us. We all need to get on Twitter *right now* and use the CriticCrew hashtag to boost support for our side. Rally the troops."

"You sound like we're going to war," Spice said cautiously. Sugar was known to have a fiery temper, and would potentially lash out if she thought her opinion was being questioned.

"You're *damn right* we are," Sugar said. "You've been *drafted*, Beth-Anne."

Some reviewers were also authors, said a critic who wrote YA horror under a pen name. What side did they fall on?

"They'd better just stand aside," Sugar snapped. Looking around to make sure they were alone, the four of them in the third-floor hallway near the ice machine, she reached into her handbag to flash the shiny chrome of a small pistol. "Sugar's got a gun and she knows how to use it. If anyone comes for *this* bad bitch," she said, meaning herself, "they're gonna leave on one of those—" She snapped her fingers. "What's it called? The bed with wheels?"

"Lots of beds have wheels. My bed frame has wheels, it's easier to move."

Sugar rolled her eyes. "The ones *paramedics* use, Beth-Anne. Jesus Christ!"

"You mean a gurney?" the writer-reviewer suggested.

"Right. If anyone comes for *this* bad bitch, they're gonna be leaving on a gurney with a gut full of lead."

FAN/DOM

1

ANDERSON ACKERMAN WAS on his—fifth? sixth?—Mai tai of the morning when the woman with the colorful braids, the sex expert from last night, approached him at the bar. He'd already participated in two panels, one on the so-called "toxic fandom" phenomenon and a seminar called "Plot Twists & How to Write Them," which he'd shared with David Ennis and a few other big names in the genre. He was very much ready for his midday siesta.

"Tell me more about this slippery slope of yours," the woman said, running an ornately manicured fingernail over his barrel chest, which was enshrouded by a fuzzy gray cardigan with pulls.

Ackerman nearly spat up his drink. He had to reach up and get a napkin from the bar to wipe up what had spilled down his beard. "I beg your pardon?"

"The slippery slope," she repeated, taking the napkin from his hand and wiping his beard with it, giving him a sultry look. "The road from call-out culture to authoritarian dystopia, to paraphrase your points from the panel discussion this morning."

"W-well, I—"

"Actually—" She crumpled the napkin, tossed it behind the bar. "—I was hoping we could chat more about it... in your room."

"Of course, my dear, of course," he said, composing himself. Many fans over the years had propositioned him, though not quite in this same fashion, under the guise of cerebral discussion.

He'd taken many of them to bed. Some had wondered, because of his chair, if all of his parts were in working order. He'd proven to them that they were quite capable, he was merely unable to use his legs.

"Would you mind very much wheeling me up?"

"Not at all," she said. "Leave yourself in my capable hands."

"Oh, I'm certain they are," he choked.

"I'm Aimee, by the way," she said, rolling him through the already packed convention hall. "That's an A-I with two Es."

"Wonderful to meet you, my dear. Simply wonderful."

2

Clay had watched the protesters follow David Ennis around all morning and couldn't help but feel a sense of pride in his work. What a magical thing the internet was: how like a virus the message spread, quickly and efficiently infecting one mind after another. What he'd started with a single post and a handful of comments from three different dummy accounts had snowballed into an avalanche, causing multiple reaction threads and arguments within arguments. He'd of course used his own email to counter the discontent, to present the voice of reason, but he'd been swiftly dogpiled, many of the commenters remembering the little story that had gotten him blackballed at the previous Gross Out contest. The story that had made him an Unperson in the so-called horror "community."

Clay didn't care about any of that anymore. All he wanted now was revenge for David's betrayal. He'd sold Clay down the river to protect his own reputation, and now he was paying for it. Clay watched the expanding group of protesters follow Ennis from panel to lobby and back. The man looked beaten down. Defeated. The protesters, Clay's unwitting minions, the useful idiots doing his dirty work for him, followed Ennis to the elevators, then hung out in the lobby after the doors closed, looking like broken-down robots, unsure what to do next.

Frank Wallis's voice came over the P.A. system a short while later, stating that David Ennis wouldn't be attending his final panel discussion of the day.

Likely, Ennis would spend the rest of the weekend watching trashy reality TV, guzzling one Pibb Xtra after another. His guilty pleasure, now that alcohol was no longer an option.

With Ennis out of commission, Clay had spent the rest of the morning looking for Moira. He texted her after his business with Ennis but she didn't reply, so he suspected she was likely watching the readings, waiting for her turn. He noticed Kendra Pleasance taking notes a few rows up from where he took a seat in the back. He spotted Moira up near the stage, recognizing her curly, shoulder-length auburn hair and pale, slender neck.

He sat through a handful of rape revenge fantasies, Fiona St. Clair's tale of a werewolf boyfriend told like Palahniuk pastiche, and a few over-the-top, grotesque stories that felt like conscious attempts at an "Aristocrats" joke.

Then Moira hurried from the room, looking ill.

Clay trailed her into the hall. She headed directly for the washroom. He knew she was likely throwing up, her pre-public speaking ritual. When she didn't leave the bathroom for several minutes, he decided to return to the convention hall. Maybe spy on Towne for a little while.

As he made to leave, Kendra Pleasance emerged from the conference room, looking busy as she hustled down the hall, tapping her teeth with her pen, peering down at her notebook.

"Excuse me, Ms. Pleasance?"

The director looked up briefly, continuing on her way. "No autographs," she said. "I'm insanely busy."

"Actually, I don't want an autograph."

"No pictures. No selfies. No whatever it is you're selling."

He followed along behind her as she hustled toward the lobby. "Ms. Pleasance, I have a friend, she's a massive fan of yours. She's seen everything you've ever done, even your student films. She's—I know it's not the best phrase for a horror creator to hear—but she really is your number one fan."

The director paused. "And *she* wants my autograph?"

"No. I mean, yes. Probably. But I saw you taking notes in there. There's a rumor going around that you're looking for young talent, young *female* talent, to nurture. To maybe make a film with. If that's true, my friend isn't just a fan of yours, she's also one of the best writers I know."

The pen clicked against her whitened teeth. "Is that right?"

"That's right."

"She's published? Agented?"

Clay felt his hopes dashed. "Not anymore. Our publisher went out of business a few years back, and she's been struggling a lot with self-doubt. But she's had some stories published since. Publications you've probably heard of."

Kendra Pleasance hummed thoughtfully. "And she's reading this afternoon?"

"A couple readings from now, yeah."

"Okay." Her gaze narrowed to slits. "It's not rape revenge, is it? I'm so goddamn tired of that awful fucking trope."

"That's not the kind of stuff she writes."

"Good." She looked him over, peering over the top of her glasses. "You're not fucking her, are you?"

The question took him by surprise. He couldn't stop himself from laughing. "Does that make a difference?"

"I'm just trying to decide," she said, "whether you're a good ally or you're using me to get into her pants."

"We're just good friends."

The director held his gaze, tapping her teeth: *clack-clack-clack.*

"This isn't about me. Her work is good. It's *better* than good. She deserves this chance, Ms. Pleasance."

The director nodded. She tucked her notepad under an arm and stuck out a hand. "Call me Kendra."

Clay shook it. "Good to meet you," he said. "And thanks for your time."

As he followed her back into the room, he glanced back at the washroom door, hoping like hell Moira would finish up soon and make it back in time for her reading.

3

2 P.M. Reading from Moira Mead,
Conference Room 3:

My little brother Nigel had Prader-Willi syndrome. I say
had because he passed away when I was twelve.

The life expectancy for someone with PWS is much
lower than someone without it, and lower still in men
than women. The leading cause of death is respiratory
failure. Heart issues is second. This is because people
with PWS tend to be overweight, due to a defining
characteristic of the syndrome: an inability to stop
eating.

This isn't to be confused with bulimia. It's not quite
an eating disorder, and it's not related to trauma or any
such thing. People with Prader-Willi syndrome have
what's called 'hyperphagia,' characterized by an inability
to feel full, meaning they're constantly hungry. A
childhood friend once said Nigel was like a panda bear:
eating far more eucalyptus than they require to feel full,
to feel nourished. I didn't think it was a very nice
comparison but from then on, I couldn't *not* see it when
moonfaced little Nigel ate his celery or carrot sticks
cross-legged on the floor in front of the telly.

Nigel would eat all kinds of things he shouldn't. My
parents had to keep a watchful eye on him to make sure
he wouldn't eat what he wasn't supposed to, and whilst
they were off at work that duty would fall to me. Nigel
was nine and I was a very mature twelve, and because
of this dynamic, I resented him nearly as much as I loved
him.

When I say Nigel would eat things he shouldn't, I

don't mean he'd be constantly getting his hand caught in the biscuit tin. God forbid if anything even remotely edible was ever left out on the counter, he'd gnash it down and spit out the bones, leaving nothing but the cellophane packaging. The fridge and the cabinet door to the kitchen bin had combination locks so Nigel couldn't pick food from the trash. The rest of the dry goods were stored high up in the cupboards so Nigel couldn't reach without dragging a chair in from the dining room. When he was three years old, he nearly choked to death on a bit of gravel from the drive. Even fag ends—that's cigarette butts for you Americans— even they weren't safe around our Nigel.

He'd sick much of it up, naturally. But even then he'd want more. Once, he'd vomited on the floor and whilst I'd scurried off to get some kitchen roll, he ate most of it, using his hands to scoop it up from the rug like he'd spilled his porridge.

I'm not telling you this to disgust you, or to make you feel like Nigel was an awful person, or that he was somehow less than human, like a dog who'd eat his own vomit. And I certainly don't want your pity for myself. We all have our crosses to bear. Nigel's was PWS and mine was our Nigel. But I loved him just the same.

One day whilst walking Nigel home from his special school, which I did from Monday to Friday, I was doubled over with the most awful pain I'd ever experienced. I felt a dampness between my legs and was so horrified I forgot about the pain and hurried Nigel along home.

When we got home, I sat Nigel in front of the telly and rushed to the loo. I didn't have to poo like I thought but there *were* brown spots on my knickers. I worried I'd shat myself, which would explain the stomach cramps, but not why my breasts were sore.

"God blimey," Da said with a chuckle, when he

overheard me telling this to Mum after supper. "The painters are in, Mum."

Mum hushed him, struggling not to laugh herself. She told me what I'd experienced was menstrual cramps. It meant I was becoming a young lady.

"What are they teaching the children these days?" Da asked rhetorically.

Of course, I'd already learned about menstrual cramps in Sex and Relationships class but they don't tell you what any of these things *feel* like, and most of us were so mortified just talking about it in those days it was a wonder they expected us to retain any of it.

Cross-legged in front of the telly, Nigel called it "minstrel cramps" and laughed until tears streamed down his chubby cheeks.

Anyhow, after supper Mum showed me how to use her tampons while Nigel and Da watched *Yes Minister* in the living room.

"You mustn't flush it," Mum instructed. "It'll clog the pipes. Cover it with toilet roll—" She demonstrated, wrapping the unused tampon like a doner kebab. "—and throw it in the kitchen bin."

These days a mother would probably take their girl to the Tesco and get them straight on the pill, I suppose, but this was the 1980s. Teen pregnancy rates weren't much lower than today, though parents were far less progressive about such things. They preferred to pretend it was other people's daughters getting pregnant, *low-class* girls, you know. No way would that happen to *their child*.

I put in one of Mum's tampons, what she called "plugs," before bed. It was uncomfortable getting it far enough up there, but otherwise I got used to it rather quickly. It turned out I didn't need it. Other than those few spots in my knickers I didn't get much of a flow for the following two days, just a few red daubs on the cotton here and there. Aside from the cramps and weird breast swelling that first day, it wasn't all that bad. I thought if this was what periods were like, Mum and all the ladies on TV sure were making something out of nothing.

It was almost two months later when my mind was changed. I didn't even have a period in between. For weeks I assumed God had changed his mind, He didn't feel I was ready to be a lady just yet. But when that second period did finally arrive, the cramps were so awful I needed to have a lie down in bed for an hour with Da's hot water bottle he used for his piles—that's hemorrhoids for you Americans—perched on my belly.

Fortunately, I was already home when it struck. It was a Sunday and I'd been doing my maths homework for Monday's class. Nigel was watching the telly, and Mum and Da both had to work overtime at the mill after church.

I made supper for Nigel and I—his food had to be weighed and calorie counted, so I often just did the same for myself and Da when Mum was out working or at her night classes—and we ate in front of the telly, this new program called *Tandoori Nights*, which Nigel enjoyed quite a lot as it was about Indian restaurants, meaning it often featured images of food and eating. I sometimes found it hard to concentrate on the telly because Nigel breathed quite heavily through his mouth—the same friend who'd called him a panda bear also called him a "mouth-breather" before I stopped being her friend. Nigel suffered from apnea due to his weight. He slept with a CPAP machine that hummed and grinded throughout the night on the other side of my bedroom wall, keeping me awake. There were nights when I *wished* for him to stop breathing, just so I could get some sleep. Of course, just thinking that kept me up the rest of the night with guilt.

Midway through dinner that evening, I started to feel an itchy dampness between my legs. I excused myself and waddled hurriedly to the toilet, like that game where you're meant to hold a balloon between your legs. I discovered the tampon string bright red, drenched in menses and staining my knickers. I took it out gingerly, wrapped it up just like Mum taught me—like a strawberry kebab—and put it in the bin. I inserted another plug, bunched up my knickers and brought them to the hamper. I gave them a scrub in the laundry sink and put in a wash, hoping that mixing them in with Da's skid-marked underpants and Mum's tatty Wonderbras would wash away any evidence of my shame.

The moment I emerged from the laundry room I sensed something amiss. Nigel wasn't seated at the table. In my embarrassment I'd temporarily forgotten him. Not sitting on the rug in front of the telly, watching the last few minutes of *Tandoori Nights*. Not in the kitchen, standing on a chair to sneak food.

I called his name. A muffled squawk came from somewhere. I assumed he'd gone to his room. Had he been hiding food in there? Stashing it away for just such a time?

His bedroom door was open, but he wasn't in there, either.

I turned. The toilet door was closed, a crack of light streaming into the hall from below. Nigel was using the loo. Another strangled squawk came from inside. I thought nothing of it—he often had trouble using the toilet due to his massive fiber intake—and I nearly scurried off in embarrassment, but a thump came at the door, as if he were beating a fist against it. The light under the door shifted. Something was pressed up against it on the floor, and thumped again.

I called out his name. The thump came twice more. I could see now the thing under the door was the toe of his dirty white tube sock. I thought he must have been lying on the floor, that maybe he'd fallen off the toilet from straining too hard and hurt himself. Knocked himself on the head.

The door was locked, but we used to keep a nail above the door for emergencies. You poke the nail through the keyhole to unlock the door. I wasn't tall enough to reach it, even on my tiptoes. I needed to get a chair from the dining room and drag it over. "Keep thumping, Nigel!" I told him, and hurried off to get one.

I heard two more thumps on my way down the hall. By the time I reached the kitchen I couldn't differentiate his weak thuds on the door from the hurried beat of my heart. When I finally stood the chair up in front of the door, half dragging, half lifting it, his rapping on the door had stopped.

"Nigel!" I called. I climbed up on the chair, reaching up as far as I could, fingers scrambling across the top of the door frame. The nail rolled off and landed on the floor, halfway under the door. I scrambled off the chair to my hands and knees. If not for Nigel's foot, the nail would have rolled right into the loo and been lost.

I got the nail into the keyhole and frantically tore the door open. Horror struck me, crippling as a thunderbolt. Nigel lay on the floor, his joggers and underpants around his ankles. Colors stood out in the otherwise drab room. The brown of his feces streaking the toilet seat. The blue in his fingers, neck and cheeks. Bright red blood stained his lips, as shocking as if he'd put on Mum's lipstick, and smeared the fingertips of his right hand. His eyes rolled back to the whites.

And on the floor beside him, the overturned rubbish. The clump of blood-soaked toilet roll I'd tossed into the bin prominent among coils of dental floss and crumpled tissues. The tampon I'd forgotten, in my haste to wash away the evidence, to bring with me to the padlocked kitchen bin.

I couldn't tell if Nigel was choking to death or if he was already dead but I remembered my emergency first aid training from school and dropped to my knees beside him, gingerly avoiding his cherubic little boy's penis poking up from under his pudgy stomach.

Move the victim to their back, arms at his sides.

I did so. His hands were already so cold.

Clear the airway.

When I pried open his jaw I saw the obstruction immediately, and gagged at the sight of it. The coiled string, still pink from my menses, lay on his purplish tongue. The tampon itself was lodged in his throat, caught beneath the uvula.

Because of his weight, Nigel could never breathe through his nostrils. The tampon, doing exactly what it was meant to, had soaked up the moisture in his throat and stopped it up.

I pulled the tampon free and tossed it aside, already beginning CPR as it landed on the tiles with a red splat.

But I'd reached him too late. Nigel, whose life expectancy had never been very long, died just two months before his tenth birthday.

When friends tell me their periods are awful, I think of Nigel, and resist the urge to tell them no matter how much pain they might be in, theirs could never be as bad as mine. My period murdered my little brother. Every twenty-eight days, sometimes less, sometimes a little longer, I've had to reckon with that, for the past thirty years.

Tomorrow marks the three-hundred and ninety-third anniversary of Nigel's death.

Tomorrow is "That Time of the Month."

4

Anderson Ackerman grinned as the lovely young lady with the colorful hair braids wheeled him down the hall from the elevator to his room. At conventions just like this, one or two in every major city across these Great United States, he'd find at least two or three of his female fans eager to ingratiate themselves, indeed *prostrate* themselves before him.

Invariably, they would mainly discuss his epic dark fantasy series, and quite often he would discover they were writers themselves, waiting on their Big Break, or looking for a mentor, or sometimes just a bit of "inspiration." Eventually he'd convince them to let him touch them and they would, reluctantly, touch him. He'd stop them mere moments before climax and have them lie facedown on the bed. Then he would haul himself out of his chair onto the mattress, climb on top of them and penetrate their anus, hurling insults at the backs of their heads the entire time, telling them they were talentless, they would never amount to anything, they didn't have the courage to write anything more complex than a grocery list, until the combination of sadism and friction became too much and he'd fill them full of his creative juices.

He'd roll off of them then, sweat and the frothy yellow-brown mixture of lube, ejaculate and fecal matter drying on his hairy belly and flaccid cock, leaking from their swollen orifices. They would roll over, wipe themselves off in humiliation, and begin to put on their clothes with their tear-streaked gaze on the floor.

Sometimes, they would say, "I'll tell."

They'd assure him, "I'll tell everyone what you did."

To that he would ask, "Tell them what, exactly? That I assaulted you? That I *raped* you? My dear, I *asked* and you *complied*. You've known where the door was the entire time."

There was a name for what he did. Producers and casting agents all over Hollywood and Miami knew it well. That word

was *coercion*. It wasn't illegal. It wasn't quite like *blackmail*—
that hideous word—but with enough power and clout it could be
just as effective.

Technically, but most importantly *legally*, he'd done nothing
wrong.

"I'm chairbound," he'd remind them. "Who do you expect
will believe you?"

The Sensuous Dirty Old Man, he thought with a sly grin,
recalling Isaac Asimov's little-known handbook for the elderly
letch. He felt her tits graze the top of his head as she rolled him
closer to his lair. Was that deliberate? He'd know soon enough.
Perhaps she'd let him suckle on them.

"You still with me?" he asked, trying to look back over his
shoulder.

"I'm here," she said, her voice breathy. She traced the back
of a finger down his bushy cheek, causing him to stir within his
underpants despite the many Mai Tais. "I'm just thinking about
all of the things I'm going to do with you when I get you into
that room."

"Well," he said, trying his best not to slobber. "Don't let me
distract you."

She pushed him a little further and he nodded toward his
door. "This is me. Room Two-Three-Seven."

The woman—she'd said her name was Aimee—wheeled
him up to it, and he unlocked it. She rolled him into the room,
leaving him facing the wall.

"Would you mind very much locking the door?" he asked,
rolling around to face her. "We wouldn't want any unexpected
visitors, would we?"

"I'm expecting some friends," Aimee With Two Es said.

"Friends plural?" The idea intrigued him. "As in, more than
one?"

She smirked. "Mm-hmm. Fans of yours, actually."

He wiped a runner of drool from his beard with the back of
a liver-spotted hand.

Her right eyebrow arched. "You like that, do you? Having

your way with more than one woman at a time?"

He nodded brusquely, his jowls shuddering. He liked the idea very much, though he'd never had the courage to put it into practice. One woman crying foul he could handle. Two or more... that could get trickier. But he was willing to try anything once. Any port in a storm, as his dear old dad had often said.

Aimee's phone tinkled like wind chimes and she responded with a flurry of clicks from both thumbs.

"Your friends?"

She smiled, not looking up from her phone. "You're going to get the royal treatment today."

Aimee With Two Es plopped down on the sofa in the entrance. Ackerman's gaze lingered on her knee-high boots, trailing her fishnet stockings up to where they crossed under her tight skirt. Good God, she was an exquisite creature. The things he would do to her....

Salivating again, Anderson. Rather like Pavlov's dog.

Aimee's phone tinkled again. She uncrossed her legs— giving him a brief glimpse of the secretive shadows within her skirt—and stood to get the door. "They're here."

Aimee With Two Es opened the door and three women entered. All gorgeous, of various body types. An Amazonian black woman with short orange hair and tattoos on nearly every bit of exposed skin, which was plenty. A slender, short redhead with facial piercings, her ample buttocks visible below the frayed hem of her cut-off jean shorts. An Asian woman with a generous waist and rump, her eye makeup smoky. Each of them held a copy of one of his books from the *Anvil of the Gods* series.

"What is this? *Charlie's Angels?*" Ackerman stammered as the four women tossed the books unceremoniously to the floor and began circling him like dancers in a Maypole ritual.

Speaking of poles, I'm hard as a standing stone.

"More like Ackerman's Demons," the Asian woman said as she passed.

Aimee With Two Es stopped before him, the others pausing in tandem. She planted the toe of her right boot between his legs, dangerously close to his erection, which throbbed like a still-beating heart torn from the chest of a ritual sacrifice. Then she shimmied to pull down her panties from under her short skirt, slipping them down over her fishnets.

"What exactly do you mean by that, dear?" he asked, surprised he was able to talk with the vision before him.

"It means," Aimee said, "today is your reckoning."

Before he could respond she stuffed the purple thong into his mouth. *Crammed* it in, shoving his tongue to the back of his throat. He gagged, then pushed his tongue through the silky, tangy fabric, simultaneously in both Heaven and Hell.

What did she mean by 'reckoning'?

They circled again, and the way they laughed and tickled his beard, squeezed his shoulders, pinched his nipples and flicked his erection, prominently displayed beneath his khakis, began to feel more like the circling of buzzards, waiting for the starving man to finally die.

"Your sophomoric writing reeks of male gaze," Aimee said, reaching down to squeeze the engorged head of his penis rather sharply.

"You rely on lazy rape tropes to be shocking," said the Asian woman, slipping a hand down his shirt and scratching his chest through the hair sharp enough to bring blood and make him whimper.

"Your characters of color are poorly drawn," said the black woman, slapping his cheek so hard tears sprang from his eyes and he cried out in pain.

The redhead tore a piece of duct tape off a roll and pasted it over his mouth. "Your female characters are nothing more than ciphers," she said, and pinched his nostrils shut.

Ackerman thrashed in the chair but the women held his arms fast. He screamed through the sodden fabric, unable to breathe, tears streaming down his face, and they *laughed*.

Oh, this would not do. He did not like this at all, and there appeared to be no stopping them.

The women, this coven of slanderers, would have their way

with him, abuse him, humiliate him, and unless someone caught them in the act, nobody would believe a single word of it.

NEVER MEET YOUR IDOLS

1

IT WAS WHAT Shakespeare would have called a "comedy of errors" getting the comatose David Ennis from his room at the Plaza Hotel to Tyler Grody's room at the Lonely Motel, but they managed it in under an hour.

First, Jackson Rawlins, the Hashtag King, went to the lobby to see if they had a wheelchair available, telling the concierge—the same jackass with the small mustache who'd given Tyler grief the day before—that Mr. Ackerman was having trouble with his chair and needed one immediately as he was scheduled on a panel in half an hour. The concierge said they had a few in the back, and when he asked for the room number, Rawlins said, "Do you expect me to *carry* him over my shoulder? One of our *finest* authors of dark fantasy? How would that look for the hotel, hmm? Hashtag Accessibility Lawsuit!"

The concierge relented—Rawlins relished in describing how the man seemed to visibly deflate—allowing him day-use for the chair, which he promptly rolled upstairs to room 501. By then, Tyler had managed, through plenty of trial and error, to dress up Ennis in the cloak he'd worn the day before. It fit too tightly in the shoulders and neck, but Ennis wasn't in a state to mind. Nor did he notice when Tyler had accidentally rolled him off the bed trying to get the cloak down under the man's ass, landing face-first on the carpet, where he still lay when Rawlins returned with the chair.

"Hashtag What the Actual, dude?"

"I got it on him, didn't I?"

Together they hoisted Ennis into the chair. The comatose man sat with his head slumped over one shoulder, carpet burn on his cheek. He was still breathing fine.

"You know, this kind of reminds me of that movie..." Tyler said. "The one with the corpse."

"Clint Eastwood?"

Tyler gave him a look of annoyance. "He needs a beard."

"Clint Eastwood doesn't have a beard."

"*Ackerman*, you idiot."

Rawlins pouted. "Hey. Hashtag Be Kind, dude. We're in this together."

Tyler didn't need reminding of that. And while he did appreciate the help, partners meant twice the opportunity for mistakes.

"I bet we could buy one off someone downstairs. I saw a few Gandalfs when I was down there this morning."

"Good thinking. I'll do that while you get your glucagon."

Rawlins looked at Ennis. "You think he'll be okay while we're gone?"

"He's not going anywhere."

It didn't take Tyler very long to find a wizard, but it took him longer to find someone who would give up their beard for less than the hundred dollars cash he had on him. His paranoia didn't make the quest any easier. He kept thinking people knew what he was up to, that he was holding a semi-famous midlist author captive, unconscious in a wheelchair, and *oh God, Tyler what have you done, you got yourself in a heap of trouble now! Shut up, shut up! Nobody knows anything. You're being crazy.*

He finally parted with all of the cash in his wallet, planning to hit a bank machine after they got back to the hotel. When he got back to the room, Rawlins was trying to hoist Ennis back into the chair.

"What happened?"

"I dunno!" Rawlins said. "Help me with him!"

Tyler did. They got him back in the chair with no trouble.

"He was on the floor when I got in."

"He probably just fell," Tyler said. "That gives me an idea, actually."

He crossed to the mini fridge. He used a tissue from the box on the dresser to open it, then remove a small bottle of Wild Turkey, which he knew from his research had been Ennis's drink of choice, the Brown Demon, he'd called it, back when he was drinking.

"Really? You're getting drunk *now*?"

Tyler held the bottle with the tissue and unscrewed the cap. He brought it to the bathroom and poured it into the toilet. Then he tossed the bottle on the floor beside the bed. "Help me with these," he said.

Rawlins seemed to clue in. He approached Tyler at the fridge and reached for another bottle.

"Use a tissue, you idiot. Do you want to leave fingerprints?"

"Oh, right." Rawlins got a tissue, and aped what Tyler did with bottle after bottle, unscrewing the caps, pouring the contents into the toilet, then leaving the empty bottles and caps on the dresser, the bedside table, the floor. They poured the contents of two bottles onto the bedsheets, which they'd messed up theatrically. Tyler broke a table lamp, crushing it under his heel on the floor. Then they flushed the tissues and alcohol down the toilet and left the lamp in jagged shards.

When the room looked and smelled about as "rock bottom" as Tyler could manage, Rawlins stepped out to make sure the coast was clear. Then they wheeled Ennis out of the room, leaving the mini fridge wide open. With any luck, Towne would think Ennis had fallen off the wagon and run off to score some more booze and coke.

Wheeling him out of the hotel and getting Ennis into Grandma's Datsun *should* have been easy. Rawlins went ahead to the lobby to distract the concierge, telling him Mr. Ackerman was very happy with the chair. Tyler waited for the next elevator.

When the doors opened, a man stood inside. His eyes went wide when he saw the man in the chair, and he reached out to hold the doors just before they closed.

"Oh. My God. I am *such* a huge fan, Mr. Ackerman."

Tyler didn't know what to do. He was caught. So he wheeled Ennis into the elevator, facing him away from Ackerman's huge fan, and stood staring intently at the closed doors, willing them to open again on the lobby.

"Could I get an autograph?" the fan asked. He held out a small notepad over Ennis's shoulder.

"Mister, uh, Ackerman is…" *Die, die, why won't you shut up and die!* Tyler screamed in his head. "Well, you know how he is with the, uh, the booze."

"Oh." The fan retracted his notepad reluctantly, seeming to know what Tyler meant. "Oh, yes. His *siestas*. He's famous for them, isn't he?"

Tyler faked a genial laugh. His warped reflection stared back at him from the brushed steel doors. *Please leave me ALONE!*

The elevator doors finally opened on the lobby. Rawlins was at the front desk, blocking the concierge from view. He glanced back and gave Tyler half nod. Tyler stepped out briskly.

"Please let Mr. Ackerman know I said I love his work," the man called from the elevator.

Tyler ignored him and rushed Ennis to the front doors, out into the snow. Once he'd reached his grandmother's Datsun, Rawlins met him there, panting heavily and shivering in his jacket.

"That was too close, dude. Hashtag Close Call."

The two of them loaded Ennis into the front passenger seat. After a brief period where Tyler was certain the car would never start, the engine turned and they got going. Made anxious by the oppressive silence, he flicked on the radio. Some guy was singing about going for a soda, assuring the listener if they did no one would hurt and no one would die. Tyler didn't tend to like old people music, but he had to admit the song was kind of soothing.

"Dude, use the carpool lane. It's faster."

"Our passenger is comatose," Tyler grunted.

"There's three of us. No one will notice, trust me."

Tyler glared at him in the rearview as he signaled to change lanes. "If we get pulled over, I'm going to literally murder you."

2

She was in the audience: *Kendra Pleasance*. Right there in the front row, with Clay Kayden sitting beside her.

Moira had sat patiently through several readings (including Fiona St. Clair's odd story about dominating her wolfman boyfriend, which she'd read straight from her cell phone and seemed to be a riff on, or straight up rip-off of, Palahniuk's minimalist, repetitive style), but midway through two writers prior to herself, she'd run off to throw up what was left in her stomach from the small lunch she'd been able to hold down. On her way out the door, she'd spotted Ms. Pleasance near the back, taking notes with her glasses slipping off the bridge of her nose.

She's taking notes. Could it be true what they say? That she's here looking to make a film from one of our stories?

When she'd returned from the toilet, Ms. Pleasance was no longer in the seat she'd been when Moira left the conference room.

Moira sat dreading the moment emcee Frank Wallis would call her name, and climbed the stage in a semi-daze when he finally did. The jitters were awful, they always were, but she pushed through her story, rushing at first, eyes on the trembling paper, making as little eye contact as possible. She didn't even notice until she was several paragraphs into her story that Clay was sitting up front, smiling, with Kendra Pleasance watching her intently beside him, chewing on an arm of her glasses.

Seeing the two of them calmed Moira. She slowed her pace, placing emphasis on all the right words, hitting the precise phrasing, reading it to the audience the way she'd read it out loud to herself countless times at home and again in her hotel room, in front of the vanity mirror.

When she finished, Clay began clapping and Kendra quickly

joined him. The whole audience clapped. A few people actually rose from their seats to give her a standing ovation.

Nigel would have been proud.

When the applause died down, Moira left the stage hurriedly and exited the conference room. She stood there catching her breath, trying to slow the beat of her heart and calm the queasy feeling in her belly. Clay met her out in the hall, with Kendra Pleasance in tow.

"That was… incredible," Ms. Pleasance said.

Moira gushed. "Oh, my goodness. I am such a huge fan, Ms. Pleasance."

"Kendra, please. Your friend here made quite a case for you." She nodded toward Clay. "Ms. Mead, is it?"

"Just Moira's fine. Thank you so much for coming, Miss— Kendra," she corrected herself, blathering and nervous.

"Relax, Moira. This isn't an interview. I loved your story."

"I'm dead chuffed, Ms. Pleasance, Kendra—I absolutely love your films, all of them, even the early ones you did in film school people rarely mention—"

"Moira." Kendra touched her shoulder, smiling gently. *The* Kendra Pleasance actually *touched* her. "I'm not blowing smoke up your ass. You don't have to tit for tat with me. Your friend already told me you're my biggest fan."

Clay smiled. Moira smiled back. With all of the thoughts swirling around in her head, she didn't know what to say.

"You may have heard I'm here writing a screenplay for my latest film, but I'm also hoping to find new talent. Fresh voices on the horror scene. That's where you come in."

"Me?"

"Yes, you. As I said, I loved your story. And I'd like to produce it. To finance it. Get it made as a short film, something we could take around to festivals."

"You want to make a film from Nige—from 'That Time of the Month'?"

"That's what this is all about, isn't it? Women promoting women?"

"I suppose."

Kendra turned to Clay, who raised his eyebrows as if to say, *What did I tell you?*

"So," Kendra said. "Don't answer me now. Just think about it. I want you to come to my room at six P.M. tonight. Room three-oh-six. Can you remember that, or do you need to write it down?"

"Room three-oh-six," Moira said, nodding shakily. "Six P.M."

"I love the trill. *Thrrree*," she said, attempting to roll her R. "That's six P.M. Eastern, not whatever time zone you're in back home. Got it?"

It seemed like an odd comment to make, but Moira ignored her gut feeling. She was still nervous and probably making too much out of nothing. "Got it," she said.

Kendra smiled. Again, she patted Moira's shoulder. Her touch was electric. Moira wouldn't have been surprised to find that her hair was standing on end as if she'd rubbed it with a static-charged balloon.

"Great. I'll see you then," she said, already beginning to walk away. "Thank you for recommending I stay, Mr. Kayden."

"No," Clay said. "Thank you. Really."

And then she was gone, entering the crowd of slow-moving bodies, leaving the two of them alone.

"Jesus *Christ*, Clay," Moira said. "You might have at least warned me."

Clay chuckled. "Relax. She loved you. She said she loves your accent's 'old-world charm.'"

"Oh, wonderful."

"I just wanted to make up for last night. I should have stayed—"

She grabbed him before he could apologize further, pulling him into a tight hug. He sank into her embrace, hugging her back just as fiercely. It was the kind of hug that held everything they hadn't done with each other and couldn't possibly in public. Finally, she let him go. He was smiling down at her.

"Oh, Christ," she said, glancing at her wristwatch. "I've got a panel in twenty minutes. Will you come?"

"I wouldn't miss it."

A wide smile spread across her face. Then she remembered the morning, the hangover, waking up with Dean Foster Towne in her bed.

"Clay, I—" She stopped herself.

"What?"

"Never mind. Let's go. I'll need a drink to get through this."

He held out his arm. "Hair of the dog?"

She slipped hers through it. "D'you mean Fiona St. Clair's boyfriend?"

They both laughed, walking off arm in arm to the bar.

3

David awoke with a stinging throb in his shoulder, like he'd just gotten his shots for a tropical vacation. He felt hungover. His mouth was drier than a nun's cunt, his heart beat rabbit fast, and his body was sore all over. The air smelled of wood polish and mustiness, along with a sour smell he couldn't define—possibly sweat? His eyes wouldn't open fully, so he couldn't verify aside from blurred shapes in the brightness where he was or if there was anyone in here with him. The space, wherever it was, felt small.

"He's awake," a squeaky, cracked male voice said.

Another man said, "Oh, thank God. We'll have to check his blood sugar levels for a little bit still. Hashtag Diabadass."

"I don't..." David groaned, his voice barely more than a croak. "I don't have diabetes."

"You were in a diabetic coma, Mr. Ennis," the man with the kid's voice said. "We gave you the antidote."

"Antidote? What the fuck is this? Where am I?"

"Room 7 at the Lonely Motel," the other guy said.

"*Don't tell him that!*"

"What? Why not?"

"Because if—"

"Because if I get out of here," Ennis finished, "*which I will*, I'll know exactly what to tell the police about you two."

Silence hung in the room, as heavy as the smell of fear sweat from his two captors.

"Well, shit," the guy with diabetes said finally.

"It's not too late to turn this around," David said, after giving the clueless guy a moment to let his situation sink in. "You want money? I don't have much. All of my money's socked away in mutual funds so I can fucking retire."

"We don't want money," Squeaky Voice said.

"What *do* you want then?"

Footfalls crossed the room quickly, nearing him. He smelled the man's sweat, the funk of his breath, but also a familiar scent. He still couldn't see well—his eyelids were crusted over and the eyeballs themselves felt like he'd been wandering the desert on a six-day coke binge—but he remembered the smell of bleach from the day before.

"I want—"

"You're that kid," David said, cutting him off. "The elf from *Lord of the Rings*."

"Shut up!" the kid screamed in his face. "It's my turn to talk. You're always talking, talking, talking. Do you ever *listen*?"

David sat quietly—*yes, I'm sitting, sitting in something uncomfortable*—awaiting the kid's next move. His hands were immobile, strapped or taped to the chair. If he'd been able to move them, he'd have wiped the kid's spit off his face.

"What I want, is for you to *pay*."

"I already told you," David said calmly. "I don't have cash sitting around. It's all tied up." He laughed bitterly. "Just like me, apparently."

"I told *you*, I don't *want* money."

"Then how am I supposed to pay you?"

"With your *life*, Mr. Ennis."

"Wait, wait." The position of the other guy's voice ascended, as if he were rising from a chair. "Nobody said anything about killing him."

"Would you *shut up*?"

"Fellas, can we all get on the same page here, please? You've put me into a diabetic coma somehow, and you've obviously kidnapped me. That's a class A-1 felony in New York State. You're already looking at fifteen years behind bars, minimum. *Life*, if you get a conservative judge."

"No, no, no—this was just supposed to be a *prank*," the clueless guy said.

David barked a laugh. "A *prank*? You could've killed me!"

He blinked hard and his vision finally cleared. Sure enough, the kid who'd asked for his autograph the other day stood with his butt against a vanity. The other guy, who looked like a hipster from a ska video with his checkered bowling shirt and black and white wing tips, stood with his mouth hanging open.

"You karate chopped me," David said, remembering in the moment before he blacked out he'd tried to throttle the squeaky-voiced kid.

"I am so, so sorry, Mr. Ennis," he said, clasping his hands together. "Hashtag Please Forgive Me."

"It's a little late for that," the kid said.

David clenched his jaw, staring down the kid. "So what now? You gonna do it quick? You think you've got the stones?"

"I've killed before."

The Hashtag King shot a glance at his partner.

"What? Mice? The neighbor dog?" he said, affecting the slight hillbilly twang the kid had obviously tried hard to lose. "Those hands haven't taken a life. They've probably never held anything but a joystick and your own pud."

The kid sneered but said nothing. The other guy let out a surprised nervous laugh.

"I thought so," David said.

The kid pushed up from the vanity. Behind him, what looked like a stack of printer paper lay on the dresser.

Christ, is that a manuscript*?* David thought. *Is that what this* *is about?*

"Let me guess… you sent me your novel to blurb and I didn't endorse it."

The kid picked up the large, poorly stacked manuscript. "You didn't even *read* it," he cried, waving the flopping pages at him. "You *ignored* my messages."

"I ignore *hundreds* of messages a week, kid. What makes you so special?"

That seemed to trip him up. The lanky guy in the bowling shirt closed his mouth audibly, watching his partner.

Finally, the kid slapped the manuscript back down on the vanity. He pulled a page from the top and brought it over to where David sat in what appeared to be a wheelchair.

Taking a page from Anderson Ackerman, he thought. *If only these little twerps had kidnapped* him *instead.*

The kid held up the title page for David to read. *The Rosehip Conundrum*, it was called. He'd been smart enough to scratch out his name below and address info in the top left corner, in case David did somehow manage to escape, but David could see hints of it behind the pen lines. Ty(*blank*) (*blank*)dy.

"Tyler?" he ventured. It was either that or Tyson, and he certainly didn't look like a Tyson. "That's your name, right?"

The kid eyes flashed with what appeared to be excitement before quickly clouding over. David wasn't going to win him over so easily.

"Even if it *was* possible for me to read every unsolicited manuscript sent my way, I'm *legally* not able to. If it's unvetted, the ramifications from that, if later down the line someone wants to claim I stole their work, or plagiarized portions of it—you see how that's just not prudent for me, don't you? It's not that I don't *want* to read it—hell, sit it in my lap, I'll read it right now. It's that I wasn't able to at the time."

"You had your chance," the kid growled.

He lashed out with the page. It caught David in the cheek, slashing him, that little sting of exquisite agony. "*Fuck*," David cried out on a sharp exhale.

"Jesus, dude," the Hashtag King said.

Tyler returned to the vanity, laid the title page upside down beside the stack, and picked up the first page. He held it up for David to read. It was a dedication. It was addressed to David, crediting him as Tyler's "inspiration."

"That's sweet, kid. Really, I appreciate it. Let me read the rest. I really am interested, I promise."

Tyler let the page dangle. "We're not going to be *reading* today," he said with a serene calmness. "Today is about pain. Have you ever heard of *lingchi*? You might know it by its more common name, 'death by a thousand cuts.'" The kid smiled. "The Chinese, up until it was banned in the early 1900s, they used this form of torture against traitors, see? Western observers reported ghastly observations of it, the torturers starting by gouging out the eyes, then slicing off bits of skin and appendages… one after another… until the traitor eventually died of their wounds. *You* betrayed me, Mr. Ennis. Therefore, I sentence you to *lingchi*."

"Kid, you don't have to—"

The kid flicked out with the page and the paper's edge drew blood on David's left hand. David flinched but wouldn't give him the satisfaction of crying out.

"This is a very long book," Tyler said, returning to the vanity for another page. "I believe it's going to require a *lot* of cutting."

For the next twenty minutes or six hours, David wasn't sure, the kid picked up page after page and used each one to make a single papercut into his victim's flesh. David had sat in dentist's chairs over the years, getting fillings and teeth removed without anesthetic. It wasn't exactly *nothing*, but the pain was endurable. This was very much like that. Bursts of pain followed by longer moments of respite, while Tyler pulled out David's earlobes and slashed the folds of skin underneath, cut the webbing between each of David's fingers several times, held his tongue and sliced it edgewise, until finally David was unable to hold in his screams.

"The walls are very thick," Tyler said, holding down David's left hand to draw a page sharply below the nail of his index finger. Both hands were already bloody, ten to a dozen little slashes on each, the creases in his skin and fingertips laced with blood, collecting in the hair follicles and cross-hatching and raised veins.

"Trust me," the kid said, "I screamed so loud the other night, if anybody was going to come for help, they would have."

The thing was, growing up in the Buffalo-Niagara Falls area, David had heard stories of this place, the Lonely Motel. It was one of those no-tell motels, where hookers and businessmen met for a few hours before or after a flight. They'd shot porn here in the '70s, from what he'd heard, when it was still illegal to star in them. Even the original owner had killed herself in one of the rooms. Hung herself in the closet, according to rumor. He remembered there'd been speculation that it was a failed attempt at autoerotic asphyxiation. Or a successful one, depending on whether or not she got off before she punched her ticket. For all he knew, it could have been *this* room. Right there in that closet, to the left of the Hashtag King.

Kids used to say it was cursed, this place. No adult David had ever known would have been caught dead frequenting the Lonely Motel. Even if their house burned down or they had bugs and needed to get it fumigated, they would stay *anywhere else* on this strip of motels and used car lots, pawn shops and payday loan brokers.

Tyler brought the next page over, dangling it before David. He could barely distinguish the paragraphs through his tears.

"This part is going to be unpleasant," the maniac said, and reached for David's face.

David turned away violently.

"Hold his head," Tyler said.

"Me? You gotta be kidding. Hashtag No Way Jose."

Tyler picked up the boxcutter that David only just noticed had been lying there beside the diminishing manuscript the entire time. "Hold his head," the kid said, "or I'll kill him right now."

The Hashtag King stood reluctantly from the chair in the

corner of the room and crossed to David. "I'm sorry, dude," he said, moving behind the wheelchair, and grasped David's sweaty, matted head with both hands.

David struggled against it, but however reluctant the Hashtag King was to perform this task, he was more reluctant to watch him die. In the end, David suspected that might prove the kid's undoing.

The man held fast. David steeled himself.

"This is going to be very painful," the kid assured him.

He reached out again and pulled out David's right eyelid by the lashes, between his thumb and forefinger.

"*Oh, fuck, dude. I can't look*."

"Kid," David groaned, looking up at him with one blurry eye, his throat raw from screaming.

"*Don't call me that*."

"Tyler," David corrected himself, blinking away tears.

"What?" The kid looked down at him, devoid of emotion.

"Your book *sucks*."

Tyler's brow furrowed. He clenched his jaw and flicked the page across David's eyelid. The pain flared, his vision going a violent red then cloudy white, the eyelid twitching involuntarily.

The kid let go and returned to the vanity. "I'm glad you said that about my book, actually. It makes it easier for me. But it won't be any easier for you. There's still… a hundred and fifty-three pages to go." He turned to his reluctant partner, who was sitting in the chair again, head in his hands, elbows resting on his knees. "What do you think, Jackson? What part should we cut next?"

4

Moira broke off from Clay after a few drinks at the bar and a bit of mingling throughout the convention, where several writers, readers, narrators and critics congratulated her on her reading. It was incredible, surreal. After their publisher had gone under, leaving both hers and Clay's first novels in limbo, she'd struggled to finish her second. She'd sold a few short stories to magazines and small press anthologies here and there, and received a smattering of praise in reviews. But it was nothing like this. The adulation of her peers, and a meeting with her favorite director. It felt like a dream. She'd told Clay as much. He'd assured her it was well deserved.

"We'll get together after, yeah?" she'd asked, before leaving him to do whatever he'd been doing prior to meeting up with Kendra Pleasance. "Have a nice dinner?"

"Sounds excellent," he'd said.

Moira decided to dress up a little for Kendra. It still felt so odd for her to say: *Kendra*. As if they were already friends. Not Ms. Pleasance. She said the name aloud again, holding up the dress she'd meant to put on for dinner in front of herself, standing at the vanity mirror. It was a business meeting, after all. "Dress for the job you want" and all that, even though Kendra herself would probably be dressed casually in her black beret, a T-shirt with another catchy feminist slogan, and requisite Doc Martens.

"*Kendra*," she said again.

Wearing her new dress, she put on a dash of makeup and stepped back from the mirror. Would Kendra appreciate the effort, or think she was too glammed up? Was this the right impression she wanted to make on a feminist icon, dressing herself in gender-normative clothing?

"Fuck it," she said. She slipped on a pair of jeans under the dress and swayed her hips a bit. That was no good either. "It looks like I'm wearing a fucking apron."

She took off the jeans again. The dress would have to do. She wasn't going to change herself to fit someone else's idea of what a woman should or shouldn't be. Wasn't that what feminism was supposed to be about? Or had she already changed to fit society's doctrine, from the moment she escaped the womb?

Whatever. The dress felt right and looked good. She'd wear it, and if Kendra thought lesser of her for it, that was Kendra's issue, not hers.

She wouldn't warp her own self-image to fit into a box. She hadn't in her writing, and she wouldn't in life, no matter if it might cost her potential opportunities. She'd rather languish in obscurity with her integrity and dignity intact than chase clout like all the sad fools chasing clout on social media in the vain hope *someone* might take pity on them and buy their lousy book.

Moira worked her way through the winding halls toward Kendra's room. Even though their rooms were on the same floor she had to turn around twice, feeling a bit like Spinal Tap lost backstage in Cleveland, until finally she found it: room 306. She rapped on the door, self-conscious about how delicately she'd knocked. Like a dainty old lady.

Nevertheless, the door opened. Kendra smiled and looked at her watch. "Right on time," she said. "I admire punctuality." She stepped aside, letting Moira into the room. "Great outfit, by the way."

"What the fuck is this?" Fiona St. Clair said from just inside the room, looking Moira up and down with a sneer. "What's *she* doing here?"

Moira noted the video camera set up in the corner of the room, aimed at the two guests, and wondered the same. "Kendra?" she asked, curious whether she'd been double-booked on purpose, and what exactly was happening here.

The director smiled and sat on the edge of the bed, tapping the tip of a ballpoint pen against her Hollywood-white teeth. "This is it, ladies. The final-act showdown. Only two women remain."

Moira's heart sank. "What d'you mean?"

"I can't exactly choose *both* of you. That wouldn't be much of a success story. So I thought, why not have the two of you decide for me?"

"I've decided," Fiona said. "Pick me."

"It doesn't work quite like that. I need to *really* know you want this. I need to know how hard you'd fight to get to the top." She nodded over her shoulder, toward the camera. "And *this* is my little insurance policy. This ensures that once I do help you break through that glass ceiling, you'll remain *grateful*. You'll remember to thank me at every award ceremony. And you'll never, *ever* betray me. Because of what's on this tape."

Fiona stepped forward. "Kendra, I don't give a shit about the camera. I will one-hundred percent get down on my knees blow bubbles in your asshole if it'll get me this movie."

Kendra laughed. "I'm not interested in… whatever that is."

"Then what exactly *do* you expect from us, Kendra?" Moira asked. Saying the director's first name no longer felt good on her tongue. It felt acidic. *Venomous.*

"I love that accent, did I tell you that? It's so… *working class*. It'll definitely help to sell your rags to riches story. If, that is, you win."

"Win *what*?"

"Win wot?" Kendra said, mimicking her. She grinned at Fiona. "Isn't that great?"

"She sounds like a British harp seal."

"I'm Welsh, you Yankee cunt."

"Whoa, whoa, whoa." Kendra held up her hands. "There's no need to drop C-bombs in here. It's not that kind of movie. But you *will* want to remove your earrings, because it's about to get nasty."

"What the bloody hell are you talking about?"

"She wants us to beat the shit out of each other," Fiona said. "Isn't that right, Kendra?"

"Right on the nose. But don't think that wins you any points. You have to be *fierce* if you want to make it in this world. This is about pure, unfettered *violence*."

"I thought this was about women helping women!" Moira cried, pulled to the end of her tether.

"It is." Kendra picked up the clapperboard Moira only just noticed had been lying beside her on the bed, and struck the filmsticks sharply together. "Now… may the best woman win."

"I'm not fighting—"

The fist connected with the side of Moira's head before she could finish the sentence. Her vision grayed, stars skittering in front of her eyes.

"You bloody cunt clot!" She slapped out at Fiona, who caught her by the wrist and twisted it.

"I'm fucking *winning* this contest, you bitch!" Fiona growled through gritted teeth. "I live in a *basement apartment* with three crust punk roommates. Do you have any idea how *expensive* it is to rent in Portland? Do you have any fucking clue how *bad* crusties smell?"

"I'm *not* fighting you."

"Fine. Be a little bitch. I'm gonna kick your ass, either way."

"*That's* the spirit!" Kendra said, jotting something down on a notepad.

Still holding Moira by the wrist, Fiona threw a jab with her left hand. It struck Moira weakly above her left breast. Outraged, Moira grabbed Fiona's nose ring with her free hand and pulled.

"*Ow!* You bitch!"

"Let go of my wrist."

"Let go of my septum piercing!" Fiona cried, her voice nasally.

"Only if you let go of my wrist!"

The director yawned dramatically. "*Boring!* I want *Caged Heat*, not *Mean Girls*. This is middle school bullshit."

Still gripping Fiona's piercing, Moira turned her rage toward the director. "I'm not brawling for your amusement, you commodity feminist twat!"

Kendra blinked behind her glasses, taken aback. Then she said, "Don't you just love how she says that? Not tw*awt*. Tw*aht*."

"Yeah, it's fucking fire," Fiona said in a nasal drone. "*Let go of my*—"

Moira let go, and while Fiona gasped in relief, Moira tore her arm free from the other woman's grip. "I'm leaving. You can have your fucking movie, Fiona."

The director leaped to her feet, glancing at the rolling camera as Moira headed for the door. "No! No, this wasn't supposed to happen like this!"

"I don't need your bloody film, Ms. Pleasance. I would rather walk barefoot through a field full of dog shite than be obliged to a vile woman like you."

She turned again and reached for the door handle.

"Wait!" Kendra called out. "Just hold on a second. *Please*."

Moira hesitated only a moment. Then she opened the door and stepped briskly out into the hall, her back still to the director.

"Moira, come on! You don't have to fight. You won. It was a *test*, and you passed. Just come back."

She turned. Kendra wore a genuine look of reprieve. Fiona just stared at the two of them, holding a tissue under her bleeding nose, seemingly unable to believe what she was seeing. The shift in the power dynamic was palpable.

"You gotta be fucking kidding me," Fiona said, her voice muffled by the crumpled, bloody tissue. "A *test*?"

"She's lying, Fiona. It wasn't a test. It was a *game*. A manipulative, nasty little game. And I've no interest in playing along."

Tears already forming, Moira forced herself to storm off, leaving behind what might have been her only opportunity to break into writing for the movies, but cherishing the one thing she had to hold on to: her dignity.

TORTURE PORN

1

AIMEE WITH TWO Es and the three other succubi lifted Anderson Ackerman out of his chair. He did his best to fight them off, twisting and jerking at the hips, lashing out with his arms, but in the end they overpowered him, and laid him out spreadeagle on his luxurious California king bed.

Ordinarily this might've been a stimulating experience, something Asimov's Sensuous Dirty Old Man would have lusted after. Four gorgeous women, having their way with him. It was the sort of premise one might discover in a *Penthouse Forum* letter, some trite fable in praise of bold women, begun with the hackneyed cliché, "Dear *Forum*, I never thought this would happen to me..."

And though he was stiff in his underpants, his engorged meatus oozing Cowper's fluid, what laypeople called "pre-cum," this was definitely *sexual* but wasn't by any tweak of imagination *sexy*. His body was merely responding to the stimulus, both visual and physical, as the succubi pulled hairs from his beard and pinched his nipples, giving casual, sadistic flicks to the throbbing head of his member.

They *laughed* at him. His frail, skinny legs and his pathetic erection. They disparaged his art, his entire career. With his mouth taped shut, the tang from Aimee's panties crammed into his mouth already absorbed by his tongue, snot oozed from his overworked nostrils and tears spilled from his eyes.

There was no dignity it this. He was helpless as a babe in arms, yet his treacherous penis gave their sadistic performance a standing ovation.

What they might do next was anyone's guess but he dreaded even considering it. Frankly, he doubted they planned to mount him, nor to allow him manual relief. Perhaps they'd take turns sitting on his face, suffocating him with their snatches and buttocks. Perhaps they'd crush his balls under their footwear, milk him to the point of near climax and let go, each of them taking their turn in an excruciating game of edge play. But perhaps what they'd planned was nothing sexual at all, merely more humiliation, stripping him bare and exposing him as the twisted deviant he clearly was, parading him around on a leash in front of the entire convention forced into some leather puppy-cosplay getup.

All suitable forms of revenge, he thought, for the young women he'd taken advantage of with his position of privilege and esteem over the years, at conventions just like this.

"I liked what you said the other day about writing with empathy," Aimee With Two Es said, sitting down beside him on the bed, draping her long, delicious legs over his own, very close to his throbbing manhood. "That when you're writing your stories, your torture porn, you're both the victim and the perpetrator. I thought that was fitting. It's *apt*, isn't it? Because you've been the *perpetrator* many times before, haven't you?"

He nodded pathetically.

"And now," she said, rising from the bed, giving him a tantalizing glimpse of her wonderful inner folds, "now, you're getting to know what it's like to be the *victim*."

The panties in his mouth muffled his screams as they rolled him over and tied his arms and legs—despite the obvious fact that his legs were entirely immobile—to the head and footboards with surprisingly soft rope likely meant for bondage.

"You complain a lot about authorial insertion in interviews. What was that quote of yours about Mary Sues in science fiction and fantasy? Right. You said navel-gazing is a symptom of youth and inexperience. Of the—what did you call it? The 'Me-Me-Me Generation'? *You* said modern writers couldn't *help* but insert themselves into their stories."

He remembered the quote. He still stood by it, but he feared there was nefarious intent behind its mention.

"Let's be honest, you do a fair amount of authorial insertion yourself, don't you? The moral posturing. The grandstanding. The longwinded speeches."

Ackerman didn't find the critique fair but remained silent, while Aimee picked up the first volume of the *Anvil of the Gods* series, rolling and twisting it until it was curled over on itself like a newspaper meant for smacking a dog on the nose.

"Since you like inserting yourself into your books so much," she said with a sadistic smile, "let's see how much you enjoy inserting your books into you."

The Asian woman—he'd heard one of the others calling her Misti—unrolled a Magnum-sized prophylactic over the book, squirted lubricant on it, then drizzled the cold and shocking liquid onto his anus. His penis had since shriveled against the mattress, pre-ejaculate chilling his belly.

This was a nightmare. What kind of diabolical sadist could have imagined such a thing?

Yes, of course. I did it myself, didn't I? In Book 3 of Anvil. The invading Ghost Cleric rapes the Anchorite with her own Holy Book. It was meant *as a metaphor.*

But this was no metaphor.

This was crude and blunt. The work of a hack like Ennis.

He felt the cold latex pressed between his buttocks. A smoothed corner edged into his rectum, not much further than he'd accidentally gone with his own fingers, while washing himself or if the toilet paper happened to split after voiding his bowels. Certainly not as deep as Dr. Tabor, the old Hungarian general practitioner, delved with his gloved fingers once a year. And nowhere near as deep as he'd let his childhood best friend go when they were still young boys, the first and only time he'd let anyone other than Tabor penetrate him.

He clenched his buttocks.

"Spread em, girls," Aimee said.

Ackerman jolted. Gloved hands gripped his buttocks and pulled them apart.

"Looks like I'm gonna need a hand for this, Misti. On the count of three... One... Two..."

On "three," God's *Anvil* punctured his pucker, spreading him wide. It entered like a driven fist, hammering his innards with all the tenderness of a railroad spike. He cried out against the bunched, damp panties as the book pressed against his organs, protruding like a massive abscess. Often, he'd compared writing and publishing a book to childbirth. But aside from a few bouts of constipation, never before had he wanted to eject something from himself so badly.

"I guess it's true what they say about you," Aimee With Two Es said, leaning into his field of vision with a lipstick-red smirk. "You like thick books."

"Dummy thicc," said one of the women behind him.

Ackerman could only weep softly into the snot and tears smeared on the bedspread.

"If you thought this was tough, Andy," she said, "you won't *believe* what happens next."

Nor would anyone else, he presumed. Aimee and her fellow succubi would get away with it, all of it, and he'd have to live with the shame of what they'd done.

2

After yesterday's whirlwind events, Archie Schneider decided to take the morning and afternoon off from the convention to further prepare for his Gross Out reading tomorrow.

He'd awakened with the sun, feeling fuzzy, at first thinking he was sick. He'd only ever had one hangover in his life, when his roommates in college convinced him to get "shit-faced" on cheap malt liquor during frosh week. This was kind of like that, only his jaw was sore from apparently grinding his teeth during the night, and his eyeballs felt like they'd been wringed out of any moisture.

He got himself a hearty breakfast, had a cold shower, and spent an hour in the hotel gym, forcing himself through a modified workout, focusing on cardio as he listened to Mozart's Symphony No. 39. He got a few interested looks from a woman in a blue spandex sports bra and quad shorts sweating it out on a treadmill. After she'd wiped off her machine she passed by his elliptical. He took out an earbud, expecting her to compliment his muscular physique.

"You're that guy, aren't you?" she said instead. "The Poo-Poo Man?"

Archie gritted his teeth. "Not me."

"Well," she said, admiring his butt as he moved, "*whoever* you are, you can periscope my ass any day."

She left Archie speechless, peering back with her eyebrows raised. "Just sayin," she called back, sashaying away.

Archie burned through the rest of his workout, wiped down his machine and hoped to see her again in the sauna or outside the changerooms, but she was nowhere in sight. He supposed she was either still in the showers or had left immediately, preferring to wash up in her own room. Whichever, he didn't plan to hang around waiting to see if she came out, and asking the guy at the desk seemed pointless.

He jerked off furiously under the spray of hot water, his mind conjuring up not the woman he'd just seen but the Turkey Lady instead. *Stuff this bad bird!* she begged him, her cry as he thrust his fist into her pushing him over the edge, his spunk splatting on the wall, oozing down the tiles to circle the drain. Catching his breath, he changed into street clothes before driving to the nearest department store, still stewing about the woman calling him by that name.

"Welcome to Walmart," the greeter said as Archie stepped through the sliding doors.

"Do you have baby laxative?" Archie asked.

The woman pouted. "Aw, does baby have a sore tummy?"

Archie ignored the woman's attempt to dig into his personal

life.

"That'd be pharmacy, aisle three."

"Thanks." He continued past her, then paused and called back: "And ponchos?"

"Ponchos? Your kid must be quite the little pooper!"

Archie folded his muscular arms across his chest.

"Um… ponchos, aisle twenty-three."

"Thank you."

"Good luck with your baby!"

Good luck with minding your own business, he thought but didn't say, heading toward the pharmacy.

3

Tyler picked up the final page of his manuscript. The other four-hundred and twenty pages he'd used were stacked haphazardly beside it, each spotted and speckled with more and more blood. He'd exhausted himself torturing Ennis, going back for page after page, having to decide which bit of exposed skin he should let the razor-thin edge of the paper bite into next. Ennis's bare arms, chest, neck, back and face were covered in small welts, weeping blood, some unintentionally crossing one another, since it was often difficult to control where the paper struck flesh. They'd stripped him down to his boxers and cut his legs, between his toes, under the nails.

Ennis himself had long ago passed out from the pain.

"He needs sugar," Rawlins said, looking at the diabetes test strip he'd swabbed against one of Ennis's thousand paper cuts.

"When I'm done," Tyler said. He nodded toward Ennis. "Pull down his boxers."

"*What?*"

"Pull them down or I'll call the police and we'll both go to jail for the rest of our lives. You heard what he said. Fifteen years *minimum*."

Rawlins groaned, "Fuck my life," and shuffled over to the

chair. He tugged at Ennis's boxers gingerly.

"Put your back into it," Tyler said, unconsciously mimicking his dead father.

Rawlins yanked the boxers off. Ennis's penis flopped out, flaccid and surrounded by salt-and-pepper pubic hair. It was larger than he'd expected, and the effect was jarring, like the time he'd seen his father's penis when was still too young to have pubes of his own.

"Hold it," he told Rawlins.

"No fucking way, dude. Hashtag No Homo."

"Hold it or I'll cut it off."

Rawlins looked mortified. "*You wouldn't.*"

Tyler reached for the boxcutter.

"Okay, okay!" Rawlins reached out hesitantly, then retracted his hand with a grimace. "Dude, it's got *crumbs* or some shit on it. Oh, fuck—*is that dick cheese?*"

"It's not—" Tyler bent at the waist to take a closer look. He reared back in disgust, nearly gagging himself. He wasn't sure it was smegma since Ennis was circumcised, but it was definitely milky white and curdled. This wasn't going to be a pleasant experience for any of them but it was a necessary component of the torture. It had to be done.

"Here." He pulled a tissue from the box on the vanity and held it out to Rawlins.

The Cuntrag King squirmed. "I'm not *wiping it off.*"

"*Hold* it with it. Just lift it by the… by the tip."

Rawlins used the tissue to pluck Ennis's fat, purple glans from its furry nest.

"Hold it up straight," Tyler said, picking up the final page.

"Aw, dude…" Rawlins lifted Ennis's penis, stretching it out. "Hey, you know, for a softie, this is a pretty big hog."

Tyler ignored him. He held the page on two corners, the edge close to the frenulum, the little flap of skin connecting the head to the shaft. "Hold it steady."

"I am," Rawlins grunted, looking away.

Tyler drew the page across Ennis's delicate dick skin. The

frenulum split open and spilled blood onto the paper, a lot more than many of the others.

Ennis roused to consciousness with a scream. He shook and pulled at his binding. The wheelchair moved back and forth by small degrees, held stationary by the wheel locks.

"Oh, good, you're awake." Tyler got down on his haunches before him. "I'm pleased you responded so well to my book, Mr. Ennis. It really was a labor of love. Don't worry, I've got plenty more copies—"

The spit flew at him so swiftly he wasn't able to react in time. It spattered on his cheek under the eye and dribbled down onto his upper lip. He gagged. All of the childhood bullying he'd endured rushed back at him like a gang of brutes in that moment of sheer disgust. He wiped the blood-streaked saliva away with the back of a hand.

"What the fuck! You just fucking *spit* on me!"

"There's more," Ennis grunted, heaving a breath, "where that came from, you twisted *motherfucker*."

Tyler stood abruptly. "Well, I thought you'd appreciate the genital torture, since your friend Lee Stark seems to enjoy it so much. A little bit of *fiction bleeding into reality*, so to speak. But I guess self-reference isn't your thing."

"*Fuck you.*"

"I thought you might say that. Go get Mr. Ennis some sugar, Jackson. An ice-cold Doctor Pibb would hit the spot right about now, wouldn't it, David?"

Rawlins nodded, clearly traumatized but happy to get rid of the blood-spattered tissue.

"There's money in my coat. You remember where, don't you? It's where you found the chloroform we didn't get to use because you decided it would be more fun to drink it instead."

Rawlins lifted the left side of Tyler's coat from the chair it hung over. He pulled out Tyler's wallet, peeled out a few one-dollar bills, then headed for the door.

"Oh, I think I saw lemonade in the machine," he called out before Rawlins could leave the room. "I bet that would hit a few spots as well. Nothing like a little lemon to soothe a papercut, right, David?"

Ennis only breathed raggedly, oozing blood from every inch of skin, his eyes glazed.

Tyler had beaten him.

But it wasn't over yet. He'd made Ennis pay, but not in full. When Rawlins came back with the Doctor Pibb, he'd give him some sugar.

Then he'd give him *sour*.

4

While Moira prepared for her meeting with Kendra Pleasance, Clay sat in the hotel bar by the fireplace, nursing a Coke Zero, sifting through the convention message board. The protesters were currently congratulating each other for "deplatforming" Ennis, but many believed the "work wasn't done" until they got the latest Lee Stark novel pulled from publication.

This was going even better than Clay could have imagined. He set his phone down on the table with a pleased smile and watched the fire.

His thoughts drifted back to sitting in front of this same fire last night, telling Moira, *Sometimes I think about burning this whole damn scene to the ground.*

She'd asked if it would make him happy. He hadn't answered her truthfully, because he thought the answer would have scared her. His mask of polite charm was the smile of a tiger. His anger, his *rage*, was the beast caged within.

I'm Fiona St. Clair's Big Bad Wolfman. Maybe I should join their group sessions?

"Christ, Kayden!" came a familiar voice. "Here you are."

Dean Foster Towne stood over him, looking distraught, the only sign of dishevelment a strand of hair loosened from his manbun, falling over his right ear.

"What do you want, Towne?"

"David's missing."

Clay stood abruptly. "Missing?"

"I suppose you must be happy with yourself." Towne gave him a dour look. "Your little plan to get him canceled worked a trick. These weird little twerps chased him around all day long, shouting lies about him and his work. After the convention announced his departure from the rest of the day's events, I went up to his room. He'd raided the minibar. Miniature spirit bottles everywhere, Kayden."

"Shit," Clay said, though he cheered inwardly. "Did you tell the front desk?"

"What exactly would I say, Kayden? A guest got drunk and left his room? That's not a crime in America, is it?"

"No, you're right. Show me."

"Show you?"

"Take me up there. I need to see it."

"But *why*, Kayden?"

"You want me to help you find David, I'm going to need to see what kind of bender he's on. Have you ever seen him drunk?"

"No."

"Exactly. I have. If he's really gone back to Brown Town, you'll need all the help you can get to find him." He gave Towne a serious look. "If you still want to, that is."

Towne nodded. "I want to."

"Then lead the way."

5

"The little bitch is *out on bail* already!"

The Critic Crew stood in a cluster in the Artist Alley section of the con, watching Kelly "Sugar" Lumpkin, the self-styled Bad Bitch reviewer with the gun in her handbag, get a tattoo of Dean Koontz on her dimpled thigh. She was currently lying flat on a table, scrolling on her phone while the tattoo artist buzzed and wiped blood and black ink from her dimpled flesh. Whether the look on her face was pain or rage was anyone's guess as she read the Facebook statement of Mr. Ortega's attacker.

"She's claiming Ortega attacked *her*!"

"Iggy wouldn't do that."

"Yes, I *know* Iggy wouldn't do that, *Beth-Anne*. But her followers don't know Ignacio like we do, and the police don't, either. Whose side do you think they're gonna take? The poor, defenseless white lady or the scary Latinx gay man?"

"Ignacio isn't scary at all."

"It's about *optics*, Beth-Anne. White lady versus male POC. Whose side do you think the media will take?"

"I still think he's white Hispanic."

"Jesus *Christ*, Elana. Get with the program here!" She slipped her phone back into her handbag alongside the pistol. "This is bad. If these writers start thinking we've got it out for them, we're gonna have to be on guard twenty-four-seven."

"Or we could just leave."

"We can't *just leave*, Beth-Anne. We have as much of a right to be here as any of them do. We can't *show them* we're scared. We have to make sure they know we're not leaving this place without a fight."

Beth-Anne and Elana gave each other fretful looks.

"All done," the tattoo artist said, wiping away the remaining ink.

The Bad Bitch rolled over onto her ass and looked down at her tattoo. "I said Bald Mustache 1980s Dean Koontz, not Hair Implant 1990s Dean Koontz! He looks like a goddamn Golden Retriever!"

The conspicuously untattooed tattooist shrugged. "Artistic license?"

Sugar reached into her handbag. Her two closest friends and the others with them flinched, certain this was the moment their volatile leader would snap for good, and pump this poor tattoo artist's guts full of lead. Instead, the Bad Bitch's hand emerged with a fistful of cash she shoved at him.

"You're lucky Sugar's in a good mood," she said.

"Seems like it," the artist said sarcastically, pocketing the cash. "Ya'll have a good night now."

"Oh, we will." She stormed off. The others followed. "We need to talk to Frank Wallis," Sugar said, leading them out of Artist Alley toward the conference rooms. "This aggression against us *will not stand*!"

PUNCH UP

1

CLAY STOOD CLOSE behind Towne as Ennis's protégé opened the door to room 501. The place was a mess: linens torn off the bed and the mattress overturned, a table lamp smashed on the floor, a hole punched in the wall beside the bathroom door. All of the hallmarks of a visit from the Brown Demon. And, as Towne had mentioned, dozens of tiny emptied liquor bottles left just about everywhere, just like that last night with David: the tables, the bed, the floor.

"You see?" Towne said, peering back.

Clay entered the room and picked up a travel bottle of vodka. "Oh, David's definitely had himself a Kentucky hug."

"A what?"

"It's what he called a binge. Wild Turkey, usually, but any drink would do if he didn't have any on hand. Didn't he make you read his biography?"

Towne shrugged. "I skimmed it. Must've missed that part."

"The last time David went to Brown Town," Clay said, "I was with him. He was like a wild animal. Like Jekyll and Hyde."

Towne picked up a small vodka bottle and looked at it with distaste. "What did he do?"

"He was constantly trying to be the life of the party, every place we went. Like Robin Williams on coke. One minute he was telling a story, the next he'd be betting strangers he could do the stupidest shit, like he'd eat a jar full of pickled eggs, then suddenly he's puking them all over this woman's wedding dress. Her husband took him outside and beat him to a pulp but he kept getting back up until the guy got bored of hitting him and left. Then he wanted to go to the zoo."

"The zoo?"

"They don't have zoos in England?"

"They have zoos in England, you muppet. I'm asking, *why the zoo*?"

"He said he was gonna fuck up a panda bear."

"Fuck *up*?"

Clay gave him an annoyed look. "He wanted to break into the zoo and wrestle a panda."

"Well, that's a relief. I thought it was American slang for a shag."

"Not this time, but after that he dragged me to the strip club. He was throwing bills at all the dancers like Jack Nicholson's Joker. Then he got up on stage with this duo, they were so annoyed with him they took turns smacking his bare ass until it was red. Before they kicked us out, he flashed his dick to an extremely unimpressed crowd."

"Jesus. Does his wife know?"

"That's not even the worst of it, the thing that almost got him divorced. That binge, that fall off the wagon—he's got *serious* demons, Towne. And when he drinks, those demons *possess* him. That's why he's always sucking down Mr. Pibbs, why he doesn't even *look* at liquor anymore." Clay peered around the room. "Or didn't. I guess that ship's sailed."

"Apparently. What are we going to do, Kayden?"

Clay sputtered. "We? Not my rodeo, not my clown."

"I thought you came up here to *help*, Kayden."

"I came up here to *gloat*."

Towne made a sour face. "Jesus. I knew you had a grudge, mate, but the man is *sick*. You may as well have handed him a loaded gun."

"Don't be dramatic, it doesn't suit you. Besides, if he does something *really* crazy, like take a naked swan dive off a fifth-floor balcony, it'll make whatever you're writing for him an instant bestseller."

Towne followed Clay's gaze to the balcony door. "Christ, you don't think—"

"I'm fucking with you, Towne. He's probably bar hopping, or trying to score coke. But who knows? Maybe he's at the Buffalo Zoo, getting mauled by a fucking panda bear."

"Have you no empathy, Kayden?"

"Me? Have *I* got empathy? David left me swinging in the wind for a handful of sales. *I* wrote his last three novels. *I'm* the only reason he's not *divorced* right now. You think I've got no empathy? You're looking in the wrong direction. Believe me, he'll sell your ass down the river like he did to me the second you stop being profitable."

Towne looked toward the balcony again.

Clay's cell rang. He slipped it out of his pocket. It was Moira. "Hey," he said.

"Clay?" Her voice was phlegmy, as if she had a cold. Or she'd been crying.

"What's wrong?"

"Is that him?" Towne said.

Clay held up a finger.

"Oh, Clay," Moira said, "it's just… it's so *awful*."

"Where are you? Are you in your room?"

She made a strangled sound something like a yes.

"I'm coming down. I'll be right there, okay, Moira?"

Towne's eyebrows rose and quickly descended, in what appeared to be an attempt to cover for his surprise.

"Okay," she said, and hung up.

Clay slipped his phone back in his pocket. "I have to go. Good luck with all of this," he said, waving a hand at the mess.

"You're not even gonna help fix the mess *you* made?"

"I'm done cleaning up David's messes. You're his lacky, aren't you? It's your job now."

With that, he turned and headed for the door.

"I shagged her, you know," Towne blurted out.

The words stopped Clay cold. He tried to remain composed as he turned back to the room. "So what? She's a grown woman.

She can sleep with whoever she wants."

"*Last night.* After you and I spoke in the lobby."

Clay made a fist. "She was drunk."

"Oh, don't be such a prude, Kayden. She wasn't so drunk she couldn't say yes. Besides, I'd enjoyed a tipple myself. There's nothing wrong with two fully grown adults enjoying each other's bodies under the influence of a little social lub—"

Clay swung. The punch connected with Towne's jaw. Towne cried out and staggered back, holding his cheek. Clay shook out his sore fist.

"She wanted it, mate," Towne said through blood-smeared teeth. "She practically *begged* me to fuck her."

"Bullshit."

"Why don't you ask her then, eh? What did you expect? *Loyalty?* From a *woman*?"

Clay jabbed a finger at Towne, who shrank back against the bed. "We're not through here," he said. Then he turned and left Ennis's room.

2

"I've got a surprise for you," the kid said with malicious glee in his eyes, holding something in a paper bag behind his back.

David was sweating, throbbing and bleeding from every pore, his breathing ragged, his mind racing, only remaining upright due to the gads of duct tape holding him in the chair. He never thought this kid would have had it in him, what he'd put David through. The cut on his prick had been the worst of it, but the lemonade the kid had poured on him had made David's entire body feel like he was on fire. His only respite was that he'd been sitting the entire time, and they hadn't been able to do anything to his asshole.

Maybe that's what this *is,* he thought dismally. *A little cornholing to put the topper on the cake.*

Would it be so bad? the voice of the Other asked.

The strangest thing happened when the kid started splashing citric acid on the hundreds of paper cuts crisscrossing David's flesh: it was almost as if he'd split from his body, a strange voice unlike his own commenting on what was being done to him while his physical self absorbed the pain. And while the agony from nearly every inch of exposed skin was excruciating, while his body remained fixed to this chair, in this awful motel room, this prison, his mind was finally *free*.

In his torture, he'd unleashed the creative instinct trapped within him, in the form of this Other. His writer's block, the mental constipation that had plagued him since his last visit to Brown Town, the big one that had almost ruined his life and his career, had finally fucked off to Timbuktu.

He was *writing again*.

All he needed now was a pen and paper on which to spew his words, like vomit, like the blood oozing from the slashes on his skin. Was it the pain that had jogged it loose? Was it the humiliation? He didn't know. All he knew for sure was that if he lived long enough to get through this, he wouldn't need to rely on Towne's subservience or Clay's silence anymore.

He'd be a *writer* again. A real, honest to God Writer with a capital W.

This kid who thought he was destroying his former idol, instead he'd become David's unwitting savior.

"Do you want to guess what it is?" the kid said, meaning his surprise, the glee in his eyes even more pronounced. His partner, the guy the kid called Jackson, was sitting with his head in his hands on the chair near the door.

That man will break, the Other said, paraphrasing the words David himself had read aloud from his upcoming Lee Stark novel the other day, a phrase Clay Kayden had written for him, from a passage that had perhaps not coincidentally gotten him chased by a bunch of protesters.

The kid's smarter than you, the Other said.

This kid? He's a fool.

Not him. Kayden. He played you like a Stratovarius.

Something about the phrasing of this felt familiar. Like he'd heard this unknown voice before. It came to him suddenly, like one of Ackerman's metaphorical Anvils from God.

Is that you, Stark?

The voice of the Other fell silent, neither agreeing nor disavowing.

"Take a guess," said the kid, Tyler, looking eager now. Like holding back his excitement might just make him spontaneously combust if David didn't say something soon.

"I don't care," David grunted. "Whatever it is, you can take a flying fuck out the window with it."

The unwitting partner raised his head from his hands with a look of deep concern.

"Aw, that's not nice," Tyler said with a faux pout. "I picked this out especially for you. I'm sure you'll like it."

"Fine. What is it?"

"*Guessssss*," the kid said, drawing out the S to sound like Hannibal Lecter.

"A .223-caliber AR-15 with a bump stock."

This surprised a laugh out of Tyler. "Nice try." The paper bag crinkled as he brought it around to the front.

David's mouth went immediately, *intensely* dry. He knew it from the shape, held by the neck in one hand, still enclosed in brown paper. Even if it hadn't made a tantalizing little slosh of liquid as it came to rest in front of him.

"Guess again," the kid said.

Stark spoke up then: *Perhaps he's not the fool you thought he was.*

"Wild Turkey," David said. His tongue had never felt so dry, like a shriveled sea sponge left baking in the midday sun. He needed something to wet it. A Mr. Pibb. A tepid glass of Lonely Motel tap water. A squirt of lemon juice. A stream of hot fucking piss.

Anything but this.

But goddamn, a Kentucky hug would feel good right now.

Stark, his nascent narrator, remained silent.

"Surprise!" the kid said, pulling the bottle from the bag, which he cast aside. "When's the last time you took a trip to Brown Town, Mr. Ennis? Could it be—just over two years ago? When you hit rock bottom? When your life nearly fell apart?"

"I see—you read my biography," David said, barely able to form the words with such dry inner workings.

"I *did*. Know your enemy, see? Sun Tzu. A favorite of Lee Stark's, isn't he?"

That's it, Stark said in David's head. *If you know your enemy and know yourself, you need not fear the result of a hundred battles. If you want to release yourself from bondage, David, you need to know your enemy. What does this boy fear? What does he* truly *fear? Better yet, what does he* love*?*

Tyler unscrewed the cap and held the bottle under David's nose. A concoction of wonderful scents—vanilla, spices, a hint of toasted oak and toffee—pricked David's nostrils, split and bleeding but still able to tease his olfactory senses. A flash flood of saliva saturated the desert of his mouth.

Whatever the kid might fear, he knew David's greatest fear: that he would lose control. That he would tear down everything he'd worked so hard to build with a single gulp.

You've already lost control, David, Stark said. *Don't let this boy beat you over a sip of bourbon.*

"You want it, don't you?"

Against his will, David nodded.

"But you won't let yourself give in."

He shook his head unconvincingly.

"That's okay," the kid said. "Let me make the choice for you. How would that be?"

David shook his head more vigorously.

The kid tilted the neck toward him, the scents flooding David's senses, the Brown Demon already beginning to possess him, but rather than bring it to his lips the kid began to pour out its contents on the stained vermillion carpet.

David wept. For the loss of liquor and the albeit momentary loss of control. He would have given up his life for a single sip.

Just. One. *Sip.*

This kid didn't know his enemy at all. If he had, he would've known the *real* torture would have been forcing David to drink it, to guzzle its contents and set fire to his life, his marriage, his reputation, his entire twenty-six-year career.

"Oh, did you want that?" the kid said, again unaware that he'd saved rather than tortured him.

"Yes," David croaked.

"Well, too bad. Don't think I don't know alcohol is an anesthetic. No, I'm gonna need you sharp and sober for this next part."

"Oh, God," his partner groaned.

"Oh, it's nothing like that," Tyler said, smiling gleefully again. "We're going to collaborate on something, Mr. Ennis. Just you... and me. We're gonna write the Gross Out story to end all Gross Outs, see? And we're gonna read it together, tomorrow, in front of the whole crowd. I think they're going to love this one, Mr. Ennis. It's gonna be *to die for.*"

3

Aimee With Two Es pried the book out of Ackerman's asshole like Excalibur streaked with shit from the stone, and held it out in front of the older writer's face, dangled between thumb and forefinger. Even its stench was relieving, knowing it was out of him, that he'd already suffered through what he hoped was the worst of it.

There couldn't possibly be more, could there?

"I remember when those mean internet trolls accused you of shitting out your *Anvil of the Gods* series after the first book's success. Well, now it's true. At least, with this book."

"They got thicker over the years," another of the women said suggestively, though Ackerman couldn't see which one it was.

"True. But I think he's had enough of that. I think he's *learned his lesson.* Haven't you, Andy?"

Ackerman nodded meekly, wincing from the stench burning his tear-dampened eyes and the excruciating tears in his anus. Never again would he use his power and position in the industry as a tool to fuck women in the ass or any warm orifice. In the previous century it was perfectly fine, even *expected*, to use one's status to get laid. It was a mutually agreeable transaction: a fuck or a blowjob for a foot in the door, a step up the ladder.

Ackerman had become a writer because it was his passion but he'd striven for fame *in order* to get young, attractive women to fuck him. Many men—and sometimes women—of his and later generations did the same. Still do, he imagined. What was the point of fame if it couldn't be exploited? The *price* of fame was a lack of anonymity, a lack of privacy, to be disparaged and have your entire character picked apart by strangers on the internet. The *privilege* of fame was being able to get whatever you want whenever you wanted it.

That was how it had always been. He'd seen no reason to change it.

But that wasn't how the world worked anymore, at least not for the generation of which these women belonged. It was the Age of MeToo, the age of Yes, All Women. The Golden Age of Hashtag Activism. A modern-day *The Crucible*. Opportunities were to be afforded through altruism. Merit? Pah! Throw it out the window. Because these days it was everyone's responsibility to "Do Better." The only personal gain should be the reward of knowing one has helped a fellow human being.

Paid for with a chuckle, as old Ebenezer Scrooge might have said.

Aimee With Two Es dropped the excrement-coated condom and hopelessly curled book into a Ziplock bag. Hiding the evidence. She was a smart one.

"Now comes the difficult part," she said, sitting beside him, looking down at him. "It's time for confession."

"You want me to confess? Yes, I did it. I did all of it, just please, *please, don't put anything else in my ass!*"

She patted his head. "Playtime is over." She held up her

phone. Silken hands pulled up his boxers. Even gently, just the slight jostling stung his torn and ravaged pucker.

"It's time to make a statement to your fans. This is *your* MeToo moment, Andy. Are you ready? You'd better be ready, Andy, or my girls are gonna start in on the sequels. *I said, are you ready to make your statement?*"

Ackerman nodded vigorously.

"That's good to hear."

She held the phone with the cameras facing him.

"*Action*," she said, thumbing the Record button.

4

Clay paused in the hall just outside the elevators as the doors closed behind him.

During the ride down he'd thought about what he was going to say to Moira, if he was going to acknowledge what Towne had said or ignore it, let her tell him if she wanted. Now, he still wasn't sure, and her door was just a few further down the hall.

Something must've happened at her meeting with Kendra, he thought. *It must've gone badly. I'll let her say what she needs to say. This whole thing with Towne... I mean, maybe he's lying. Maybe nothing happened. Or maybe it did, and she doesn't remember. She was pretty drunk. Towne, though. Of all the fucking people in this place it* had *to be Dean Foster Fucking Towne. She might as well have fucked Ennis himself.*

He told himself to relax, smoothed down his jacket, and tried to stroll casually toward her door. Stopping in front of it, he took in a deep breath through his nose, out through his mouth. "Play it cool, Clay," he muttered to himself.

The door opened as he reached out to knock.

"Oh, gawd, Clay," Moira said, running into his arms. In that glimpse he'd seen her eyes were very dark. Either her mascara had streaked from crying or she had a big black eye. He held her trembling body with one arm as she squeezed him tightly. After a moment, he patted her back with his free hand.

"What happened?" he asked finally.

She pulled back from him, looking up with—he was right—a great big shiner barely concealed by streaks of mascara. Her hair was a mess, her stockings torn and one delicate strap of her black dress had fallen off her shoulder.

"Did he do that to you?" Clay spat, realizing in the moment he'd said it that she hadn't said anything about Towne yet.

"He?"

"Never mind. What happened?"

She took him by the hand and lead him into her room. He only just noticed her knuckles were bloody and split.

"It was awful, Clay." She pushed the door shut and latched it, picked up a plastic glass filled with booze and ice and guzzled its contents, directing Clay to sit on the bed, which he did. She sat in the chair opposite, opening another small bottle and pouring it over the remaining ice.

As she sipped it, she told Clay what she'd gone through, about how Kendra had invited both her and Fiona St. Clair—of all people—up to her room without telling the other. How she'd pitted them against each other. How Moira had refused to fight and Fiona had sucker-punched her. How she'd made Kendra beg for her to return, and walked off with her head held high.

"Good for you," he said. "You did the right thing. She's probably kicking herself right now, missing out on that story of yours."

"Right," Moira said sullenly. "But then, when I got to my door I thought, if I don't do something what's to stop her from doing it to someone else? If I didn't do anything I'd be giving her carte blanche to continue humiliating and controlling women just like Fiona and me. And I thought about all of her protégés over the years, and I wondered if she'd put them through the same sort of shenanigans, all the punching down she must've done behind the scenes."

"It seems likely," Clay said.

"So instead of going to my room, I went back to hers."

"Oh?"

"Yeah." She sighed heavily, her chest hitching. "I didn't even bother knocking. I just stormed right in. And lo and behold, there was Fiona St. Clair, eating Kendra Pleasance's bum from behind just like she'd promised, the director's trousers bunched around the knees."

"I didn't know she was gay."

"Maybe? I don't know, Clay, I don't even think it was sexual. It was probably just for the blackmail, like what she'd said about the tape she wanted to make of Fiona and me."

"So…" Clay didn't want to pry for details, he didn't want to seem like he was leching after a Fiona-and-Kendra lesbian session. But he needed to know what happened next. And truthfully, he did want details. He was leching, a little.

"I just got so *mad*, Clay. Like, not just mad at Kendra but mad at Fiona, too. I'd given her an out. I changed the dynamic. She saw it, I could tell. I took away Kendra's *power*, Clay. But Fiona went back to groveling, to kissing her arse. *Literally*. I suppose I also felt sorry for her, but Kendra wouldn't learn anything if she still got what she wanted, and I knew Fiona wouldn't learn either if I didn't intervene."

"Jeez," Clay said, wondering where she was going with all of this.

"So I yanked Fiona back by the hair. And I slammed a fist right into her bloody nose."

"You didn't," Clay said.

"I did," Moira confessed, clearly ashamed. She downed the rest of her drink. "Then I whipped her around by the hair and she landed over the vanity. Her forehead cracked the mirror."

Clay was impressed. He had no idea Moira had it in her. "You're like John Wick."

"Did John Wick ever kick a woman's bare arse so hard her O-ring bled? In heels?"

"I think they're saving that for *Chapter Four*."

Moira uttered a bemused chuckle. "Clay, I absolutely *pummeled* her. Fiona just stood there astounded, bleeding from her forehead and nose, while I kicked and clawed and punched until Kendra Pleasance didn't look quite so pleasant anymore."

"You were waiting to use that one, weren't you?"

"It is a good line," Moira admitted. She stood, put her drink on the top of the fridge and crossed to the bed. She sat down beside Clay, taking his hands in hers, soft yet bleeding. They'd both punched someone tonight for different reasons. Clay's punch had been in anger, unadmirable. Hers had been for good, for justice.

"I've never done anything like that before," she said. "*Hit* anyone. I went absolutely mental, Clay."

"She's the one playing Gladiators and Emperor. Everybody wants Maximus to get revenge on Commodus. They'd get it. They'd understand. Unless… shit, Moira, she could cut the footage. Make it look like you were beating on them because you were jealous or gay bashing or something."

Moira nodded at the bedside table, where a little red flash drive lay. "I didn't know how to remove it so I made her do it. She practically *begged* me to take it, only so I wouldn't hurt her anymore."

"Moira, you don't need to be ashamed of this," he told her. "You punched up."

Moira smiled sadly, blood in her teeth. "I punched up."

Plot Twists &
How to Write Them

1

ANDERSON ACKERMAN'S TEARFUL apology on Instagram
passed around the convention like a bad cold. Colleagues,
fans of his work, friends and enemies, all began discussing
the ramifications of his confession. What would happen to him?
Would his Big Four publisher drop him? Did coercion count as
rape in a court of law? Would he go to prison? Would they *ever*
see the final book in the *Anvil of the Gods* series?

Once the news reached Frank K. Wallis, he took a few
minutes to write a statement denouncing Ackerman's behavior
and promising to "do better" in addressing sexual assault and/or
harassment allegations and concerns in the future, which he read
over the convention hall P.A. system.

Two heavy hitters in one day, he thought, putting aside the
microphone. *At least Ms. Pleasance will probably be back next
year.*

Unbeknownst to Frank, Kendra Pleasance had already left
the Plaza Hotel quickly and stealthily through an emergency exit
just after nine, wearing a large hat and oversized sunglasses. One
observer, a dishwasher for the hotel restaurant out back for a
smoke, said to his coworkers she was hobbling "like she just
shitted her pants or something."

Kelly "Sugar" Lumpkin was livid upon hearing the news
about Ackerman. It was all Beth-Anne "Spice" Roe could do to
hold her longtime friend back from finding out where Ackerman

was right this minute and pumping his gut full of lead.

"They probably won't even tell you which room he's in," she reminded her temperamental friend.

"I know that, *Beth-Anne*. Do you think Sugar's stupid?"

Beth-Anne didn't think Sugar was stupid but she sure did have an itchy trigger finger. Which made it fortunate that she'd been in the toilet when the police arrived to bring Ackerman in for questioning.

The protesters—who'd included Aimee's friend Misti With an I, until more important matters needed to be taken care of, ie. "taking that pervo writer down a peg"—had fallen into a funk after David Ennis disappeared. They'd gotten what they wanted, they'd deplatformed the fascist, decolonizing the convention one Shitty White Male at a time, but with the fash hiding in his room there was nothing more to be done outside of the usual internet hashtivism. Ennis refused to even respond to tweets calling for him to apologize for all of his many transgressions, despite the publisher for his Lee Stark novels releasing a statement assuring their readers that they "denounce bigotry in all forms" and would "work with Mr. Ennis to assure he feels the same."

"I know how we can get that coward out of his room," Misti With an I said once she'd reunited with the others. She was still buzzing from what they'd done to Ackerman, feeling the high of a good power trip. Sure, he used a wheelchair and it had been four against one. But Misti had found power and privilege were amorphous concepts, depending largely on circumstance. In a room full of women writers, Ackerman, with his prestige and respect in the community and his cishet white maleness, held all the power, even considering his disability.

Until he no longer did.

"*How?*" one of the protesters asked Misti.

She winked in reply. Leaning against the wall, where the group had gathered just beyond the tattoo booth in Artist Alley, she casually reached up and pulled the fire alarm.

The effect was immediate, alarms blaring throughout the convention hall. Artists and writers began removing their stock and tucking the boxes and stacks safely under the table, likely to prevent the sprinklers from soaking them if they came on. The crowd, mainly annoyed to have been interrupted, began slowly milling out through various exits, directed by the hotel staff. Only a few attendees seemed genuinely concerned, shouting excitedly at the crowds ahead of them, "Get moving," "Speed up," and "If this was a real fire would you walk so slow?" Et cetera. Some speculated it might be a bomb scare, while a few jokers took the opportunity to shout "Fire," as if to disprove the old adage about yelling it in a crowded public space.

Misti Tan and her companions, twelve of them in all, waited outside in the shivering cold, stationed at the various points of egress, watching the crowds exit the building while two firetrucks and a cop car pulled up out front. They called the police "pigs" and shouted "All Cops are Bastards!" as the two officers entered the building along with the firefighters.

The protesters reconvened in the lobby after the firefighters gave the all-clear to return, having discovered no evidence of fire, that it was likely a "false alarm, and the person responsible will be charged if found out," according to the hotel's night manager. None of them had seen David Ennis.

"Maybe we scared him off? Like, *really* scared him?"

Misti didn't believe that. Men like Ennis, men like Anderson Ackerman, they didn't change unless force was applied.

She thought about asking Aimee and the others to help her work on Ennis tomorrow, after the Gross Out contest, and started to brainstorm what sort of torture would be most fitting, like they'd done with Ackerman.

Frank Wallis knew he had to do *something*, but he wasn't sure what. Even after ingesting a microdose to calm his nerves, he couldn't escape the feeling that events were coming to a boil at the convention. Despite all of the new rules he'd put into place since the last in-person affair to prevent monsters like Ackerman from doing the awful things he'd done over the years—*And thank the Flying Spaghetti Monster it didn't* only *happen at my Splatterfest*—the harassment and assaults, both physical and sexual, were still ongoing.

First, there'd been the unfortunate incident with that awful self-published writer and Ignacio Ortega, then those protesters— and while Frank believed sincerely in the right to protest he did feel they'd crossed a line this morning—causing David to run off on a bourbon bender somewhere. Would he even show up to emcee the Gross Out contest tomorrow? Who knew? And finally, the excrement icing on this cake of shit, his good friend Anderson Ackerman, whom Frank himself, along with a crowd of writers and reviewers, watched escorted from the premises by two Buffalo Police detectives.

It was clear *something* had to be done to mellow out this crowd, so Frank got out his microdosing kit, which he often used to *macro*dose on a free weekend or evening, and asked the hotel staff to open up the stockroom for him, where the Splatterfest-branded water bottles were stored. "It's still locked," the desk clerk said. "Just pull it shut when you're done."

Once the desk clerk left, Frank began to dole out his own acid using a hypodermic syringe, taking a page from the CIA, who during the MKUltra era had dosed unwitting colleagues and civilians with loads of purest-quality LSD. A very small amount in each bottle would produce the desired effect, he thought: that being a nice, clean high of introspective calmness, without the possibility of a "bad trip."

When he was finished, he'd used up nearly all of his supply for the month, and the pinprick holes through the plastic casing and into the divots in the lids were barely observable, even from close up.

He removed a single bottle for himself, turning it upside-down to see if it would leak. Only after shaking it several times, jumping up and down in the storeroom like some tweaker maniac, did a single dribble eke out, like sweat oozed from a pore. Frank suckled from it, then tore off the cap and guzzled its contents. If anyone deserved to feel calm after today, it was Frank K. Wallis.

Tomorrow, everyone who drank from a con-branded water

bottle would feel calm, as well.

At least, in theory.

2

"I slept with Towne."

Clay was holding Moira, smoothing her hair when she said it, the two of them still sitting on the edge of the bed, too nervous to do anything else. He paused the movement of his hand only a moment before resuming. "I know."

She pulled her head away from his chest, looking up with one tearful eye, the other blacked over, puffy and squinting. "You *know*?"

"He told me. Moira, you were drunk. He took advantage of you."

"No, he didn't. I remember exactly why I did it, Clay. I was tamping—"

"Tamping? Is that a menstrual thing?" he asked, recalling her reading from earlier.

She smacked his chest. "Fuming mad, Clay. With you. After you walked out on me, I was so angry. We've been dancing around going to bed together for two years now, you and me. Then that handshake when we finally reunited... A bloody *handshake*, Clay."

"Yeah, I, uh... that was a bit awkward, wasn't it?"

"A *bit*." She scoffed. "Anyway, I was angry and I'd planned to use Towne to hurt you. If it's any consolation, I regretted it come morning."

"It doesn't matter," he said. "It's just funny. I left you to meet with Towne."

"You what?"

"That was the 'business' I was taking care of. I wanted to get dirt on Ennis."

"And did you? You weren't gone ten minutes before he found me in the lounge."

"I did. He's writing all of Ennis's books, just like I thought. You remember what I told you about Ennis hitting his 'rock bottom'? He couldn't write anymore, that's what it was about. As far as I know, he hasn't written a word of fiction since I started writing for him three years ago."

"Three years? Wait, didn't he just get canceled for his new detective book? Spark or Snark or whatever?"

"I wrote it, Moira."

"*You* did?"

He grinned. "I know a thing or two about how to get canceled."

"So you did it on purpose—"

"Because they came after me so hard after the Gross Out story, a *nobody*, I figured they'd go after him even worse. And they did. And now he's fallen off the wagon again—"

"Oh, Clay."

"That wasn't my intention, but I don't feel bad about it. He *burned* me, Moira. He could have defended me but he just walked away and let them tear me apart. And did he ever reach out, just once, since then? No." He reconsidered it. "Actually, yeah, he did, through an email from his lawyer, to cancel our contract."

"You went pretty hard on the liquor yourself after that, didn't you?"

"For months. Then I cleaned myself up and started writing again, for myself this time. Started publishing again. Signed a three-book contract with a Big Four publisher."

"And you still can't let this go."

"When this weekend's over, I'm done, Moira. With Ennis. With all of it."

"But what if he *confesses*? What if he tells everyone you're the one who wrote the book, not him?"

"And admit he's been using ghostwriters? I guess he could." Clay shook his head. "But it's not likely. He's the working man's horror writer. If his fans found out he was cheating them…"

"Damned if he does, damned if he doesn't."

"Exactly. I could've sued any of those people who went after me online, for the things they said about me. I could've sued Fiona for libel. Thanks for kicking her ass, by the way."

Moira gave him a tight smile, unamused. "Technically, it was Kendra's ass I kicked."

Clay chuckled. *Christ, I'm thirsty as hell all of a sudden*, he thought. "Any bottled water in the minifridge?"

Moira nodded. "I picked one up from the con when I went looking for you. Help yourself."

Clay padded across the carpet to the minibar. Dozens of small liquor bottles caught his eye, and a few cans of pop. The Lonely Motel had no luxuries like minibars and room safes. Even the coat hangers in the closet were mismatched, from plastic with dry-cleaning service labels to wire. He found a semi-chilled Splatterfest-branded bottle in the door, cracked it open and took several healthy swigs. The squat bottle was almost empty. "Okay I finish it off?"

"I'll have a drink from the tap if need be."

He chugged the last few sips from the bottle and tossed it into the recycle bin, then sat beside Moira.

"I just wish you'd learn to forgive him," she said, running her fingers through his hair. "Holding all of that anger inside of you, it's *poison*, Clay. It's terrible for your health, mentally and physically."

"I promise, Moira. Once this weekend's over, it's done."

She held his gaze with her one good eye long enough to see he was sincere, then nodded.

"You know there's one other thing that kept me going these past two years, besides the writing. And the booze, I guess, back when I was still drinking."

"What's that?"

"You," he said, brushing back a curly lock of hair from her swollen eye.

Moira tilted her head toward him, her lips parting. He leaned forward. Just as their lips were about to meet, a blaring rattle startled the both of them. They pulled apart from each other, shocked, upset and laughing at the absurdity of the timing.

"Saved by the bell," she said, with a nervous chuckle.

"I guess we'd better go."

She sighed. "I suppose."

"It could be a real fire."

"It could be a false alarm.

"I guess we won't know until it burns us alive or the alarms stop."

The sound of distant sirens reached them from outside.

"I am a little hot," Moira said, fluttering the neckline of her dress.

Clay grinned, peering down at the cups of her bra. "More than a little, I'd say."

She smiled back. "We should check the hall at least."

He nodded. They stood together, crossing the room to the door, both of them reaching for the handle and brushing hands.

"It's your room," he said, stepping back.

She reached again and opened the door. A family passed by them, rushing down the hall, pulling on their jackets and beanies. The father's had a Canadian flag emblem so he supposed they'd called them "toques."

"I hope we get to see a fiyatwuck," the smallest of the two boys said as they headed for the stairs.

"I s'pose we should go," Moira said reluctantly.

Clay agreed. They grabbed their jackets and headed into the chilly stairwell, following the young family down the stairs in a line of annoyed people.

Outside, they huddled together among a small crowd, Moira shivering against him, her legs bare from mid-thigh down, watching the first responders around the side of the building where they'd exited.

"I guess the timing could've been worse," Clay said.

Moira raised the only eyebrow she could manage. "How so?"

"We could've been naked."

"If you think I'd have jumped out of bed for a bloody fire

188

alarm, you've lost the plot."

After ten minutes standing in the cold, commiserating with the others in the group about the weather and the length it took to figure out whether or not it was a false alarm, someone around the front of the hotel shouted, "All clear! You can head back inside now!"

People started milling back inside. Clay and Moira followed the herd, letting them go ahead, in no mood to rush. That was when he happened to look up and see someone standing on a fifth-floor balcony.

"I'll do it, I swear!" the man called down. He was holding a liquor bottle, wobbling slightly. Clay recognized his accent before he was able to distinguish the man's features in the relative darkness.

"Is that *Towne*?" Moira said.

"Shit," Clay muttered. It was that night all over again, only with a different writer on the balcony.

"*I'm gonna fucking jump, I will!*"

Clay let go of Moira's hand and returned to the parking lot. Cupping his hands around his mouth, he shouted, "Towne, get your dumb ass back inside!"

Towne peered over the edge. "Kayden? Is that you?"

"And me!" Moira called up.

"Moira? Bloody hell, shit timing for a reunion."

"Why are you threatening to kill yourself, Dean?"

"Because it's over," he said, genuine sadness cracking his voice. "It's all gone to shit, innit? David's fucked off somewhere, piss drunk. He was my foot in the door!"

"He's *using* you, Towne! You think he wouldn't dump you the second he's done with you like he did to me?

"No." Clay could just make out the man shaking his head over the balcony railing. "No, we're mates, he and I. He wouldn't abandon me."

"But he did! He could've gone to you for help when all this happened. Instead, he left you to sell his books while he took a trip to Brown Town!"

"Brown Town?" Moira asked.

"Long story."

"He did do that, didn't he?" Towne said, as much to himself as to Clay. "But that's worse, innit? If I've no value to him aside from our contract, what's to stop him from dropping my arse like a sack of shite when our contract's done? Then I'll be nothing! I'll be no one again! I'll be Dean Towne, proprietor of a fucking barber shop catering to beta males," he said, pronouncing it *beeta*, not *bayta*, as Clay would have. "—pretending to be alphas! Fuck it, I'm jumping."

He tossed the bottle over the railing. It fell quickly and smashed several feet from where Clay stood. Then he climbed drunkenly over the railing.

"For fuck's sake," Clay muttered. "Towne, we're coming up!"

He turned to Moira for confirmation. She nodded.

"Don't jump before we get there," he called up.

"I'll be dead before you reach the lift, Kayden. I'll be flat as a pancake on the tarmac."

"Then just try not to hit my car. It's the black Cutlass."

"You callous prick, just for that I'm aiming for it," Towne said as Clay and Moira returned to the building.

"Think he's bluffing?" Clay asked on their way up the stairs.

"Most likely, but I'd feel shit if he did jump and we'd done nothing. He was likely hoping to have a crowd, but they all went back inside before he could check if his hair was fine."

Clay chuckled.

They reached Towne's room less than five minutes later. Clay banged on it with a fist.

"Door's open!" Towne called from somewhere beyond. From the distance, Clay figured he was no longer on the balcony. As it turned out, he was right. Towne was lounging on the bed with his jacket and shoes off, pointing the remote control at the TV, where a dung beetle rolled a ball of shit along a forest floor. On his jaw was the shiny bruise Clay had left him with.

The surprise lay against pillows stacked in front of the

headboard: Fiona St. Clair, wearing nothing but a silk bathrobe, gave the two of them a bored sneer. Her hair was up and her face shiny as if she'd just come from the shower. She had a bandage plastered to her forehead where it had struck the mirror in Kendra Pleasance's room, her nostrils packed with bloody gauze.

"Oh great, look what the cunt dragged in," she said in a nasal tone.

"Bit late for an orgy, Kayden," Towne said with a wink.

"You asshole, what the hell were you trying to prove out there?"

"Just trying to spoil your night, mate. Like you lot spoiled ours. I saw you two down there, thick as thieves." He grinned, showing teeth. "I just couldn't resist."

"I hope you didn't kiss Fiona on the mouth," Moira said. "She just had her tongue stuck up Kendra Pleasance's bum."

"Which means by six degrees of separation, *I* had my tongue up Kendra's bum. Nice bit of minge, that. Don't mind at all."

"So, what?" Clay said. "The two of you were in cahoots the whole time?"

"*Cahoots?*" Towne laughed heartily, and Fiona joined him. "Americans say that still, do they? I'd have thought that went out with the Old West. Yes, Fiona and I bonded over our mutual dislike of you at a writing event quite some time ago, Kayden. Seems you inspire that in people. Whereas me, I've got charm. I've got charisma. People *like* me."

Moira sputtered. "People *pretend* to like you because you're chums with David Ennis. But that won't last, will it, Fiona? Not with your Spanish Inquisition after his head."

"I don't cancel people anymore," Fiona said flatly. "That's the old me."

"More like you only do it when it suits you."

"Whatever, bitch. You want another black eye?"

"Ladies, please," Towne said, holding out his hands in a gesture of peace. "No need to fight over me. There's more than enough Towne to go 'round."

"Yeah, there is." Fiona reached over his shoulder and

grabbed his dick over his pants.

Towne grunted, then flashed a smile at Clay. "You can stay, Kayden, but you'll have to sit in the corner."

Clay rolled his eyes. "All right, I've had enough."

He and Moira left.

"If you change your mind, Moira, the night is still young," Towne called after them, as Clay slammed the door.

"What is it that makes women want to sleep with that guy?"

"Well, I told you why I did," Moira said. She ran her fingers through his hair, paused with her hand near his crown and gave him a quizzical look. "Have you ever thought about growing a twat knot?"

Clay laughed. "Fuck off," he said amiably.

"Seems like the universe is conspiring to prevent the two of us from sleeping together," Moira said as they reached the elevators and stopped there, holding hands. "Doesn't it?"

"It does."

The elevator dinged. The doors slid open.

She nodded suggestively at the empty car. "Going down?"

"That's not all I'll be doing."

They started making out the second the doors closed, two years of pent-up sexual energy held at a distance of some eight-thousand miles. When the doors opened at the fourth floor, the woman attempting to get on was so startled she nearly stumbled over her own shoes stepping back into the hall, muttering an apology.

They laughed as the doors shut again, holding in their passion for the moment, allowing it to simmer. Once the elevator reached her floor they walked briskly hand in hand to her door.

"Give me a moment to freshen up," Moira said, glancing at herself in the vanity mirror.

"You're gorgeous."

"Even with the black eye?"

"*Especially* with the black eye. I'm into some freaky shit, Moira."

She laughed and entered the bathroom. "Two minutes."

Clay took off his shoes and sat on the bed. He took off his shirt and began to unbutton his pants, then thought better of it. She might want to leave that as part of the foreplay. Easy enough to remove them as desired. He sat back against the pillows on the headboard, suddenly reminded of Fiona St. Clair in one of Towne's bathrobes, and he shuddered at the thought of the two of them together, bumping uglies.

"See if you can find some music?" Moira said from the bathroom.

Clay turned on the radio, scanning the stations. After a while "The Safety Dance" by Men Without Hats came through on a clear signal. It was either that or modern pop or some hipster song with plenty of claps and "hey-ohs," so he shrugged and left it on.

"Could you turn down the lights?" Moira called over the music. Clay leaped out of bed, flicked on the table lamp in the corner of the room, and turned off the overhead lights.

The bathroom door opened once he'd set the mood and Moira stepped out, her hair unpinned in loose ringlets, her skin shimmering in the moonlight. She'd taken off her dress and wore nothing but a thong.

"Jesus," he muttered.

"I thought you'd have taken yours off."

"I didn't want to assume."

She laughed, approaching the bed. In the time it took her to cross the room, he'd already taken his pants off.

"Odd choice," she said, nodding at the radio.

"It was either this or Justin Bieber," he said. "We're close to the border, I bet it's gonna be a lot of Canadian stuff. Not that there's anything wrong with that."

"No," Moira said, slipping under the heavy comforter. Clay took off his socks in the semidark and then remained seated on the edge of the bed, naked, looking at the socks on the floor.

"Do you plan to join me?" Moira said.

He sat up abruptly, wondering how long he'd been staring at the lumps of his socks on the floor, and why. He slipped under the covers. Their lips met. After what seemed an appropriate amount of time, Clay reached for a breast, giving it a soft squeeze, caressing her hardened nipple. She moaned into his lips, rubbing herself against his thigh.

"You mentioned something—about going down," she said between kisses.

"Next floor, ladies' undergarments."

"We call them knickers."

He slid beneath the covers, into the dark, kissing his way down her body, burying himself in the scent of her perfume. He flicked his tongue into her belly button, causing her to giggle and bring her knees up into his chest. The tips of his tongue and fingers felt tingly, as if just brushing against her skin was like touching a live wire.

"Are you trying to tickle me?"

He wasn't sure why he'd done it, truthfully. Rather than reply, he kissed further down her stomach, not ignoring the light c-section scar, aware she had a daughter back home, about nine years old, staying with her mother at the moment, but trying to push that thought aside and attend to the matters at hand and tongue. He slipped down her thong, and she raised up from the sheets to allow him to remove it, revealing a thatch of dark pubic hair and smooth labia. She smelled like fresh hotel soap. He assumed she must've washed up while she was in there, though with the radio playing he hadn't heard the faucet running. He thought of her beating the shit out of Fiona St. Clair in her little black dress and his dick throbbed so hard he had to pause for a moment to suppress the urge to just fuck her brains out right then and there.

When he turned back, ready to get down to business, Dean Foster Towne's smirking face smiled up at him from between Moira's legs. His manbun rose from the curls of Moira's pubic hair, a literal twat knot.

"Told you I'd been here first, Kayden."

Clay reared back in insurmountable terror, barely able to stop himself from screaming. He blinked and rubbed his eyes, having never experienced a full-blown hallucination outside of a bad acid trip or two in his college days, thinking now was a helluva time to have a flashback.

His erection wilting, he peered back with one eye, hoping to find the horrifying vision had dissipated, mortified to discover it had not.

Towne winked. "C'mon. Give it a go, mate." His lips parted, just about where her vagina would be, and he flicked out his tongue lasciviously.

Moira patted Clay on the head. "Fall asleep down there?"

"No, I—" He swallowed. "I don't feel so good."

"Oh," she said, clearly disappointed.

"Don't give up yet, mate. I think she's ready. Might as well stick it in." Towne opened his mouth wide like a Roman emperor awaiting a grape, then seemed to notice Clay's hesitation. "Don't worry, I've got an excellent gag reflex."

"I can't do this!" Clay cried out.

"You're not a *homophobe*, are you, Kayden?"

Clay struggled to throw off the comforter and sat up, his heart thrumming and stomach churning. With her lower half covered it was easier to think of what he'd just seen as a hallucination. *What the fuck caused that? Am I losing my mind?*

"If you're sick, we don't have to do anything." Moira sat up and scooched over to him. Her hand on his forehead felt incredibly cold. It was all he could do not to cringe, thinking about the British barber buried between her legs.

"You don't have a fever. Maybe it's something you ate?"

"Maybe," he said, and let out an acidic burp. "I think I need to go."

"You should lie down."

"No, I need to go. I don't wanna get you sick."

"Clay, you shouldn't be driving."

"I'll take an Uber." He was already trying to put his socks back on, though they felt like tree bark scratching his feet and ankles. *Must be food poisoning*, he thought. Then he said, "Did I say that out loud?"

"About taking an Uber?"

He stepped quickly into his pants. *Oh God, this is worse than I thought.*

"Clay, maybe you should go to hospital."

"No, I just—I just think I need to be alone. I'm sorry, Moira." He buckled his belt as he crossed the room, thinking how weird the name Moira felt in his mouth. *Mweyerah. Muh. Why. Ruh.*

"Why d'you keep repeating my name like that? Clay, are you having a stroke?"

"Huh?" He turned, startled. Had he said all of that out loud? *Maybe I am having a stroke. I can't feel my heart beating. Is that what happens when you have a stroke? Oh God, I THINK MY HEART STOPPED BEATING!*

He stumbled forward and caught himself by the door. He'd slipped his right foot into his left shoe. Correcting his error, he looked back at Muh-Why-Ruh in the bed, holding the comforter over her breasts. The shadows on her face moved and for a split second she looked like a goblin, like something that had crawled up from the sewer and slipped into bed with him, like a corpse rotting in an open casket.

He shrieked.

"Clay, just stay. I'll sleep on the sofa."

"No!" he yelped. "I have to go right now!"

He stepped out into the hall, shying at the incredibly bright lights. He leaned against the door briefly, trying to tie his shoes, forgetting how to make a knot. *Fuck me, what the hell is happening to me?*

Clay mangled his shoelaces and hurried toward the elevators. The father of the family they'd seen earlier peered out into the hall, still wearing his Canadian flag toque. "You okay there, buddy?"

Clay shied away from him, suddenly feeling very paranoid, the hallway light having taken on a yellow, runny egg quality, the man's face looking ghoulish. He fumbled with his phone in the elevator, hoping it was going down, though the doors opened again on Moira's floor, and he thumbed the ground floor button.

Somehow, he managed to schedule an Uber—he'd almost put in his home address in San Diego, which would have cost him a fortune—and before he knew it, as if the film cut and he'd lost the ten minutes it said it would take for the ride to arrive, he was sitting in the back of the car, staring at a text message from Moira.

hope you feel better, maybe tomorrow? was all it said.

He didn't know how to answer it. Tomorrow, maybe, if he was still alive by then. If Towne wasn't still taking up residence in her downstairs flat. He Googled "food poisoning causing hallucinations." Judging by the first few results it was a definite possibility. *Should I go to the hospital?*

By the time he decided, *Yes, I should go to the hospital*, he was already standing in front of the door to his room at the Lonely Motel. The Uber had driven off. The slushy parking lot had only a handful of cars in it, including the rude kid's from this morning. He remembered the woman from Room 6 telling him if the light was on above the door to knock. Even if the light *was* on, he wouldn't have subjected himself to someone else's company at the moment, nor them to his. Fortunately, the light was off.

His heartbeat—which had returned sometime during the Uber ride, beating like the undead against their coffin lid—had resumed its normal rate as he fumbled with the key on its fob. Once inside, he pulled the door quickly shut, locked it, latched it, and flopped down on the bed, staring up at the tobacco-stained popcorn ceiling, the room swimming.

"I'll just lie down for a little while, try to relax," he told himself. He couldn't tell what time it was. The numbers on the clock were in constant flux, as if he was already dreaming. He could only hope he was able to live through whatever this was, and that Moira would forgive him in the morning.

3

Four doors down from Clay's room, David Ennis roused once more from unconscious ness to sound of the kid's raised voice.

"What are you doing?" the kid asked sharply.

For a moment, David thought the kid was talking to him. His heart beat faster. He didn't think he had it in him to abide more torture tonight. Then the reluctant partner, he answered, "I'm reading."

"That's not reading."

David opened one eye, the lid sore and stuck together with dried blood and tears. He saw the one called Rawlins still in the chair, pulling an earbud from his right ear. "Huh?"

"I said that's not reading," the kid, Tyler, said. "You're being *read to*. You don't say 'I'm cooking dinner' when you go eat at a restaurant."

Rawlins sighed heavily. "Fine. What do you want me to call it then, dude?"

"Reading is an *active* process, see?"

Tyler started pacing around the room. David peered out through a squint, not wanting the kid to know he was awake.

"You construct meaning from words on a page, see?" the kid said, on yet another of his many rants. "What you're doing is called *listening*. That's passive. Reading is acting, listening is *re*acting to something someone else is doing to you."

"Hashtag Okayden."

"When your parents read to you when you were little, did they express *pride* that you could *listen* to a story?"

"I never knew my dad and Mom worked nights, so no."

"See, that's why you think you're *reading* when you're really just *listening*."

"What difference does it make?"

"What *difference* does it make?" The kid threw up his hands, as if pleading his case to an unjust god. "It's night and day!"

"Whoa, dude. Hashtag Frankie Say Relax."

"Writers who don't read drive me up the wall," the kid said through gritted teeth. "That's all I'm saying."

"I *am* reading."

"We'll ask Ennis then, huh? Might as well wake him up."

"I'm awake," David said, his throat scratchy.

Tyler flinched, nearly leaping backward at the sound of David's voice. David grinned, his lips split in half a dozen places, weeping blood.

"Well," the kid said, composing himself, "what do you think? Is he reading or listening?"

"*Technically*, he's listening. But listening to a story is only passive if you're not paying attention," David said. He'd been asked this question before, by fans and on panels, and knew this diplomatic response by rote. "Sure, there's the extra act of decoding printed words, but both are just ways of processing language. Would you say a blind person isn't reading because they use their fingers? No. And what the fuck's it matter to you how he chooses to consume story as long as he's doing it?" he added, going slightly off script.

"Because he's *cheating*!"

"Last I heard, reading isn't a fucking contest. Not since those Scholastic things you probably did in grade school. What are you listening to, Rawlins?"

The Hashtag King startled. He looked down at his wingtips. "Uh… T-*Twilight*."

"*Twilight!*" Tyler cried, sounding vindicated.

"The sparkly vampire book?" David asked.

"The sparkly vampire book."

"Okay. That's fine. Reading is reading."

"I'm researching for this series I want to write."

"A vampire series," David said, his sympathy for the kid's reluctant partner beginning to wane.

"*Zombie* vampires."

David exhaled patiently through his chapped and bleeding nostrils. "Tell you what, guys: I've got a better story for you. A *true* story. It's about this motel, actually. In fact, the two of you couldn't have picked a better place to do this to me. This place has a *history*. It's got a lot of stories."

"How would you know?" Tyler said with a suspicious sidelong glare.

"I'm a Buffalo native. I grew up around here. I guess you missed that part of my biography."

The kid grumbled something David couldn't hear and sat against the vanity, gripping its edge.

"It wasn't in this room, at least I don't think it was, the story we heard as kids. It was in one of the double-digit rooms. Eleven or thirteen, I dunno."

"What happened?" Rawlins asked, leaning forward in his chair in the corner of the room, the earbuds entirely removed. That was how you knew you had a young person's attention these days, *really* had it: they removed not one but both earbuds.

"This area, we used to call it Motel Row. Just this big long strip of no-tell motels, pawn shops and payday loan joints. They used to shoot porno here in the '70s, back when it was still illegal to shoot porn. Who knows, they probably still do."

Tyler sneered at the bed. "Gross."

"You think that's the only place they're fucking?" David said, and the kid abruptly pushed off of the dresser, looked at it with distaste, then used a Lysol wipe to clean a space for himself.

"Anyways, when we were kids this place had this *mystique* to it, like the local haunted house where every kid knows the old witch lives, only she actually turns out to be a sweet old lady who just never gets out much, probably has one too many cats and hoards all kinds of junk since her husband died."

Rawlins nodded thoughtfully.

Every kid had their own haunted house, their own witch or boogeyman. David knew this intimately. It was what started him on this journey, his decades-long career in horror. Every kid learned about fake monsters before they learned about the real ones—if they were lucky.

The Lonely Motel was *his* haunted house.

It just so happened to also contain real monsters.

"Fellas, I'm crashing," he said on a dramatic heaved sigh.

Rawlins's shoulders slumped. "Aw, you're just gonna leave us hanging like that? Hashtag Not Cool."

"I'll tell you," David said. "But first, I'm thirsty as hell. I think my blood sugar's still low. I need another Pibb."

"No more Dr. Pibbs," the kid said. "You've had enough Dr. Pibbs."

"It's *Mister* Pibb, kid."

"Whatever. No more. You'll be up all night and we need you *bright and cheery*—" He said this with a sarcastic grin. "—for our reading tomorrow."

"This story—*this* is the story, kid. For the reading."

Tyler narrowed his gaze. "It's gross enough?"

"Oh, it's gross. And it's mean, and it's terrible. And it's *true*. At least, the gist of it is. I looked it up to confirm it about ten years back for that novel I wrote about urban legends."

"Come on, man," Rawlins whined. "After everything I did today, I just wanna hear this one story."

"All right. One more *Mister* Pibb," Tyler said, snarling on the honorific, as he pushed himself up from the vanity again. "Got any change, Rawlins? I used my last dollar on the other one."

Rawlins raised up from the chair, took out his wallet from his back pocket, attached to a chain that linked to a belt loop on the front of his slacks. He opened it and counted out two bills. "Can you get me a Pepsi while you're out there?"

Tyler snatched the bills. "Anything else you'd like, your Majesties?"

Rawlins took out another two bills. "A bag of Gardetto's, if they have em. If not, Chex Mix is fine," he added, with an air of disappointment.

The kid took the other bills and went to the door. "You're lucky I'm feeling generous." He headed for the door. "Oh, and by the way—" He pointed to the vanity mirror. "—everything we did here today, it's being recorded. The hard drive's locked in my car. So don't even think about trying to convince Rawlins to turn on me, because if I go down, he goes down with me. That's my black box. You got it?"

"Crystal clear, my friend," David said.

The kid eyed the two of them for a long, suspicious moment. Then he unlocked and unlatched the door, quickly stepped out, and closed the door behind himself.

"Is he bluffing?" David asked.

Rawlins stood up, beginning to pace. "I don't think so, man. *He made his own chloroform.* I wouldn't put anything past him, he's pretty fucking crazy."

"You don't say. Check the mirror."

Rawlins crossed to the vanity. He pressed his face against the wall and peered behind the mirror. Then he reached down and tugged a black cable out.

"Shit," David said.

"There's a little chip in the mirror stuff on the back of the glass. He's got this little spycam-looking thing pointing right through it."

"Double shit. Look, Jackson. You're name's Jackson, right?"

Rawlins nodded glumly.

"Jackson, you're going to jail whether or not this turns out poorly. You know that, don't you?"

"Hashtag Caught an L."

"But here's the beauty of the law: you can change what kind of sentence you get, if you turn on Tyler. If you help me get free, I will ask them for clemency. You didn't really *do* anything, did you?"

"Well, I hit you with the—"

"*You didn't do anything, did you?*" David repeated, glancing sidelong at the camera.

"No, sir. I was a, uh… Innocent Bystander. Hashtag."

"Right. If I *don't die*, your sentence is automatically lessened from first-degree murder to kidnapping. With my testimony—"

David stopped speaking. He'd only just noticed the curtain must have moved slightly when Tyler closed the door. He found himself staring at a pallid face looking back at him through the window.

It wasn't Tyler—that was his first thought. That the kid had caught him in the act, that he'd been watching the footage from his "black box" in whatever beater car he drove and had come back to put an end to his scheming.

But it *was* a face he recognized.

"With your testimony what?" Rawlins said.

But his testimony didn't matter. If he could signal to the man outside the window that he was in trouble, he'd get out of this hellhole and both Tyler and Rawlins would go down for what they'd done to him. Maybe, after he'd healed, he'd write a tell-all novel about what he'd experienced here. He'd be back on top again, despite what those kids at the convention tried to do to his career this morning.

The eyes in the window widened and blinked harshly, as if the man outside couldn't believe what he was seeing.

Then he disappeared into the dark, making David wonder if his own unresolved guilt had caused him to hallucinate it.

Less than a minute later, before he'd even gotten a chance to start in on Rawlins again, the door opened and his enemy-savior returned.

He just had to hope his former friend had enough sympathy left in him to call the police.

4

Clay didn't know how long he'd been lying in bed on top of the covers. Long enough to imagine an entire world of microbes in the yellow-brown archipelago on the popcorn ceiling.

When his swirling thoughts finally died down, he was left with only queasiness and a vague sense of disconnection from his body, like he was wearing a skin suit that didn't quite fit. It tingled and rubbed against his bones unpleasantly.

He got up and hurried to the bathroom, flipping up the lid and seat of the toilet just in time to puke. It splashed up the back of the bowl, a torrent of undigested Clams casino, slippery bits of chewed clam and bacon and caramelized shallots and brown liquid he assumed to be the two or three Coke Zeros he'd had in lieu of alcohol.

There's the culprit, he thought, coughing on the acid stinging the back of his throat. *Who the fuck eats Clams casino, anyway?*

He wiped the back of the bowl with toilet paper and flushed. Then he stood and washed out his mouth in the sink, spat and checked his eyes. The pupils were still pretty dilated and his face still had a slight waxen quality to it, but he felt better.

Food poisoning. What a wild trip, man.

He was still buzzing, though. He didn't think he'd be able to get to sleep any time soon.

If you're around later and the light's on above the door— we're in six—feel free to knock, Shyla had told him this morning. *Maybe we could... share some stories.*

Clay pushed the heavy curtain aside and peered out through his window. The parking lot was indeed lonely, the night quiet. Sporadic vehicles passed by on the highway.

Sure enough, the light above Room Six was on.

Clay stepped out of Room Eleven. The night had warmed enough he didn't need his coat. He was starting across the lot when the door to Room 7 opened, and the rude kid he'd seen that morning stepped out briskly, slammed the door and locked it.

Clay ducked behind a van parked at the angle. Something about the kid gnawed at him, but he couldn't say exactly what. Maybe it was the animosity with which he'd responded to Clay's offer of assistance with his car, and the flat expression his face had taken on while his voice remained cheery. He had the look of a sociopath. Or *worse*.

But he was probably just some ugly kid. Maybe he was a writer. That would explain the misanthropy.

Clay watched as the kid went to the pop machine and fed in a few bills. One can tumbled out. The kid thumbed the other button and nothing happened. "C'mon. C'mon, you *cocksucker*! You motherfucker!" He punched the machine. "Come on you *cocksucking motherfucking piece of shit*!"

In any other motel, this might have woken up every guest. At the Lonely, the rooms had apparently been built soundproof. Clay hadn't heard a single noise while inside his own, not even the traffic. Not even the television in the next room, or the toilet flushing.

The kid gave the machine a swift kick before storming off, heading for the office. The light was on inside, the blinds drawn.

Clay crossed the parking lot, meaning to head for Room Six. But something the kid said made him pause and listen.

"There's no *goddamn* Mr. Pibb left in the machine," the kid said, "and it ate my dollar!"

"You want your dollar back," the night manager said, "you have to call the number on the machine."

Clay bet the night manager, the old guy with the coke nail who looked like a character from something by R. Crumb, was wishing he'd stayed home tonight.

"I don't want my *dollar*, it's not even *my* dollar—*I want the goddamn Mr. Pibb*!"

Mr. Pibb, Clay thought. *That's David's favorite.*

"It can't be," he said.

He hurried down the walkway, running soft-footed, creeping as he reached the door to Room 7. Peering across the lot, he saw the rude kid still arguing with the night manager, his back turned. The night manager was trying to explain that the machine wasn't under his purview, but the kid wasn't having it. He just kept getting angrier, ranting about everything that was wrong with the motel.

Emboldened, Clay approached the window, where a crack of light shone through an opening in the curtains, feeling like a peeping tom but not caring, only hoping he didn't get caught by the kid. If he did, what would he say? Could he talk his way out of it?

In the next moment, none of that mattered. Clay didn't know exactly what he was expecting to see, but it definitely wasn't this. There was David Ennis, or at least what *looked* like David Ennis, duct-taped to a wheelchair in a soiled pair of boxers, his body and face entirely covered in blood and sweat. His head hung low, until he caught Clay's eye—then he sat up rigidly, staring directly at him.

Clay blinked and rubbed his eyes. Was it really him? Or was he hallucinating again?

"Well, *fuck* this place and fuck *you*!" the kid shouted. The office door whipped open with a jingle of the bell above it and he stormed out into the cold, slamming it behind him.

Clay swiftly moved to the door to Room 6 and knocked, praying the kid was too into his own grumbling anger to notice he'd been peering in through the kid's window. He held a bag of what looked like chips and a can of Pepsi.

Come on, Clay thought, willing Shyla to open the door. He knocked once more, slightly louder.

The kid looked up. His rage disappeared and took on the flat expression it had this morning. "Can I help you?" he asked.

"I'm good, just—"

The door to Room 6 swung open. Shyla looked annoyed at first, then brightened when she saw it was him. "Speak of the Devil and here he is," she said.

Clay smiled with an inward sigh.

Maybe it really is David in there? But why? What reason could this kid possibly have to kidnap an aging mid-list writer when there's millionaires walking around at the same con?

The kid frowned, then pulled out his keys and stopped in front of the door to his room, looking down at them with his brow furrowed, as if to decide whether or not Clay's presence there at that exact moment meant him harm.

Does he recognize me? Does he know who I am to David?

"Thanks," the kid said.

"Huh?"

Shyla peered out from the doorway with a raised eyebrow and a slight grin.

"For helping me with the car this morning," the kid said. "I forgot to say thanks."

"No problem. Have a good night."

The kid smiled queerly. "Yeah. You too." With that, he tucked the pop under his arm, stuck his key in the lock and twisted it. He opened the door, took one last look at Clay, then stepped inside and pulled the door shut.

"He's a weird one, huh?" Shyla said.

"That's an understatement," Clay said. "So I was thinking about what you said this morning, about complicated stories. I'd love to listen, if it's not too late."

Shyla smiled. "It's never too late."

"Good," Clay said.

Shyla stepped aside, allowing him in.

Clay glanced once more at the window to Room 7.

I could save him right now, he thought. *One call to the police and he'd be free.*

But he had to admit, seeing David like that, bleeding and vulnerable, afraid for his life, after everything he'd put Clay through, letting him twist in the wind when a single word in his defense might have spared him, even if he *had* just hallucinated it, it was more than a little satisfying.

Maybe it'll wait until morning, he thought, as he stepped into Room 6.

SPLATTERFEST, DAY THREE
SUNDAY, NOVEMBER 28TH

BEDTIME STORIES

1

CLAY ENTERED ROOM 6 and the woman who'd called herself Shyla closed the door behind him. "Take off your shoes," she said. "Don't worry, I steamed the carpet."

This room actually looked livable, compared to his own. The vermilion carpeting was clean, as she'd said, and the popcorn ceiling appeared to have been given a fresh coat of white paint. Nice furniture, too. A proper vanity and dresser that didn't look like the drawers might fall out under any amount of weight. The bed was a sturdy king, with nice linens and a frilly skirt. The artwork, rather than the standard cheap hotel paint-by-numbers, was somewhat tasteful, aside from the Jonah and the Whale painting above the bed, which looked similar to the painting in his own room of children in a playground.

"Is this the honeymoon suite?" he asked.

"Angel's a permanent resident. I stay with him some nights. When I can't, I have nurses come check on him."

The man himself, bald and thin, sat in his wheelchair in a pair of clean pajamas, staring vacantly at the floor ahead of him. He had no real expression, his face entirely blank aside from the long, jagged scar running up the left side of his face.

"Is he...?" Clay didn't know how to ask without sounding rude.

"Traumatic brain injury," she said, with a sympathetic look toward her companion.

"Is that the scar?"

"No, that was from before he was born."

"Before…" Clay frowned and stopped himself from asking. He didn't want to imagine what might have caused such an injury *before* birth.

"Make yourself comf'able," she said, indicating the chair as she sat on the edge of the bed. "You mind if I vape?"

"Go ahead."

She picked up her e-cigarette from the bedside table and took a puff. "You asked me this morning about my relationship with Angel."

"And you said 'interesting is an understatement.'"

Shyla smiled secretively with a pull on her e-cig. She exhaled a cloud that smelled like cinnamon buns. "Angel was a client."

"Of the Hair Club for Men?"

Shyla blinked.

"Sorry, bad joke. Go on."

"Like I said, Angel was a client. This was back in 2016 when this happened. I got called out to the Lonely Motel. I'd heard about it in stories, everyone has. But I'd never been on a call out here before, so I took a cab out, expecting I don't know what."

"You were…" Clay didn't know the proper terminology for it these days and didn't want to insult her.

"An escort," she said, nodding and exhaling a cloud of sweet and spicy vapor. "My boss said Angel was specific: he wanted a plus-size woman. In my experience, that could mean all kinds of things. I never knew whether the guy just wanted a little more curves or he's into some kinky shit, but I guess that's the same for anyone. You hear lots of stories in my line of work, that's for sure. Except when you're a curvy woman you sometimes get guys who are into sploshing or feedism or adult babies, which isn't something I'm into.

"Anyways, aside from the scar, Angel seemed like a typical client. No immediate red flags. We get a lot of businessmen on layovers who just want a quick lay. But Angel didn't want to fuck, he wanted to tell stories."

"Stories?"

Again, she nodded. "About this place, this motel. And a guy named Johnny."

"Is Angel Johnny?"

Shyla frowned. "That's not the important thing but I didn't figure that out until it was too late. All the while he's telling me these stories, he's using sex toys on me. Bigger and bigger."

"Jesus," Clay said.

"It's okay. I enjoyed it." She exhaled and held his gaze, as if daring him to judge her. "But these were real graphic stories. About drug abuse and abortion, suffocation and mutilation. Not the kind of thing you read for sexual pleasure. I mean, I'm the last person to kink shame, but they definitely weren't *my* thing. Maybe someone who gets off on other people's trauma, that's not for me to judge."

"Was he a writer?"

"No. He's independently wealthy. He won a lawsuit, against this doctor who was smothering people."

"Smothering them?"

She raised her penciled-in eyebrows. "Started some wild cult of rebirthers, driving around the country in white vans with tinted windows, suffocating people in rugs. Anyways, these stories, they're all true. They all happened. In the late-'60s, a woman died in that bathtub giving herself a coat hook abortion. The baby survived. That's Angel. He grew up in an orphanage, lived there until he was old enough to leave on his own. When other kids got picked to live with new parents, nobody wanted him."

"Because of the scar? From the abortion?"

"I guess so. Can't say for sure."

"So he hooked up with the rebirther cult because he never knew his real mother."

She nodded. "And when *that* didn't work he dreamed up a new plan. Apparently, he already tried with two or three other girls before me, that's just from the agency I worked for. There coulda been more. But none of them were the right fit."

"The right… fit." Clay remembered what she'd said about

adult babies. He considered attempting another guess but decided to let her tell it herself. "So he was just a client. But you feel responsible for his well-being?"

"Because *I'm* the reason he is how he is. It wasn't my fault, but—do you believe in Fate, Clay?"

"Not really, no."

"Well, I didn't either until I met Angel. See, him and me, we're two halves of a whole. I was exactly what he wanted. And he's what I wanted, only I never knew I wanted it."

"Which is what, exactly?"

"Responsibility, I guess. Someone to care for, aside from yours truly. I could never have a kid of my own, and I'm no good with pets, but I have him. And he has me."

"And how did that happen, exactly?"

She smiled proudly. "I gave birth to him."

"You... excuse me, you what?"

"That was what he wanted. He wanted someone to listen to his stories, not to pity him but to *empathize*. He wanted someone, he wanted *me*, to *want* to give birth to him. To give him new life. He wanted to start over from scratch and to do that he needed me to be his mother, not the relationship, but the *physical act* of being his mother."

"I don't understand."

"Neither did I. But then he *made* me understand. He used chloroform on me, just like the Mannequin Girl used on him, and when I woke up, he was filling me up like a new mommy. He was *inside me*, Clay."

"He was..." Clay's eyes went wide as he began to understand what she meant, and the image of Dean Foster Towne's smug face between Moira's legs came back to him, making him cringe. "No, that's... that's not possible." His gaze fell to where her legs met. "...is it?"

"If it hadn't happened to me, I wouldn't think so either. But it did. And that's how come he is like he is. He assfixated inside of me," she said, mispronouncing the word as an unintentional double entendre. "He was just about dead when I birthed him, right there on the carpet between us."

Clay looked down. The carpet was clean, but she'd said she'd had it steamed, and it likely hadn't been the first time.

"This room has seen its share of trauma, Clay. But I'd like to say it's seen healing, too."

"And you *forgave* him? *How?*" Clay asked, incredulous. He couldn't imagine forgiving a man who'd drugged and then forcibly—what? Inserted his head into her vagina? Deep enough to lose his breath?

"My mother used to say, 'Hug your enemies, sugar. Make them into friends.'" Shyla smiled, not quite wistfully. "So that's what I did. I hugged him closer than I'd hugged anyone in my life. It's like what some parents do when a kid's having a tantrum, or deprogramming cult members, only it was me who was freakin out inside. There's still times I want to kill him for what he did to me. For stickin me here with him. When I do, I just think about my mother. 'Hug your enemies.'"

"She sounds like a wise woman."

"Oh, she was a lousy, two-timing bitch. But she knew how to drizzle on the honey after she splashed you with vinegar."

"This happened back in 2016. Have you been here the whole time then?"

"I have a condo across town. But Angel and me, we actually got famous for a while there."

"Famous? On the *news*?" He wondered how the local news might have framed the story. It wasn't exactly a puff piece.

Shyla shook her head. "Underground sex tapes. See, Angel's friend Charles, he used to do gonzo porn before he became a legitimate filmmaker. All kinds of weird stuff. He did some mainstream stuff too, but the *gonzo* stuff, if you wanted it and it didn't exist, he'd make it happen for you. This one day a month or so later, Charles comes around to the room, wonderin where Angel's at. And he sees me, and his eyes go real wide, like he *knows*. And then he sees Angel, in his chair where he is now.

"He goes, 'So he finally did it?'

"I asked him, 'Finally did what?' Actin innocent but feeling guilty, like it was *my* fault what Angel did to me. But still, he coulda just meant 'got married' for all I knew. I wasn't about to show my hand.

"'He finally got *reborn*,' he goes, all excited. 'It worked!' And before I could say either way, he hugged me. 'You don't know how long he's been wanting this,' he says. Then he asks me how I was doing down there. I told him not that it was his business but I'm healing up fine.

"He never straight up asked me that day. He came around every couple of days after that to check in on Angel, and me and him got to be friends. Then one day he asks me if I want to make some money. He's been asking around to his big-money clients if anyone would be interested in seeing a grown man get birthed. And apparently, a lot of them did."

"You're serious," Clay said.

"He was going to pay me—pay *us*—a hundred grand to… *recreate* what we did that day. One time only."

"Jesus Christ," Clay said. He couldn't imagine doing it once, let alone *twice*, as birther or birthee. But a hundred-thousand dollars was a lot of money. Most people would do just about anything for that kind of cash.

"Angel had a fair amount of money from the settlement, but it was dwindling fast, with the nurses and doctor fees. By then, what happened that night was kind of like a distant dream. I could remember the pain, sure, but there was also the orgasm. Honestly, Clay, it was the best I've ever had. And believe me, I've had a lot of great orgasms. Given plenty, too," she said on exhale.

Clay didn't doubt either claim.

"Mothers and midwives call them 'birthgasms.' It's rare but it's real. The baby's head hits the G-spot and *bam*," she exclaimed, slapping her palms together sharply. "Instant, leg-shaking, earth-shattering orgasm. That's what I had when I pushed him out. The kind people literally die to have, choking themselves hanging off of hotel doorknobs. Like addicts say about that first hit of heroin."

"I guess I'm vanilla. I prefer a nice normal ejaculation."

She chuckled. "I'm not one to judge. *Obviously.*"

"So you did it, then."

"I asked Angel. I gave him the *courtesy* of consent, unlike what he did to me. See, we have a system. I ask him yes or no questions, and he blinks twice for no, once for yes."

"So he's not entirely..." Clay stopped himself from saying *a vegetable*, not solely for Shyla's benefit. If the man could hear him and understand, what must he be thinking right now? *Is he actually thinking?* Clay wondered. Or was his brain so low-functioning he could only process what was immediately said or seen? It made Clay think of the Trumbo novel *Johnny Got His Gun*, with the soldier whose conscious mind was trapped within a body unable to communicate. He wondered if it was cruel irony Angel had chosen the name "Johnny" for the stories he'd told Shyla about himself, or if Shyla might have been right about Fate.

"No, he hears us. Don't you, Angel?"

The man, not looking up from the place on the floor he'd been staring at vacantly, blinked once.

"See? Blink once for yes. So I asked him, I said, 'Angel, we don't have to do this if you don't want to but we're getting low on cash and Mama can't spread her legs for everything around here,' which in retrospect was a funny thing to say, considering what I was asking. I go, 'Angel, will you do this with me?'"

"And he blinked," Clay said.

"He blinked. It wasn't exactly a 'yes' blink, it was more like an 'okay,' like he didn't exactly *want* to do it, but he knew he didn't have much of a choice. Do you want to do the thing that almost killed you last time? Okay. Kinda like that."

"And then..."

"And then the day came, Charles set up his cameras. One right here, pointing down at the bed and the other over by the vanity on one of those three-leg thingies."

"A tripod."

"Right. Like a short guy with a big dick."

Clay laughed.

"It was just the three of us. Charles said he wanted a 'closed set' for this, because we were all friends. But also, because he didn't want anyone seeing what was about to go down that they could tell their friends, pass it on like a chain letter. He said we were making *porn history*, but these underground sex videos only worked if the people paying for em knew they're the only ones watching. After that first pop, it didn't matter who else got to see it. They pass around, somehow. Someone makes a copy or a screengrab like they call it, like how private camshows end up on Pornhub, and suddenly they're making references to *2 Girls 1 Cup* on your favorite network sitcom.

"I told Angel, 'You take a deep breath and tap my thigh when you feel like you've had enough.' I was already used to this. By then, I had a regular client with a smother box."

"What's a smother box?"

Shyla exhaled through her teeth as if she wasn't ready to get into that. "It's a long story," she said. "Anyway, Angel blinked 'okay,' and we got started. I laid him down on the bed, his head all shined up with lube, and I straddled him, and Charles said 'action,' and with a couple of good pushes, after I got the positioning right, Angel was in up to his eyebrows. That's when the first wave hit me."

Shyla gripped the headboard with one hand. "I'm shaking, holding on to the headboard with both hands, both my legs quivering uncontrollably, squatting over poor Angel's head. That's not easy to do on a mattress in high heels, which is what they wanted me to wear, whoever was on the other side of the cameras, watching us. Like I said, I'm not one to judge but I got to wonderin who these people were and what they were getting out of this as I worked Angel's head into my pussy. Were they getting off on this? Or did they just want to see a carnival freakshow? That got me mad, thinking about it, so I just tried to shut off my brain and concentrate on the task. If you think too much about what these guys might be thinking, that's a rabbit hole, and you need to be focused on the work. You gotta be a no-nonsense bitch or they'll walk all over you, make you cross lines you don't wanna cross.

"Anyway, I worked him up inside me after five or ten minutes, I don't know how long. Angel tapped out pretty quick, and when the time comes for me to birth him, I came so hard I squirted all over the camera and poor Charles standing behind it. He just shrugs and goes, 'Hazard of the business,' and said he shoulda thought to wear goggles and a poncho but he didn't know I was a squirter.

"After it was all over, the cameras off and the lube and whatnot all washed off Angel and myself, Charles said his clients were all super impressed but they did say Angel looked a little 'lifeless,' and it would've been better with a guy who was more 'into it,' like there are guys who would be into that, having their whole heads swallowed up by a pussy." She shrugged. "I guess maybe there are. If there's one thing I've learned as an escort, there's a fetish for everything. Just before Charles leaves he goes, 'If you wanna be a star, call me.' And overnight, one-hundred and fifty-thousand dollars showed up in my account. For ten minutes of work, a half hour of reverse Kegels, and a mind-blowing birthgasm on top."

"That's wild," Clay said, unable to fathom such a thing had happened in real life let alone in some underground porn world. He'd gone down some dark web rabbit holes but had never come across what Shyla was talking about, a literal rebirthing. He had seen a somewhat convincing fake, while researching a story, but with a bit of careful study he could tell for certain it was what the film industry called a "life cast" when the man gripped the woman's leg to pull his head back out.

"So the video got around?"

"You could say that, yeah. If videos like that got royalties, Angel and me would've been sitting pretty right now. But we're doing okay. This place is rent-free. The night manager, Mr. Bronson, the old dude with the coke fingernail, he's the one who found Angel in the tub after his mother died. And he's the one who stopped him from bleeding to death when that crazy girl tried to make him into a mannequin on prom night."

In his chair, Angel whimpered, his eyes closed as if he was sleeping.

"What do you mean, make him into a mannequin?"

Shyla gave her companion a look of pity. "Some other time, maybe. It's getting pretty late. Anyway, I guess Mr. Bronson feels responsible for him. He's kind of like the father Angel never had."

"And you're the mother."

Shyla smiled lovingly at her companion, her man-child, her Angel. "I'm the mother," she said.

They sat in silence for a long moment, the only sounds the ticking of the wall clock, and Shyla's occasional cinnamon-scented exhale.

"Did you know in German, the word *traum* means dream?" she said finally. "I looked it up. *Trauma* comes from the Greek word meaning *wound*, but what if it comes from *traum* instead?"

"You think he's dreaming?"

"He only ever makes noise when he's sleeping," she said, speaking quietly now. "I wonder sometimes, if he isn't reliving all those things that happened to him in his dreams. If he isn't living through those traumas over and over, on some kind of a loop. I wonder sometimes if we're ever really over the past. If we're not just living the same moments again and again, not even until we get it right, just until we..." She shrugged. "...learn to live with them, I guess. I mean, if being *reborn* doesn't make the pain go away, what chance do the rest of us have?"

Clay regarded the sleeping man in the chair. "I guess we've just gotta find a way off that Merry-Go-Round, try to make good for what we've done, forgive others for what they've done to us. You can't take any of it back, but you can change how you react to it."

Shyla nodded. "'Hug your enemies, sugar.'"

Clay smiled sadly. "Mother knows best, doesn't she?"

"Yes, she does."

2

The Turkey Lady stood over Archie's prone, naked body, his rock-hard boner oozing precum like an overfilled baster, her goose-fleshed labia in full view, glowing blue-white under the moon.

"*This is my body, given for you*," she said. "*Eat this in remembrance of me.*"

Directly above his open mouth, her lips parted and moist, fragrant stuffing began oozing out of her cunt, plopping onto his tongue in savory gobs. He tasted onion and sage and raisins—he hated raisins, the sickly sweetness made him gag—and he swallowed the mouthful.

"*You need to check the spring, Archie, baby. You've got to make sure it works.*"

More stuffing squeezed out of her, pouring into his mouth, far too much to swallow, making him choke. It came out of his nose and he came so hard he felt it in his bones, but the cum spurting from him wasn't white it was brown, caramel brown like turkey gravy and—

He woke up, coughing. His room at the Plaza was dry but his boxers were moist. Archie couldn't remember the last time he'd had a nocturnal emission. Probably not since high school, when he still used to prematurely ejaculate from close proximity to girls.

The Turkey Lady was right. I need to check the spring.

He got out of bed and crossed to the dresser. He used the combination on the briefcase, then opened the latches. Inside the case, the spring-loaded trap was loose. He'd tried it three or four times already the previous day—it was nearing two a.m. now—once when he got back to the hotel room from the gym, again when he returned from his trip to Walmart, and once more after his shower, before he climbed into bed.

He set the spring, his erection wilting in the cold splat of semen on the inside of his boxers, and picked up the closest thing at hand: the hotel's Gideon Bible. He laid it on the catapult and gently closed the briefcase, latched it but didn't lock it.

It was disconcerting how much he'd thought of the Turkey Lady since the show the other night. Seemed every so often in a moment of silence his mind would drift to her performance. He'd imagined donning the apron and gloves, being the butcher who filled her with stuffing, night after night offering his savory sacrament to her holy of holies.

He'd considered taking a cab out there tonight. He'd been unable to get her out of his mind. He *needed* to see her again, his Vixen. Instead, he'd masturbated again, been unable to climax, and had fallen asleep with the same hard-on he'd woken to.

Standing at the dresser, he stepped briskly out of the way and unlatched the briefcase.

The Bible sprang from the briefcase, flew across the room like a Holy Bat, and struck the painting over the headboard—a modernist Buffalo skyline as seen from Lake Erie—knocking it crooked.

"It still works," he said aloud.

And it will work tomorrow, the Turkey Lady assured him. *In the name of the Butcher, the Bird and the Holy Stuffing. Amen.*

"Amen," Archie repeated reverently, climbing back under the covers. Despite the cold stickiness in his underpants, he was asleep again in minutes, dreaming once more of his Gobbling Madonna.

3

"We used to avoid this place, the Lonely Motel, when we were kids. As an adult, you get trapped out here in a snow storm, unable to make it home to the wife and kids, you trudge through the snow to one of the other motels on the down the block."

That was how David had always begun this story, the few times he'd told it before, to Towne and Clay and his handful of protégés before them. He'd changed the name, never told them the actual source of the story, had always told them instead it was whatever motel they'd been staying at, in the room Clay or Towne had been about to spend the night.

They'd each gone to bed assuring him the story hadn't affected them, but by morning they'd looked harrowed, like they'd had trouble getting a decent night's sleep—and they certainly hadn't *showered.*

It had been fifteen minutes since he'd seen—or thought he'd seen—Clay Kayden peering in through the window at him. The sight had *seemed* real, but he supposed it could have been a hallucination, brought on by his own unexamined guilt and the suffering he'd undergone in the past six or seven hours.

"This story's gonna make you feel dirty," he said, "but you're not gonna be able to shower once you hear it. You know, *Psycho* from 1960, with that one single movie Hitchcock made everyone afraid to take a shower. Even grown men. Ablutophobia, it's called. Sometimes it's a specific fear of showers or tubs, sometimes it's a fear of washing altogether. It's a real thing, feel free to look it up when we're done.

"This *specific* story, though, I heard about it when I was… ten or eleven years old, maybe? The same year my folks and I moved to Stratford, Connecticut, where Uncle Stevie grew up before his mother moved them back to Maine."

"He means Stephen King," Tyler said to Rawlins.

"Hashtag No Shit, dude. I'm not dumb."

Tyler scowled, his fingers making tiny creaks in the wood as they gripped the edge of the dresser tighter.

"Between 1971 and 1973, I think it was, there was a serial killer in the Rochester area, just an hour's drive to the northeast. The Alphabet Killer, they called this guy. He killed three girls, ten and eleven years old. They say he chose his victims because their names were alliterative. Like from old comic books, how characters had names that started with the same letter or sound. Clark Kent. Bruce Banner. Peter Parker. My guess is, it was a pathological thing. But since the killer's never been caught, might even be dead by now, we'll probably never know.

"When we were kids around that time, I remember a kind of urban legend going around about the Alphabet Killer. You used to see billboards on the expressways asking 'Who killed Carmen Colón? Please help before it happens again,' with a six-thousand-dollar reward for tips and a picture of this sweet, innocent dead girl smiling out at you as you drove past on your way to the office or a drive-in movie.

"That sort of thing hits you different when you're a kid, I think. Like the pictures on milk cartons. I used to stare at those pictures wondering what happened to these kids. Did they run off? Were they kidnapped? Did they get hit by a car and die in a ditch or just get lost in the woods, their remains picked apart by carrion? When you're a parent, I guess it hits you in a similar way but when you're a kid you wanna solve all of those unsolved mysteries. You wanna discover the Lost City of Atlantis, find evidence of bigfoot and help capture the Alphabet Killer. At least I did.

"I remember a friend of mine, Joey Germain, we used to scare the crap out of him telling him he'd be the Alphabet Killer's next victim. Even though the victims had all been girls, at least the ones the authorities knew about, it got so poor Joey couldn't sleep at night and his mom made him go to a hypnotherapist.

"This story takes place a few years after all that. It was the same year I left town, I think, so it would've been 1974 or '75. This all went down in a specific room but it's actually connected to a whole wing of the motel. Maybe this one. Over a period of a week or so, guests at the Lonely kept complaining about issues with the water. It tastes funny. It smells bad. Black crud's gurgling up from the drain or the water coming out of the shower head is the wrong color, too dark, but not like loosened rust or sediment. The final nail in the coffin, so to speak, according to what I could piece together of the story, was this guy dropped his wedding ring in the sink drain in one of the rooms. Eleven or thirteen, I don't remember. You can probably guess what his ring was doing off his finger, at a place like this. It's not like the hooker cares he's married but to some guys, it's a psychological thing. I guess it'd be worse if you're left-handed and you gotta use your ring hand to get things on and get em off, if you get my meaning.

"This guy, instead of going to the manager and making a scene, he gets a wire coat hanger from the closet, he pulls it apart and bends it into a hook at the end, then he starts feeding it into the sink, trying to reach his ring.

"After a bit he hits something. A little metallic clink that doesn't sound hollow, like the pipes. He think's he's got it, so like a fisherman—which is something they used to call pedophiles like the Alphabet Killer, I don't know if you know that—like a fisherman but not that kind of fisherman, he starts pulling on the wire but it's tough going. It's snagged on something. He pulls real hard, using a sawing motion to get it unstuck, pretty sure by now he's lost his ring but desperate.

"Then the coat hook suddenly springs free with a little twang like a door stopper. Splatters this black gunk on the wall, the mirror, all over his clean dress shirt and his fresh shave and little clumps of it sticking to his lips. He spat it out and ran hot water to scrub it off his face and neck but the water comes out dark, the same color as the gunk stuck all over the bathroom. He was probably worried about coming home with lipstick stains on his collar but there's no way he's getting *these* stains out of his shirt.

"Gross," Tyler said with a sneer.

Rawlins was sitting forward, elbows on knees, enthralled.

"Yeah. But that's not the worst of it. He's pissed off, and he goes to the night manager to make him aware of the situation. 'You've got to call a plumber in here, stat.' So the night manager, he calls in a guy he knows will cut him a deal, who just so happens to be my friend Joey's dad, Alphonse, or Alfie as we called him when we were teasing Joey.

"Alfie was a helluva good plumber. You wanted something difficult done, you called Alfie Germain. Everyone knew that. He made decent money, running his own business out of the garage. Enough that he could afford to let his wife take their son to a hypnotherapist, despite him thinking it was 'hippie garbage.'

"So Alfie heads out to the Lonely Motel, assesses the situation. The businessman who lost his ring, he's hanging over Alfie's shoulder while he does. 'You're gonna wanna stand back,' says Alfie. The john who lost his ring, he doesn't need to be told twice. Alfie's heard the story from the night manager, he knows he's not just looking for some john's ring, so first thing he does is removes the pipe under the sink at the U-bend, fishes out the john's ring and the clump of crud its stuck in and hands it over, still shiny with bits of black goop. He tells the guy, 'You're gonna wanna wash that,' says the gunk it was stuck in is clumps of hair, maybe a decade's worth, all gummed up with black bacteria from soap and dirt and lotion and toothpaste, spit and snot and probably even some 'jizzum from the last ten or a hundred guys through here,' he says. That gets the guy off his back so the real work can get done.

"Alfie starts snaking the pipe, using this little doohickey they had back then, something like a fishing creel. He feeds it into the pipe, down and down, and finally he hits a real tough blockage. By now he knows he's probably closer to where the sink pipe hits the one for the tub. So he reels up the snake and decides to go right to the source.

"First thing he notices, there's a lot of scratches and nicks on the tub drain strainer. Like somebody's been trying to get it out. Its rusty around the edges, too. He gets his screwdriver and it pops out too easily. Then he takes a look in the pipe with a flashlight. Right away he sees why there's all those little scratches, why the strainer came out so easy. There's this little loop of string, jute twine, down just far enough somebody could reach in with their finger if they were dexterous or they had a long enough fingernail to fish it out.

"Alfie had fat fingers, never were good for much aside from plumbing. So he grabbed a pair of needle-nose plyers and used them to pinch the little loop and start pulling whatever it was that was clogging up the works out of the tub drain.

"It's about six or seven inches before the thing attached to the twine pokes out of the drain, pulling up a clump of the black crud with it. Alfie grabs it, slender and hard—"

"Was it a penis?" Rawlins asked excitedly.

David frowned. "It wasn't a penis. What's with you two and penises?"

Rawlins shrugged. Tyler merely scowled.

"Don't interrupt me, okay? Goddamn it, you messed with my flow."

"It was a tampon!" Rawlins cried out, raising a finger.

"*Shut the fuck up and let the man tell the story*," Tyler hissed.

"Thanks, kid." David took a breath, and regained his footing. "So Alfie grabs this thing, and he sees its attached to more string, like a chain of it leading into the drain. He turns on the tap a little, gets a trickle going, and rinses this thing off, tied with twine on both ends.

"When he sees the fingernail, he drops it like a hot potato, beyond mortified. He's seen a lot of things stuck in drains that shouldn't be, he's seen live snakes and clumps of turd the size of newborn babies, but this is the first time he's seen a *human finger*, the cuticle chewed down to the quick. A *child's* finger, to be exact, hard to tell from the size of it but probably the pinkie.

"Now like I said, Alfie's got a boy at home, Joey, who hasn't been able to sleep since we teased him so bad about the Alphabet Killer. He's looking at this finger, tied on both ends, around the top knuckle and the base where it's been severed, where the meat is beginning to rot but it's still somewhat fresh. Like it hasn't been there all that long. The cut is clean, not sawed, like maybe it's been snipped off with boning scissors, or a cigar cutter, or garden shears.

"'Jesus,' he says, crossing himself with his crud-caked hand, looking down at that finger on the porcelain while dark water trickles on it, all the while he *knows* there's something else in the drain, tied to the other end of that string. 'Jesus Hortense Christ.'

"So he turns off the faucet and gets back to it. He's climbed all the way into the tub now, squatting in there, tugging on this twine. Pulling it up, inch by inch. And after about six inches of twine, up comes another clump of this stuff, gurgling out of the drain, with yet another hidden treasure.

"He runs the tap again, cleaning it off delicately. It's another kid's finger. Maybe the same kid, maybe not. Could be a girl's or a boy's. Alfie's not a coroner, so it's impossible for him to tell. But he knows this one's been down there longer than the first, maybe just a few months, maybe as long as a year. The flesh is rotten and gray and the nail's turned yellow.

"And this one's tied with another piece of twine to something else, deeper in the drain.

"By now he's so determined to solve this, he can't stop. He's like a kid with a mystery. He's got to be the one to solve it. So he keeps pulling on that string, pulling out more of that black gunk and more kid's fingers. He keeps washing these things off, and tugging on the next piece of twine, hoping like hell the next one will be the last.

"All in all, Alfie Germain pulled up eight fingers that day in 1974 or '75, each in different states of decay. The last finger, it was practically all bone, only held to the previous one by a ridge of skin protected by the twine. This finger, these bones from a kid who could've been dead as long as a few years, these trophies of some serial killer, some sick sadist, they pulled up with them the last clump of bacteria, and all the crud behind the blockage starts spewing up at poor Alfie like crude oil, like Texas tea, and in seconds he's *covered* in it, shiny and black from head to toe, spitting it out, this *filth*, the human waste and decomposition juices, snorting it from his nostrils and wiping it out of his eyes.

"In desperation he turns on the shower, not thinking about the fingers or the twine or the crud still bubbling up from the drain, just wanting to get the awful shit off his face, out of his eyes. Only he forgot about the complaints of black water, the reason he was here in the first place, and it washes off the crud, sure, but he took a mouthful to get the gunk off his teeth and tongue and swished it around before he realized it was probably something similar rotting in the water main. He's *gargling* with it. The second he realized it he puked it all right back up into the drain between his feet.

"Needless to say, that was the last time Alfie Germain gave the night manager at the Lonely Motel a deal. And when it was all over, after the cops questioned him and sent him home to his wife and son, he decided it might be a good idea to try this hypnotherapy thing himself."

Rawlins stared at David for a long moment before starting a slow clap, rising from the chair for a standing ovation. "That was genius, Mr. Ennis. Hashtag Gross Out Win Secured."

David didn't think it was "genius," exactly. But he took the kid's praise graciously.

Tyler, meanwhile, sat frowning against the vanity. "Okay, so it's gross. But what was the point of it?"

"The point? I don't get what you mean, kid."

"There needs to be a *point* to a story, see? It can't just be a string of disgusting things that happen, excuse the pun. That's juvenile."

"Oh, here we go."

Tyler's expression went flat. "Here we go *what*."

"With the 'juvenile' argument. You don't know how many reviews I've gotten saying my work is something a thirteen-year-old boy would write. Well, you know what? I was a thirteen-year-old boy once. And sometimes, I write for me at that age."

"Did they ever find him?" Rawlins asked. "The guy who did it?"

"They matched the fingers, the first five, at least, with the bodies of boys who'd been found in New York and neighboring states. The killer, the Pinkie Ripper they called him, he was never caught. Neither was the Alphabet Killer." He turned back to Tyler. "You need a point, kid? There's your point. Awful shit happens in the world, and sometimes there *is* no point to it. What's the point of all this, huh? You think doing this to me is gonna get you what you want? I thought you wanted to be a writer."

"I *am* a writer."

"Then *write*. Give yourself up, before it's too late. I'll ask for clemency."

Tyler's scowl returned. "Are you going to make me the same offer you made to Jackson?"

David's heart sank to the bottom of his chest. Rawlins shot him a nervous glance but he didn't dare make eye contact. "That offer still stands. I'm willing to let this go, I *promise* you that. If you let *me* go."

"Why should I believe you?"

Tell them, David, Stark said. *Tell them about me.*

David sighed through his blood-encrusted nostrils. "Kid, I didn't want to tell you this, but you've *inspired* me. I haven't been able to write in years, not since I got off the sauce. But right now, I feel like I've got a *dozen* novels in me, just bustin to come out. That's because of *this*, 'cause of this horrible thing you did to me. I don't wanna say good always comes from bad, all you have to do is look at all those poor dead kids who've never been found, those parents who never got closure—but you can't *heal* if you haven't been *hurt*. When I quit drinking, I lost my *edge*. I went *soft*. Then I hit what I thought was rock bottom, and I *still* couldn't climb back up out of the shit. I still couldn't find my muse. *You* did that for me today, Tyler. Jackson. You two could let me go right now and I swear, I won't tell a goddamn soul. But I'll dedicate my next book to you, if you want. My next six books. I'll get both of your novels in the hands of my editor. I *swear* to you. *I swear on my mother's life.*"

That was it, that was everything he had in him. He was spent. His head hung heavy from his shoulders, swaying slightly, awaiting his captor's response.

The kid seemed to mull it over. His reluctant partner gave him an imploring look.

"No," Tyler finally said, through gritted teeth. "We follow through with the plan."

"What *plan*, kid? Seems to me, you've been making this up as you go along."

"What *is* the plan, Ty?" Rawlins asked, disappointment and desperation in his eyes.

"Tomorrow, David Ennis makes a surprise appearance at the

Gross Out contest. His *final* appearance. And when I'm certain we've got their attention, when all of their eyes are on *me*, I'll cut his fucking throat for the whole audience to see. They want *gross*? I'll *give* them gross." He turned to David with a sadistic grin. "How's *that* for a fucking point, David?"

You have to admit, Stark said, *the kid has a flair for the dramatic*.

THE DAY OF

1

CLAY WOKE SHARPLY at nine A.M., lying on the covers of his double bed in the Lonely Motel, to an alarm he didn't remember setting. His head felt much clearer than it had last night. He remembered feeling electric, his mind buzzing like an acid trip. He couldn't recall drifting off, let alone how he'd gotten from Shyla and Angel's room to his own, but he did remember a vague sense of a dream as he was waking, of being trapped in a womb the size of a grown man, and being birthed onto this very bed feeling refreshed. A brand-new man.

Remind me never to eat Clams casino again, he thought.

Standing under a hot shower, he remembered the story Ennis had told him when they were on the road together, at a hotel in Tallahassee, about the Pinkie Ripper and Alfie the plumber. The story never failed to make him step out from under the spray and check the color of the water, if it was clear or dark as tea, as liver-damaged urine. Thanks to Shyla and Angel, he now had bathtub abortions to add to his distaste for hotel bathrooms.

Thinking of David's story made him remember what he'd seen—or thought he'd seen—in Room 7. Was that really David he'd seen? The light had been dim, a single yellow table lamp casting much of his face in shadows. It could have been anyone. At a place like this, maybe the kid was some Mafia torturer, the man in the chair not Ennis but someone with a similar build. The kid didn't look like a "made" guy, but Clay couldn't be sure he'd ever seen a mobster outside of a TV show or news photos. Or maybe the guy—whoever it was that looked enough like Ennis to confuse Clay's food poisoning-addled mind—was into sexual sadism? It could've been a consensual thing, all that cutting. If Shyla's story had taught him anything it was that there was no telling what kinks people were into. Maybe the kid was a dom instead of a Dominic. Did he really want to get involved in any of that?

After toweling off, a quick shave and dressing for the day, he stepped out into the unseasonably warm November weather. The light in Room 6 was off. The kid's car was still parked where it had been last night. A light snow had fallen overnight, melting already, but enough of it was left to see a pair of footprints from Room 7, ending at a set of tire tracks that came in from the road and led back out. The kid must not have been able to get his car started again, took a cab to wherever he was going.

Curiosity got the better of Clay, and he crossed the lot to Room 7, creeping again as he neared the window. This time, the curtains were fully closed, not even a crack of the room visible from outside.

He kicked aside his tracks and returned to his room, having forgotten he'd left his own car, the rental Cutlass, at the Plaza Hotel. He ordered an Uber and sat at the small table in front of the window, watching a light snowfall, waiting for his ride.

The door to Room 7 opened.

He leaned back out of the window, peering around the window frame. The kid he'd seen the other day stepped out in jogging pants and boots and the same heavy winter coat with the furry hood he'd been wearing yesterday. He went to his car and sat behind the wheel. It looked like he was hunching over, studying something.

It couldn't have been David, Clay thought. Whoever it was had likely left in the car whose tracks he'd seen. *Or maybe*, he thought, *maybe he got into the backseat of a black Cadillac, wedged in between two meatheads with guns, and he's getting fitted for concrete shoes right now.*

Whatever it was, there was no reason for concern.

His ride showed up a few minutes later. He went out to meet

the driver. As he climbed into the vehicle, the kid got out of his car and caught his eye again. This time the flat expression the kid tended to wear became narrowed eyes. He was suspicious.

Clay gave him a single wave and got in the backseat.

2

Moira hadn't slept well.

It was hard enough trying to sleep with a headache but the black eye made it worse. She was a side sleeper who often rolled over during the night, flipping from one side to the other. As a result, she'd awakened several times to excruciating pain, her eye and cheekbone throbbing. The bitch Fiona had really landed a good one with that sucker punch.

Perhaps worse, Moira had no idea what had happened to Clay after he left. She'd texted him but he hadn't responded. She supposed he could have been in hospital. Perhaps the battery in his phone had run out.

What an awful time for food poisoning, she thought, glancing again at her phone. *After everything we went through to get into bed together.*

A small part of her, barely worth listening to, wondered if Clay might have been making an excuse, running out the way he had. If maybe he'd thought something was wrong with her fanny, if he wasn't used to pubic hair on a woman or he'd encountered an odor he couldn't bear.

That same small, hardly-worth-considering voice wondered if he'd been reacting to her reading from earlier in the day. If by telling a story about her little brother who'd died choking on her used tampon, she might have turned him off entirely. Even though the story wasn't true. Even though Nigel was still alive and as well as possible, living with their mother, likely watching late-afternoon telly with Mum and Genevieve right now.

Sod him if it did, she thought, pitching a sigh. *Well, best get on with it.*

The Gross Out contest would start in three hours, David Ennis emceeing. The final day of any convention was always bittersweet. There were old friends she wouldn't see until the next one, possibly not for years, and new friends she'd promised to keep in touch with over social media. The Gross Out contest was the last chance many of these people would have to unwind and enjoy each other's company, enjoy one another's art. After that, they would present the awards for best readings over the weekend, as judged by Frank Wallis, David Ennis and… well, now that Anderson Ackerman had taken himself out of the picture with his disgusting behavior, who knew who they'd tap to judge these stories? Kendra Pleasance, perhaps?

Moira hoped her story would be acknowledged, after what she'd gone through with that horrible woman and Fiona St. Clair, but really the crowd's reaction to it had been an honor unto itself. Perhaps she'd be able to sell it to a publication for a decent per word amount.

Since Clay hadn't responded to her text, she decided to get brekkie with her friend Aubrey, who wrote under the penname Jessica Tuffet to avoid repercussions at her day job. They met at the convention breakfast buffet. Moira picked up a plate and started loading it with carbs, eggs and greasy rashers of bacon.

"Jeez," Aubrey said, giving her side eye from the coffee station. "What happened to you?"

Moira sighed. "Long story."

"If it has anything to do with why Fiona St. Clair has cotton balls stuffed up her nose and a bandage on her forehead, nice going, girl."

Moira chuckled halfheartedly.

"You missed a crazy show the other night," Aubrey said as they searched for a table. "Honestly, I've never seen anything like it in my life but I couldn't look away."

"At the lap dancing club?"

"Is that what you call it in the UK?"

Moira shrugged. "We don't talk much about them in the circles I run in."

The two of them sat at a table beside a bald man with no neck to speak of and a woman with colorful braids. The woman was breaking small pieces off of a croissant and eating them with quick little chews like a rabbit, the man over-stirring a packet of apple-cinnamon porridge.

"This show," Aubrey said, shaking her head as she smeared plain cream cheese on a barely toasted bagel, "I'm gonna lose my shit in front of Nana and Pops and the cousins at Christmas when Dad starts scooping stuffing from the turkey. They'll all think I'm insane." She shrugged and took a bite. "More insane than they already think I am."

Moira wasn't sure she wanted to hear the details. Instead, she asked, "Where are the boys?" Meaning the other Gorehounds: Conor, Shawnders, Steve and Mike.

"Sleeping it off, no doubt. They went back to the club last night, last I heard."

"It must've made quite the impression."

Aubrey rolled her eyes. "Boys," she said, a statement that didn't require further explanation. "How'd things go with you and Clay? That's not where this came from, is it?" She indicated her own eye with her plastic knife.

"Gosh no," Moira said. "No, Clay and I had an… interesting night. That is, before he left."

"Girl, he didn't even spend the night?"

Moira told her friend everything that had happened last night, from her own perspective, from the meeting with Kendra Pleasance—"That manipulative *bitch*," Aubrey said—to the fire alarm, to trying to stop Towne's fake suicide attempt.

"What an asshole," Aubrey said to that. Moira hadn't told her they'd slept together the night before, only Clay and likely Fiona knew about that, but she did tell Aubrey that Towne had tried to cajole her into a threesome now, and then about making out with Clay in the lift, and Clay beginning to go down on her.

"And he just left you hanging?"

"He said he felt sick."

"Ooh," Aubrey said with a wince. "That's not good."

"He was acting strangely. To be honest, it sounded like he was high on something. But he's been staying sober, since the incident. I suppose it could've just been food poisoning."

Aubrey shrugged. "So are you gonna hook up with him today?"

"My flight's at three. It doesn't seem likely."

"Star-crossed lovers, huh? Bummer." She finished the last bite of her bagel.

"Apparently it wasn't meant to be."

"Well, you'll always have Splatterfest. Maybe they'll stick us in Jersey next time," she said derisively, wiping her hands with a serviette. "You could stay with me."

"That would be nice."

Aubrey laid a comforting hand on Moira's shoulder. "Listen, if you and Clay were meant to be, you'll make it happen. If not, at least you had some fun together."

"True."

They picked up their trays and brought them back to the buffet.

"Hey, Conor's gonna try and snag us front row seats for the Gross Out contest," Aubrey said, dumping her serviettes and plastic cutlery in the rubbish bin. "We could probably save a seat for you, if you want."

Moira smiled. "I'd like that, thanks."

"Good." Aubrey held open her arms. "Hug?"

Moira stepped into her embrace, hugging her friend back.

"Archie," Aubrey said, breaking their hug. "You know, the Poo-Poo Man?"

"From last time? The periscope in the loo?"

"That's him. I think I'm gonna try to fuck him after the Gross Out contest."

Moira laughed. Aubrey was bisexual, according to her social media profiles, though she tended toward dating women. "So that's what rings your bell these days?"

"Hey, a girl's gotta get hers. Everyone else is getting a piece, why can't I? He's just so sweet and shy, I gotta admit, it's my weakness when it comes to boys. But *man*, has he filled out since last time." She waved a hand in front of her face, as if to prevent the vapors, as they left the dining room.

"Bit of a beefcake, is he?"

"The kids call it *swole* these days."

"I don't think this conversation would pass the Bechdel test," Moira said wryly.

"Fuck the Bechdel test. Anyways, I'm not talking about a *man*, I'm talking about getting some *dick*."

Moira laughed. "Well, I hope it happens for you."

"Fingers crossed," Aubrey said, demonstrating with both hands. "I'm heading over to the Gorehounds table. Wanna join?"

"I'll come round later. I'm going to pack up and see if I can check in early for my flight."

"Good idea. Don't forget: front row, eleven. Me, you and the Gorehounds crew."

"I'll be there," Moira said, waving as she headed for the lifts.

3

Archie woke with morning wood and a smile, reminding himself that today was the very last day anyone would dare to call him "the Poo-Poo Man."

He'd spent the majority of the last two years working out, gaining mass, trying to put the shy dweeb who'd just wanted to entertain a few people with a disgusting story at a Gross Out contest behind him. Hoping when they saw him again, Conor and the others, they'd be so impressed and intimidated by what they saw they'd forget all about the silly story he'd written on a lark over the same weekend he'd read it aloud for the first and final time.

He'd only wanted to impress them but instead they continued to mock him. He was a laughing stock. A mascot. And he'd never be anything more than that… until he took action.

The briefcase was ready.

The contents of the briefcase were ready.

He dressed in a nice suit, his grandfather's suit, the one Opa had worn across the Atlantic Ocean from Yugoslavia after the war. The briefcase had belonged to Archie's father.

Once he'd placed his folded poncho on top of it, Archie was ready, too.

4

Jackson Rawlins, the Hashtag King, had taken a Lyft back to the Plaza Hotel at just past nine in the morning. He hadn't slept much, lying on the motel room floor on a single lumpy pillow under a stained bedsheet, worried Tyler might decide to kill him in his sleep. He must have gotten *some* sleep, though, since he'd woken to the sun blasting in through a crack in the curtains, and felt like he'd been dreaming something vaguely sinister about shower drains and tortured children.

David Ennis seemed to be barely hanging on to his last shred of consciousness, and the slashes all over his body looked angry, but Tyler was refreshed, having slept in the bed, and almost seemed happy, a smile cracking his flat expression here and there. He was eager to attack the day, and that meant sending Jackson back to the Plaza.

For his part, Jackson couldn't say why he'd gone along with Tyler's plan, if he'd even had a plan to begin with, if he hadn't just been making it up as he went along, as Ennis seemed to suggest. He'd always been cowardly, but that wasn't an excuse. Tyler was menacing but he was *small*. Jackson could easily have overpowered him if he'd wanted to, cowardly or not.

He supposed the truth was harder to admit: that he was jealous of David Ennis, and the writer's success. Seeing him brought to his knees had been a bit of a *rush*, yep, Hashtag Guilty as Charged—but he'd never wanted to see the man *harmed*. He'd *especially* not wanted to hold up the tip of Ennis's pickle while Tyler gave him the Mother of All Paper Cuts.

The torture, that was all Tyler. Events had spiraled out of

control from the moment Jackson had taken the little bottle from Tyler's coat and, thinking it was some kind of hillbilly moonshine—judging by the slight twang Tyler tried so hard to hide—he'd slugged it down. That it would turn out to have been *chloroform* had never crossed his mind. Who would carry around chloroform in their pocket?

Well, now he knew. Hashtag Lesson Learned. Hashtag Too Little Too Late. Hashtag Somebody Please Put Me Out of My Fucking Misery. Tyler Grody was a maniac, a sociopath or a psychopath or whatever -path was the kind to torture and plan to kill his former idol in front of a live audience for the pettiest of reasons, forcing Jackson to help him because he was already in too deep to climb out without penalty.

He considered calling the police during the entire drive from the Lonely Motel. Or telling the convention security officers as soon as he got back to the Plaza Hotel. But he'd done neither of those things.

He could have erased the footage from the recording device, removing his participation in the crime entirely, aside from David Ennis's testimony, who wouldn't be alive much longer to testify against him. But who knew if Tyler hadn't already backed it up on *another* hard drive?

So he didn't do that, either.

What he did instead was go directly to Frank K. Wallis, the convention manager, and ask if it was okay to set up some audio-visual equipment in the conference room ahead of the Gross Out contest.

Frank seemed frazzled, much less mellow than usual. His head twitched around with jerky, birdlike movements. He asked who would be calling in their reading.

"My f-friend," Jackson said warily. "Tyler Grody?"

Frank pulled out a clipboard from under his vendor table and blinked his bleary eyes, apparently having trouble focusing as he ran a finger down the list. "Ah, yes. Last on the docket."

"That's him."

"Sure, you go ahead. Jackson, was it?"

Swallowing a hard lump, Jackson nodded, suddenly certain Frank knew something.

"You look tense," Frank said. "Would you like some water?" He indicated a flat of stubby bottles with the Splatterfest convention logo on their wrappers, a few already taken.

Jackson shook his head. "I'm a Powerade guy. Hashtag Go Stronger for Longer."

Frank put on a false-looking smile. "Wonderful. Let me know if you have any trouble setting up your equipment."

"Will do, thanks."

Jackson headed for the conference room with his bag slung over his shoulder. He glanced back to be sure Frank wasn't watching him from his table, but the man was busy signing one of his books for an eager fan.

It was all too easy. Someone had to be watching him, setting him up, waiting for him to get the video linked so they could trace its source. Then they'd swoop in and arrest him, and he'd be on trial for the kidnapping and torture of David Ennis, Undisputed Master of Splatter Horror.

Better than being on trial for murder, isn't it? Hashtag Lawyer Up and Plea Bargain.

Jackson opened the double doors to Conference Room 1. This was the biggest of the four rooms, where they'd held the opening ceremonies on Friday and where they planned to hold the Gross Out contest and award presentation. The trophy for the winner was a woman's head with a stick protruding from her mouth, reminiscent of one of many gruesome scenes from the '70s horror classic, *Cannibal Holocaust*.

Didn't the director almost go to jail for murdering the entire cast?

Jackson pushed those thoughts aside and concentrated on the work. As an experienced wedding videographer, he knew his way around a room like this: stage, podium, seating. He knew the best places to set up his stationary cameras, and how to avoid getting in the way of them while moving around with his handheld. He'd connected and set up projector systems in hotels and churches and bingo halls and just about anywhere someone might think to host their wedding. He'd even shot a wedding on a bridge where the bride and groom said "I do" and bungee-jumped hand in hand a hundred feet above a river.

Tyler's equipment was simple to set up yet pretty genius in its application: a video camera that streamed directly to a dual recording device and monitor via a secured, password-encrypted transmission. The signal wasn't *impossible* to intercept, but it was unlikely that someone could eavesdrop unless they were very good at their job.

What made it simple was a set of connections in the back of the recording device for output in HDMI, coaxial and RGB. All Jackson had to do was find the cable for the projector's input and Hashtag Plug and Play.

Which he did easily, discovering a coiled HDMI cable on the shelf of the projector stand.

He FaceTimed Tyler on his way down the aisle to the doors. Tyler picked up on the first ring, the angle close, his expression returned to its state of blank-slate nothingness.

"Is it set up?"

Jackson turned his phone, giving Tyler a good look at the empty conference room, the podium, stage and projector stand.

"I'm just gonna check to make sure the doors are locked." He did. They were. He crossed back to the podium, where he'd set up the projector stand. "Ready?"

"*Yes*, I'm ready. What do you think?"

"Hashtag *Chill*, guy. I'm just trying to make sure you're not in the middle of something you don't want projected on a twenty-foot-tall screen."

"Check the monitor if you're worried, dummy."

Jackson couldn't fault him there. He had considered checking the monitor, but he wasn't sure if somehow Tyler didn't have some way to know when the monitor on the record box was turned on. If he wouldn't think Jackson was showing his video stream to the cops at the police station.

"It's not too late to put an end to this," Ennis called out, from wherever Tyler had wheeled him.

"Oh, but it is, David. It very much is. The only way this ends, *David*, is with one or all three of us in body bags."

Ennis said nothing further.

Jackson swallowed hard.

"Go ahead," Tyler said.

Jackson turned on the projector. The interior of Room 7 at the Lonely Motel appeared on the projection screen, the colors somewhat muted but it still felt almost as though he could climb right through the wall into the room itself. Tyler stood in the center of the room, where Ennis had been this morning. The edge of the bed was on the right side of the screen, the television and dresser behind Tyler, the chair Jackson himself had been sitting in most of yesterday on the left.

Tyler made a single wave. "See me okay?"

Jackson turned the phone so Tyler could see himself. On the big screen, Tyler squinted at his phone. "Tilt it a bit?"

"The projector?"

"The phone, you halfwit."

Scowling, Jackson tilted the phone.

"Looks good. What about the sound? It's like hearing my own voice through a tin can here."

"Sound's good. Hashtag All Systems Go."

"Good. Unplug everything, pack it up, and call me when it's done so I can see."

"But I just set it all up."

"And I don't want you *showing* it to anyone who shouldn't be *seeing* it in the meantime. It's a surprise, see? Just you and me and David makes three."

Tyler uttered a creepy little giggle that chilled Jackson to his ska-loving core. Would Tyler really go through with it? *Murder* David Ennis, the Gross Out emcee, in front of a live audience? Just cut his throat in front of everyone?

On the projection screen, Tyler Grody's smile faded and his expression resumed its dead-eyed flatness.

Yeah, Jackson thought. *He'd do it. Hashtag Muy Loco.*

Jackson unplugged the cable, causing Room 7 to vanish. But the anxiety it caused him remained. He supposed that would only go away once this was all over and done with, when David Ennis was dead and he and Tyler were taken to the police station in handcuffs.

Though he guessed the feeling might *never* go away.

TRUTH IN FICTION

1

CLAY TEXTED MOIRA an apology and a promise to explain himself while heading to the Plaza Hotel in the back of another Uber. She replied swiftly, saying she was just glad he wasn't dead. The text was curt, and he wondered if she wasn't actually upset, like she'd been about the handshake the day before.

At least she probably didn't hook up with Towne again. Not with Fiona's patchouli stinking up the room.

But how could he explain what had happened last night? And how much of it really had? Obviously, Dean Foster Towne taunting him under the covers had been a hallucination. But had he really seen Ennis in that room? Had he really listened to the woman in Room 6 tell him a story that couldn't possibly be true, and actually *believed* it?

I'll tell her everything and hope she believes me. Oh hey, Moira, did you hear the one about the catatonic who got his head stuck in an escort's vagina? No? Well, neither did he, because he's in over his ears! Ba-dum-bum.

After responding to Moira, letting her know he'd be at the hotel shortly, he checked the convention message board one final time. With David MIA, ostensibly on a Bender to End All Benders, it no longer mattered. But he was curious what his Inquisition had gotten up to while he'd been indisposed.

It turned out they'd been busy little bees. They were planning to stalk the conference room where the Gross Out contest would be taking place, awaiting David's return to emcee the event.

They would start their protest the moment he arrived, demanding he be removed as judge and MC and have someone of their choice take his place, preferably a "woman or nonbinary author of Color, disabled if possible." Clay wondered if they would be party to the disabling themselves or if they preferred to leave that task to someone else, perhaps a neurodivergent or otherwise historically marginalized leg-breaker.

Aside from this, there was chatter about the woman who'd allegedly attacked Ignacio Ortega trying to clear her name on social media. This caused several long threads of arguing, name-calling and threats before the mods closed the comments. From the look of it, trouble was brewing in the critic community, or the "Critic Crew," as they often called themselves, always one word and usually hashtagged.

One comment was a thinly veiled threat that critics should protect themselves and one another by "any means necessary." An author—obvious not from their comment but from the word "author" as a suffix in their username—suggested this comment could be considered intimidation. The first commenter, a person who called themselves Sugarmama, replied: "If it sounds like a threat, you're probably one of the ones we need to watch out for."

"Yikes," Clay said to himself.

"Pardon?" the Uber driver asked.

"Sorry. Talking to myself."

Another poster speculated the fire alarm last night had been intentional, that someone—they didn't know who and weren't about to point fingers, "but probably some busybody Bible-thumper with a grudge"—was trying to stop the convention. There were families staying here, and it was clear to this poster that the "Horror People" were not welcome, especially after the violence on Friday night, the alleged "loud partying," and the "crazy SJWs trailing Mr. Ennis like a bad smell" on Saturday. They were "sick and tired of the Liberal Gay Agenda constantly paraded around and rubbed under our noses. Can't we just have horror without all the sex?"

This puritan soul was then dogpiled, naturally, by several of the usernames Clay recognized from the Inquisition thread and other helpful individuals, several asking pointedly if the OP agreed with the constitutional right to protest or not, and if they were in fact a fascist themselves. Other courageous crusaders jumped in to defend the poster. After plenty of back and forth, with both sides resorting to ad hominem attacks, strawmen and whataboutisms, this thread's comments were also closed.

The message board also had a few innocuous posts, mostly attendees voicing appreciation about convention guests, book signings and particular readings. Moira's story received a thread of its own, with at least a dozen positive comments (and one, from the puritan, who wished stories from "lady writers" didn't always have to be "about their vaginas," a comment that was quickly shouted into oblivion). But the angry posts received the most attention, and since Clay was partly responsible for the inception of at least one of them, he couldn't exactly complain that the internet was functioning as intended.

It's a feature, not a bug, Clay thought.

All of this pointed to a bad day ahead for Frank Wallis and the convention, and Clay began to feel a little bad about his contribution toward it. After last night, talking with Shyla—he'd never gotten her last name—he'd started to think maybe it was time to give up his grudge against Ennis. Like Moira said, it was a poison, eating him up inside. And he'd certainly had enough of *that* for one weekend. Enough for a *lifetime*.

I'll see if I can corner him before the Gross Out contest. Try to summon up some sort of forgiveness, even if he doesn't feel it on his part. If you can forgive the people who've slighted you even when they don't express remorse, like Shyla and Angel, even for your worst enemies, that's the true spirit of forgiveness, isn't it? That's why authentic compassion is so difficult. Because it often only goes one way.

Besides, he had plenty enough to apologize for himself.

He never should have accompanied David on his last trip to Brown Town, almost three years ago now. That was his mistake. He'd thought he was being a good friend. A *supportive* friend.

But as an alcoholic, it was the sort of support David didn't need. After Vanessa, Ennis's wife, had staged the intervention, with all of David's closest friends and family, Ennis had gone running to his latest drinking buddy. The one person he knew wouldn't judge him, because he drank heavily himself. Clay knew David was one of those writers who relied on alcohol to fuel his muse, that going cold turkey was likely to dry up his creative well, and so he'd humored him, he'd taken David out on the town.

It was the blowout to end all blowouts. He hadn't told Towne everything about that night. He'd left out the worst part. Clay had suspected David thought it might be his last binge—but part of him wondered, later, if David hadn't intentionally been trying to sabotage his marriage, his friendships and career, just to keep the Brown Demon in his life. Clay didn't believe addiction was a disease but he did know that one sip of booze was enough to send David Ennis on an unending spiral, tearing down anything and everything in his path. He lacked the ability to say no. And after their stunted trip to the zoo, to "fuck up a panda bear," stopped by a tall fence and a bewildered security guard, they'd gotten a hotel room to sleep it off, with the intention of getting up and hitting the bottle "as soon as the sun comes up."

They'd crashed, each in their own double bed, just like they had on countless nights on the road.

In the middle of the night, Clay woke to the sound of sobs. David wasn't in his bed. He wasn't in the bathroom, but the light was on. The minibar had been raided, empty bottles all over the bed. It was likely he'd blacked out and continued drinking while Clay had slept.

The balcony door was open, the curtains fluttering.

The sobs came from outside.

Rubbing sleep dust from his eyes, Clay got out of bed and crossed to the balcony in his socks and underwear. He pulled the heavy door open and saw David had climbed over the railing. He stood in his sock feet on the edge of the cold cement, holding the top railing behind himself, seven floors up from the parking lot below.

"David, what the fuck?"

David turned, his face red, tears shining on his cheeks under the lights from the highway. "I'm gonna do it, Clay."

"David, you're drunk. Come inside, for fuck's sake. It's too early and too goddamn cold for this bullshit."

"I can't," David sobbed over his shoulder. "I can't write for shit, Clay! Not without my Kentucky hug, I just can't! I *need* it, man! But Vanessa's gonna divorce me. If I don't quit she'll divorce me and take half of *everything*!" He wept. "I love her, Clay!"

"Then come inside. We'll get you clean."

"But I love writing *more*, and I can't write for shit without the Brown Demon!"

The desperation in his voice was clear. He truly intended to jump. In his mind, it was the only choice he had.

"Bullshit," Clay said. "It's a *crutch*, David. The booze isn't your muse, all it's doing is holding back your inner critic! Christ, man, you've been at it almost thirty years, *you don't need booze to write*!"

"I do, though. You don't understand! I've tried to quit before! I couldn't write a word! This was the last straw, Clay. That's what she told me. Quit or get out."

"Then *quit*."

"I *can't* quit, Clay. I have to keep writing. My books are my fucking retirement plan."

"Then I'll write them for you," Clay said, voicing the only suggestion he could think at the time to get David off the ledge and back inside. "I can mimic your style, David. You know I can. Lee Stark fanfiction was how I taught myself to write. Let me write your books for you, just *come back inside*."

"You'd do that… for me?"

"If it'll get you off the ledge. If it'll keep you and Vanessa from getting a divorce. If it'll get the Brown Demon off your back. Of course, I'll do it. You're my best fucking friend, David. I'm not gonna let you jump and I won't let you burn your whole life down, either."

David sniffled, looking back. "I couldn't let you do it for free," he said.

Clay reached out to him. "Give me your hand."

David had come in off the ledge and they'd drawn up a contract that same night. Clay agreed to write David's next three books, and however many more until David could train himself to write without depressants or stimulants, for half of any advance and a third of the royalties.

Clay had a coffee ready for David when he'd awakened groggily shortly after noon, though he'd had to heat it up in the microwave. "What the hell happened last night?" David asked. Clay told him he couldn't remember much of it himself after the fight outside the bar, but there'd been something about David wanting to fight a panda.

David laughed, his fog apparently clearing enough to recall that part. "Oh, right. Stupid fucking panda bears."

"We're lucky the security guard stopped us," Clay said. "Imagine the headline, 'Midlist horror author dead after mauling by cute, cuddly panda.'"

"Nah," David said, scratching his ass as he sipped his coffee contemplatively. "I would've won. I fight dirty."

"Tell that to the newlywed whose fist made that dent in your forehead."

David looked at himself in the mirror. "Jesus. We really tied one on last night, huh?"

"That we did," Clay admitted.

David picked up the contract, still on the table from the night before. He glanced at the balcony door. "You really wanna go through with this, huh?"

"If you want me to. If you need it."

David nodded. "Maybe Vanessa's right. Maybe I should quit drinking."

Clay shrugged, not intending to join him. "Likely wouldn't be a bad idea."

So David had quit, cold turkey. He'd done surprisingly well at it. It was almost like a switch had flicked in his head, from

Addict to Clean. They remained friends for nearly a full year, and as per their contract, Clay wrote two novels for him, an apocalyptic novel and the latest in the Lee Stark series. He'd started plotting the third by the time of the Gross Out contest, and had already begun working on it when David's lawyer had reached out to cancel the deal.

Clay had written the Stark novel straight, figuratively and literally. He'd had no reason to burn David Ennis at that point. It wasn't until after the Gross Out contest and Fiona St. Clair's crusade to get him canceled for his entry, when David betrayed him, that he'd decided to take his revenge, using the groundwork Ennis himself had laid out.

The timing for its publication couldn't have been better. He'd known David wouldn't be able to resist reading from his latest novel, which he likely thought was sure to be a hit. Since Clay had never mentioned him publicly, nor sought to contact him after their "separation," he likely thought the whole situation was water under the bridge. What reason would Clay possibly have to begrudge him, the man who'd given him a leg up in the industry, who'd paid him a substantial amount of hush money to write two new novels?

Neither of them thought Clay's story about a male writer who got off beating his meat to female writers over video chats would get the reaction it had. David had said it was "brilliant" and "sharply satirical." Clay had felt that sympathy for the devil was a staple of the genre, that with all the stories of molestation, rape, torture, animal and child abuse, a story about a man pulling his pud to unsuspecting women would be tame in comparison.

Maybe it was a bad idea to simulate the masturbatory actions during the reading. But David had laughed his ass off during those parts, as did much of the audience. And maybe it was ill-timed, coming on the heels of several anonymous harassment complaints against an alleged well-known author (who, it turned out, was likely Anderson Ackerman). But Moira had said that was precisely the reason he needed to tell the story, that it was timely and clever and was actually feminist.

Besides, others had done worse. Hadn't they?

Fiona had felt differently. She'd thought it was "tone deaf" to write from the perspective of a male sex criminal at the height of the MeToo movement. She'd also presumed, because the character's name "sounded black," according to several people, that the reading was some sort of racist screed disguised as fiction, perpetuating the harmful trope of the black male as a "hypersexualized savage," which Clay had obviously never intended. He'd never given the character, whose name was Rodney, any implication of racial heritage. The story itself was simply a male writer trying to jerk off to a female writer over his webcam. Rather than express shock and horror, as Rodney expects and probably wishes for, perhaps even laughter, the intended "victim" tries to understand the pathology of his fetish, psychoanalyzing his need to shock and perhaps be laughed at in order to get off.

It was a simple Reversal of Expectations story with the twist being that the woman actually gets off on belittling men, so in the end, while Rodney is left humiliated and unable to climax, the female writer—who'd remained nameless throughout the story, another bone of contention from Fiona's crowd—ends up having an orgasm herself.

The outrage that followed was shocking to Clay, David and Moira, and it had spiraled out of control, with writers who'd been there and had clearly been entertained deciding they'd been laughing from shock at the audacity of the performance. Any claims that those who didn't want to be present could have left the room at any point were told they were "shitting on the idea of consent," and that "people respond to trauma differently."

With near-constant accusations of racism and misogyny hourly for days on end, Clay had left social media altogether, and the contract for the novel he'd expected to have published the following spring was nixed within a week. They hadn't asked for the advance on royalties back, at least they'd afforded him that concession. But the fact remained, he'd been unable to find a publisher for his novels for nearly two years, until finally, a few weeks ago, he received an offer on his previously published novel, which he'd managed to parlay into a three-book contract.

The advance was scheduled to be paid next week. It wasn't a ton of money, but with his day job it would be enough to get him back on his feet. If he hadn't paid in advance for Splatterfest he never would have been able to make it out here, short of crowdfunding, an idea that didn't appeal to him.

But here he was, despite every ounce of opposition stacked against him, standing in the lobby waiting for Moira Mead, the only person who'd stood by him throughout the entire scandal and quite possibly the love of his life, on what could end up being the last day they'd ever see each other.

The Gross Out contest was scheduled to start at eleven, in less than an hour. Moira's flight was at five.

It didn't give them much time alone together, outside of the drive to the airport Clay had promised. But he intended to make the best of it.

Someone clapped him on the shoulder from behind. Startled, he turned quickly, expecting to find an angry face. But the short, well-dressed Hispanic man with the bandage wrapped around the top of his head smiled widely. "Clay Kayden? I just wanted to say, I personally loved your story at the last Splatterfest. Don't listen to the haters." He held a hand to his heart. "Always follow the muse."

Stunned silent, Clay stood immobile as Ignacio Ortega, famed horror critic, likely just released from the hospital, grabbed his hand, shook it fiercely, and walked off, entering the convention hall.

"Thank you, Mr. Ortega," Clay called after him.

"My friends call me Iggy," Ortega said, turning with the same wide, genuine smile. "I expect to see you at the Gross Out."

"Yeah, uh… wouldn't miss it."

"Wonderful. *Hasta luego*, Mr. Kayden."

"Call me Clay," he shouted across the lobby with a wave.

Ignacio Ortega liked my story. Loved *my story. Wow.*

He marveled over this a moment, thinking things really did

seem to be turning around for him lately. Maybe today would be a good day after all.

THE TICKING CLOCK

1

SUGAR AND SPICE, the misnamed reviewer duo, decided to get in the lineup early to snag front row seats for the Gross Out contest. They called Iggy Ortega over when he entered the hall, eager to hear the truth about what had happened with that awful self-published author.

Aimee With Two Es and their friends stood outside the line, waiting for David Ennis to coming crawling back. Misti With an I, who stood right behind Sugar and Spice, had promised to save them seats. Dean Foster Towne also didn't bother with the line. As the Plus One of the Guest of Honor and MC, he'd sit up front beside Frank K. Wallis and Jane Cockcroft. He just hoped David would get his drunken arse back to the hotel posthaste so Frank, who sat with Jane at a table set up by the doors, waiting to hand out water bottles and ballots for the Gross Out awards, wouldn't try to coerce him into taking over the job of emcee.

The Gorehounds were right behind Misti With an I, though Mike Miller had an emergency at home he'd needed to handle and "pussied out" yet again, according to Aubrey. Moira met the group as the queue had reached about fifty or sixty people, a much larger gathering for this year's contest. She suspected it might have to do with the controversy surrounding Clay's contribution at the last in-person con. Whatever the reason, they would likely have to start turning people away at the doors, or at least allow for standing room in the back.

Clay arrived just as the line reached the convention hall. There had to be at least a hundred people waiting for the awards.

It was a big conference room, but Clay was certain there was no way it would hold that many people. He spotted Moira, and Moira's friend Aubrey nudged her and chuckled. She must have told Aubrey at least a bit about what happened last night. He supposed she would've at least had to explain the black eye.

"Hey, Stud," Aubrey said with a smirk.

"Yo, what's up, Clay Dawg?" Conor said. "You gonna lay down some words today or what? Get up on stage and start air masturbating like last time?"

Clay said, "Probably not," then returned his attention to Moira. "I'm really sorry about last night."

"It's okay."

"I don't understand what happened. And if I tell you what happened, you'll probably think I'm crazy."

"Yeah, you're crazy all right, dude," Conor said. "Fuck the Man, am I right? But you gotta ignore all that noise. Write what moves you, no matter what."

Again, Clay ignored him. "Can we talk for a minute?"

Aubrey encouraged her with a nod. "We'll hold your place."

Moira went along with Clay, past the table where Frank and Jane sat waiting to open the doors, and headed around the corner.

"How's your eye?"

"It's fine. It only hurts when I blink."

"Good. You're not mad at me, are you?"

"I'm not mad, Clay. I'm just confused."

"Moira, what happened last night—"

"It's not *just* last night though, Clay. It's been odd between us the whole weekend. Things keep getting in the way. Things keep popping up, getting weird."

"I know. I really wanted us to be together this weekend, Moira. But I let my anger get in the way, and I'm sorry for that. I should've been here with you but I was with Ennis, up here." He tapped his temple. "The whole weekend, he's been inside my head. For *two years*, he's been there. That ends today. I'm gonna tell him I forgive him, and I guess that means I'm gonna confess to what I did. Hopefully put this all behind me. Leave it in the past where it belongs."

"Oh, Clay." She smiled, the lids of her bruised eye fluttering. "I'm so glad to hear that."

"Moira, I know we haven't put a label on this, whatever it is between us, and last night was a mess, and I can't really explain what happened—"

"It wasn't your fault."

"Maybe not directly. Maybe you were right though, maybe anger really is poisonous. Maybe that's what happened. It doesn't make sense but I don't think the Clams casino was bad, either. What I'm trying to say is, I love you, Moira. I've loved you since we met two years ago, I just didn't know how we could do this, how we could make this work with eight-thousand miles or thirteen-hundred kilometers between us."

"Something really *must* have happened to you last night," Moira said, grinning, touching the side of his face. "Knocked you on the head or something."

"I'm serious, Moira."

"I know. And I love you, Clay."

Clay felt his heart swell. He'd had a feeling before, but hearing the words, knowing she loved him back, it was the best feeling in the world. Revenge paled in comparison. He took her hands and kissed them.

"We'll make this work," she said, smiling up at him. "We sort of have to. I've already told Genevieve and Mum and Nigel all about you. They're expecting you to pop by any day now."

"I'd like that," Clay said. He looked into her big brown eyes, full of love and compassion and hope, and he kissed her, the kiss they should have had when he'd picked her up from the airport, filled with love and promise and not just the explosion of lust from last night.

They returned to the line hand in hand to find a stranger had joined their group. The old-fashioned tweed suit, forest brown, barely fit the young man's muscular frame. He held a briefcase in one hand, and something made of clear plastic folded and tucked under the same arm.

"Clay, Moira, this is Archie," Conor said. "The Gorehounds are cheering him on today. We're like his entourage."

"We're his poopy groupies," Aubrey said, causing the others, aside from Archie himself, to laugh.

"Oh, right," Clay said. "You told the toilet periscope story at the last Gross Out, didn't you?"

Archie nodded, smiling strangely. "That's me. Conor and his friends like to call me the Poo-Poo Man."

"That's not very nice," Moira said with a pout.

Conor frowned. "Aw, it's not like that. We're just busting his balls, is all."

"We just really loved his story," Steve Pilkington added.

"It's fine," Archie said. "I'm fine with it."

"You're going to be reading today?" Moira asked.

"Yes, that's right. It's more of a performance piece, really. Postmodern."

"My man Archie's got his finger on the pulse," Conor said. "He's tapped into the shitegeist."

The others laughed. Even Archie himself cracked a smile.

"I mean, just look at this suit! It's perfect! Dressing up all classy to tell filth. The man's a genius."

"Where the fuck is Ennis?" Steve wondered aloud, looking at his phone. "It's almost eleven."

Clay looked at his watch. It wasn't like David to be late. Even after his worst binges, the man was typically half an hour early.

Maybe he won't show, Clay thought. *Maybe my Inquisitors scared him off.*

Or maybe it really was him in Room 7. What if I didn't just hallucinate seeing him because I felt guilty? What if that creepy kid's been torturing him all night? What if he killed *him?*

"Moira, I have to do something. Will you come with me?"

She looked at the others. Again, Aubrey gave her a nod of encouragement.

"Save us a spot?" Moira said.

"We'll hold two seats as long as we can but this crowd looks rabid," Conor said. "Don't be long."

Moira followed Clay as he hurried down the hall. "What's wrong, Clay?"

"I think something might have happened to David."

"Happened? Did he get himself in trouble again?"

"I think… I think he might've been *kidnapped*."

Moira laughed. Then she frowned. "You're serious?"

Clay told her what he thought he'd seen through the window, the man, bleeding from every pore, duct-taped to a wheelchair.

"We should call the police," Moira said.

"This is America. You hear of this thing called 'swatting'? If I call the police, they could kill this kid based on something I thought I saw while I was *hallucinating*. I need evidence."

"What sort of evidence?"

"I don't know. I'll know it when I see it. Towne," Clay called out, approaching the man, who was leaning casually against the wall at the far end of the line. "I need your keycard."

Fiona St. Clair sneered at them.

"Why on earth would I give *you* my keycard, Kayden?"

"Because I don't think David's with the Brown Demon. I think he's in trouble."

Towne pushed off from the wall, a slight look of anxiety breaking through his cool exterior. "In trouble?"

"Just give me the keycard, Towne. Or come with us."

"Shit. You know I can't bloody come with you, Kayden. I have responsibilities." He waffled a moment, then let out an angry huff and reached into the back pocket of his houndstooth slacks, pulling out a brown leather wallet. "You'd better not be fucking with me. If you shit under my pillow or some such nonsense, I'll personally shove my size-eleven loafer up your arse."

Clay took the card. "I'll bear that in mind."

"Keep me in the loop, eh?" Towne called after them. "You Americans still say that, don't you?"

While they headed for the lobby, Clay told Moira the gist of what had happened to him last night, from Towne the Talking

Twat to peering in through the window of Room 7 after hearing the kid argue with the motel manager about Mr. Pibb.

"Who's he?"

"It's a pop."

"A fizzy drink?"

"Uh-huh," Clay said, watching Moira clue in. "It's David's favorite. If he didn't want to get too smashed, he'd mix his Wild Turkey with Mr. Pibb. But why would David need Mr. Pibb if he was on a bender?"

"You lost me."

They headed for the elevators, Moira a few steps behind.

"I figured David fell off the wagon because of the protesters, because of what I did. But he *never* mixed his drinks when he was on a black-out bender. He always drank it straight from the bottle. Or *bottles*. And from what I saw in his room last night, he was heading on a non-stop trip directly to Brown Town."

"So, going to Brown Town is having a piss up?"

"That's what David called it, yeah. I mean, maybe he was trying to sober up so he'd be fine in the morning. But the David I know wouldn't stop drinking even after he blacked out. He'd *literally* drink until he was unconscious, and *keep* drinking 'til he was out on his ass."

The elevator doors opened. Clay stepped in, Moira right on his heels.

"So what are we looking for, Clay?"

"I don't know. I just need to see his room again. If something is off, I'll know."

"But what if David just met up with that boy you saw after? He could still have gotten into trouble."

"True."

"Maybe we should go to your motel instead?"

"And do what? Knock on his door and ask if he's seen David Ennis, Undisputed Master of Splatter Horror? If David's in there with him, what do you think that kid'll do? And what if he's got a gun? You've got a little girl at home to think about."

"I don't know, Clay. I don't know. I've just got a bad feeling about it, that's all. This whole weekend, something's felt... *off.*"

He nodded, looking at his warped reflection in the brushed steel doors. "I know what you mean."

The elevator chimed. The doors slid open on the fifth-floor hallway. Clay and Moira shared an anxious look, and stepped out together.

2

Despite doubling his dose of LSD this morning, Frank Wallis was anxious.

David Ennis was late. David was *never* late. And on the very minimal chance he was running a little bit behind, he'd call ahead. It must have been the protesters. They'd rattled his cage.

What if he's drinking again? Frank thought.

This was not good. This wasn't good at all.

"I'm going to make an announcement," he told Jane. The round woman with short-cropped silver hair nodded sagely for him to proceed. "People! People!" He clapped his hands sharply. The sound left a ringing in his ears. "May I have you attention, please?"

The crowd quieted.

"We'll be opening the doors shortly, but we're still waiting for our Guest of Honor to arrive—"

A collective moan of disappointment filled the hallway.

"Rest assured, the Gross Out contest *will* proceed with or without David Ennis. This is one of our favorite events of the weekend, and the show must go on!"

Cheers rang out. People clapped. A few whistled.

Frank smiled, feeling a little less anxious.

"In the meantime, you must all be thirsty," he said, returning to the table for the flat of dosed water. He hefted it into the crook of an elbow and carried it down the line, distributing bottles to whoever wanted one.

When the box was finished, he approached Towne, who was

busy typing something on his phone.

"Dean, have you spoken to David this morning?"

While David's protégé offered a nonchalant shrug, Fiona St. Clair flashed Towne an anxious look. *Seems like she could use a microdose, too*, Frank thought.

"I haven't heard from him since last night," Towne said. "Why? Has he not said anything to you?"

Frank sighed. "Not since the incident yesterday afternoon. He wasn't in his room?"

"No, mate. Wish I could help."

Frank put a hand on Towne's shoulder. The man looked at it like he thought Frank might have a contagious skin disorder. "Thank you, Dean. You'll let me know if you hear from him?"

Towne nodded. "The moment."

Frank looked up and down the line. It was clear people were starting to get restless. He'd have to open the doors soon, with or without his Guest of Honor.

There weren't nearly enough microdoses to keep this crowd from getting rowdy.

3

David Ennis had managed to live through the worst night of his life, worse even than his last visit from the Brown Demon, when he'd awakened with very little memory of the night before, only a vague sense that he'd threatened to jump off the hotel room balcony and the contract they'd written up waiting for him on the table in the kitchenette.

His entire body was covered in micro-scabs that cracked and splintered like walking barefoot on a field of broken glass with every tiny movement. Many of them wept puss. More still, fresh blood. It would take weeks to heal, likely. If he lived that long, of course.

The clock on the wall by the vanity showed the time at five past eleven. Frank Wallis would be shitting himself right about now, and probably have to open the doors shortly without David. Would he emcee himself? David had written a nice little speech for the event, something reverential and sweet about the horror community that had embraced him when he was a nobody and accepted him even at the lowest points in his life, a community he still believed in, despite what had happened to him over the weekend. The bad stuff was just blips on the radar. The heart of the community were the readers, and writers without an agenda, like Clay and Moira and himself.

If he was to do that speech now, he thought he'd likely confess. Not to implicate Clay—even though Clay clearly hadn't called the police, which meant David was likely going to die in this shitpit little room at the Lonely Motel—but to clear his own conscience.

If he lived through today this was the end of it. No more lies. No more cheating, on his wife or his contracts. No more spending months at a time on the road, slinging books. Just a quiet, simple life at home with Vanessa and Bo, their six-year-old Rottie mix. They weren't rich, but it wasn't like they didn't have money. Now that the muse was back with a vengeance, he thought he could live like that.

Of course, he'd have to break yet another contract with a mentee. Towne would be all right. With a bit of tweaking, he could release the novels on his own, if he wanted. But it wouldn't sit well, especially after he'd left Clay high and dry after the Gross Out contest.

He had to admit, Clay had gotten him back pretty good with that novel. David hadn't even realized how gay he'd written Stark until Stark himself began speaking up in his head last night. Even the protesters hadn't broken through his denial.

But maybe he could write that into the books. Make it a series character arc, Lee Stark coming to terms with his own sexuality. Would that be okay? Would his readers buy that? It wouldn't be the driving force of the novels, of course. Just, you know, a subplot. Could he sell that to his publisher? Everything seemed to be gay these days, anyway—Kurt Cobain said it best.

And it wasn't like he didn't have personal experience to draw on, as minimal as it was. He considered himself about a two on the likely outdated Kinsey Scale. A three if he was drunk.

The kid was talking to his partner on the phone again. David had been sure Rawlins would turn on Tyler the second he got far enough away from the motel. But again the police never showed, and Jackson had called a short time later to let Tyler inspect the audio-visual setup in the conference room, then once more to show his paranoid partner that he'd packed the receiver back in his shoulder bag.

David couldn't hear what Rawlins was saying, but it sounded like he was having doubts, judging by how Tyler responded. It was a normal call this time, not video.

"*Because*, Jackson, I don't want you accidentally turning that thing on before we're ready." He paused, listening. "Just read the program. Hook it up the reading before I'm set to go on. Just don't turn on the projector until you've called me. *You got it?*" He paused again, shorter this time. "Then repeat it back to me." He nodded, listening. "Good. Now don't call me again until that poop-loving freak starts his reading. *Goodbye.*"

He hung up with a forceful push of a button.

"You really think you can go through with this, huh?" David asked.

The kid turned to him with burning rage in his eyes. "I've never been more certain of anything in my life."

"You know, this isn't gonna get you what you want. You go to prison for the rest of your life, you can't profit off your story."

"That's the difference between you and me, David," the kid said, waving the lethal end of the boxcutter as he approached where he'd pushed the chair in the corner of the room. "Ellison was wrong, see? I don't *care* about money. All I want is to be *read*."

"*Harlan* Ellison? That no-talent son of a bitch."

Tyler sputtered. "You're one to talk. You couldn't even read the subtext in your own work if it was…" The kid thought a moment before adding, "…if it was the top line of an eye exam!"

Get him angry, David, Stark said. *If he kills you now, he'll be a footnote. He'll get nothing.*

"What about you, kid? *The Rosehip Conundrum*? What kind of pretentious fucking title is that? I mean, talk about overcompensating."

Tyler's expression went flat. "What do you mean by that? Overcompensating."

"Trying to convince people of your quiet brilliance. Of your articulateness. But that's the thing, kid—"

"Don't call me that."

David forged ahead regardless. "—the literati, they don't care how *flowery* your prose is. To them, you're just another lowly horror writer, like me or anyone else. You're gutter trash."

"That's not true," Tyler said through gritted teeth.

"Oh yeah? When's the last time you saw a decent horror section at a brick-and-mortar bookstore? A *comprehensive* one, more than just a couple of stacks of King and Koontz and a few flavors of the month. Or how about, when's the last time you found a book from your pal Ellison that wasn't in some discount bin at a used book shop that makes more money selling coffee than it does from books?"

"That doesn't mean anything."

"Doesn't it? We're the bastard stepkids of Poe and Shelley, man. If it was up to the suits in marketing, they'd lock us in the attic, pretend like we don't exist. They *know* they're slumming it, that's why they disguise all the new horror books with bullshit modern minimalist art and big thriller and romance fonts. That's why indie and small press are killing it, selling straight to the fans."

Tyler tightened his lips, taking a step back, the boxcutter still held out. "I know what you're doing," he said after a moment. "You're trying to provoke me into attacking you. Maybe you think I'll slip up and you'll get free somehow. But this is happening, David. In front of all your fans and peers, I'm going to bleed you like a hog. Nothing you do or say will stop me."

The kid walked away from him and sat against the vanity

again, laying the boxcutter down beside his blood-stained manuscript.

Eleven eleven, David thought, looking at the clock above the kid's head. *Frank must've figured I'm MIA by now and started letting people in for the Gross Out.*

The typical contest, at least the ones they'd had in person prior to the pandemic, lasted about two-and-a-half hours, including the awards ceremony and closing speech.

Meaning, Stark said, *you've only got that long to live.*

SHIT HITS THE FANS

1

Frank opened the double doors to Conference Room 1 and beckoned people forward. The line moved quickly, critics, authors and other attendees stepping up to take their ballots from Jane Cockcroft, some taking a bottle of water she offered. Only the first case had been dosed, but Frank hoped those twenty or so people would be mellow enough to serve as a ballast for the rest of the group. The protesters from the other day had already finished theirs and tossed the bottles into the recycling bin at the ballot table. Frank loved a good protest but he'd seen firsthand how quickly a rousing chant could turn into a battle cry. If David finally *did* show up, it could easily trigger them. The microdoses in their water would make the chance of violence far less likely.

Sugar and Spice took seats on the left side of the front row, closest the aisle, with Ignacio Ortega on the inside. Beth-Anne, aka Spice, had started feeling a little queasy the moment the line moved forward. She let out an acidic belch behind her hand. Ignacio was kind enough to ignore it, but Sugar, aka Kelly, said, "Excuse *you*," as if Beth-Anne had done it on purpose.

"Sorry."

"Maybe you shouldn't have inhaled so many sausages at breakfast, *Beth-Anne*."

Beth-Anne nodded obsequiously, not wanting to upset her friend and colleague.

"It's perfectly normal to overindulge now and then," Ignacio said soothingly, giving Beth-Anne a sly wink. She hid her smile behind a hand as Kelly scowled, watching as the seats around them filled up.

Misti With an I took a seat in the right-hand row, front and center, draping her friends' coats and purses over the three seats next to her. When Steve saw this, he was livid. "What the fuck is this shit, eh? You can't *save seats* at the Gross Out contest!"

"I can *save seats* wherever I want," Misti told him. "It's still a free country, isn't it?"

"Are you even a writer? You *look* like a hooker."

Misti popped her heavy eyelashes. "*Excuse the fuck me?*"

"It's *escort*," Aubrey said, trying to smooth things over. "She looks like an *escort*."

"Look, bitch—"

"People, *please*," Conor said, pointing at the very prominent sign beside the stage. "*Relax*. Zero tolerance policy, remember? No violence, no names, no fighting."

"I'm not tryna let a *sign* tell me what to do," Misti said, still half out of her seat, ready to fight.

Conor shrugged. "Fine, start a fight. See how fast you get your ass kicked out and lose *all* of these seats. We only need one for the five of us."

"Don't forget Moira," Aubrey said.

"Those two won't be back, they're *obviously* going upstairs to bang or shag or whatever they call it. Now, can we at least have *one* of those seats?"

Misti scowled, weighing her options. "Fine," she groaned.

"*Thank* you," Steve said, mock genuflecting.

Misti removed a purse with a huff from the seat furthest from her and Aubrey sat in it, giving Steve a buffer, since he was often the most hot-headed of the group despite being Canadian. Archie sat at the end of the aisle, briefcase and poncho in his lap.

The rest of the seats filled quickly, and standing room was indeed allowed. Frank spoke with the hotel staff, who informed him fire safety required the occupancy remain at or below one-hundred and fifty. With Jane on the tally counter, she cut off admission at exactly that, to a choir of disappointed moans from the remaining twenty or thirty people in the line.

Once the packed room had quieted, Frank took the stage to a massive round of applause. "Thank you," he said, stepping back as the microphone whined. He thumped it. "Sorry about that, folks. Last-day jitters."

This received more chuckles than Frank expected. "And once again, I truly apologize for the absence of our Guest of Honor, Mr. David Ennis." After Frank spoke with Dean Foster Towne, he'd called David's phone multiple times in a last, frantic attempt to get a hold of the man. It rang and rang. He'd even called David's agent, Gloria. The woman hadn't heard peep from him since last week and was as surprised as Frank to find he'd ditched an obligation. "I know many of you would have liked the opportunity to chat with him after the awards," he said from the podium, "but I'm afraid he's… *indisposed* at the moment."

"Where is he?" a woman called out from the back.

"Probably getting drunk!" Conor shouted behind a hand, and looked around innocently while many in the audience laughed.

"I doubt that's the case," Frank said crossly. "Now if David *were* here, I'm sure he'd mention the 'Gross Out movement' has a long and storied history, dating as far back as 16th-century France with the novels of Rabelais, featuring the character Gargantua, who was often shown vomiting in buckets and pissing in the streets from a penis larger than most living rooms. The French especially are masters of the Gross Out, from the Marquis de Sade's *120 Days of Sodom* to the modern comics in *Charlie Hebdo*. Ribald limericks carried the tradition through the 19th century, as did the old vaudeville joke 'The Aristocrats,' and you can find elements of the Gross Out in the parody films of the Zucker and Farrelly brothers, Monty Python and John Waters, television cartoons like *Ren & Stimpy, South Park* or *Family Guy*, even in live-action reality series like *Jackass* and *Fear Factor*.

"As for the Gross Out contest itself," Frank said, "no one is quite certain where and when they began. In the horror world, at least, the tradition seems to have first appeared in the 1980s at the now-defunct World Horror Convention, which hosted its last Gross Out contest in 2016, I believe. But a now-debunked legend has it that famed musician Frank Zappa won a Gross Out in the '70s when his opponent—alternately said to be Alice Cooper or Ozzy Osbourne—literally *defecated* on stage, whereupon Zappa ate the result."

Frank allowed for laughter.

"Obviously that story isn't true. But wherever and *when*ever this tradition was started, we've carried on the torch here at our little convention for the past ten years, and we intend to continue for as long as Splatterfest remains running—which of course we all hope will be for decades to come, don't we?"

A cheer started in the front row and ran through the crowd. Frank smiled proudly, glad for the vibe shift, and said, "Without further ado, let's begin the contest, shall we?"

From there, the first contest took the stage to a rousing round of applause.

2

A "DO NOT DISTURB" sign had been placed on Ennis's door, likely by Towne, to allay suspicion. Clay used the keycard on Towne's door and entered the room. The pungent scent of Towne's cologne, Fiona's patchouli, and sex sweat made him cover his nose. The bedding was rumpled, the comforter lying in a heap on the floor. A used condom lay beside it, oozing semen and lube on the carpet.

Moira tried the adjoining door. It opened easily on the same scene Clay had witnessed the night before, but something he'd missed caught his eye this time: a dark stain on the carpet near the door. A half-empty bottle of Pibb Extra lay on the floor in the corner of the room, with smaller stains leading to it from the larger one, as if it had been kicked aside, spilling as it rolled. Clay got down on his hands and knees to smell the stain.

"Better hope the last guests didn't smuggle in a dog," Moira said.

The stain on the carpet smelled sweet. Not sweet like dog urine, sweet exactly like Mr. Pibb.

Clay stood up. "David must've just come in from the pop machine when he dropped the bottle at the door, but he didn't pick it up. He let it roll over there, into the corner. It's possible he was getting mix, but like I said, David didn't mix when he drank like this." He indicated the mess of tiny bottles. "And this wouldn't have gotten him drunk enough to leave half a bottle of Mr. Pibb on the floor."

"So you think someone maybe attacked him as he entered his room?"

"It's possible. That kid... there was something really *off* about him." He looked over the room again. The liquor bottles really were all over the place. Unlike when he'd seen David on a hotel room binge, where most of the bottles would end up on or around the bed. Almost as if it were staged.

He didn't think a kid that size could take on David on his own, but if he'd incapacitated him somehow, and if he'd had a partner...

The footprints in the snow. That could've been someone else, whoever helped the kid get David from here to the Lonely Motel.

"What are you thinking, Clay?"

He was thinking he messed up. He was thinking he should've done what needed to be done last night, when he'd seen David through the window.

He was thinking it might already be too late, and the guilt over letting his former friend die would hang over his head for the rest of his life.

But he told Moira, "I think we should call the cops."

3

Writers rose to the podium, one after another, and did their three-to five-minute prepared readings, some far less prepared than others.

The first contestant told a story about a man who bought an experimental drug off the internet to impress his new boyfriend with what was promised to be a "massive load." The ejaculation, it was told, shot out "like a firehose," covering every inch of his tastefully decorated condo. The descriptions of the thick, sticky, and foul-smelling chemically-enhanced semen striking objects around the room in Bret Easton Ellis-level obsessive detail were met with plenty of cringes and laughs, and the author received rousing applause as he left the stage.

The second entry featured a fair amount of what Anderson Ackerman often called "useful grimness," set in a Hieronymus Bosch-like Hell where the damned were forced to live in the bellies of giants, force-fed bodily fluids and excrement, while their own bodies were picked apart by insect larvae. A handful of moments caused a few listeners to grimace, but the story didn't have quite the same effect as the first. The applause it garnered at the end was more polite than earned.

The third writer told another humorous story, which seemed to do better with this crowd than full-dark, about an underground "shock" video that would turn its viewers into mindless, puking zombies. The contestant employed fake vomit with pitch-perfect timing to maximize comedic effect, and the audience roared with laughter.

While the stories unfolded on stage, several members of the audience found themselves restless, tapping their feet or grinding their teeth. Some shuffled uncomfortably in their seats, others were struck with sudden, pervasive feelings of dread or depression, or with the idea that the people around them had been preprogrammed by a cult or some L. Ron Hubbard-esque "Typewriter in the Sky," to laugh and cringe and howl at the exact right moments—because certainly *they* weren't getting the same effect *these people* were out of the stories being told. In fact, they could hardly focus on the words at all, as deeply absorbed as they were in their own intrusive thoughts and paranoia.

Up front, Beth-Anne "Spice" Roe had found herself deeply attracted to Ignacio Ortega. She knew the man was gay, that he had a husband and a cute little Pug puppy at home. But for some reason she thought he might feel the same way about her as she did for him. The sensuous way he'd repeated her name earlier, and his closeness now, felt intense. She was also certain Kelly "Sugar" Lumpkin would be deathly jealous if she knew, and kept her eye on her friend's handbag, tucked between the woman's feet on the floor, where the shiny chrome handgun was nestled.

Misti Tan—who'd been joined by her friend Aimee Skinner, while the other would-be protesters sat in the back row waiting to give them the signal should Ennis eventually show his face— seemed to see faces of her own just about everywhere: in the gross wall-to-wall carpeting, in the wood knots on the podium, in the patterns of her Helmut Lang leggings, even in Aimee's multicolored yarn braids. Worse still was when the faces opened their mouths as if to tell Misti their secrets…

"What are you looking at?" Aimee whispered hoarsely.

"Nothing," Misti muttered, sinking into paranoia. Her mouth suddenly dry, she finished the water the convention manager had given her and tucked the emptied stubby bottle into her purse.

Aimee gave her friend a suspicious glare, applauded as the latest contestant left the stage, then went up herself when Frank called her name. She told her story of a conference room just like this one, where a female employee decided to take revenge on all of the incompetent men in her company, who'd leered at her, made lewd comments behind her back, and stole her ideas, presenting them as their own. She'd locked the doors, set off the fire alarm, and hacked them all to death with a fire axe. As she described in great detail the oozing entrails and splattering gore, she enacted all the hacks and slashes with well-choreographed movements.

Her story, while told well enough, was only gross enough to receive a few squeamish looks and chuckles and a smattering of applause. The following contestant was something of a "Weird

Al" Yankovic enthusiast, singing a medley of popular songs with lyrics twisted into humorous filth, from "Cum on Eileen" to Pat Benatar's "Hit Me with Your Best Shot." Repeating any portion in a written work would surely get the author sued for copyright infringement, though performed on stage was no less legal than karaoke. He encouraged the audience to join him in several rousing choruses, which most participated in happily. His performance earned many jeers and cheers, as well as the loudest round of applause yet.

The walls are breathing. That was what Shawn "Shawnders" Anders thought as he sat awaiting Archie Schneider's story. *The walls are breathing and I'm the only one who can see it.*

Was the hotel itself alive? Had they all been swallowed by a massive beast of concrete and steel, like that story about Hell? Was this room a living, breathing tomb?

Room rhymes with tomb but it's spelled different, Shawders thought. *What else rhymes with tomb? Gloom. Doom. Womb. Zoom. Bloom. Sploom....*

Across the room, a writer named Wendell Abrams dreaded his turn to take the stage, his hands fidgeting in his lap. He'd found he suddenly couldn't remember the words to the story he'd practiced again and again in the mirror over the past several weeks. The entire thing was gone. He couldn't even remember the opening sentence, the one that had made his wife laugh uproariously, then caution him that it was too gross even for a contest devoted to such things. He looked it up on his phone but he found his eyes too jittery to focus on the screen. It was almost as though he was trying to read in a dream.

Wendell shot up anxiously from his chair, causing those around him to give him strange looks. "Excuse me," he said quietly, and made his way down the row, avoiding drawn-up knees and annoyed glances. He scurried down the aisle to the doors. Once out in the hall, he vomited in the closest trash bin, woozy and disoriented.

Frank watched the man leave the conference room with a slightly perturbed frown. He was only mildly buzzed himself, but of course, he'd been using LSD since he was a teen in the '70s. His tolerance was quite high. Yet it did feel like a different trip this time. He felt *zoomier* than usual, for the dosage, and his peripheral vision, whenever he turned his head, was swimmy and somewhat out of focus.

Still, he'd consumed three to four times more than he'd put into the water bottles. No cause for alarm. In fact, the contest seemed to be going quite well, aside from the jarring interruption by the man who'd scurried out.

The Gross Out contest wasn't for everyone, and it certainly wasn't for the squeamish or faint of heart. Better the offended or overly disgusted party leave the room than have a repeat of the Clay Kayden Incident.

God forbid, Frank thought, unknowingly grinding his teeth.

The next contestant told a rollicking tale of a necrophiliac cannibal hooked on "munging," which the storyteller explained to be a variation on the standard "felching," in which the felcher sucks their own sperm—or the sperm of a group in an orgy—from the anus of the felchee. What made munging different from felching was that the jism was sucked from the anal cavity of a corpse.

This story sickened a great deal of the audience, making them shiver and shake their heads and laugh in disgust as the writer described first the intricacies of sexual congress with a cadaver, followed by the churned, frothy "milkshake" slurped from its cold and festering rectum.

Misti Tan couldn't hold in her nausea any longer and threw up a little in her mouth. She swallowed the bitter, chunky mess—mostly green smoothie and last night's Buffalo hot wings—and risked another glance at Aimee, whose tangled, vibrant hair had indeed begun whispering to her.

Thoughts of food poisoning rippled through the audience, one by one, as the paranoid delusions and mild to severe auditory and visual hallucinations became more difficult to ignore.

Food-and-book-review blogger Sandy Watson, who called himself and his blog "the Reading Gourmet," looked at the faces of those around him and wondered if everyone here felt as awful as he did. Certainly, their skin looked a bit yellow, sallow and waxy, almost corpselike.

It must have been the convention buffet. He'd thought the sausages had smelled a bit off, but he'd eaten them anyhow, priding himself on his "iron stomach." That iron must have been hit with hydrochloric acid this morning. He was not feeling well *at all*. His vision was swimmy, as if he was drunk, and his guts felt like they were full of hot, bubbling lava.

But his oft-professed iron stomach when it came to extreme horror as well as spicy foods wouldn't allow him to leave the room. People would think he'd wussed out, and his reputation would go down the toilet, where he'd forcibly eject what he'd eaten this morning directly after the contest was over.

No, he would stay until the bitter end.

He just hoped it would come *soon*.

4

"I just hope the police get to him in time," Clay said as he and Moira left David Ennis's hotel room.

"We've done all we can," Moira said, taking his hand. "All we can do now is pray for the best."

Clay nodded, deep in thought as they sauntered down the hall. How much of this was his own fault? Would the kid have been able to kidnap David if Clay hadn't done what he had, causing Ennis to leave the convention? Would he have found another opportunity? And who was the partner, the footprints in the snow? Was he here at the con, too? Was he a danger, as well?

Moira pressed the button for the elevators. "You're blaming yourself, aren't you?"

He sighed. "If I hadn't been so goddamn petty, this might not have happened. If I'd called the cops last night—"

"You said it yourself: you weren't certain. And you were ill, Clay, let's not forget."

He shrugged. "True. But a part of me was *glad*."

"Clay, there's always a dark part of us happy for the misery of our enemies. There's always that voice telling us to run with scissors or step on a crack to break our mother's backs. But the simple fact that you didn't give in, that you *moved beyond* it, means it's not who you are. If you don't let those evil thoughts define you, dictate your behavior..."

Moira trailed off as the elevator doors opened. He followed her in. She pressed three.

Clay gave her a curious look. "What about the Gross Out contest?"

"Fuck the Gross Out contest. You've got—" She looked at her watch. "—just over an hour to give me the best shagging of my life, Clay. Up for the challenge?"

He grinned. "I think I'm gonna win this time."

She smiled and tucked her head into the crook of his shoulder, the two of them looking at their warped reflection as the doors slid closed.

"In that case, we both win," Moira said.

5

After the munging enthusiast came a tale about "cockvore." Like Rabelais's Gargantua, this "kaiju" attacking an unspecified city had a monstrous dong, as big as a city bus and as voracious a sucker as the previous contestant's felcher. The giant creature sucked up fire hydrants and trash and mailboxes and pedestrians into its massive glans like a fleshy Hoover, and masturbated with them inside its urethra, a technique the author called "sounding." The poor victims smothered within the kaiju's penis beat and pounded on the hot, wet fibromuscular tissue while the monster fucked a subway entrance, "lizard-balls deep," according to the storyteller. They were finally spared from suffocation when the beast ejaculated them into the tunnel upon the unsuspecting throng of passengers leaving the eastbound train.

Matt Shaw took the stage next, regaling the audience with a suitably disgusting stream-of-consciousness tale that garnered many gags and much laughter. He mooned the audience as they applauded him. This was followed by a horrifying true tale of a spider bite infection that blew a scrotum up to the size of a cantaloupe. The infected tissue had to be excised, the wound—which the patient called his "mangina"—large enough to reach into and clean. Another told the tale of a patient with maggots squirming in their skin folds, who smelled so foul the nurses had to put toothpaste under their noses to clean them out. The next was in a similar vein, about a man finding the breakfast cereal he'd been happily munching was crawling with woodlice.

Five or six subsequent entries later—with topics ranging anywhere from eating babies to sex with barnyard animals—a man dressed in a blood-smeared butcher's apron took the stage. He held in his gloved hands a plastic bowl which, from its fragrant smell, was clearly full of stuffing. Conor and the other Gorehounds—aside from Shawnders, who'd consumed the contaminated convention water—were shocked and appalled as the "writer" blatantly ripped off the Thanksgiving Special show they'd witnessed at the Canadian Ballet. Beat for beat, the story was exactly the same. Conor suspected the plagiarist must have been in the audience somewhere while the creep in the butcher's outfit stuffed the Turkey Lady. Aubrey shook her head in disgust. The others crossed their arms, refusing to applaud out of protest.

Jackson "the Hashtag King" Rawlins had been sitting behind the Gorehounds during the entire show, anxiously fiddling with his shoulder bag. He knew the guy in the old-fashioned brown suit—whom people called the Poo-Poo Man or the Poo-Poo Guy because of his poop-periscope story at the last con—was on right before Tyler. Which meant, as soon as the Poo-Poo Man's name was called, Jackson would quickly call Tyler to be sure he was ready and set up the projector.

Archie "the Writer Soon-to-Be Formerly Known as the Poo-Poo Man" Schneider bid his time, barely listening to the stories unfolding on stage. But when the blasphemer began spreading filth and lies about his beloved Turkey Queen, it took nearly every ounce of willpower, gripping his father's briefcase so tightly his fingernails made divots in the leather, not to leap onto the stage and throttle the man to death.

Finally, it was Archie's own turn to take the stage. When Frank called his name, Archie stood, placed his briefcase on his seat, adjusted his suit and tie just so, to the chuckles of the audience. Then he picked up the clear plastic poncho, let it drape out before him, and stuck his arms through one after another. He buttoned it up, *snap snap snap*, causing more curious laughter. Then he picked up his briefcase and ascended to the stage.

The audience applauded.

When the applause died down, Conor shouted, "Go Archie!"

This was met by more laughter and light clapping.

Archie began, "It's thought that Wolfgang Amadeus Mozart might've been a fecalpheliac. See, Mozart wrote letters to his mother and father, his sister and a female cousin, which featured funny little rhymes and poems about poop." Archie paused for light laughter. "'Into your mouth your arse I'll shove,' and 'I shit on your nose, so it runs down your chin.' His 'Canon in B Flat,' and undeniably lovely composition, features a line that translates to 'Lick me in the arse.'"

This received a few confused laughs.

"Me, personally, I think this theory, that Mozart was fixated with feces, is a gross misrepresentation of an inside family joke, and a cultural phenomenon of that time and place. I think people sometimes take things people write too seriously. The idea the subject of a song or a story is indicative of the writer themselves is naïve and simplistic. It's armchair psychology. Mozart's good name was *besmirched*, and for what? For people's amusement? For a slightly humorous anecdote to tell strangers at parties?"

The blank stares this was met with made him smile.

"Take me, for instance. Archie Schneider. When I was a kid, people called me Archie *Schiesse*, which is German for 'shit,' not because I pooped my pants or did anything weird with poop, just because it sort of rhymed with my last name. How fair is that? Now you all call me the Poo-Poo Man. *For two years*, you've called me that," he said, addressing the Gorehounds in particular, picking up his briefcase from the podium and holding it out in front of him.

"Well," he said, "that ends *right now*."

And he flicked open the latches.

The lid of the briefcase flung open violently, nearly striking his chin. The heavy plastic bag stayed within, attached to the inside of the case, the tightly coiled spring flinging its contents at the crowd.

No one saw it coming until it was too late to turn away.

Thick, stinking chunks and foul, wet splatters of festering feces, two whole months' worth of bowel movements Archie had heaped one upon the other, holding his nose from the stench each time he opened the reinforced, smell-proof plastic bag, struck the people in the first several rows like the wake of a garbage truck running over a puddle at high speed.

The Gorehounds seemed to think it was a joke, prop poop meant for showmanship—until the ungodly stench hit them. Their amusement turned quickly to shock and finally disgust, as they wiped the putrid filth from their lips and eyes and nostrils. The attractive women sitting to their left sat mortified, Archie's excrement clinging to their hair and fake eyelashes, streaking their cheeks like shit-colored blush, spattering their name-brand clutch purses and trashy-chic clothes.

"Shit!" someone a few rows back from the front cried. "It's *actual shit*!"

The gags and retches came rapidly after that, flowing back through the room like the wave at a baseball game.

A pug-faced woman in the front row stood and screamed, Archie's septic defecation dripping from her hair and shoulders and the bag she clutched in both hands.

That was when the shit really hit the fan.

THE LAST GROSS OUT

1

WHAT HAPPENED AFTER Kelly "Not-Actually-All-That-Sweet" Lumpkin stood and screamed, the news would later describe alternately as "pandemonium," and "sheer chaos." But neither of those terms aptly described the scene that followed the explosion of feces onto the crowd, in the eyes of those who were there.

Too many people in the first several rows were absorbed in their own horror and disgust or drug-induced self-obsession to notice when Sugar pulled the small chrome handgun from her purse—not even her best friend, who'd only moments ago been obsessed with the man seated next to her, and was currently trying to fathom how she'd suddenly become covered in this stinking, cloying feculence. Archie certainly didn't notice, so consumed was he with gloating over the priceless reaction to his Gross Out entry, his diabolical plan finally come to fruition.

Only Jackson Rawlins, facing the crowd with Tyler Grody's video receiver plugged into the projector, noticed the gun. Yet even he was too late, shouting, "*Look out!*" just as the deranged woman fired at the man on stage.

In his haste, Jackson accidentally flicked the Output switch, projecting Room 7 of the Lonely Motel on the wall to the right of the stage. Tyler stood in front of the dresser drawers, the boxcutter in one hand, looking at his phone in the other. He said, "Is it time? I can't see anything. Turn the fucking phone around."

But Jackson, who'd been fortunate enough not to get hit with what looked like a port-a-potty explosion, had left his phone on

Mute, lying on the projector stand.

The bullet struck Archie in the guts, causing him to drop the briefcase, the last of its loathsome contents slopping out over the stage. He fell to his knees, clutching his stomach, acutely aware of what a gut-shot could do to a person's insides if not treated quickly.

The crowd reacted instantly to the gunfire, having seen what could happen in such a situation on videos of shootings that made headline news again and again, by screaming and rushing for the doors. No one knew *what kind* of gun the shot had come from. For all they knew, the shooter planned to put a bullet in any one of them, their pockets stuffed with ammunition and their AR-15 fixed with a bump stock, which truthfully only a few gun enthusiasts at the Gross Out knew anything about. The others only knew that it was bad, and something they didn't plan to be around for very long.

As a result, the mad dash to the doors looked much like the Black Friday rush at a Walmart, only many in the charge wore layers of fecal matter caked on their faces and clothing. Chairs toppled. Elbows were thrown, connecting with ribs and faces and teeth. People pushed and people fell, and others toppled over those who did. Still more trampled the fallen.

Jane Cockcroft had the foresight to get up and pull the fire alarm, while Frank Wallis remained rooted to his seat in stunned silence, unable to fathom how his microdosing experiment had gone so horribly wrong. He was already dreading what the police would think once the toxicology reports came in and they found his fingerprints all over the water bottles left in various places around the conference room.

Ignacio Ortega struck the crazy woman's wrists with a sharp downward chop before she could fire the pistol again. He'd seen her leap from her seat and scream, but with the shock of the explosion from the lunatic's attaché case he hadn't understood what he'd been seeing until it was too late to stop her. The pistol dropped from her hands, skittering along the carpet to the foot of the stage, and she whipped her head around in unbridled fury.

Ignacio had suffered enough at the hands of *mujeres locas* for one weekend. As a young man in Cartagena, he'd learned the Brazilian art of dance fighting, *capoeira*. D.M. Carpe might have surprised him with the bottle, but he didn't intend for this woman to put him back in the hospital. He took a defensive stance as Sugar advanced on him.

"*Iggy!*" Spice cried, leaping at Ignacio like a DNI agent protecting *el Presidente* from assassination. She was skinny but nearly a foot taller than him, and her weight shoved him back. He struck his head on the floor, his brain still rattled from the bottle attack, and immediately lost consciousness.

Draped over the esteemed critic's prone body, Spice took the opportunity to profess her undying love for the poor man, kissing his lips, his dimpled cheeks, his eyes and chin, hoping to wake him. "Oh, Iggy, Iggy," she moaned.

On stage, while screams erupted in the audience and the stampede began, Jackson Rawlins dropped to his knees beside Archie Schneider. The man had fallen sideways into a spillage of shit and appeared to have stopped breathing. Jackson, who'd learned CPR to work summers as a lifeguard, began to resuscitate him. *Clear the airway*, he thought, opening Archie's mouth and sticking two fingers inside. He pulled free a glob of mucky brown shit. Flinging it away in disgust, his mind focused on saving this man, no matter what he'd done—not that Jackson was faultless, he'd eat as much shit as he had to if it would buy him a single ounce of good grace—he pinched Archie's nose and breathed into his mouth.

While the crowd around him stampeded toward the doors, the Reading Gourmet watched as a tall white woman in the front row attacked a small, well-dressed Hispanic man with a bandage on his head. With her back turned to him, all Sandy could see was her shoulders moving back and forth as the man lay docile on the floor. It reminded him of something from *The Walking Dead*. The heavyset woman she'd been sitting with stared at her in disbelief a moment before turning toward the stage. All three of them, as well as many in the crowd, appeared to have brown rot oozing from their waxy, corpselike faces.

A man on the stage leaned over the guy with the briefcase who'd apparently been shot. He raised his head, his lips streaked with the same brown rot as the others, moving soundlessly, then plunged toward the dead man's face again.

Sandy remembered the Miami Zombie, the guy who'd eaten a man's face while high on some designer street drug. It had been all over the news at the time. All anyone could ever talk about.

"*BATH SAAAAALTS!*" he screamed.

He pushed and shoved through the throng of bodies pressing forward, until he finally broke free and pulled the fire extinguisher off the wall. He ran with it, held in both hands, to the front row.

"Get off him, you zombie bitch!" he shouted, and slammed the fire extinguisher across the tall woman's back.

The woman yelped and collapsed over the man on the floor.

"What the fuck did you do to *Spice*?" the heavyset woman on her hands and knees at the foot of the stage barked.

"Huh?"

"That's my best friend you just hit!"

"She was…" He looked down at the man and woman on the floor, clearly unconscious, not undead at all. "…a zombie?" he muttered.

"I knew you people were out to get us!" Sugar snarled. She picked up her pistol from the floor and fired.

Sandy yelped and held up the fire extinguisher as a shield. The bullet struck it, puncturing the metal, and Sandy let go as a massive cloud of sodium bicarbonate erupted from the cannister. Within seconds the stage and the first four rows on the left side of the podium were obscured as if by a sudden sandstorm. Sandy coughed and gasped, waving his meaty hands as he staggered backward, out of the cloud, and the fire extinguisher rolled along the carpet in front of the stage, propelled by the pressure erupting from the bullet hole.

Throughout all of this pandemonium or sheer chaos or the myriad of other descriptions those who were there would later apply to it, no one saw Tyler Grody's look of surprised panic as the door to Room 7 was kicked inward. Over the screams and the fire alarm, nobody heard a man shout, "*POLICE! PUT THE WEAPON DOWN!*" Nor did they hear Tyler's whining plea of "*This isn't fair!*" Nor the staccato bursts of gunfire that followed.

With the baking soda cloud obscuring the projection, not a single soul at the Gross Out contest witnessed Tyler spasm as the volley of bullets riddled his body, filling him with holes, and the SWAT team storming the room as he eventually collapsed out of the camera's view.

2

Clay and Moira lay in her hotel bed in the afterglow of their respective orgasms, holding each other, hearts racing, just living in the moment, glad for the time they'd had together.

The fire alarm began blaring.

Moira laughed. "You've got to be kidding me."

"Forget it," Clay said. "It's probably a false alarm."

She snuggled her head into his chest and he held her that way until the alarms were finally overtaken by sirens.

3

In the aftermath of the mass exodus from the last annual Gross Out contest, twenty-six people suffered broken bones, from ribs to limbs to eye sockets, this last from a particularly hard-soled boot worn by Misti Tan. Twelve people were hospitalized with concussions, including Beth-Anne Roe and Ignacio Ortega, who suffered second impact syndrome, and sadly passed away from rapid brain swelling on the way to the hospital. Twenty-eight people were treated for possible drug overdoses, despite being unaware they'd ingested anything. Thirty-eight were given ointment for acute conjunctivitis, otherwise known as pink eye.

Three would receive diagnoses, after several weeks of upset stomach, bloating, and bloody diarrhea, of intestinal parasites, including Aimee Skinner, who was pleased to shed the last few pounds of belly fat despite the discomfort.

Kelly "Sugar" Lumpkin was arrested for attempted murder and led out of the Plaza Hotel in handcuffs. At her trial, she would claim self-defense, attempting to use the assault against Ignacio Ortega as proof. The district attorney pointed to her posts and comments in the message board which they argued clearly showed premeditation. Following the brief trial, she was sentenced to twelve years in prison, which she would serve in the Bedford Hills Correctional Facility for Women.

Jackson Rawlins managed to resuscitate Archie Schneider, who underwent many hours of complicated surgery to save his life. When he awoke from anesthesia, he found bandages taped over his belly button and a tan-colored pouch attached to his abdomen on the left side. Tugging on it hurt his already swollen innards.

A nurse entered his room a moment later. "You're awake."

"What is this?" Archie asked, indicating the pouch. Of course, he *knew* what it was, having had to empty and clean them hundreds, if not *thousands* of times at the care home. He simply couldn't believe it was attached to *him*.

"The surgery went well," the nurse informed him. "But due to a few minor complications, the surgeon needed to create a stoma. I'll leave that for Dr. Demetria to explain in detail, but the gist of it is, this little bag there collects your poop."

The moment the nurse left his hospital room, Archie began to weep.

Tyler Grody was pronounced dead at the scene, having been pummeled by over a dozen .223-caliber rounds from the Buffalo Police SWAT Team's AR-15 semi-automatic rifles. David Ennis witnessed the shooting, but as they wheeled the kid out in a body bag, he felt no satisfaction or *schadenfreude*. He was merely glad he'd survived. When the paramedics got him onto a gurney, he was equally glad to get the hell away from the Lonely Motel.

Tyler's slightly unwitting partner, Jackson Rawlins, was sentenced to serve two years less a day for aiding and abetting a kidnapping and torture. His habit of adding a hashtag to just about every sentence was beaten out of him in the first two days. Hashtag Lesson Learned.

After several weeks of deliberation, in light of her partner Frank K. Wallis's involvement in drugging multiple people with what was deemed to be a "bad batch" of LSD, and the attempted murders, the actual deaths, the sexual assaults and violence, Jane Cockcroft decided to cancel any further conventions. She posted the announcement with a heavy heart to the Splatterfest website, and the convention itself was mourned, along with the lives of those lost, until the next controversy in the scene came along to replace it.

It lasted about a week.

4

Clay pulled up in front of the Departures terminal at the Buffalo-Niagara International Airport. He turned to Moira in the front passenger seat, bundled up from the cold with her coat and knit hat with the pom-pom, the way she'd been when he'd picked her up on Friday.

"I'm gonna miss you," they said together, then laughed at the coincidence.

"I'll come out to see you as soon as I'm able," Clay said.

"You'd better." Her eyes went wide. "Oh, my *gosh*, I forgot to tell you!"

"What?"

"A woman from Kendra's production company rang me this morning, right before you showed up at the hotel. She wants to produce my story in a female-led anthology film."

"That's great!" He backtracked. "Wait. It is, isn't it?"

"They've offered me *ten-thousand dollars U.S.* for the rights, Clay. Of course, I said yes right away. I may despise the woman but there's loads I could do with that cash."

"That's incredible."

She smiled. "And I've got you to thank."

"Nah. If it wasn't her, it'd be someone else later on. Big things in your future, Moira."

"And yours."

Clay shrugged. "Things do seem to be getting better."

"Modest," she said, smacking his chest with a glove.

They sat a moment in silence, smiling at each other.

"We should probably…"

"Yes," Moira said, unbuckling her seatbelt. She got out first. Clay unbuckled and popped open the trunk—or the "boot," as Moira called it—then stepped out into the late-November sun.

He grabbed her bag from the back. When he rolled it around, she was waiting on the sidewalk. She took it from him.

"Well, it really was great to see you," Clay said, reaching out to shake her hand.

Moira regarded his extended hand in horror.

"*I'm kidding,*" he said.

She laughed and smacked his chest again.

They stood there a moment, smiling again.

"It'll just be a few months," she said.

"It'll feel like nothing."

"It'll feel like forever."

Clay nodded. "Yeah." He reached out, cupped a hand behind her head and kissed her, a kiss tinged with love and sadness, anxiety and hope. Though their time together was over, for now, it didn't feel like an ending. It felt more like the beginning of something different. Something new.

"They say revenge is sweet," Clay said, once they'd broken their embrace. Moira gave him a quizzical look. "I'm glad I chose love, in the end."

"I'm glad, too."

They hugged once more, so fiercely he thought they might break each other's ribs, and she went on her way, waving back at him as the doors to the terminal closed behind her.

5

David Ennis was treated at EMCH Hospital for blood loss and dozens of infected wounds. They had him on fluids, but on his second day they let him eat solid food. He was spooning Jell-O delicately into his mouth, nearly every inch of skin wrapped in gauze and bandages, when a familiar face showed up to his room with a vase full of white-and-yellow flowers.

"You shouldn't have," David said, laying down the spoon and crossing his arms over his chest. He winced in pain and lowered them to his sides again.

Clay Kayden placed the vase on the bedside table. "They're daffodils. The guy at the shop said they symbolize forgiveness."

"So you bring me flowers—what? I'm supposed to forgive you? Just like that?"

"I'm sorry I tried to end your career, David. It was childish. I was hurt. After you broke our contract—"

"Which you fucked me with, by the way."

"I'm here to apologize. To make amends. Whatever."

"It was you I saw in the window the other night, wasn't it? You could've made amends then by calling the fucking cops."

"I did call them. You're alive right now because I had a change of heart. When I saw you, I was tripping balls because of your friend Frank Wallis."

"Shit, he got you too, huh? Crazy hippie bastard. Okay, so you called the cops. Thank you for that. But that doesn't excuse everything else you did."

"You're right. And I'm trying to do better, David. I just hope that we can move forward together in a positive direction—"

David laughed bitterly. "Don't give me that P.R. bullshit." He picked up the spoon, tried and failed to scoop up a square of green Jell-O. He threw the spoon down in frustration.

"Can I give you a hand?"

David shrugged petulantly.

Clay approached the bed. He picked up the spoon, scooped

up the pesky square, and fed it to David. "It's not like I didn't have any reason to be angry. You could've stood up for me. You could've had my back."

"And risk my career?" David said with a mouthful of gelatin.

"I saved your life. *Twice*. You still can't admit that you might have fucked up just a little?"

David chewed the sweet dessert, mulling over what Clay had said. He swallowed. "Fine. You're right. And I felt like shit about it, believe me. I kicked my own ass over it for months."

Clay fed him another square. "Then why didn't you ever reach out to me? You could've called. Or emailed. You got your *lawyer* to cancel the contract. You didn't even have the decency to say it was over to my face."

"I felt guilty," David said, his mouth full. "Take it easy with the Jell-O, huh? You're gonna make me puke."

Clay put the spoon down.

"On the bright side," David said, chewing the last of his dessert, "at least we weren't at the Gross Out. Can you imagine how bad that musta stunk?"

"They'll be washing their hair in tomato juice for a month."

Clay laughed. David joined him.

"Goddammit, I am sorry, kid. I treated you like a shmuck, and I'm sorry."

"I'll tell people it was me who wrote that book, if that's what you want."

David shrugged. "Nah. I'm gonna run with it. See how it lands. I was thinking, maybe Stark's gay after all."

"I hope it sells hundreds of thousands of copies."

"Hey, same for you. I saw the write-up about your three-book deal. Nice going."

"Thanks. So we're good?"

"Yeah." David nodded. "I think we're good."

"Well, I'm real glad you didn't die," Clay told him, grinning. "I still need to know how the Stark series ends."

David smiled. "Thanks, kid. Keep in touch, huh?"

"I will."

Clay left him then, and David lay in bed, thinking about all that had happened over the weekend. He had to admit, of all the things he wouldn't have expected, it was for Clay to show up and apologize. And they were really nice flowers.

You know what we have to do now, David, Stark spoke up in his mind.

"Yeah, what's that?" David said aloud.

Kill the smug bastard, that's what.

Murder Clay Kayden, David thought, and barked a single laugh. *Yeah. You know, maybe I will. I'll kill him off in my next book. That's the best kind of revenge, isn't it? It's not like killing someone for real. This way, you can do it over and over and over and over....*

David picked up the pad and pencil beside the flowers and began to write.

THE END

ANOTHER AUTHOR'S NOTE

This novel was a huge departure from its predecessor. If you've read both, you already know that. If you've skipped through the novel to read this, shame on you. (Kidding, this is a shame-free zone. But there may be spoilers.)

There were a few reasons for this shift. The biggest was that every attempt until this one to continue the story of the Lonely Motel felt like a vain attempt to recreate everything that made *Woom* special to those who enjoyed it. The *Cult* novella—another two people in a room novella—wasn't working. The prequel I started felt overly supernatural. The novel told from the perspective of the Night Manager, our elderly friend with the coke fingernail, felt like I was trying too hard to meld *Woom* with *Tales from the Crypt*.

And I realized what I was doing wrong. I was writing what I thought readers might enjoy. First and foremost, I had to write for me. If you liked it, that's awesome. I'm very glad you did. But I'm my first reader, and if I can't please myself I feel like there's little point in writing something. I certainly didn't want it to be a "cash grab" (even though I'm sure some will accuse me of doing just that, despite me having decided to write more about the Woomiverse since 2017 at the latest).

Another reason was, I didn't want to suffer from the dreaded Sophomore Slump. The literary equivalent of "whiskey dick." Sequels most often don't live up to their predecessors. The process of trying to make this a direct sequel was stifling. How could I get grosser, more shocking, than *Woom*?

That's where the idea for *Gross Out* came from. *Woom* was

a story about two people telling stories. I decided *Gross Out* would be that times ten. It's *all about* stories. The people who tell them, the ins and outs of them, the stories themselves and how they affect us. That was a concept I thought I could run with for a couple of months at least, until I ran out of steam and moved on to something else.

But once I got into the thick of it, I didn't *want* to move on. Now that I have told these stories, I feel like it's opened up the Woomiverse to be much more than Two People Telling Stories in a Room. It can be anything I want it to be. And that's very exciting to me.

I've already got a story brewing featuring those people who pay for Chuck P.'s (Charles's) gonzo porn videos. I think it will be very dark, very shocking, and very fun.

Keep an eye out for it.

There are *thousands* of people I need to thank. Unfortunately, I don't know many of your names. If you've bought a copy of *Woom*, add yourself to that list. If you've reviewed it, or shared it with friends or colleagues (or enemies), put yourself up near the top. This book wouldn't exist if not for the appreciation I've seen for that demented little brain baby of mine. So *thank you*, sincerely and forever.

As for specific people, of course I must as always thank my amazing parents for encouraging even filth like this, and my wife for putting up with me while I hash out these bizarre ideas aloud, often over lunch. I'd also be remiss if I didn't thank the illustrious Matt Shaw, for getting me into this whole thing in the first place.

Marie Kirkland (Book Nook Retreat), Corrina Morse, the Mothers of Mayhem (Marian Elaine & Christina Pfeiffer), Stephanie Gagnon (Books in the Freezer podcast), Brandon Baker (Baker Reads), the guys from the Written in Red podcast (featuring awesome authors Aron Beauregard, Rowland Bercy Jr., Carver Pike and Daniel Volpe), Frank Spinney, Dawn Shea, Andrew Lennon, Erin Sweet-Al Mehairi, Mort Stone, Anna R. Reid, Mary Keifel, Patrick Reuman, Steve Stred, Richard

Gerlach, Jesse Thibodeau, Danika Meyerson. Special thanks to Regina Watts, whose ridiculously fun novel *Mayhem at the Museum* convinced me I could get away with a certain plot point I'd been deliberating over.

Big thanks to Marisa Ammerman, Nikki Fontana, and Kurt Wilde, whose stories had the unenviable task of following the fictional Matt Shaw at the Gross Out contest. And thanks of course to everyone in the Woomies Facebook group. It's been great fun discussing the book and sharing laughs with you all!

If I've forgotten anyone, please forgive me.

Until next time—keep it freaky.

D.R.
March, 2022

For more delicious dark fiction,
visit **www.duncanralston.com** and
www.shadowworkpublishing.com.

Made in United States
Orlando, FL
21 March 2024

45032739R00163